THE
BROTHER

THE BROTHER

by
Dorothy Clarke Wilson

THOMAS NELSON PUBLISHERS
Nashville • Camden • New York

Published in Nashville, Tennessee, by Thomas Nelson, Inc. and distributed in Canada by Lawson Falle, Ltd., Cambridge, Ontario.

Printed in the United States of America.

Library of Congress Cataloging in Publication Data

Wilson, Dorothy Clarke.
  The brother.

  1. James, Saint, brother of the Lord—Fiction
I. Title.
PS3545.I6235B7   1984   813'.52   84-2020
ISBN 0-8407-5890-1

To
MY MOTHER

Contents

PART ONE
Comrade

1

From the top of the hill where the boy lay, his thin, vibrant body half hidden by an overhanging shelf of rock, there was a long, clear view of the road from Jerusalem. Unthreading itself from the knotted mass of gray-green mountains on the south, it coiled downward in a thin, white ribbon out of the distant foothills; then, passing over the broad, flat triangle of the great Plain of Esdraelon, it suddenly straightened itself like a curtain cord drawn taut, baring the stage for its ceaseless pageant of the centuries.

And no mean pageant it was. For there on that broad arena of plain land act after act of history-making drama had been revealed. Kingdoms had been made and lost, nations freed and enslaved. Civilizations had met and clashed in mortal combat. The black, thirsty soil had drunk so deeply of blood that its very substance seemed tinged with red.

Out of the narrow mountain passes had marched army after army, scoring the black-red earth with the marks of Philistine ox carts, Syrian horses, and Egyptian chariots—the hot sun glinting in turn on Assyrian breastplate and Grecian spear and Roman eagle. Deborah, Gideon, Saul, Antiochus, Alexander, Maccabaeus, Antony, Pompey— there on the plain their ghostly, heroic, marching shapes still lingered. And mingled with them were others, still more intangible yet no less real, the shadowy actors of heroic episodes yet to come, born of an age-old, racial foreboding of future Armageddons.

Young as he was, barely six, the boy was almost as keenly aware of this shadowy pageant as of the present colorful panorama constantly unfolding beneath him. For he had been suckled on the hero stories of his race. The undulating wave of camels moving east to west and carrying nobody knew what treasures stirred his pulses not one whit more than the shadowy caravan of Deborah and Barak stealing from the strongholds of Mount Tabor, not five miles away, to keep their deadly tryst with Sisera. The band of Bedouins moving northward from Gilboa on their Arab stallions were no more real than Gideon with his creeping handful of loyalists bearing their pitchers and torches.

But at the moment he found them more interesting. His alert, dark eyes went questing over the broad vista, their agility fully compensating for the unnatural stillness of his slim, lithe little body. They were intelligent eyes, set rather deeply in a long, narrow, intent face, and they reacted to each fresh stimulus like flames played upon by varying air currents—kindling into curiosity at sight of a merchant caravan swinging slowly down along the River Kishon; flickering into disinterest as they lighted on the familiar image of a wandering shepherd, but flashing into immediate speculation over the sight of a lone horseman riding hard toward Endor; then, as a glittering scimitar of a Roman soldier unsheathed itself from the passes of Mount Carmel and swung southward, flaming into a swift, consuming hatred.

But today the curiosity, the speculation, even the hatred, were purely incidental to a steady, burning expectancy as the boy's eyes returned, again and again, to the groups of pilgrims slowly making their way northward along the great three-track road from Jerusalem. The quietness of his body found its source, not in indolence or lethargy, but in the tense desperation of waiting.

There was a sudden scuffling of sandals on the rocky ledge above his head.

"James!" shrilled a childish treble, which the wind caught and magnified into a plaintive wail. "Ja-a-ames!"

The boy frowned and wriggled deeper into his burrow beneath the rock. Of course! Jude would have to follow him and come snooping about, just when he happened to be up here for a very special reason and in his most secret hiding place! He had come upon it one day by accident, crawling through an almost imperceptible crack between two boulders and discovering to his delight a small, grassy nook beneath an overhanging shelf. Lying here on the soft grass with a bed of yellow anemones for his pillow, he was invisible to all interlopers from every angle save one. But trust Jude with his four-year-old plodding tenacity to find that one!

"James!" This time the treble was nearer, dangerously near the slit between the two boulders. The boy tensed himself in a motionless agony of suspense, the blood pumping so violently through his slender body that he thought the beat of it must be heard. This was his place, his secret, his holy of holies, like the one the high priest had in the Temple in Jerusalem. If his stupid, blundering four-year-old brother dared to thrust his blunt, prying fingers—

"Oh, look, Tamar! Come here!"

"What is it?" Another voice, this time a girl's, was drawing nearer. Jude wasn't alone, then. He was with Tamar, their older sister.

"Look, Tamar! A little door! A hole right through the rocks! I'm going through!"

James stared at the rock wall despairingly. He couldn't see the narrow fissure, but he knew just where the short, stocky form of his small brother would emerge, just where he would burst into shrill, excited crowings of discovery. At the moment he felt that he hated his brother, hated his round, good-natured, healthy face, by contrast with which his own looked so dark and narrow and sullen, hated his slow, deliberate movements and unhurried good humor, hated, above all, his blunt, prying fingers that were already more apt with the tools than his own.

What was it his father had said the other day, impatiently?

"Not that way! You hold the hammer as if it were a writer's reed! Look at Jude there! He can drive a nail better than you!"

Something blind and hot and quivering had seized his whole body, just as it seized him now, and his small hand had clenched the wooden mallet. Now he wriggled noiselessly forward and felt his fingers closing about a round, smooth stone.

"Hole too little! Can't get through! 'Most got stuck!"

"Let's go back down again, then. There's nobody up here. It's funny. I was sure I saw James—"

The scuffling of sandals and murmur of voices died away. The boy's tense form relaxed, limp and sweaty and exhausted. For a long time he lay trembling from sheer relief, not so much at freedom from discovery as at his sudden release from that blind, all-consuming fury that a moment before had possessed him. Each time it came it filled him with a torturing fear. Perhaps, like poor Gad, the herdsman's son, he was possessed of a devil. Gad was an ordinary boy, most of the time just like himself, but when the demon came into him it would throw him on the ground and make him foam at the mouth and do all sorts of strange things. Conscious of the rock still in his hand, the boy flung it away from him with a gesture of violent loathing, heard it bounce and thud and thud and bounce again on the rocks far below. Then he snuggled down into the grass already flattened to fit the contours of his body, cupped his small, pointed chin in his hand, and settled himself again into the attitude of watchful expectancy.

By the time the afternoon sun had begun to dip toward the nearer ridges of Mount Carmel his thin, intense features were showing signs of worry. As the shadows lengthened beneath the moving caravans, they showed desperation. His eyes did no wandering now; they only clung to that white ribbon of highway, kindling hopefully as each approaching mass of shapes resolved itself into the distinguishable outlines of donkeys and camels and patient, plodding individuals. The groups of pilgrims were becoming fewer now, scattered sparsely like broken beads along a chain, for in less than an hour's time the sun's descent behind the long ridge of Mount Carmel would mark the beginning of the Jewish Sabbath.

"They must come," repeated the boy audibly over and over, as if in magic incantation. "They must come. They must, they must—"

Again he counted the days on his fingers, as he already had done a hundred times. Three days to go, three to come, and three more for the feast in Jerusalem, with one extra for the Sabbath. Ten in all. And this was the tenth. He knew. On the doorpost he had scratched them, each one painstakingly, with a bit of soft limestone. And tonight was the Sabbath. If they did not come today, they would have to stop over somewhere, and to endure this aching suspense for another day and two more nights—

"They must come," he incanted patiently. "They must, they—"

Suddenly his alert muscles grew taut, for the straggling, shapeless mass just emerging out of indistinctness was slowly taking on familiar contours. Those six donkeys tied together in the lead, the limp in the pack driver's gait—Old Jonathan limped like that, with his clubfoot.

The boy squeezed hastily through the narrow crevice, not even stopping to see if anyone was watching to detect his hiding place. He ran the length of the ridge, down into a grassy depression, then up another sheer incline, not minding when he stubbed his toes nor even when he fell once and scraped his knees on a scattering of loose pebbles. He was straining for breath when finally, his small legs still pumping furiously, he came charging down the hill into the town's first narrow, winding street.

"They're coming!" he shouted eagerly to the first person he saw, a woman nursing her baby in a doorway, and sped on down the street, not even turning aside for his usual detour to avoid the house of Malluch the carpenter, whom he feared even more than he hated.

At this supreme moment there was no room in his small body for either fear or hatred, for they are both cold things. And he was all warmth. It coursed through him in wave after delicious wave, leaving his whole body vibrant and tingling, flooding him with an almost unbearable happiness.

At last he burst into his own house and blurted out the news.

"You'll be glad to see your father and mother again, won't you?" said Deborah, the next-door neighbor who had been taking care of the children during their parents' absence.

Yes, of course he would be glad to see his father and mother. He had missed them. But that was not the reason for the blessed surge of warmth. It was because after ten long days of separation he was going to see his Brother.

Even after the tired travelers had assembled in the marketplace, separated their possessions from the common baggage carried by the pack donkeys, and exchanged last, excited comments of the trip before going wearily to their homes, James couldn't believe that it was really true, that his parents and Brother had not come. On the way home he clung to the hand of his older sister, Esther, deriving obscure comfort from her superior ten years, an admission of weakness which he would ordinarily have scorned.

"It's nothing to worry about," she assured him easily, touched into a kinder tone than usual by the sight of his stricken face. "They probably just decided at the last minute to stay over the Sabbath with Uncle Clopas."

"But Old Jonathan said he was sure he saw them," interposed the more practical Tamar, whose short, fat legs were as usual having difficulty in keeping up with her sister's, "after they left Jerusalem."

"He must have been mistaken," returned Esther. "Anyway, I don't blame them for wanting to stay in the great big city house. They say it has seven whole rooms and a courtyard with a real fountain." She sighed wistfully. "Cousin Susanna doesn't know how lucky she is."

"I don't think so!" The vehemence of Tamar's reply consumed some of her much-needed energy, and she had to run a few steps to catch up. "She hasn't nearly such a nice mother as we have, and even if Uncle Clopas is father's brother, sometimes he—he's *mean*."

James had no interest in their arguments. He plodded along beside them miserably, the narrow, dusty street stretching ahead of him as interminably as the empty day yet to come.

When they entered the house, Deborah, already apprised of the news, was cheerfully reconstructing her plans. Herself a childless woman and big of heart, she was not at all averse to mothering her neighbor's five children for another two or three days, especially since it involved the care of little Simon, who was not quite two and dimpled and altogether adorable. She was seated on a mat now, the baby in her lap, her ample figure relaxed and comfortable.

"It's all right," she assured them, smiling. "I don't mind staying one bit. I've sent Daniel home for the food I'd cooked for the two of us, and there's plenty here to last us all over the Sabbath. We'd just as soon sleep here as over home."

Something startled James out of his apathy. It was the mention of the word "Sabbath." He looked swiftly about the room, his keen, discerning child eyes taking in all its minutest details—the dishes from the noonday meal still piled on the low table instead of hanging in neat rows on the wall; the lamps not only unlighted but untrimmed and unfilled; the round loaves not yet stored away in the Sabbath chest; the general lack of cleanliness and order. He remembered the sun which, when they had climbed the hill, had been almost touching the tops of the sycamores. And panic surged within him.

"B-but—" he blurted, stammering in the unaccustomed rush of speech, "it's the S-sabbath, and the house isn't clean and the food isn't put away and the lamps aren't cleaned and lighted and—and we aren't any of us washed and our clothes aren't changed."

Deborah stared at the boy curiously and reluctantly put down the baby. "That's right, lamb," she murmured good-naturedly. "There is a lot yet to be done. I suppose I'd better get busy."

She moved with her usual deliberation toward the cook bench and without apparent haste began to hang the clay vessels on the wall, one by one.

Only Tamar, following his glance about the room, shared his dismay. "Oh!" she gasped, hurrying to lift one of the lamps down from its stand. "What would mother say! Fill the other lamp quickly, Esther!"

"Mother isn't here," returned the older girl indifferently. "Deborah's taking care of us now."

Jude, his round face unconcerned, watched Tamar curiously. "It isn't dark yet. Why do we light lamps, anyway, on the Sabbath before it's dark?"

James stared at Deborah's good-natured face. It was unbelievable. He had known, of course, that there were people—even people in Nazareth, like Malluch the carpenter—who were lax about keeping the Law, who even deliberately broke it. But to think that one of them should be his next-door neighbor! He felt very small and futile and deflated. They, the family of Joseph, son of Jacob, who traced his lineage back to the great King David, were going to be lawbreakers, sinners, no better than Malluch! For did not the Sacred Writings say that if a man failed to keep one single provision of the Law, he failed to keep it all? Only last week in the synagogue school Rabbi Nathan had made that very plain. Not that James had needed Rabbi Nathan to tell him! A reverence for the Law had been instilled in him with the very milk that he had suckled at his mother's breast.

Desperately he turned to his brothers and sisters, who had been nurtured in the same reverence, from Esther's indifference to Jude's placidity, from baby Simon munching a crust of bread to Tamar, anxious and willing to do something, but still fumbling helplessly at the lamp. And even at that moment the sun was sinking farther into the sycamore.

Then all at once something happened to James. He felt it stirring within him, something conceived long ago within the passionate loins of his race, felt its birth pangs, its sudden swift growth to maturity. One moment he was a small, six-year-old boy, helpless and tonguetied. The next he was an Israelite, superbly conscious that he was the oldest male present in the household, passionately proud in the dignity of his heritage.

"Listen," he said clearly, "all of you! I'm the head of this house tonight, and I command all of you to listen. We wouldn't be breaking the Law if father and mother and big Brother were here, and we're not going to break it now. We're Israelites, understand, and we're going to obey God's laws."

He stood there in the middle of them, his dark eyes flashing tiny rapiers, his thin body looking absurdly small. But nobody laughed. Even Esther regarded him with startled respect.

"Now get busy, all of you," he told them abruptly, "because there's no time to waste. Esther, you get the broom and sweep the floor. Jude, you help Tamar to get the lamps filled and lighted. And while

Deborah is putting the food away in the chest, I'll wash Simon and change his clothes."

Strangely enough, to his amazement they all did as he said, quietly and without any objection. And when a few minutes later the sun sank behind the hill, the house of Joseph, son of Jacob, descendant of the great King David, was, as usual, ready for the Sabbath. The room was swept and dusted, the lamps trimmed and lighted, the food laid away beneath white napkins in the storing chest, the children all freshly washed and in clean raiment. Even Mary herself could not have done better.

Later James lay on his pallet in the dark, holding his thin body stiff and taut as a bowstring so the others would think he was asleep and wouldn't talk to him or ask him questions. He didn't feel like talking, and he couldn't have answered their questions if he had wanted to.

"What in the world came over you, James? You're usually so quiet, I couldn't believe it was you!" That would be Tamar, gently but proddingly inquisitive.

"So you think you're the head of the house, do you?" Esther could be withering and cutting even in the dark, without the aid of her black, mocking eyes. "Pretty soon you'll be bossing father and mother around too, I suppose."

Or Jude: "What made you look so funny, James? Why did you get mad at Deborah, and why didn't she punish you? Where were you when I was hunting for you this afternoon?"

He could feel the words already, as if they had been spoken, rudely penetrating the frail armor of his loneliness, probing into the tender flesh of this newborn thing within him, this unexplainable, nameless something, the very knowledge of which gave him such a strange new sense of power.

At last there came an end to the suppressed giggling and whispering over in the girls' corner of the room, and Jude began to twist and make little muttering sounds in his throat the way he did when he was asleep. Now he could stretch his cramped body, draw long breaths, turn his head so he could look out the narrow opening high up in the wall and see the glimmering of the stars.

He must have slept then, for the next thing he knew he was waking to the sound of voices close by, low but penetrating. It took him a few moments to realize that it was Deborah and her husband Daniel talking together on their pallet.

"Should have seen him.... Stood right up on those little spindly legs of his.... Told us what was what.... Didn't know he had it in him...." The snatches of phrases were broken by a chuckle. "Thought he was one of the old prophets come to life."

James' body tensed again. His cheeks grew hot. He strained forward in the darkness to hear Daniel's reply. It was low but very distinct, every word intelligible.

"Maybe he is. You can't tell. Stranger things have happened. I always knew the boy was made of good stuff, in spite of his queer, moody ways. He's a lot like his older brother. I shouldn't be surprised if he had the makings of a patriot."

They changed the subject then. Deborah's voice lowered still further, and James caught only two words: "Today ... Sepphoris."

The boy's heart leaped in a great surge of gratitude. He had always liked Daniel in spite of his ugly face with the scar that drew his mouth down on one side. Now he would love him. Not, of course, the way he loved his Brother. That belonged all by itself in the very inmost holy of holies. But he would give him a sort of "outer court" kind of love, like that which he felt for Jude—sometimes—and for Rabbi Nathan and for the little lamb he had owned for a pet the summer before. For Daniel had not laughed. He had not even chuckled. Daniel had said: "I always knew the boy was made of good stuff.... He's a lot like his older brother. I shouldn't be surprised if he had the making of a—a—"

While James was struggling to recapture the unfamiliar word, he heard it again.

"There are plenty of people right here in Nazareth who are good patriots," Daniel was saying, "if we could only find them. Of course we have found some of them. There's Johanan the tanner and—" His voice lowered again, becoming a cautious mumble.

"Joseph?" suggested Deborah softly.

"No. Not yet, at least. He's with us, I believe, in spirit, but he won't commit himself. He's a good Jew—none better—but not all good Jews are good patriots."

"Patriots!" Ah, there was the word again! Something his father was almost, but not quite. Something that he himself might be. He listened more closely, missing Deborah's next mumbled words.

"Soon," said Daniel, evidently in reply to a question she had asked. "We're all ready now. The spears have come, five thousand of them, smuggled in from Damascus. And as many patriots to use them.

Every man has his orders. All we're waiting for now is the word from Judas."

Soon after that Daniel and Deborah must have gone to sleep, for he heard no more. The room was very quiet except for the sounds of uneven breathing and Jude's little mutterings in his throat. James tried to lie awake, to discover some meaning in this strange conversation he had overheard, but it wasn't long before all the events and emotions of the day became jumbled in his mind. He drifted off into a meaningless whirl of repetition.

"They didn't come.... James is made of good stuff.... I'm the head of this house tonight.... He's a lot like his older brother. He has the makings of a—the makings of a—I'm an Israelite, the head of this house I tell you.... James is made of good stuff. He's like his brother—his Brother, who didn't come ... He has the makings of a patriot—a patriot—"

2

Jesus had been at home again for half a day and one night. At first he had seemed almost a stranger to James, much taller than he had remembered him and wearing a strange aura of remoteness because he had traveled so far and had had so many new experiences. Now, however, as he walked between Jesus and his father along a familiar road in the early morning, he felt like laughing at himself for that feeling of strangeness which during the whole preceding evening had kept him awkward and tongue-tied.

Of course Jesus wasn't any different. He certainly wasn't any taller. In fact, James was sure the top of his own curly dark head came level with a little higher spot on the other's striped tunic. And as for being remote—"Tell me again about the Temple," he said gaily, "and about the priest who goes up on the tower every morning to watch for the dawn and blow three notes on his silver trumpet."

And while Jesus told him, in that deliciously exciting and altogether fascinating way in which he always managed to tell a story, James traveled along in six-year-old fashion at his side, sometimes walking, sometimes running, now stooping to pick a pebble out of the dust-filled space between his toes and his sandal, now taking a few little flying leaps into the air just for the sheer joy of motion, but always keeping his small, slim fingers tightly clasped in his Brother's hand.

He always thought of him like that—"Brother," spelled with a capital. It had always been so, since the day he had taken his first tottering steps away from his mother's arms and had steered unerringly toward a safe haven of warm, challenging brown eyes, laughing red lips, and a pair of strong boyish hands that didn't keep him from falling down but were always ready to help him to pick himself up and start over again. Jude and Simon were his brothers too, of course. But he had only one Brother. In his company James was a different person. The shy reticence that so many, even the members of his own family, mistook for a sullen moodiness seemed to dissolve completely, and he became the normal, healthy, uninhibited boy who was now skipping along the dusty five-mile road between Nazareth and Sepphoris.

Only one thing marred his otherwise perfect sense of well-being, the grim, unsmiling face of the short, heavily built, bearded man who walked on his other side. Joseph was always a silent man, his tongue far less fluent of expression than his short, blunt fingers with their adz and hammer. But this was the silence not of reticence but of disapproval, and it filled the small James with dismay. For Joseph was displeased with Jesus.

It was connected in some way with the reason for their coming home late from Jerusalem. His father and mother had had to let the caravan go without them. And it had been his Brother's fault. After the Passover feast, it seemed, they had left the house of Joseph's brother, Clopas, and spent the night with other Nazareth pilgrims in the encampment outside the city, in order to be ready for an early start the next morning. Jesus had got up long before dawn and departed without permission on some mysterious errand—James hadn't been able to find out what—and had returned to find the encampment deserted.

"We thought he was with some other part of the caravan," his mother, Mary, had explained simply. "And when we found he wasn't, we just had to turn around and go back after him, that's all. We found him in the Temple. Suppose—suppose we don't talk anymore about it."

It was only when they had traversed the three miles of intervening valley and had started to climb the long, steep hill crowned by the imposing city of Sepphoris that Joseph broke his silence.

"We were due here three days ago," he said worriedly. "I promised Jared the merchant that I would start work on the finish of his new house the day after the Sabbath. Jared is a hard employer, and he won't like this delay."

James caught the accusing glance that Joseph cast toward his oldest son, and his small heart began to hammer with a fierce, instinctive loyalty. He knew that his father was blaming Jesus for the delay caused in their journey home from Jerusalem, and every fiber of his thin little body pulsated with the compelling desire to defend his Brother.

"Jesus didn't mean to be late," he said stoutly, surprised at his own audacity. "He thought he'd get back to the caravan in time. I know he did, because he told me all about it. Jonathan told him they wouldn't be starting until after the morning sacrifice."

"Jonathan was not the leader of the caravan," returned Joseph obstinately, obviously addressing his older son over the younger one's head. "He took his orders from Rabbi Nathan. And they had to start early in order to reach Nazareth before the Sabbath. As it was, they had less than an hour to spare."

"But he meant to get back," James was amazed at his own daring stubbornness.

"He shouldn't have gone," said Joseph sharply.

James looked up despairingly into his Brother's face. Wasn't he going to say anything, defend himself against what James felt sure was unjust criticism? Why didn't he tell his father what he had told him last night, when they had lain on their pallets looking up through the slit in the wall at the stars? What was it he had said? James tried to recall the words his Brother had spoken, but it was hard, for he had not understood them, yet he was sure they would help to explain this distressing thing that had happened.

"You see, little one, they tell us the Temple is God's house, but I was not sure men were truly serving Him there. I needed to be there alone with the teachers and ask them questions."

James wet his lips. "He had to go," he struggled desperately to explain. "There was something—something he had to find out—" Then he felt a quick, strong pressure on his fingers and was silent once again.

Something in the quiet firmness of his Brother's touch caused him to look up quickly. He saw the eyes of his Brother meet those of his father, the man's stubborn and hurt and baffled, the boy's clear and straightforward and just a little pitying. And he knew suddenly that he had been wrong. Jesus was different. The trip to Jerusalem had changed him. Instinctively he tightened his grip on his Brother's hand, attempting, as it were, by that possessive gesture to bring back the child in him which, he vaguely sensed, had vanished.

"We'll go this way," said Joseph, turning inside the gate toward the street that went straight up the hill. "It's nearer."

James' eyes glinted with anticipation. This was an unexpected treat, for his father usually insisted on taking a long, circuitous route through the city. James knew why, of course. On the crest of the hill rose the magnificent palace that Herod Antipas had built for himself after becoming tetrarch of Galilee, and no Jew could pass its towering arrogance without muttering a curse and spitting in the dust. Even more than the bristling Roman arsenal halfway down the hill did it arouse their bitter hatred, for it was a symbol of that most despised of all hybrids—a Jew who had gained favors by fawning and bowing to Rome.

James spat in the dust along with his father, even while his dark eyes glittered and his pulses quickened in tribute to the little subject monarch's arrogant display of power. For the first time in his memory the great gates stood open, and, while Joseph strode on up the street, he stood staring, helplessly fascinated by the great frowning turrets, the unfamiliar fluted columns, the massive, ornate carvings with their forbidden images. Then all at once a queer, clashing din was in his ears, a dull pounding like waves growing louder and getting ready to break, as a small garrison of Roman soldiers swept, double-quick time, around the corner of the gate and out into the street straight toward him.

Too stupefied to move, he felt himself lifted by their sudden impact, tossed rudely on the crest of a hard, metallic wave, and flung violently against some unyielding surface. The tide swirled past with a glittering flourish of spears and a triumphant flare of trumpets, utterly indifferent to the small, bruised, flattened little figure crouching against the wall.

A firm hand lifted him to his feet, brushed the dirt from his tunic, passed gently and surely over his body to see that he was unharmed. Without a word he trudged down the street beside his Brother, completely unconscious of his aching shoulder and of the warm, thick trickling of blood moving slowly from his bruised knees to his ankles. Still silent, he quickened his pace to keep up with the long, measured stride of Joseph, taking two steps to his father's one. But after Herod's last frowning battlements were passed, he kept his silence no longer.

"When I grow up," he said clearly, "I'm going to kill that old fox Herod, and I'm going to make every Roman sorry he was ever born. And I'm going to—"

But he said no more, for a hard, calloused hand was placed over his mouth. "Hush!" commanded Joseph hoarsely, darting swift eyes about the narrow street to see if the boy had been overheard. "Do you want us all to be measured for crosses!" His voice lowered to a whisper as his hand relaxed. "Think such things all you will, but don't let even the air you breathe or the earth you tread on hear you say them."

For the second time that week James felt within him that swift surge of exultation, that amazing glow of self-discovery. "I am an Israelite," he had said on that evening before the Sabbath, and the words had opened the floodgates of a whole vast reservoir of possibilities. Now he had discovered the secret password of another source of power, an even mightier reservoir whose vast energies even his childish mind could realize had barely been tapped. He repeated it over to himself silently, with satisfaction. "I hate. I hate my country's enemies. I am an Israelite. I hate."

So tremendous was this sudden sense of self-discovery that he looked up eagerly to see if his Brother was not sharing some of his emotion. But Jesus' face registered no trace of hatred.

The house that Jared the merchant was building for himself was in a desirable location, about halfway down the western slope of the hill, and it commanded a splendid view of the highlands of Upper Galilee, stretching away in the distance to Mount Hermon. It was constructed of the finest limestone, the blocks chiseled into one another so carefully that the walls showed scarcely a crack. Joseph regarded it with keen satisfaction. Setting his box of tools down outside the unfinished opening in the wall, he measured it appraisingly, his fingers already curved in anticipation to fit the worn handle of his adz.

"The door and lintels are to be of cedar," he told the boys proudly, "the best Lebanon cedar that can be secured. No knots or imperfections. Jared is sparing no expense. And on the inside panels there are to be carvings of vine leaves." He looked quizzically at his younger son. "Do you suppose your brother and I can do it well enough to suit?"

"Of course," returned James promptly, adding with proud importance, "you're the best carpenters in southern Galilee, and everybody knows it."

"Better than Malluch?" suggested Joseph in one of his rare bursts of humor.

"Malluch's no good," put in James hotly. "You're a thousand times better."

The sharp, staccato sound of hammering brought a swift, startled question to Joseph's eyes. Abruptly picking up his toolbox, he entered the new house and passed through the empty, unfinished rooms into the inner courtyard, the two boys following. In the center of the enclosed space had been set up an impromptu carpenter's bench, and a man was working at it—a short, stooped, wiry figure, bent to its labor like a bow drawn taut.

"Malluch!" exclaimed Joseph in amazement.

The taut bow relaxed itself to a thin curve, the man's face twisted into a smile of recognition that was almost a leer, and he lifted a bony hand in salutation. "That you, Joseph? A bit late, aren't you? Or was yesterday the Sabbath over home in Nazareth? Not being a devout man like you, I'm apt to get my days twisted."

"You—" Joseph's perplexed eyes traveled slowly downward from the mocking face, the stooped shoulder, the thin arm, to the expert fingers curved about the mallet. Then he saw what lay beneath—the long, smooth, perfect lengths of finest Lebanon cedar chalked with an intricate pattern of vine leaves. "What are you doing here?" he demanded furiously.

James shrank back beside his Brother and clutched his hand. Never before had he seen his father really angry. He could see the cords tighten in the hand next to him, clasping the handle of the toolbox, and he thought for an instant that Joseph was going to lift the heavy thing and bring it crashing down on Malluch's head. Jesus' hand pressed his reassuringly. He knew Joseph better than James did.

"Go ask Jared," replied Malluch indifferently, lifting his mallet deliberately to drive another pin. Then, as a tall man came around the corner from the outer courtyard: "Ha! You don't need to. Here he is now."

Joseph listened in silence to the merchant's smooth explanations. He was sorry, but his house had to be finished as quickly as possible. And, since Joseph had not appeared when he said he would and Malluch had kindly offered his services, it had been quite the natural thing to hire him in Joseph's place. He was sorry, but he had no other work that needed to be done now—none, that is, that Malluch, who seemed very capable, could not handle. Sometime in the future, no doubt . . .

As they left the house, a boy about James' age, so thin and ungainly of body that he looked almost a cripple, sidled timidly toward them around the corner of the building. Seeing him, Jesus turned with a quick, warm gesture of greeting. James moved on hastily after his father. Hearing his Brother call his name, he stopped, but grudgingly and without turning around.

"I see him," he said sullenly, kicking at the dust with his sandals.

He knew what Jesus wanted. His Brother was always trying to get him to be as friendly to Malluch's son as to the other children he played with. As if all the other Jewish boys in Nazareth didn't treat Zeri just the way James did! And why shouldn't they? Didn't their fathers treat Malluch the same way—call him names, spit after him when he walked down the street, mutter prayers if they were obliged to go too close to him—because they knew he only pretended to keep the Law and did business with Gentiles whenever he got a chance? Why shouldn't they be allowed to treat Malluch's son the same way— laugh at his weak, bleary eyes and hunched shoulders, ape his queer, awkward motions and halting speech? Certainly it was nothing for his Brother to be so concerned about!

It had been a sore point with James ever since a certain memorable incident several months before. Jesus had promised to meet him after finishing his afternoon work in the carpenter shop and take him for a long ramble up on the hilltop. James adored these intimate pilgrimages alone with his Brother almost with the passion of a religious devotee. They were always delightfully varied. Sometimes he and Jesus would hunt rocks or different kinds of grasses or wild flowers or explore one of the excitingly gloomy caves that honeycombed the hills about Nazareth. At other times they would climb to the topmost point of the hill, which they called the "Lookout," and lie on the sun-warmed rocks, watching the caravans and the white triangles of sails on the brief bit of dazzling blue beyond Mount Carmel. This day had held a special treat in store. His Brother had promised to show him a hidden path he had discovered leading down beside the precipitous cliff at the extreme western edge of the hill. It was to be their very own secret, and no one else in all the world, not even Jude, was to know about it.

James had found the waiting hard that day. He had played half-heartedly with a group of schoolmates in a vacant lot behind the house of Laban the merchant, one eye on the cleft between the buildings so he would not miss the first glimpse of his Brother. Then Zeri had appeared, slinking timidly along the wall in that eager, furtive, apologetic way he had, and the boys had pounced on him.

"O-ho! Look who's here!"

"Son of the heathen swine!"

"Hello, there, you Squinty Eyes!"

"We've missed you. Where've you been lately?"

"You know what happens to lawbreakers? The earth opens right up in front of them and swallows them up. My father said so."

"You'd better be careful, Squinty Eyes! Look where you're going! Your eyes are so bad you might fall in without knowing it!"

"Let's let Squinty Eyes play with us. We can play Garden of Eden, and let him be the serpent."

"No, let's play funeral, and he can be the corpse!"

"I've got a better idea! Let's make him say the Shema!"

"Yes, yes! The Shema!"

Zeri had stood cowering while the boys, James among them, had surrounded him, and to their intense delight he had begun to make the queer, fluttering motions with his arms that made him look like a grotesque bird trying to fly.

"The Shema!" they had cried loudly, closing in about him so he could not get away.

Making him repeat the Shema had been James' idea, and the other boys' instant approval had filled him with a warm glow. Never too popular with other children on account of his moody reticence, he had welcomed this sudden flow of approbation with alacrity. Dancing gleefully, he had let his voice shrill out high above the voices of the others.

"The Shema! If you think you're a good Jew like us, then let's hear you say the Shema!"

Zeri had opened his mouth twice before any sound came out. Then he had made a little gasping noise. The boys had chortled gleefully. It was because of his halting speech that they were always seeking new devices to make him talk. This idea of James' had been a master-piece.

"H-hear, O Israel—" The words had finally escaped the boy's quivering throat in a series of choking gasps. "The L-Lord our G-God is one L-Lord—"

Then suddenly James had felt a firm hand on his shoulder, and he had looked up into his Brother's eyes—not warm and brown and filled with little flecks of sunlight as they usually were when they looked at him, but cold and stinging and slate-colored like sharp barbs of winter rain.

"It's time you went home, little one," he had said abruptly. Then very gently he had taken the thin, cowering boy by the hand. "Come Zeri. You and I are going to take a walk up on the hill. Just you and I, together. There are some beautiful things up there waiting for us."

Even now, months afterward, James could remember the way he had felt at that moment, all hot and cold—hot because of the swift fury of jealousy that had swept through his veins at the sight of Jesus and Zeri going up the hill together, cold because of the chilling certainty that for the first time in his life his Brother had been angry with him. It had all been Zeri's fault, and he had hated him for it.

Now, try as he would, he could not keep his back turned. He had to know how his Brother looked at Zeri, what he was saying. Surely now, after what Malluch had done to their father, Jesus would treat Zeri as he deserved. Reluctantly, but hopefully, he turned to watch them.

Zeri was standing awkwardly, first on one foot, then on the other, the color coming and going in his thin cheeks. There was a certain wildness about him, an elusive quality that suggested an animal both untamed and hunted, yet he stood quietly without his usual fluttering motions. In his weak, squinting eyes there was nothing wild or elusive. Their warm candor, as he lifted them to the face of Jesus, was nakedly illuminating. It was pure hero worship.

"I—I did what you told me," he said shyly. "I w-went up on the hill at night all alone and—and let the stars talk to me. And—and now I'm not afraid of the dark at all."

The older boy smiled down at him, answering him in a few friendly, simple words. James listened, aghast, hardly believing his ears. That his Brother, after witnessing the mean trick that Malluch had just played on their father, could still treat Malluch's son with friendliness, and not only friendliness but intimacy! It was unbelievable! When

Jesus joined him again, he muttered an excuse and ran back. Zeri was still standing at the corner of the house.

"You son of a heathen swine!" James said contemptuously. And, stretching himself to the extreme limit of his six-year-old stature, he spat in Zeri's face.

Joseph found other work to do that day in Sepphoris. He mended a sill on the house of Jacob the tanner and adjusted a door for a poor widow whose husband had been a distant relative of his wife, Mary. They ate their lunch under a gnarled olive tree behind her house—the round barley loaves and fig cakes that Mary had prepared for them, and some gourds of fresh, warm goat's milk which the widow brought them.

While they were at the widow's house a messenger came, saying that Eleazar the king's steward had heard that Joseph was in town and would like him to do some work for him. James thought the messenger rather a peculiar person, in spite of the fact that he came riding on a horse and was dressed in far more splendid fashion than was customary for servants. For all the time he was speaking he kept looking down at the ground and making queer little marks with the blunt end of his whip.

"Tell your master I will come," said Joseph after some hesitation.

Even James' young eyes widened in surprise. For had not the messenger said Eleazar was the king's steward? And was it not a well-known fact in the family that unless circumstances compelled him to do so Joseph did no business with anyone connected with the Roman government, especially one like Eleazar, who had deliberately sold his Jewish birthright by making himself a tool of the emperor's vassal king?

While Joseph was casting about in his more slowly working mind for an adequate explanation to give them, James made an interesting discovery. "Look!" he cried gleefully, pointing at the little marks the messenger had made with his whip in the dust. "If you look at them this way, they're just like the head of a fox. Here's the nose—"

But he said no more. For the second time that day his father's rough, blunt fingers closed firmly over his mouth. "They look like nothing of the sort," Joseph retorted sharply. "They are just marks, nothing else, understand?"

And he scuffed them out with his sandals.

The house of Eleazar was much grander than any in which James had ever been before. Instead of having just one or two rooms and an inner courtyard partly roofed in, like most of the homes he knew, it seemed to have at least a dozen courtyards, with rooms opening out of them in every direction. Into one of these the two boys were taken to wait while Eleazar held audience with Joseph. It was entirely unroofed and looked like a garden, with shrubs and flowers growing all around and the whitest boy he had ever seen standing in the center blowing great streams of water out of his nose and mouth.

James stared at this startling motionless creature in incredulous amazement until his Brother, seeing his look, told him what it was—not flesh and blood at all, but one of the statues, or life-sized figures, that the Gentiles were accustomed to make out of stone. James knew that the Jewish laws forbade the making of images. That was why he had never seen such a thing before.

He backed away but continued to stare, now in horrified fascination. "Who—who is it?" he asked, thinking that so lifelike a thing must have a name, a personality.

When Jesus explained that it was Apollo, the Roman god of beauty, James turned his curious glance from the statue to his Brother. How was it, he wondered, that Jesus knew so many things that were not written in the Law or in the Prophets, or even in the Mishnah? It was Rabbi Ben Azel, he supposed, who had told him, the old man who had conducted the synagogue school before Rabbi Nathan, who had come to Nazareth only a year before. Jesus still studied with Rabbi Ben Azel instead of going, as James did, to Rabbi Nathan.

As his Brother sat on the edge of the basin, looking up at the statue, so close that the poised white marble fingers were almost touching his shoulder, the likeness between the two still figures was startling. There were the same slender, graceful bodies whose very attitude of repose seemed but the still expression of an abundant, overflowing vitality; the same slim molded columns of throat and shapely heads, each crowned by its smooth crest of finely waving hair, parted in the middle and falling just below the shoulders; the same high, arched forehead and eagerly parted lips; even the same dauntless yearning for adventure in the wide-set, youthful eyes, the one pair hard-white and coldly penetrating, the other warm and brown and sun-flecked. Then the seated figure relaxed and turned, and there was no longer the slightest resemblance between them. For one of them was keenly, joyously, vibrantly alive, and the other was dead.

James turned resentfully away, because the statue was so achingly beautiful and because he knew that there was nothing in the bare austerity of the synagogue—perhaps not even in the Temple at Jerusalem—that could quite compare with it. "Why doesn't the true God smite down all the other gods and show how strong he is?" he cried hotly.

The brown eyes lost their warm flecks, turned black and impenetrable, like a spring sky overcast with sudden shadow.

"Perhaps he will," replied Jesus slowly. "But where would he start? In Rome or in Jerusalem?"

"But I thought you were going to do some carpentry work for that Eleazar," said James, after they had left the great house and were going down the street.

"It was only a small thing he wanted," replied Joseph evasively.

"But if it was only a small thing, how could it have taken you so long?" persisted the child with more than his usual obstinacy, for it was getting near the end of the day and he was tired. "It seemed as if we waited in that courtyard for hours."

And indeed he was right, for when they had gone in, the sun had been only a little past the zenith, and now it was casting long, oblique shadows down the street ahead of them.

"Besides, you didn't even open your toolbox at all. I know you didn't because it was sitting there in the courtyard where we were all the time."

Joseph frowned, his slow-moving mind bewildered by its unaccustomed effort to wrestle with two problems at once. His strong, patient, immobile features, so unlike those of either of the two sons who walked beside him, were drawn into strained and weary lines. He looked even more tired than James.

"I—I guess he just wanted to ask my advice," he stammered in answer to his small son's persistent queries. A plain, hard-working man, except in rare moments unimaginative and taciturn, he was possessed of a surprising and extraordinary patience toward his children. "Yes, that was it." His troubled brow cleared slightly. "He wanted to ask my advice. He was telling me some plans."

"Some plans for a house?" persisted James. "Is Eleazar going to build a new house, and does he want you to help him?"

"Eleazar is going to build something," said Joseph slowly. "You can call it a house if you want to, a house for a people robbed of their birthright and shamed and crushed by an enemy and driven out of their own home that their Father gave to them. And—you are right. He wants me to help him."

"And are you going to, father?"

James felt a firm, quieting touch upon his shoulder. He mustn't ask questions now, his Brother told him softly. Didn't he see that their father was trying hard to make up his mind about something?

Joseph shot a sudden quick glance at his oldest son, but the boy was gazing innocently away over the narrow, winding, dirt-infested street, over the square, flat roofs of Sepphoris to the distant horizon, where Mount Hermon, white-crested and remote, stood guard over the northernmost bounds of Israel. He shifted his heavy toolbox to his other hand and sighed. If the boy were only a little older and could understand the fiercely terrifying issues of this problem with which he was wrestling! But, no, he was only a child, just barely past his initiation into youth as a "son of the Commandment," and, he feared, with the trip to Jerusalem still fresh in his mind, an imaginative and irresponsible one at that.

Jesus turned suddenly toward his father, a little of the sun-crested glory caught and enmeshed in the clear warmth of his eyes. His voice as he spoke was eager and compelling. James, plodding along patiently beside him, looked up into his radiant face and tried to understand what he was saying. He was talking about Mount Sinai and Mount Hermon, one on the north and the other on the south and their little country in between. Wouldn't it be strange, he was asking thoughtfully, if all the time their people had been looking in the wrong direction? Perhaps God wasn't like Sinai, after all—thundering and belching out smoke and sometimes even boiling out over the top and killing people. Perhaps he was like Mount Hermon, quiet and serene and shining and patiently willing to wait.

Joseph looked wonderingly at his oldest son, then on over the square, flat roofs to the distant, sun-crowned crest. To his near-sighted eyes, long focused to fine detail, it was only a dim, shining blur. But it was enough. He squared his shoulders and drew a long breath.

"I have to stop just once more," he said, "to tell a man something. Then we'll go home. James, poor little lad," he laid his big hand tenderly on the boy's thin shoulder, "you must be tired."

As they approached the gate leading to the Nazareth road, the streets became narrower and more cluttered with refuse, the houses smaller and dingier and closer together. James always dreaded this part of the trip, especially on the way home, when his sensitive stomach was tired and empty and revolted both at sights and smells. He wished they could hurry. But in the most unsavory section close by the gate Joseph turned and led them up a narrow alley, hardly more than a slit between two buildings, at the end of which was a heavy, tightly shut wooden door. Joseph knocked on the door, and a very old man came to open it. James could hear his shuffling steps long before there came to his ears the rusty creaking of a bolt.

"Well?" The old man eyed Joseph keenly.

Amazed, James saw his father's finger slowly trace something on the doorpost. His bright eyes unerringly followed each little point and curve. "A fox!" He mouthed the word soundlessly this time, knowing better than to speak it aloud.

The old man opened the door wider, and they entered a spacious courtyard, seemingly as far removed from the neighborhood dirt and squalor as had been that other indoor garden in the house of Eleazar. "This way," said the old man, indicating a tapestry hung doorway, and Joseph, setting down his toolbox and bidding the two boys wait for him, followed the stooped figure. As the curtain was drawn aside, James thought he caught a glimpse of Daniel's scarred, homely face in the room beyond, but decided he must be mistaken. Daniel was at home, of course, in Nazareth, busy selling raisins and figs and dates in his little booth in the marketplace.

When Joseph returned through the curtained doorway, a man came with him. He was a small man, not so tall as Joseph or so broad-shouldered, yet so dominating was his gaze, so arresting his personality, that the carpenter seemed like a dwarf beside him. His eyes swept over the two boys with the sharpness of a keen-edged sickle.

"Your sons, Joseph?" he demanded crisply.

Joseph nodded. The man crossed the room swiftly, bent his searching gaze on each of the boys in turn, then placed his thin, nervous hands for a moment on the older boy's shoulders.

"You have it," he said abruptly. "There's a fire within you too, only it doesn't consume you yet, as it does me. Mine is nearly spent. God of Abraham, to be young again like you! To have another life to spend on Israel's freedom!" His deep-set eyes became blazing pits. "Remember this—always—will you? That fire within you—don't try to quench it. Don't even try to master it. Let it master you if it will. It is far better to be consumed yourself than to let the inner fires go dead."

"I will remember," said Jesus steadily.

The man turned abruptly and placed his hand for an instant on James' curly black head. His face, swept suddenly by a brilliant smile, was like a somber cloud edged with sunlight.

"Perhaps sometime," he said, "you will like to remember, little lad, that you once looked into the face of a strange man called Judas the Galilean."

He turned quickly and went through the curtained doorway.

"There!" said Joseph, as they passed again through the heavy wooden door and heard the rusty bolt slide with rasping finality behind them. "Now we shall go home. Your mother will be waiting."

As they emerged from the narrow cleft between the two houses, Malluch and Zeri were just passing on their way to the city gate. At sight of Joseph and his two sons, the eyes of the little carpenter widened in surprise, then narrowed craftily. He hobbled forward and thrust his thin, eagle-shaped features almost into Joseph's face.

"So," he hissed softly, "Joseph of Nazareth also has business in the house of Judas the son of Hezekiah. It is a good thing to know."

Again and again that day Mary left her work and went to the door, shading her eyes and peering hopefully down the street, even though she knew there must be hours yet before they would arrive. Never, she thought, had a day seemed so long. Since that moment last night when she had overheard Joseph and Daniel talking together, time for her had stood still. Even the joy of being reunited with her children, of feeling her arms close once again about the sleepy, chubby baby Simon, had been poisoned by this dull, aching, inexpressible fear.

Her arms about him now, her lips pressed against the softness of his forehead, gently so as not to awaken him from his nap, she tried to remember just what it was they had said. She had stepped out into the tiny garden at the back of the house to see how large the almond pods had grown in their absence, and, reaching up among the young leaves to feel one of the long, flat, downy objects, she had heard the two voices just beyond the tree—Daniel's first, clipped and cautious; then Joseph's slow, measured reply.

"How did you find things in Jerusalem?"

"Quiet, for the most part. The opposition to the census of Quirinius seems to be dying down in Judea. Joazar, the high priest, has persuaded the people to submit quietly to the registration."

"Let him speak for Judea, then, but not for Galilee! By all that's holy, we'll have no census-taking here! Exact tithes from us, shall they—those vile heathen Roman dogs! Make us pay a tenth of all our grain and two-tenths of all our wine and fruit in addition to all our other taxes!"

"You're right, Daniel. Our tithes belong only to Jehovah. He who demands them of us is an enemy both of God and Israel!"

"Then you're with us, Joseph? You'll rise up with us to drive out these damnable invaders?"

"I—I'm not sure—"

"We aren't just a handful any longer, you know. We're ten thousand strong. All Galilee is seething. Before we bend our necks to this despicable yoke any longer, we swear we'll water the earth with the blood of our children."

"You can well say that, Daniel—you who have no children."

"You'd rather see them crushed by this miserable burden of taxation? Lashed into slavery like our fathers in Egypt? Ground into the dust beneath the heels of these wretched foreigners?"

"I—I don't know, Daniel. I haven't been able to decide."

"Well, you'll have to soon. Promise me one thing, Joseph. Let Eleazar talk to you. You're going to Sepphoris tomorrow—"

They had moved away from the tree then, toward Daniel's house, and Mary, her frozen body slowly regaining strength enough to move, had crept back into the house, the almond pod that she still held in her hand crushed into ragged, unrecognizable pulp.

She had gone about her daily tasks as usual—putting up lunches for Joseph and the two boys; folding the sleeping mats and putting the house in its usual order (which was no small task after a week of Deborah's indifferent housekeeping); kneading the dough that Deborah had mixed the day before and shaping it into round, flat loaves and baking it, for it had been her turn today to use the village oven; giving the children their noonday breakfast of bread and cheese and fig cakes; going to the village well with Esther and Tamar for the day's supply of water; sewing on the new striped woolen cloth that Mary, Clopas' wife, had given her in Jerusalem, enough to make cloaks for all the children.

She had found time, also, to take two of the freshly baked loaves to Milcah, a widow whose old age and lameness prevented her from getting to the oven; to settle at least three quarrels among Jude and his playfellows, who seemed unable to decide whether they wanted to play wedding or funeral; to mend a rent in little Tamar's girdle; to give patient, comprehensive answers to both girls' innumerable questions concerning Jerusalem, their Uncle Clopas and Aunt Mary, and their cousins, James and Joses and Simon and Susanna.

But all the time she had been thinking: "He's in Sepphoris now. Perhaps at this moment he's talking with Eleazar, whoever he is. Perhaps he's being convinced. O dear God, don't let him be convinced! Don't let him—"

While she was still holding Simon and watching the slow, creeping shadows of the plane trees, Deborah came over from next door. "I'll hold Simon for you," she offered cheerfully, "while you start supper. Daniel isn't coming home tonight."

Mary surrendered her sleepy burden reluctantly. It wasn't often that Simon wanted to be held, and after that ten days' absence her arms still felt empty. "Where is Daniel?" she asked dutifully, the mere mention of his name bringing a coldness to her lips.

Deborah seated herself comfortably, the sleeping child pillowed loosely against her ample bosom. "In Sepphoris," she said, an odd gleam in her eyes. "He went late last night on business. And he may not be home very soon, not for a long, long time."

Noting the sudden gleam and the tone of suppressed, exuberant excitement, Mary thought: "She knows. And she's glad. She's like Deborah of old, stirring up Barak to fight her nation's enemies. It was the Canaanites then. Now it's the Romans. Sisera ... Quirinius—what matter which? She'd be glad to drive a tent pin through Quirinius' head, as Jael did through Sisera's. And if she did she'd be a heroine. Her name might even be put in holy scriptures."

Aloud she said: "I'm having lentils for supper. And cheese. And new bread. Joseph likes a hot supper after he's been working all day." She set the table, placed several of the round, thin loaves on a plate, poured out mugs of goat's milk for the children, stirred the big clay pot of steaming lentils.

"Deborah's a better woman than I am," she thought. "I love my husband and my children better than my country. I don't care if we have to pay taxes. I—dear Father, forgive me—I don't even hate the Romans!"

"They're coming," said Deborah. "Look at Joseph, carrying that big six-year-old James on his shoulders!"

"Come," echoed Simon, squirming down out of her arms and running out into the path. "Father—come!"

Mary flew to the door, the spoon still in her hand. She was in time to see Joseph set James down, open his great arms wide, and close them hungrily about baby Simon. Then they came up the path toward her, her husband and her three sons, each one stopping in turn to touch the mezuzah, the little metal case fastened to the doorpost containing the words of the sacred Shema, and to lift their fingers reverently to their lips. Simon laughed gleefully and kissed his in her direction.

"Sorry we're late," said Joseph, stooping to kiss her. "I stopped in Sepphoris to see a man. He wanted me to do a piece of work for him, and I had to tell him I couldn't. Mm! What's that I smell? Lentils? It's good, Mary, to be home."

3

The news spread like a fire. Kindled into flame by that mysterious "underground" that is ever present in occupied countries, fanned into a blaze by the reports of secret couriers, casual travelers, passing caravans, it swept through Galilee in a fierce and mighty conflagration.

Judas, the son of the great patriot Hezekiah, had revolted for a second time against Rome. Marching from Gamala, his native town on the great lake, he had swept like a whirlwind across Galilee, swelling his ranks of hot-blooded young loyalists from every town he passed into a veritable storm cloud of fury. With the aid of his henchman spy, Eleazar, the king's steward, he had seized the royal arsenal at Sepphoris, used its contents to supplement the armor of his ten thousand followers, and overpowered the small resident Roman garrison. Herod and his whole court had fled, leaving a victorious Judas in complete possession of the capital city.

Before this welcome news the swift, hot passion of the Galileans blazed like tinder. Town after town marshaled its bands of loyalists, some of them marching at once to join Judas at Sepphoris, others organizing in secret and waiting for reinforcements and weapons to come to them from the royal city. For the first time in ten years of inactive but sullen submission nationalism reared its head unscathed, and hope flared high. The day of vengeance, awaited so long, had come at last. Jehovah had risen in defense of His people to cast out the heathen invader. And his destroying angel was Judas the Galilean.

Nazareth, so close to Sepphoris that the hot breath of the struggle struck full upon it like heat on an already fevered cheek, seethed with rumor, suspicion, lawlessness, and intrigue. Since the bolder of the able-bodied young men had already joined themselves with Judas, there was no active display of violence in the town, but the air quivered with excitement and expectation. Men wore openly upon their cloaks small replicas of fox heads, symbols of Judas and his band. There was open hostility against the small constabulary of Roman soldiers quartered in the town.

James was in school when the news of Judas' rebellion came to Nazareth. Rabbi Nathan heard the sound of the runner's outcry even before it reached the sharper ears of the boys. A flush overspread his dark, thin face like crimson banners suddenly unfurled. He strode to the door of the synagogue, his long, blue-bordered Pharisee's cloak trailing behind him, his fine, narrow nostrils quivering like those of a race horse scenting the track. The boys, sitting cross-legged in the semicircle about the empty dais, sensed the crisis of the moment even before the shrill, long-drawn accents of the messenger were punctuated by the sharp, staccato beat of his footsteps.

"It's come!" Rabbi Nathan's hoarse whisper was far more emphatic than if he had shouted. He came back into the synagogue, remounted his dais, and sat down, his breath coming in short, labored gasps, his long, thin fingers trembling. "The day of the Lord's vengeance has come at last," he continued in the same hoarse whisper. "Praise be unto Him who has lifted His hand to strike the yoke from Israel! Go out and celebrate our deliverance, boys. And don't be afraid to lift your voices in thanksgiving. There will be no more school today."

The boys stared uncomprehendingly. Then, their teacher's final words possessing far more of penetrative power than those which preceded them, they unbent their small, curved legs, tiptoed tentatively toward the door, and, once outside, burst into wild, shrill whoops of delight at their unexpected freedom.

It was a day cut to the pattern of a small boy's dreams: mad, glorious, clamorous, unleashed confusion. Noise that was not only tolerated, unfrowned upon, but put suddenly at a premium. Adults with their dignity forgotten, their fiercer instincts unbridled, dancing in the streets, tossing their garments into the air, conducting themselves with the wild abandon of children. Better even than the Feast of Lights, when there was wholesale rejoicing and every house in town was ablaze! Or than Purim, with all its boisterous merriment!

James reveled in the excitement. He tore to the top of the hill with the rest of the boys to see if Sepphoris looked any different now that it was in the hands of the Jews instead of the Romans. Then he tore down again to see what had happened to their own village in their absence. Things were becoming more delightfully confused every moment. It was like a feast day, only infinitely more so. Most of the shopkeepers were closing their booths in the marketplace, feeling, no doubt, that greater values than the earning of shekels were at stake. A crowd of idlers was standing outside the Roman barracks, jeering and throwing stones and shouting brazen threats. Presently the handful of soldiers emerged and marched, double-quick time, down the street leading to the town gate. The boys followed them, ducking behind buildings, slinking along walls, in order to reach the gate ahead of them. James, always fleet of foot, was in the lead, Levi, the son of Johanan the tanner, close behind. They peered around the corner of a building, their heartbeats accelerating to the quickened tempo of the soldiers' approaching footsteps.

"I dare you," whispered Levi, his voice hissing in James' ear, "to throw a stone at them!"

James' heart lunged. Swiftly he leaned over and picked a handful of pebbles from the ground. Levi's eyes bulged.

"You wouldn't!" he hissed again. "You really wouldn't dare!"

By now they had been joined by other boys. In their eyes James beheld the same flattering incredulity that he saw in Levi's. Recklessly he leaned over again and, dropping the pebbles, picked up a good-sized rock. The flattering incredulity changed to derision. The boys mocked him silently. They didn't believe he'd really dare to throw it. All right, then. He'd show them!

His heart pounding furiously, he watched the soldiers approach, waited until they were even with the building, a little past it. His fingers closed like a vise about the rock, and he tried to move his arm, but it seemed paralyzed.

"I knew you wouldn't dare!" hissed Levi softly.

Suddenly his arm made a swift arc in the air, and he saw rather than felt the motion of the stone as it left his hand. It spun crazily toward the band of soldiers, striking the last one full in the middle of the helmet, toppling it to the ground. Most of the boys shrieked and ran, but James stood paralyzed, unable to move a muscle. He stared horrified while the soldier turned, picked up his helmet, put it on again, and, without even drawing his sword from its sheath, went on after the others. The world rocked about James' head, then settled evenly back into place. He felt a vast, heady triumph.

"Come on!" he shouted, waving back the retreating bevy. "They're afraid of us! They don't dare to touch us! Come on! After them, boys!"

Down through the streets of the town they ran, a wild, hooting mob, not bothering now to hide behind buildings, but flaunting their brazen audacity at the very heels of the enemy. No longer a group of unruly boys, but a horde of townspeople of all ages, flinging volleys of stones and fierce epithets of abuse, a long-pent volcano suddenly aroused from its slumber, spilling its hot, deadly vintage on whatever happened to lie in its path! And the handful of soldiers, most of whom had known previous experience with the Galilean temper in eruption, wisely kept their swords sheathed and their faces turned immovably toward the safe center of Roman authority in Caesarea, until, meeting no resistance, the enthusiasm of the mob wore itself out, and most of them, including James and his now staunch admirer, Levi, straggled back toward Nazareth.

It was by far the most exciting day James had ever spent. He enjoyed every minute of it. Tomorrow he might—probably would—have to resume his role of a too thin, too quiet, much too flabby-muscled small boy, his only claim to prowess a facility of mind which made him none too popular with his schoolmates. But today was his. There was something in his small, keenly imaginative being that was amazingly akin to the mad, reckless audacity of the moment, something that other boys his age, strangely enough, did not have, something born from those two brief flashes of self-discovery—"I am an Israelite." ... "I hate."

Only one thing marred the day's perfection.

"My father is with Judas," Levi took pains to inform him proudly.

"And so's my big brother. They're patriots, they are. They're heroes. They're fighting to free our country from the enemy."

"My Brother isn't old enough," retorted James defensively. "He's only twelve."

"Mine's only thirteen," replied Levi with satisfaction. "But he's big for his age. And he's terribly brave."

"Mine's brave, too," countered James hotly. "There's nobody in the world braver than my Brother. And my father—" He choked on the big lump of his anger.

Levi smiled, a maddening, skeptical little smile. "Where is your father now?" he asked innocently.

"He—he—he's in the carpenter shop, I guess."

Levi smiled again. Remembering the episode of the rock and James' hot temper, he kept his mouth firmly closed. But he did not need to say anything. The smile was sufficient.

For two months Judas the Galilean held the hilltop citadel in triumph. The fires of rebellion blazed unchecked from southern Judea to the northernmost bounds of Galilee, and hope flamed high. Israel was to be free again. The usurper had trampled the sacred dust of her heritage for the last time. The Messiah, the long-awaited national Deliverer, had come.

James lived these days in a passion of pleasurable excitement. Fresh from his long days in the synagogue schoolroom under the tutelage of the ardently patriotic Rabbi Nathan, who seized this opportunity to imbue in his young pupils a wider knowledge of their nation's heroes, James would hasten with his schoolmates to the top of the hill, where, still dreaming of Samson and Gideon and Barak and the Maccabees, he would breathlessly and for hours keep his gaze fixed on Sepphoris and the valley between, hoping for a glimpse of the rebel army. When, occasionally, a contingent would appear to march in disorderly array off into the hills in some direction or other, he would leap high into the air with the other boys, tearing off his girdle and waving it, and shouting at the top of his voice: "Hail, Judas! Hail, Lion of Judah! Hail, great Deliverer! Blessed are you who comes in the name of Jehovah!"

Then, tiring of this diversion, they would descend to the village, to find that their elders had devised some sport even more fascinating and diverting, such as the burning of an effigy of the Roman governor, Quirinius, in the marketplace. Even the daily services of worship in the synagogue were colored by an unusual excitement. The hymns of Israel's past triumphs were sung frequently and with an abandoned lustiness, and prayers were offered each day for the victory of Judas.

It would have been perfect, James felt, if only his Brother had shared his enthusiasm. Not that Jesus ever said he wasn't enthusiastic. That was just the trouble. He didn't say anything at all. He went with James and the other boys sometimes to the top of the hill and watched the horizon as intently as they—more intently, it seemed. But he never jumped into the air as they did, or waved his girdle, or joined them in their loud, savage cheering.

"Aren't you glad?" James demanded of him once, half resentfully. "Don't you want our country to be free?"

Jesus' reply was simple and straightforward but, to James' hot, demanding ardor, not very satisfactory. Of course he wanted their country to be free. He wanted all people to be free. But he wasn't sure yet that this was the way. Rabbi Ben Azel thought—

But James wasn't interested in what Rabbi Ben Azel thought or didn't think. He was so old-fashioned, anyway, not like Rabbi Nathan, who had come to Nazareth the preceding year straight from the School of Shammai in Jerusalem. Jesus was always listening to Rabbi Ben Azel, going to his house, reading his parchments. James was glad he didn't have to go to school to the old rabbi, the way Jesus had.

Joseph too was silent. He went about his work as usual, making tables and cedar chests and benches, painstakingly shaping the long, curved handles of plows, fashioning yokes of such careful shape that they would not gall the necks of patient oxen. And if, as the weeks passed and the success of Judas' exploit seemed more and more assured, he regretted the decision made on the day's trip to Sepphoris, he gave no sign.

"Anyone would think you weren't interested in your country's freedom," Deborah accused him, a transformed Deborah these days, who brandished her husband's heroism like a gauntlet. "What we need now are spear handles and bludgeons, not yokes and cradles."

"We'll be needing yokes and cradles later," said Joseph briefly, the smooth, even flow of his adz piling up the shavings at his feet.

And when Mary came back from the village well to announce breathlessly: "They think Judas is the Promised One, Joseph—the Deliverer—the Messiah! O Joseph, do you suppose he really is?" he replied patiently, "Perhaps. Let us wait and see."

James' secret, gnawing shame because of his father's seeming apathy was partially atoned for by the possessive pride he felt in his next-door neighbor, Daniel. The morning he awoke and learned that Daniel had returned late the night before and had asked for him was one of the proudest of his life.

"How's my little patriot?" the big familiar voice boomed as James burst excitedly into the house next door. "I hear you're the bravest boy in town! Led a bold assault and drove the Romans out of Nazareth!"

James flushed and looked hard to see if Daniel was making fun of him. He felt he could not bear it if he was. But the bright eyes held no mockery, only genuine admiration. Then he flushed again from sheer delight. "You're the real patriot," he said proudly.

Daniel hoisted him to his shoulder and carried him through the streets of the town, while all the villagers gathered around to admire his new weapons, ask questions about how the rebellion was going, and give advice as to what Judas and his men ought to do next. James' small heart pounded until it felt near to bursting. His thin fingers stroked the scar on Daniel's face, and he wondered how he could ever have thought it ugly to look at. It had become all at once a badge of heroism, of victory. He almost imagined that the little points and curves that cut white furrows into the lean brown smoothness of his cheek were shaped in the likeness of a fox!

Two months had nearly passed before Rome bothered to reach its long arm into the little subject province to snuff out the small, troublesome flame of rebellion. Then the Roman legions swept down upon Sepphoris, routed its untrained army of rebels, drove most of its inhabitants over the hills to the coast to be sold abroad into slavery, and set fire to the city. On the adjoining hill, not five miles away, huddled together in silence, the people of Nazareth stood one night and watched it burn, able by its flaring light to read the terror on each others' faces.

"What are you making, father?" asked James curiously.

He had thought at first they were the crossbeams for a house—the two long, irregular timbers that were too awkward in shape to be laid on the workbench. But crossbeams were placed side by side, or at least end to end, not crossing each other the way these two were. And, besides, when Joseph made the frame for a house, the beams were taken to the place where the house was to be built, not here to the shop to be worked on, certainly not stacked all about the courtyard. Why, there were enough—James counted them, bewildered—there were enough here for a half dozen houses! Something surely must have happened while he was at school, something—

"What are you making?" he repeated with mounting excitement.

Joseph's hand, heretofore as steady as the firm crossbeams of his houses, trembled so that the adz bit deep into the wood. He opened his mouth, but no words came. Jesus, who was working at his father's side, took James gently by the shoulders. He must go into the house, his Brother told him kindly but firmly. Father had a difficult job to do, and James could help him best by keeping out of the shop and not asking any questions.

James went into the house. He had a queer feeling in the bottom of his stomach, the same feeling that had been there, more or less, ever since that awful night when he had stood shivering on the hilltop and his small body had been racked with sickness over and over again. He would have died, he was certain, if it hadn't been for the sure, warm steadiness of his Brother's arm about him. Sometimes he woke up in the night now, having dreamed that that awful flaring was again in his eyes, that this time the world had surely come to an end, and lay breathing hard, his thin little body taut and sweating. Then somehow, miraculously it seemed, his Brother would sense his terror and move closer on the pallet, and the sure, warm steadiness would be again around him.

He opened his mouth to ask his mother what was going on out in the carpenter shop, then, seeing her face, closed it again. It frightened him at first to see her look so white. And he was sure she had been crying. If he hadn't been so sure, he probably would have done so himself. Instead, he told her all the funny things that had happened in Rabbi Nathan's school that day, chattering away, quite volubly for him, until he suddenly discovered from the white, cold stillness of her face that she wasn't even listening.

It was Jude who gave him his first information about the strange, long timbers. "A great big soldier came," he told him importantly, "on a great big horse. And he told father he'd have to make something, lots of somethings. Father didn't want to at first. He looked all white and his hands doubled up—like this—the way they do when he's angry. But the big soldier said he had to—or else! And mother cried. And the big soldier rode away. And then pretty soon a big cart came with all that lumber and unloaded it. And—and—what are they making, James, anyway? They won't let me go in."

Before the day was over, the two boys made another discovery. Whatever the strange "somethings" were, Malluch too was making them. When they went by his shop that afternoon, there were piles of the same sort of lumber in his yard, and the door leading to the place where he worked was wide open. They hid around the corner of an adjoining house and watched what he was doing. He laid a long timber on the floor, then laid a shorter piece on top of it, going the opposite way, and nailed the two together securely with wooden pins. That seemed to be all there was to it, for after that he dragged the queer-shaped object outside the shop and hoisted it on top of a pile of others just like it, puffing and groaning and straining until his thin, wiry body looked ready to snap. Then he went into the shop and started the same routine all over again.

"Do you suppose," whispered Jude, his eyes wide and eager, "that they could be pillars or something for a fine new temple?"

Within a few hours they found out just what they were. For before the next dawn the hills about the charred ruins of Sepphoris were dotted with those long, heavy timbers, each with a shorter cross-piece halfway between the top and middle, and each bearing a human sacrifice more ghastly than those fair, green hills had ever seen offered to preceding Molochs. It was the Roman method of meting punishment to rebels. Death by crucifixion.

James stared at the grim, gaunt shapes, toylike against the clear blue morning sky, his child eyes widening in unbelieving horror. Then, after being suddenly, violently sick, he tore back down the hill, the great acrid lump filling his throat, growing bigger and bigger and almost choking him. Regardless of his orders to keep out, he flung himself into the shop.

"Daniel—" he gasped. "Have they—will they—"

And then, without any warning, there in the smooth, curling shavings beneath the big timber that Joseph was planing, he was sick again.

It was his Brother who comforted his small, racked body, held his quivering shoulders with strong, steady hands. For Joseph was both dumb and helpless before the boy's misery. The days just past had taken something from him, left him weak and defenseless, while, strangely enough, they had made his oldest son, working beside him, stronger. Even James could feel it—some indefinable new strength— in the firm, quiet touch of the hand on his shoulder.

"Come here, little one," said Jesus. And he led him across the shop to where one of the finished crosses stood against the wall. When the child shrank away, the boy took his fingers firmly and, raising them, passed them along the surface of the big upright piece. The wood felt very even and fine-textured and unbelievably smooth to his touch.

James lifted his eyes to the deep, warm brown ones above him. Desperately he tried to understand what his Brother was trying to tell him. And finally he did, a little. They hadn't wanted to make the crosses, he and Joseph, but as long as they had to, they had made them the very best they knew how. It was the only thing they had been able to do right then to make things any better—to see that at least there wouldn't be any splinters.

"But Daniel—" whispered James again, convulsively.

Daniel had been a brave man, Jesus told him gravely. Perhaps he had known this might happen to him, but he had not been afraid. And they were not going to be afraid, either, when the time came for them to do their work.

"Our work?" echoed James wonderingly.

Suddenly his Brother was down on his knees in front of him, his bare legs among the shavings. Their eyes were on a level. James had a strange feeling that this was the most important thing that had ever happened to him, that all his six years had been lived just for this one moment—the quiet pressure of those firm hands on his shoulders and the clear, fathomless depths of those brown eyes looking into his.

Afterward James could not remember just what his Brother had said. He knew only that Jesus had told him about some great work that the two of them were going to do sometime, somewhere. Daniel had believed he had found a way to save his people, but he had been mistaken. James and his Brother must find a better way. They must work together.

"Together." That was the only word James really remembered, was sure of. It sang through his numbed senses. Warmth came flooding back into his small, chilled body. His universe slowly righted itself. And so it was that in the boy's bruised, sensitive spirit the Dream was born, kindled there by the flame in a pair of intense brown eyes, the amazingly steady young-old eyes of a twelve-year-old boy kneeling in a pile of shavings, a newly finished Roman cross stretching its two gaunt arms above him.

4

The harvest was plentiful that year. It was as if the ancient gods of the land, long dormant, had quickened to the familiar savor of human sacrifice on the old "high places" and bestirred themselves to fresh labors on behalf of their mortal suppliants. Mary, her sensitive spirit bruised and raw and quivering, for the first time in her life found no joy in the constantly unrolling scroll of the seasons. Usually she was breathlessly, joyously aware of each delicate undertone in the shifting panorama of color—soft, tender greens becoming dark and rich and lush, ripening into sun-drenched gold, paling slowly to the parched tints of silver. Watching the field whitening toward the harvest, she wondered if the bread kneaded from their grain would have the taste in her mouth of human flesh. And later, when the rich, crimson flow began to come from the wine presses, she gazed at it in horror, knowing that whenever the harvest of this vintage touched her lips, its warm tang would for her be that of human blood.

The eyes of the women whom she met at the well each day followed her resentfully, displaying their belief that because her husband and son were still alive she was immune to their suffering. They did not know that every glance pierced her like a knife thrust. They blamed her too, because of the gaunt shapes that went out of the carpenter shop and were loaded on the lumbering oxcarts that passed through the town at regular intervals. The thing that hurt her most of all was the look in Deborah's eyes.

"What shall I do without Daniel? I—I can't stand it, Mary!" The big, strong body that had seemed to harbor the spirit of the ancient prophetess looked suddenly flabby and helpless and carried its strength like a burden.

"I know," said Mary gently. "It seems more now than you can bear. But just wait patiently if you can. The suffering will pass, Deborah."

The dark, tear-filled eyes shone with a sudden glitter of resentment. "That's all very well for you to say, you who still have your husband and your sons. If Joseph weren't such a coward—"

"Joseph is not a coward," returned Mary quietly. "You know he isn't, Deborah."

"Well—maybe not. But—don't forget—he's making those horrible things!"

As if she could forget it, when her whole body cringed at the sound of every hammer beat, and the sharp rasping of the saw set every muscle quivering! Once when Joseph came into the house and, brushing the sawdust from his hands, reached toward her with a clumsy gesture of affection, she instinctively recoiled from his touch. The look on his face was frightening.

"You think I *want* to be doing this?" he asked thickly, the sweat standing on his forehead in great drops. "You think I wouldn't rather be dead, like Daniel? If it were only myself—"

She stood looking at him, conscious that beneath his heavy, silent kindliness burned fires which, if they were ever allowed to flame unchecked, could be terrible and devastating. She made a futile, frightened attempt to quench them.

"I'm sorry, Joseph. I didn't mean—please, please don't look like that! You frighten me!"

"You think I should have refused to make them?" he demanded in the same thick voice.

"No—oh, no! That is, I—Oh, I don't know what I think!"

It was all so bewildering, she thought, desperately trying to find an answer to the questions she was continually asking. She had no doubt about Joseph's refusal to join Judas. She knew that had been the right thing to do. Some sure, instinctive wisdom deep within her told her that bloodshed was not the way to win freedom. But this matter of the crosses—that was different. Suppose Joseph had refused to make them. Would that have helped the situation? The Romans would have found others to make them. They had requisitioned all the carpenters for miles around. Joseph would merely have been nailed on one of the crosses, and perhaps her oldest son. Her heart lurched sickeningly at the thought. No—not that!

And then suddenly she understood. "If it were only myself—" Joseph had said. It was for the sake of their son that he was keeping the fires within him carefully guarded—their firstborn, who was destined, they both felt, to rise to heights of achievement which they had never hoped to attain. She felt faint at the thought of what might have happened. Jesus—and a cross—

Her vision slowly steadied. Deep, tender gratitude welled up within her, and a consuming pity. She reached out and gently touched her husband's hand.

James was watching when the big cart came lumbering up to take away the last of the finished crosses. He and Jude hid around the corner of the little lean-to shop and watched them being loaded. They must be very heavy, he thought, for the driver of the cart tugged and grunted over his burden, and he always carried the lighter end. Joseph and Jesus bore the heavy end between them, fitting their shoulders beneath the crosspiece and straining forward like oxen pulling a load up a hill, Joseph always careful that his own broad, stocky back was placed well beneath the middle.

A big, burly soldier on horseback was directing the loading in none too good a temper. Mortally sick, no doubt, of the long orgy of espionage and bloodshed, his patience rubbed raw and ragged by the hot stubbornness of the natives of this little two-by-four province that had caused Rome more trouble than any other occupied area in the whole empire, he was anxious to get the whole business over with as quickly as possible. He gave his orders curtly, punctuating them with threatening flourishes of his spear.

James watched him, small fists clenched, heavy dark brows drawn tightly together. He wished he dared throw another stone. He knew where he would hit him, not on the helmet this time, but where David had hit Goliath, right between his eyes. But those hot, brief days of stone-throwing, together with their agreeable popularity, were past. He was no longer a hero—only a small, spindly-legged boy, just turning seven.

It was when they were loading the last cross that James suddenly saw his Brother stumble and fall, the big soldier lift his spear and strike it hard across his back. He saw his father's heavy hand clench and the blood rush to his white face. Then things happened so quickly that he could not follow them. One moment his father was standing there, his strong, square body trembling. The next he had reached for the big, heavy wooden mallet that hung at his belt and was beating out with it furiously.

"Strike my son, will you! You contemptible heathen dog! I've stood just about all I can. I've kept silent under your yoke, paid your ungodly taxes, even made your crosses for you! Now take this—and *this*!"

His voice rose to a scream of fury, his mallet pounding all the while with well-aimed directness at the amazed soldier, who, while knowing that in this despicable province he must be prepared for anything, had not been at all prepared for this. A stodgy, plodding, middle-aged carpenter who had not given the slightest trouble! Recovering himself quickly, however, he raised his spear and struck Joseph soundly over the head. The carpenter dropped heavily to the ground.

"Father!" James heard Jesus' voice rising high and clear, saw his Brother disentangle himself from the heavy wooden frame pinning him down and run to his father's side. Before he could reach him, however, the big soldier had seized the boy and flung him violently to the ground, the slim body striking the stone side of the lean-to.

"Load him on the cart!" he ordered the driver curtly. "No, not the boy, the man. One's enough to bother with. Confound the dog! He'd have pounded me to a pulp. Did, almost. By Jupiter, if I find he's broken any bones—"

James stood watching, dry-eyed and paralyzed, while the cart lumbered up the street, the big soldier curbing his high-stepping horse to keep behind it. Then he followed Jude, who had run screaming for his mother. They had not far to go, however, for Mary, who had watched the entire scene from the shelter of the doorway, was already bending over the limp, slender figure on the ground.

"Help me," she said briefly to James, her stiff, frozen lips forming the words with difficulty. "We must—get him into the—house."

James obeyed, his muscles seeming to move without his will. He stared, terrified and fascinated, at the slow trickle of blood moving down the wide, white forehead. And in that moment his child soul plumbed another depth in its probing quest of self-discovery—the sudden knowledge that he loved his Brother, would always love him, better than he could ever love any other person in the world.

There was not much sleep in the little house that night, though Mary, with Esther and Tamar to help her, laid down the pallets as usual. After James was sure that his Brother was all right and that the terrifying trickle of blood came only from a surface bruise, he crawled into bed and pulled the covers up, but he did not sleep. He strained his ears and tried to listen to the muted voices of his mother and Brother and older sisters, but he could not hear what they said. He was grateful when Jude crept over to his pallet and snuggled close to him for comfort, though usually he would have resented this familiarity.

"Where's father?" The stocky little body was shaking.

James gulped. "You—you know as much as I do. You saw them take him away."

"Will they—will they—kill him?"

"I—I—" James' throat tightened. He could not answer. His whole body felt cold and numb. Long after Jude had fallen into a troubled sleep, he lay strained and taut, his ears tensed with listening. He knew that the others were listening too. That was why their voices were muted. They were waiting, as he was—waiting for something to happen. And finally, toward dawn, it came, the faint sound of heavy, dragging feet outside the door. Mary flew to open it.

"Oh, thank the Lord!" she sobbed. "You're still alive! My dear—oh, my dear!"

Her arms went about his bruised, battered body, half lifting, half dragging him into the house, her tears falling upon the ragged, bleeding flesh of his naked back and shoulders. But they were tears of joy and gratitude as well as of pity. For Joseph was not dead. Having found none of his bones broken, the big Roman had been lenient. He had ordered merely that his assailant be beaten with a scourge of leather thongs, heavily loaded with lead.

The grim harvest of the rebellion had not been fully garnered. Each dawn the gray shapes on the surrounding hills stretched their gaunt arms to receive new victims from those suspected of complicity with Judas. But their number was getting fewer. And Joseph's part in it was over. When he had finally recovered sufficiently from his bruises to return to the carpenter's shop, it was with an eagerness and zest for his work that he had not felt in months. From now on he would not have to think each time he raised his hammer, "This is perhaps for Daniel, or Johanan, or Abdiel, or Eleazar."

"Now," he said slowly, conscious that he was breaking a long silence, "I can build that new house for Eliah the potter. I can make a cradle for Hannah, the young bride of Joshua ben Nathan. I can mend the lintels of the synagogue." And to his oldest son, who understood him well, it was as if he had said, "Now I can help men to live instead of die."

The weeks had taken their toll of his body as well as his spirit. He looked much older. His black hair and beard were streaked with white. But it was with an almost boyish eagerness that he picked up his saw and a length of white wood to start work on Hannah's cradle.

"Well, well!" He had sawed the frame and was fitting the pieces together with pins of oak when a familiar, disagreeable voice broke in on his work. "So the son of Jacob is making a cradle! Don't you know coffins are more profitable than cradles, Joseph?"

Joseph eyed the thin, stooped figure steadily. "What do you want here, Malluch? You've never stepped inside my door yet without bringing trouble, and I'm sure this is no exception."

The little carpenter leered. "Just a friendly visit, Joseph. I was interested to see if you were still here, that's all. So many of the friends of Judas the Galilean have not been so fortunate."

"I was not a friend of Judas," retorted Joseph hotly. "When you saw me coming from his house that day—"

"Oh, so you admit you were coming from his house! Have you told the Romans that you paid Judas this visit, Joseph—the same day that you spent nearly the whole afternoon with Eleazar, the king's steward?"

"How did you know—"

Malluch's crafty little eyes gleamed. "Ah, so you admit that too. The Romans would certainly be interested to know of these little visits, Joseph. Especially after this other little trouble you got yourself into."

Joseph wet his lips. "Listen, Malluch," he said, "I went to Judas' house that day to tell him I would have no part in his rebellion."

The other nodded. "Very interesting. But can you prove it? Have you any witnesses?"

"I—I think so. Daniel—"

"Ah, but Daniel is dead, my friend."

Joseph lifted his big hand to wipe the sweat from his face. "You—you must believe me, Malluch," he said desperately.

"Oh, of course I believe you." The small eyes narrowed craftily. "But would the Romans, Joseph? Just in case I should consider it my duty to tell them."

Joseph regarded him steadily. "Just what do you want?" he demanded. "Why are you here?"

Malluch leaned forward, the thin, curved bow of his figure stretched taut for the shooting of its missile. "I want more work in this town, Joseph," he said abruptly. "You're popular with the townspeople. I'm not. But I'm going to be. You're going to make me. You're going to start by telling Eliah the potter that on account of ill-health you're not going to be able to build his house, and you're going to recommend me for the contract. Later you're going to do other things. You understand, my friend?"

Joseph understood. His big hand closed about the handle of his hammer. He lifted it slowly. Malluch eyed it mockingly.

"Better think twice, Joseph. A man should before he adds murder to insurrection. The last time you used that hammer, you know, wasn't so profitable."

The big hand dropped helplessly. The hammer clattered to the bench. "I'm a poor man, Malluch," said Joseph hoarsely. "I have children. My oldest son—I want him to go away to school."

"And I have a son too, Joseph." It was as if a mask had dropped suddenly from the little carpenter's face. The mocking light gone from his eyes, they looked vulnerable and naked. "It's for his sake I'm doing this. I'd sell my soul for him."

After Malluch had gone, Joseph took up his hammer. His shoulders were again bent, and his big hand trembled. He felt suddenly very tired. But he fitted the pieces of white board carefully, painstakingly together. At least, he thought grimly, Malluch would not want to make cradles.

As the months passed, the revolt of Judas the Galilean slipped farther and farther into the past and was almost forgotten. Slowly the gaunt shapes on the hillsides lost their grim, ghastly significance. Some of them were used as wall and roof timbers for the new houses that sprang up out of the charred ruins of Sepphoris. Others, after a fall and winter of seasoning under the mild Galilean sun, were taken down and sawed up and carted away to be used as firewood. The few remaining became inconsequential landmarks, of no more importance than dead trees, except to passing children, who, forgetting or not knowing that they had once been trees of death, found their square mainposts and straight crosspieces choice treasures for shinnying up and straddling. The brief, hot efflux of nationalism subsided, and Galilee settled back into its normal peace—that of a serene, pastorally beautiful, but inwardly seething volcano.

Rabbi Nathan prudently veered back from his heroic aberrations to the prescribed formulas of the Mosaic Law and the Mishnah, that vast body of lesser laws which every Jewish boy was required at an early age to learn by rote, through a method of endless oral repetition, and keep at his tongue's end. James excelled in the schoolroom. His swiftly lengthening body barely kept pace with his hungrily absorbing mind. If out on the playground a natural shyness and reticence made him acutely self-conscious, here in the glibness of the classroom he found full compensation.

And when at the age of six young Jude appeared to cross his small, stocky legs humbly on the floor before Rabbi Nathan, the vindication of James as a personality was complete. For poor Jude was no scholar and never would be. His slow tongue stumbled helplessly even on the Shema, that primer of Jewish religion which every child learned to lisp at his mother's knee and the majestic words of which were enclosed on parchment in the little box on every doorpost. Jude's stubby little fingers might curl around the handle of an adz as if they had been born holding it, but they certainly fumbled awkwardly with a scroll or stylus. Watching his patient attempts, James felt a new emotion stirring within him. "I'll help you," he whispered when Rabbi Nathan's back was turned. "I'll teach you later when we get home. Don't worry about it, little one."

That night he took Jude up on the hill and showed him his secret hiding place, which he had never shown to anybody before, not even his Brother. That is, he tried to show him. Jude wasn't able to crawl through the narrow opening in the rocks any better than he had been able to two years before, though he squeezed and grunted and attempted it at all possible angles. But, then, James discovered that now he himself couldn't either. So they played Samson and the Philistines among the rocks instead. He even let Jude be Samson and make-believe kill him with the jawbone of an ass!

5

James was sure he had never been so happy—nor so miserable. He was happy because he was nine years old, because it was springtime, and because he was on his way to Capernaum, where he was going to spend a whole week. He was miserable because soon after their return home his parents and his Brother were to go to Jerusalem for the Feast of Weeks, and his Brother was going to remain there.

He had known about it even before Jude and the other children, because he had happened to be playing in the courtyard just outside the door of the carpenter shop the day his father and his Brother had been talking. So vividly had the moment etched itself upon his consciousness that even now he could almost remember the words they had said.

"Oh, but I couldn't, father! What! Leave you here to do all the work by yourself?"

"I can manage. And James is getting old enough to help."

"James?" He had pricked up his ears at the sound of his own name, then flushed as his sensitive intuition had sensed the smile of good-natured skepticism that must have accompanied it.

"Well—Jude, then."

"Jude is only seven. You know he can't help much yet."

"There's no more than I can handle easily. You know how little work there's been since—since Malluch—"

"Yes, I know but are you sure you're quite well, father? Sometimes I've wondered—"

"So!" His father had pretended anger at this. "You think I'm getting old, do you, weak and infirm! Can't do my work well anymore!"

"Of course not, father. You know I don't think that. Only—"

"Your mother wants it very much, son. She has dreamed of it for years. I suppose it's always that way with mothers, especially with their firstborn, but she's always thought you were something—something pretty special. It's almost an obsession with her. She thinks there's some great work you're intended to do."

"Yes, I know. She's told me. And I've felt it too, father."

"Your mother's set her heart on your being something more than a country carpenter. A rabbi, perhaps. All mothers, you know, want their sons to be rabbis." There had been a hint of humor in Joseph's voice. "Probably she even has a faint idea somewhere in her mind that you're the great Anointed One, the long-looked-for Messiah."

James' heart had been beating fast by this time. He had listened breathlessly for what his Brother would say next.

"What would you like for me to be, father?"

"I? Oh, I—" In the brief pause that followed James had heard the smooth, steady strokes of his father's adz. "What I want really doesn't matter. It's your mother who counts, son. And she wants you to go to school in Jerusalem. It's all arranged. You are to live with my brother, Clopas. And you're not to worry about us, understand? You *must* go, my son."

"I understand, father."

James had slipped out of the courtyard quietly, wanting to be alone with this disturbing piece of news that threatened to upset his whole, even, well-ordered plan of life. It had been impossible to imagine what life would be like without his Brother. No long walks in the late afternoon up on the hilltop, no enthralling stories to while away the irksome hours that he was obliged to spend each day now at the carpenter's bench, no comforting arm to steal about him when he awoke out of a bad dream in the middle of the night!

But he had told no one of his misery, for he was getting to be a big boy now, nine years old, three quarters of the way to being a "son of the Commandment." He had even managed to look pleased when Joseph had broken the news to the family at the evening meal, though the piece of barley bread in his mouth had almost choked him. Jesus had understood, however, in spite of his silence, and that night after they had gone to bed he had tried to comfort him by telling him again about the Dream and how they must get ready for it together.

Today, however, even though the time of his Brother's going away was drawing very close indeed, James' happiness outweighed his misery. For the week's visit to Capernaum stretched enticingly just ahead of him, and to a boy of nine a week is a long time, practically endless.

They were taking their own little donkey, Graylegs, for Mary to ride on, and another, which they had borrowed, to carry the clothes, tools, and camping supplies. It was not a pleasure trip. Joseph was going on business. Zebedee, his brother-in-law, had sent word that he had some work for him to do, and Salome, Zebedee's wife and Mary's sister, had asked the whole family to come to pay a visit. So here they were, making quite a respectable caravan, James thought. Only he didn't want to think about caravans, because they reminded him of what was going to happen soon after their return home. He preferred to think about his cousins, James and John, and about the big lakeside city to which they were journeying, and about the increasingly exciting Way of the Sea over which they were traveling.

It seemed strange to be a part of the vast, colorful stream of traffic which from the hilltop had looked like an endless toy parade silently moving between the eastlands and the Sea of Galilee. Down here on the road the great gliding camels looked like anything but toys, and their voluble, sharp-tongued drivers were anything but silent. Used though he was to the sight of caravans in the marketplace, James never tired of watching the tall, patient, loping beasts with their endless variety of human companions, nor of speculating on the treasures that they carried in the great bales swung at their sides—spices and fruits and fragrant woods and silks and jewels and swords and carved ornaments, from Arabia and the cities of the Decapolis, from Damascus and Baghdad and those mysterious lands even farther toward the rising sun.

At night they made camp in a little valley between two high, pointed hills. Jude said they looked like two horns sticking up, and Joseph and Mary both laughed and told him that was the name of the two hills, the Horns of Hattin. While Mary and the girls were getting supper over the campfire, Jesus took the three younger boys up the side of one of the hills, little Simon riding on his shoulders. About halfway up they came to a broad, level place, and James and Jude, already tired out by the long day's walk, sank down in the grass to rest.

"Let's run," whispered Simon in his brother's ear. "Let's run to the top of that little mound and beat them!"

And they did. Triumphantly the little boy looked down from the slightly superior height of his two older brothers.

"Look!" he cried in delight. "Look, James and Jude! It's just as in the synagogue. You're the people, and I'm the preacher up on the platform."

Jude grinned up at him mischievously. "Why don't you preach us a sermon?" he asked slyly.

The little one shook his head vigorously. "No. Not me. I know what. Let's let Jesus tell us a story!"

The eyes of the two boys in the grass down below quickened with interest. "Yes, do," urged Jude. "Tell us the one about—about—"

"About the little lost lamb," said Simon happily. "I like that one best."

So Jesus sat down on the little mound, and, smiling down at his two brothers who sat on the wide level space below, he began his story.

As they traveled on the next day after leaving the Horns of Hattin, the country became more wild and forbidding. Great cliffs reared themselves beside the road, their faces honeycombed with caves, their bleak, seamed, terraced surfaces untouched by vegetation. Joseph bade his company draw closer together.

"Are there really robbers in those caves?" asked Jude, looking up at them with fearful fascination.

"Yes," returned Joseph, "the cliffs are full of them. It's almost as bad here as on the road between Jerusalem and Jericho. Sometimes they roll down huge boulders on passing caravans and then rush down to loot them. We don't need to worry much, though. It's just the rich caravans they're after."

Little Simon shivered and edged close to his father. "I'm glad we're good and poor," he said heartily.

They all laughed then, especially Joseph, who seemed more like himself today than he had for months. The spell of brooding silence, which had hung over him of late, seemed momentarily to be broken.

"Tell us some more about the robbers," urged Jude with frightened relish.

"Well, there are plenty of stories I might tell about these cliffs," said Joseph, more voluble than usual. "And they aren't all about robbers, either. Not so many years ago these caves were filled with Galilean patriots, like Judas, and they used to hold up the armies of the great King Herod, not the one who is our king now, but another who lived years ago, when Jesus was born. Finally it became so bad that Herod made great cages, filled them with soldiers, and let them down over the mountainside. When the cages got opposite a cave, the soldiers would stick long iron hooks into the hole and pull out the rebels, then drop them to death down on the rocks below. If they couldn't get at them that way, they sent smoke pouring into the caves, and the poor men inside, rushing out to get away from the smoke, either were killed by Herod's soldiers or fell over the precipice. But I shouldn't be telling you all these gruesome things," he reminded himself suddenly, noticing the younger children's frightened faces.

"I should say not," said Mary, shivering. "You'll have us all wishing we were back home in Nazareth." She turned to Jesus with a smile. "You tell us a story, son, why don't you, to take the bad taste out of our mouths? And do make it a different kind!"

"But not too different," said Jude quickly. "Make it have robbers in it!"

Jesus laughed, his deep brown eyes fixed fondly on the child's round, eager face. He wasn't sure, he told his little brother good-naturedly, that he knew one with robbers in it.

"Then make one up," returned Jude promptly.

Jesus walked along thoughtfully, his hand on the donkey rein, while three pairs of eyes—five, in fact, for Esther and Tamar were still young enough to be fascinated by a story—gazed at him in anticipation.

As Simon shivered delightedly, Jesus began a story about a certain man who was traveling on a barren, lonely road, where there were great high rocks on either side.

"This road?" demanded Jude.

Jesus shook his head. It was the road father had told about, the one going from Jerusalem to Jericho. When this man reached the loneliest part of the road, he fell among thieves, who stripped him of his clothes and beat him and left him beside the road to die.

Joseph's attention wandered. His face, lightened for a little and relieved of its now habitual anxiety, slipped back into its former grooves. His mind began to wrestle with the problems that for many months now had haunted both waking and sleeping hours.

It was three years since Malluch had stood in the door of the carpenter shop and played his first little game of blackmail. Joseph had obeyed Malluch's direction. He had told Eliah the potter that he was ill and could not build his house. Later he had been forced to make other refusals—a barn for Reuben the herdsman, some new wine presses for a large vineyard over toward Mount Tabor, a new set of booths in the marketplace for Laban the merchant, a large contract in the construction work going on over in Sepphoris. Soon Malluch's threats had become unnecessary, since the townspeople had started to whisper.

"Have you noticed how poorly Joseph is looking?" "They say he has had to refuse a great deal of work." "Have you seen how unsteady his hand is getting?" "What a pity, and he used to be such a good carpenter!" "I heard a queer story about him too, the other day. Not that I believe it, but they say there are things in his past." "Of course, we don't approve of Malluch, but after all he's a good carpenter."

The irony was that it was true. Almost as if Malluch, who had probably started the gossip about his competitor's ill-health, had actually willed it into being! For, since that drain upon his energies and emotions three years before, Joseph had not been himself. His hand was not steady. He had grown infinitely older in looks. And sometimes there was that odd pain in his chest. He hadn't had to tell anybody about it yet. So far the attacks had come when he was alone. He was sure they were unimportant, but if Jesus knew about them, he might not be willing to leave him to go to school in Jerusalem. In fact, Joseph knew the boy would not be willing. As it was, it had been hard enough to persuade him. And Mary's heart was so set on his going. He was glad it was settled.

Joseph sighed, half with relief, half with regret. Education was a good thing, he knew, and he wanted his boy to have the best. Perhaps he would be a rabbi. Perhaps he would come back sometime to Nazareth and speak in the synagogue, the way his mother dreamed of his doing. He would be proud of him. But it was a good thing to be a carpenter. There was that feeling of rightness that came when you had tools in your hands, the oneness you felt with all creators of good things everywhere, including the great Creator. And Jesus was a good carpenter. He had something, a certain vision, imagination, which he, Joseph, had never had, which he was afraid none of his other sons had, except possibly James, and James did not have the skill to go with it. Jesus might—he might even have built a temple!

Joseph sighed again. He would miss his oldest son—miss his quick slender figure at the bench, his light step beside him when he went into the country, his fresh, clear young voice telling stories to the children, as he was telling them now. His mind came back abruptly.

"And on the next day," Jesus was saying, "when the man departed, he took out two pieces of money and gave them to the innkeeper and said, 'Take care of him, and if you need anymore, I will give it to you on my way back.' "

"Is that all?" asked Simon. Then, as Jesus nodded: "I liked that. It was a good story."

Jude looked doubtful. "Are you sure it was a Samaritan?"

"Quite sure, little one."

James said nothing. The story had aroused in him a feeling of uneasiness. He wasn't at all sure he liked it. It sounded as if Jesus thought the Samaritans were just as good as the Jews, that some of them might even be better. And everybody knew the Samaritans were sinful, unfriendly people. James wished Jesus wouldn't say such things.

The road plunged abruptly. Mingled with the oaks and olives, the sycamores and walnuts, could be seen palm and fig trees and thick, luxuriant oleanders. The air became hot and sultry. Then suddenly the road emerged from a glen, dipped over the crest of a hill, and there lay before them the Plain of Gennesaret, broad and rich and fertile, teeming with industry and commerce, pulsing with the flowing life streams of two rapidly mingling cultures, Jew and Gentile, Asiatic and European, East and West.

"Oh!" cried Simon delightedly. "There's the lake!"

It lay before them like a gigantic harp, crossed and recrossed by dancing, shimmering strings of sunlight, sometimes muted by a hot, clear stillness, sometimes strummed upon by cool, refreshing breezes from Mount Hermon. It was so beautiful that they just stood for a while and looked at it, letting the slow-moving blood stream of merchants, tourists, artisans, fishermen, farmers, soldiers, Jews, Arabs, Greeks, Romans, flow through the great traffic artery about them.

"Get along there, peasant!" shouted somebody in passing. "Can't you see you're blocking the road?"

It was hot in Capernaum, with a heat so heavy, sultry, and oppressive that James wondered at first how his two cousins, James and John, could have so much exuberant energy. James, the older of the two, was already a muscular young giant at thirteen, while John, two or three years younger, made up in keenness of mind and alert swiftness of body what he as yet lacked in strength. A swift-tempered, volatile pair, they were remarkably facile at devising mischief and might easily have been on the Capernaum blacklists if their father Zebedee had allowed them more leisure. After hearing of some of their exploits James thought it no wonder that among their playmates they had been nicknamed "sons of thunder."

And if Zebedee, who in his slow, ponderous way did a good deal of rumbling, was the thunder thus referred to, his wife Salome was certainly the lightning. A nervous, energetic woman with black, flashing eyes and fingers that were constantly busy about something, she was as unlike her younger sister Mary as two women having the same parents could possibly be. She was a passionate devotee of the hearthstone, one of those women who are forever scrubbing and forever changing things.

"Zebedee has decided at last to open a big wholesale in Bethsaida," she told Mary with a somewhat misleading emphasis on the first word, it being Salome's decision, not Zebedee's. "I've been telling him for years that he should be spreading out, and Bethsaida's really the center of the fishing industries now, not Capernaum. We might move over there in time, though I doubt it, because I've just got this house fixed to suit me. You do like my new guestchamber, don't you?" She flitted from one subject to another the way a bird hops, aimlessly but with an admirable dexterity of motion. "They're going to call it 'Zebedee and Sons, Wholesale Fish.' Oh yes, and did I tell you, they're selling fish now to the salteries down the lake at Tarichaea? Zebedee's making twice as much money now as he was two or three years ago, when you were here last. The boys will be rich men someday. Oh, and that reminds me, we didn't get you down here, you know, just to do a few odd repairing jobs on Zebedee's boats. We have other plans. But perhaps I'd better let Zebedee tell you."

Mary dutifully admired the new guestchamber which had been built on the flat rooftop. She was glad they would not have to share the sleeping quarters with the rest of the family, even though Zebedee's house was much larger than theirs in Nazareth, and had more than the usual single room. She was not feeling so well as she might, and the intense, sultry heat and ever-present aroma of fish seemed to aggravate her occasional spells of nausea. Some deep reticence within her shrank from her sister's kindly but mercilessly probing eyes.

"My dear, so that's the way things are!" She knew just what Salome would say and just how she would say it, in a voice hearty, matter-of-fact, and a trifle envious, for Mary already had four sons to Salome's two. "Why didn't you tell me? Let's see, how old is Simon now? Nearly five. And Jesus is fifteen. It doesn't seem possible. I suppose Joseph is pleased, and why shouldn't he be? Well, at least I can be thankful mine were both boys."

No, she didn't want Salome to know. She didn't want anyone to know yet, not even Joseph. She wanted just for a little while to keep it deeply hidden within herself—this blessed awakening of new life, this sweet ecstasy of fulfillment, this exquisite foretaste of pain that was somehow akin to the life-creating travail of the Infinite. She had felt it first, long ago, before the coming of her firstborn son. Now years afterward, in the rich fullness of her maturity, she was feeling it again—that awakening consciousness of the presence of Divinity, that faint stirring within her body that was in some mystical way the pulse beat of all mankind.

And again, as long ago, the thing within her became rhythm, poetry, the sound of singing, and she repeated sometimes, softly:

> My soul magnifies the Lord,
> And my spirit has rejoiced in God my Savior . . .
> For he who is mighty has done great things for me.

"No," said Zebedee the morning of the third day of their visit. "I can't take you boys out on the lake today. Joseph and I are going over to Bethsaida to look at the new warehouse site. Wait until later, and you can go out with one of the men in the fishing fleet."

"Then let us go alone," suggested John quickly, his swift mind leaping ahead, as usual, to forestall the objections that he knew would be forthcoming. "You've told us yourself we could handle a boat as well as some of your best apprentices, and you know you like us to be independent. Besides, the lake's as quiet as a dead fish. Nothing could happen."

Zebedee shook his head. "You don't know that lake the way I do. It might be all right for you boys, but your two young cousins—"

"Oh, they'll be all right," James assured him easily, flexing his big muscles in a gesture of defiance. "Besides, Jesus is going with us."

"Oh, well, of course, if Jesus is going. But keep close to the shore and watch the weather."

There were seven of them in the boat, Jesus and James and Jude, the two sons of Zebedee, and Simon and Andrew, two boys who lived nearby and whose father was a partner of Zebedee in the fish business. James liked them at once, though he thought Simon rather a queer fellow, always doing awkward and impulsive things, like pushing the boat out from the wharf too far and falling into the water when he tried to jump the intervening distance. He was good-natured about it, however, the smile never once leaving his big-boned, angular face, and his short tunic soon dried in the hot tropical sun.

The lake was as smooth as glass, but even so James disliked the rhythmic, unfamiliar motion of the boat. The smell of fish was so strong that it made him feel almost faint. He was suddenly, horribly afraid that he was going to be sick, when Jesus suggested to his cousins that they stop for a while and fish. He was curious to see how the nets worked.

"All right," agreed Cousin James, "only we won't catch much. It isn't the right time of day."

James huddled gratefully down into his seat, the nausea gradually subsiding. It was like his Brother to know somehow, without being told, how a person felt. It was like him too to be interested in every little detail of everything anybody did, from throwing a net over the edge of a boat to kneading bread or shearing a sheep.

There were two casting nets in the bottom of the boat. John and Simon threw them out, one on each side, with a skillful turn of the wrist. James envied them their smooth, muscular strength, their easy grace of motion.

After watching them cast a few times, Jesus asked if he might try it. They taught him how it was done, laughing at his first clumsy attempts, applauding as he became a little more expert. "You'll make a fisherman yet," they told him generously.

A twinkle appeared in the deep brown eyes. He *was* going to be a fisherman, Jesus told them. Only he was not going to catch fish. He was going to catch men.

"What kind of men?" asked John gravely, as if Jesus had not intended the words as a joke.

James looked up at his Brother sharply. He wasn't sure just what they were talking about, but he was sure that he did not like the intimacy of his cousin's tone. After all, what concern was it of John's what his Brother intended to do? He saw the brown eyes lose their twinkle and look steadily into the fiery black ones. "All kinds," Jesus said.

"I'll tell you what," said James, John's brother. "We'll all help you. We'll form a partnership and call it 'The Galilean and Company, Fishers of Men.' "

They all laughed heartily, Jesus included. Then the brown eyes kindled. When the time came, he told them with a smile half whimsical, half serious, he would remember.

James felt small and left out and more than a little resentful. He knew vaguely that Jesus was talking about the Dream—*their* Dream—that belonged to just the two of them; that he was even sharing it with these big, boorish cousins who, he wouldn't be surprised, had already forgotten parts of the Mishnah they had learned. Besides, the Dream was something to be visioned awesomely from a hilltop, like Elisha's horsemen and chariots in the clouds, or whispered about in the Temple, with the memory of Isaiah's coals of fire hot on one's lips—not to be bandied about informally in a smelly fishing boat!

An innocent-looking cloud billowing down from the direction of Safed and allowing itself to be sucked into a deep valley funnel became suddenly ominous. The smooth, glassy surface of the lake cracked into jagged splinters, crumpled into sharp, white-crested waves, reared itself in great, threatening, pointed masses. The little fishing boat tossed helplessly like a frail bit of parchment. One moment, it seemed, James was looking at his own thin, wavering image in the smooth water over the side of the boat, the next he was clutching terrified at something, a blinding spray in his face. Miraculously the thing he clutched became a hand, firm and familiar, and unbelievably steady. Jesus' smile said, "Don't be afraid."

But James knew he was not the only one who was afraid. Even though he dared not open his eyes to look at their faces, he could tell by the sound of their voices that his big cousins were frightened.

"Pull hard!" shouted James from the other end of the boat, his voice barely carrying above the fury of the storm. "Face up—into the wind!"

"We—we can't!" replied John faintly from his place at the forward set of oars. "We—we aren't—s-strong enough!"

"And we've lost an oar!" It was the impulsive Simon's voice, thick and terrified.

James felt himself lifted and set down carefully beside Jude in the bottom of the boat. He clutched again, but his fingers found only Jude's hand, shivering and clammy. Cold spray swept over him again, leaving him choking and gasping, the tossing of the boat flinging him helpless against first one side, then the other. In the din of the waves he could hear the frightened cries of his cousins and their two friends, then another voice, quiet and penetrating, giving orders. His Brother's. He closed his eyes tightly, thinking: "This is dying. This is what Daniel did."

Then all at once he was conscious of a difference. The floor beneath him steadied. The beat of the waves against the sides of the boat became more rhythmical. It was as if a firm hand had been placed beneath them, holding them straight and poised. He opened his eyes. In the center of the boat James and John were pulling on one oar with all their might, Simon and Andrew on the other. His Brother was standing up, holding the one remaining oar, steadying the motion of the boat by long, firm, even strokes. By sheer strength of will, it seemed, he was holding the frail craft straight into the wind.

James lifted his eyes to his Brother's face, and what he saw there made him marvel. "Why, he's not afraid," he thought. "He's not afraid at all."

Like so many of those quick, furious storms on Gennesaret, the tumult ceased as suddenly as it had begun. A few moments later the boat was riding easily, the motion of the waves against its sides nothing more than the heaving of a gentle sigh after a wild tempest of weeping.

"Well," said Cousin James, pulling lustily toward the wharf, "that was quite a storm. They're always coming up like that, though, on this lake, and then going down again so quickly you'd never believe they were there. Lucky we didn't get panicky and forget to keep pulled up into the wind!"

"I guess father'll be pretty proud of us when we tell him!" boasted John loudly.

So that was it, James thought. Storms had done that before, then stopped with a suddenness that was almost unbelievable. He had had a queer feeling for a minute, looking at that quiet, serene, upright figure with its utterly fearless face. He had had a queer feeling that it was his Brother who had stopped it!

"Yes, it's just as Zebedee has been telling you," said Salome, proceeding in her usual way to tell it all over again. "There's work enough here in Capernaum to keep Joseph busy for months. What with the new wholesale to be built over in Bethsaida and the warehouses and boats to be repaired here, we could almost hire a carpenter permanently. And as soon as our work runs out, there's plenty more to be found. Capernaum is a coming city. You might just as well make up your mind now and move right up here, Joseph. Now don't begin to shake your head, because it's all settled. In fact, Zebedee and I have our eye on a nice little house right around the corner. It's bigger than you're used to, but it ought to be. Your sons will be growing up and marrying soon, and you're not being fair to Mary to keep her cooped up in a little place like that."

"Oh, but I'm not cooped up!" Mary thought in sudden panic of the cool, green hills around Nazareth, the coziness of her small, square house, the friendly group of women who met around the village well. "I love Nazareth. I—I—"

"But you wouldn't want to stand in Joseph's way, dear, would you, if he had a chance to better himself! And he certainly has. Besides, he's not looking well, either. Something's worrying him, and, if I'm not mistaken, it's the way business is going in Nazareth. You can't tell me, Joseph, that things have been going well."

"Well, I—It's true I haven't done so much work in the last few years. There's another carpenter there named Malluch—"

"There! I thought so. Things *aren't* going well, and it's time you made a change. You'll make twice as much money here, and you're going to need money with your oldest son away at school. So now it's all settled, isn't it?"

Joseph turned a worried face toward Mary. He felt very tired, much too tired to make a decision.

"I—I don't know," he said wearily. "Maybe—maybe you're right. I seem unable to think what's the best thing to do. I've told Zebedee I'd stay long enough to put up the framework for his new wholesale building. Before I get that done, I'll decide."

But it never became necessary for Joseph to make a decision. For, a few days later, while he was working on the warehouse framework, the pain came upon him so suddenly, so blindingly, that he fell, striking his head against Zebedee's strong stone foundations. So it was not a gay, adventurous caravan that climbed back up the steep incline, past the towering, honeycombed cliffs and the Horns of Hattin, along the Way of the Sea toward the far green uplands of Galilee. It was a funeral procession.

6

"It was that Malluch who killed him," said Salome spitefully, her dark eyes fully as sharp and piercing as the needle with which she was busy fashioning another black garment of mourning. "You told me yourself he's tried every trick imaginable to hurt Joseph's business, and a man can stand just so much. He's worn Joseph down the way a woman grinds grain between her two millstones. I tell you, Malluch was Joseph's murderer, just as surely as if he'd killed him with two hands. And you can't deny it."

Mary did not try to deny it. She said nothing, just sat patiently plying her needle, while the pile of black garments beside her grew steadily higher. Finishing the cloak on which she was working and carefully folding it, she stopped to count them. One, two, three, four, five, six, seven. Enough for every member of the family, except one. No, she kept forgetting. There were only seven of them now. There was an extra one for each of them, besides the ones they were wearing. Surely this was enough to last during the period of mourning. She folded her hands in her lap and sat very still.

James, who had been listening, crept out of the courtyard and found Jude and Simon playing beside the street. They had made a caravan out of sticks and were marching it slowly up and down. James watched them for a few minutes in silence, his hands clenched at his sides.

Then: "I hate Malluch," he burst out suddenly. "Sometime I'm going to make him sorry for what he's done to my father. May the curse of Jehovah rest on his horrid, mean old soul!"

The words, such a curious mixture of the childish and the adult, fell strangely from his young, innocent lips. Jude stared, his round face puckering in amazement. Simon only laughed and turned back to his play.

"Look!" he cried, pointing to the long formation of sticks. "It's a funeral, James. Those black sticks in front are the family, and those behind are the hired mourners. Look what a long string of them we have! And the flat sticks in the middle are the bier. Come on, Jude, let's begin wailing again."

"All right," assented Jude. "Only not so loud, or mother will hear, and it will make her feel bad."

James turned and ran as fast as he could, afraid that his brothers would see the hot, scalding tears that came to his eyes; afraid too that if he stayed he would yield to the sudden blind impulse to strike them. He realized vaguely that they were not to blame for the tumult of emotion that was sweeping through him, that in the game of the little black sticks they had meant no disrespect. Probably Simon had forgotten already that the white-bound figure on its wicker bier, with its shrill, terrifying, wailing company of mourners, had been his father. And Jude never showed how he really felt.

James ran blindly around the house through the narrow gate that led into the little garden. But his cousins, James and John, were there, clambering about among the branches of the almond tree, boisterously noisy as usual. He backed noiselessly out again. Finally, confused and lonely, his slender, nine-year-old body torn by conflicting emotions of uncertainty, insecurity, and hatred, he crept into the carpenter shop.

Here, unbelievably, there was normality. Familiar sights, familiar sounds. The smooth, even flow of the adz, the pile of crinkly shavings, the white, oval shape of a yoke slowly taking form. Jesus turned toward him, smiling, his warm brown eyes seeming to leap out and enfold the small, black-clad figure in their enveloping warmth. Their father, he told James simply, had promised this yoke to Ben Ephraim the farmer before this month should be over, and he was helping him to keep his promise.

James moved slowly forward and, leaning his elbows on the bench, cupped his chin in his long, slender fingers. Fascinated, he began to watch the hands of his Brother—so firm and slim and quick, like his own, yet infinitely more skillful. His father's hands had been short and square and blunt. Yet all at once, as he watched, it was Joseph's hands that seemed to be fashioning the yoke—carefully, patiently, lovingly, smoothing away every hint of roughness, until it was a thing of perfect symmetry and balance.

Long ago, before James was born, Joseph had taken a piece of terebinth wood, carved it lovingly at each end with a graceful pattern of vine leaves, and carefully inscribed in the center these words: OUR YOKES ARE EASY. It had hung over the door of the little lean-to carpenter shop ever since James could remember. It was hanging there now, its carved ends overhung with living vine strands, its letters a bit faded by the long succession of summer suns and winter rains, but still proudly legible. As long as Joseph had sons to make yokes as he had made them, carefully, patiently, lovingly, it would hang there.

And suddenly James knew that here in the little shop, with its familiar shapes and sounds and smells, there was a rightness about things. There was rightness in the tall, slender figure of his Brother going quietly about his work, in the smooth, sure touch of his hands, in the satiny white ovals of the yoke taking shape beneath his fingers. There was rightness even in life and death.

With sudden alertness James looked about to see what he could do to help. He plunged his hands deep into the shavings. He filled his arms with them, ran quickly to the big wooden box in the corner where they were stored for kindling, spread them smoothly inside, and came back for more. After three trips there were only a few scattered swirls and a heap of fine dust on the hard, earthen floor. He ran to get the broom. Father always liked to have the shavings swept up neatly, the floor left smooth and clean.

Before the thirty days of mourning were past, Clopas, Joseph's brother, arrived from Jerusalem with his wife, Mary, and two of his children, Simon and Susanna. Their coming created quite a stir, not only in the family, but also in the whole village, for Clopas was a wealthy and important person in his home city, and when traveling he took no pains to hide either his wealth or his importance. He and his family arrived in a carriage, accompanied by a small caravan of pack donkeys, driven by a servant. After their arrival the village guest-chamber, which had been prepared for the use of the dead carpenter's expected relatives, was hastily exchanged for one larger and better furnished on the housetop of Laban the merchant.

James had never seen these Jerusalem relatives before, and he was shy and awkward, especially with his little cousin Susanna, who was different from any child he had ever seen. Her small dainty features and perfect manners made his own two sisters, with their strong, healthy bodies and darkly vivid coloring, seem uncouth and over-grown and boisterous. And her expensive embroidered clothes, the tunic made of fine linen and the cloak of real silk, made him ashamed of his own homespun garments. He wondered how his Brother could treat her as he did the other little children of Nazareth, hoisting her on his shoulders for a brisk run up the hill, telling her the names of all the different kinds of flowers, showing her how to make mud cakes out of the red-brown clay of an old brook bed.

Mary, Susanna's mother, looked with disfavor on the green and brown stains that appeared on the embroidered silken cloak during these expeditions, but Mary seemed to look with disfavor on a great many things. In spite of her fine clothes and the solicitous attention everyone gave her, her thin, nervous face was etched deeply with lines of worry and discontent; her pale, sensitive lips twisted into a constant curve of petulance.

James got along better with his cousin Simon, who was only a year older than he. Simon desired only one thing of this trip to Nazareth—to discover everything he could about Judas the Galilean. When he found that Sepphoris was less than five miles away and that he could actually make the trip to the spot where his hero had staged his last fateful revolt, Simon's delight knew no bounds.

"I'm going to be a patriot someday," he told his cousin boastfully. Then, with an air of great furtiveness, he stooped over and traced some marks with his finger on the ground. "Know what that is?" he whispered secretively.

James felt his mouth grow dry, as something long buried in his memory leaped suddenly into life. "Yes," he whispered back. "It's a fox."

"Sh!" cautioned Simon. "No so loud. You aren't supposed to speak it, you know."

"Aren't you?" whispered James.

After that there was a bond between them. James revived his childhood memories and pointed out all the landmarks he could think of that were connected with Judas the Galilean. He even managed to find one of the old crosses, sagging and half-rotten, on one of the hillsides, its long upright overgrown with bushes, it gaunt arms become long ago a nesting place for birds.

Clopas was a busy man and wanted to get back to his work in Jerusalem as soon as possible. He was also a man accustomed to making plans for others and having them carried through immediately and without question. He had come to Nazareth for two purposes: first, to accord due respect to the memory of his older brother, with whom for years he had had little in common; second, to do his duty by the family of that brother. Since arriving and becoming acquainted with his sister-in-law's relatives, Zebedee and Salome, he had added a third purpose to these two—that of combining a fish wholesale with his many other business interests in Jerusalem.

These three purposes having been accomplished, he was now ready to return home, only one final duty remaining, that of acquainting his sister-in-law with the plans that he and Salome had made for her and her family. Having gathered Mary and her children together in the main room of the miserable little hovel where his brother had lived and plied his trade and brought up his family, Clopas performed this one remaining duty. He explained it patiently, but clearly.

Mary was to take her two girls and little Simon to Capernaum, where she would become a part of Zebedee's household. He, Clopas, would take his brother's three oldest sons and bring them up with his own. Jesus, as Joseph had desired, was to go to school. Clopas' keen, appraising eyes encompassed the tall, fine figure of his eldest nephew with an already possessive pride. The younger boys—his eyes traveled dubiously over James' thin, nervous features, narrowed speculatively as they rested on Jude's sturdy, compact little body—would probably learn some trade. All three of them would later on have an equal share in his business along with his own three sons. Certainly no one could say that he was not being generous to his dead brother's children.

Mary listened in silence. The springs of speech seemed frozen within her. So impassive was her body these days, so devoid of feeling, that she wondered sometimes if that new life within her had not become dead. She opened her lips to tell Clopas how kind he was, to tell him they would accept, of course. What else could they do! But no words came.

James stared, horrified, at his uncle, his small world slowly crumbling about him. Leave Nazareth, the hilltop with its broad vistas, the familiar little house, his beloved synagogue school! Exchange his lovely, serene-faced mother for the woman with the complaining voice and thin, petulant lips! In an agony of apprehension his eyes scanned his mother's face. Why did she look so? Why didn't she say something? Surely she wasn't going to let Uncle Clopas—

But it was his Brother's voice that broke the silence. He was sorry, Jesus told his uncle quietly. They were grateful to him and to Salome, but they didn't need any help. He and his mother had things all decided. He was going to stay here to carry on his father's work and keep the family together.

"Bu—but—you can't do that!" Clopas was unused to opposition. It amazed him, left him speechless. "Why—you—you're only a mere boy of fifteen!"

Jesus made no attempt to argue with him. He cast a reassuring glance toward his mother and a fleeting smile toward his younger brother. "James will help me," he said.

James' body felt suffused with a warm glow. He sat very straight and tall, stretching his narrow shoulders until it seemed as if his muscles would burst. "Of course," he asserted with what he hoped was a vast amount of dignity.

Clopas was not a gracious loser. "B—but," he spluttered, "your plans—your education—this—this work you seem to want to do, whatever it is—"

Jesus smiled. This was his work, he told his uncle simply. It was the thing that needed to be done. Therefore it was what his father would have wanted him to do.

James looked with exultant triumph at his uncle. Think he could come up here and tell them what to do, did he, just because he was their father's brother! He might be able to order people around down in Jerusalem, but up here in Galilee where folks had minds of their own—

Clopas turned to his sister-in-law, his face a stubborn, defiant red. "You're a sensible woman, Mary. Surely you're not going to let this child make your decisions for you!"

Mary felt the frozen silence melting, the feeling slowly creeping back into her numbed body, the new life that was a part of her, and yet not a part, beginning again to stir.

"Yes, Clopas," she said steadily.

It was a hard summer and winter. Life was not easy in the house of Joseph, nor was there always bread enough to eat. While the people of Nazareth were kind and neighborly and wished the carpenter's children well, they were not anxious to spend their good shekels on tables and yokes and cradles fashioned by the immature hands of a fifteen-year-old boy. Ben Ephraim the farmer took his yoke and paid for it and said that it was good. It was as Joseph's yokes had been, well-shaped and nicely balanced and carefully smoothed in the right places so that it did not chafe the necks of the oxen. He ordered another to be delivered in the autumn. But other people were slow to follow his example. Old habits are hard to break, and the path had now become worn to the shop of Malluch.

During the months following the death of Joseph Jesus seemed to grow steadily in stature. He slipped easily but with dignity into his father's place as head of the household; standing at the bench by day, leading the family prayers each night, taking his rightful place among the men of the synagogue at the daily services and on the Sabbath. And when, early in the winter, Mary brought forth her last-born son and wrapped his tiny, crimson shape tightly in swaddling clothes, calling his name Joseph after his dead father, Jesus quietly took on the added burden of another mouth to feed and welcomed the small newcomer into the family circle with all the affection that Joseph himself would have given him.

Silently and in secret James nurtured his hatred of Malluch. Instead of avoiding the house now as he had done in the past, he went by it as often as he could, sometimes inventing excuses to pass it, seeming to derive a morbid pleasure from each glimpse of the despised, familiar figure stooping over his bench or sitting with his bare feet curved tightly about the wheel. Each time he passed he muttered an imprecation, occasionally varying his usual, "May Jehovah curse his mean old soul!" to "May his seed wither up and die!" or "The Lord make his sons to eat dust and stones!" The latter epithet sounded well but couldn't possibly come true, since Malluch had only one son, and James didn't believe anybody could ever make Zeri eat stones, and as for his eating dust, he himself could attend to that.

The other children of Nazareth might have forgotten much of their aversion to Malluch's son, or at least have tired of seeking new avenues of expression for it, had it not been for James. He did not allow them to forget. Not that he ever took any active leadership in their clever little schemes of persecution. He was too reticent and silent, and, besides, the memory of his Brother's displeasure was still too vivid in his mind. But he did not need to lead actively. Whenever a group of boys were together and he saw Zeri hovering somewhere about, like a fluttering moth drawn irresistibly toward a flame, he had only to nudge Levi or one of the others and whisper, "Look! There's the lawbreaker!" or, "What do you say we play funeral? There's the corpse!" And they would take care of the rest.

Sometimes it would be the old pastime of standing him up against a wall and making him repeat the Shema, his difficulties of speech becoming more and more aggravated and ludicrous, it seemed, each time the performance was repeated. At other times they would include him in the game they happened to be playing or make up a new one for his benefit, making him play the part of Sisera or Pharaoh or Goliath or Pompey, or whoever happened to be the villain at the moment.

Once they were afraid that they had gone a little too far in their sport. Pretending to play "hide-and-seek," they let Zeri be "it," an unusual honor which he accepted with almost pathetic delight. Then they blindfolded him and, instead of conducting him to the usual starting point, led him into an inner hollow of a deep cave and left him. When later they went back after him, they found him still wandering around in the dark, the girdle that he had worn about his eyes torn to shreds in his hands. Out in the light again, his eyes looked wild and staring, and when he opened his mouth and tried to speak no words came. Once they got him back down in the village, however, he seemed normal enough.

James took a fierce, morbid delight in this constant persecution of the son of the hated carpenter, not because of any innate cruelty within himself but because in some small measure it satisfied his deep child thirst for justice. And when, late in the winter, a plague of sickness swept through Galilee and, visiting Nazareth, chose Zeri, the son of Malluch, as one of its first victims, James was secretly elated. Surely now his prayers were being answered. Malluch was going to be punished for his sins. But when his brother Simon also fell sick of the same plague, his elation turned to terrified misery. For if

Zeri's sickness had been caused by Malluch's wickedness, then whose sins had caused Simon's?

It was his Brother who nursed the sick boy, for Mary, with her new baby at her breast, dared not go near his bedside. Jesus laid aside his adz and saw and hammer, moved Simon's pallet into the carpenter shop, and stayed with him continually. For days the child lay tossing with the fever, his small face red and swollen, strange, unintelligible sounds coming from his lips. James hung miserably about the door of the lean-to, waiting for a chance to run errands, straining his ears for some sign of normalcy in the rambling childish treble, straining them even more intensely when the treble ceased.

Sometimes in those rare moments when Simon was asleep, usually toward evening, Jesus would come out and ask James to wait outside and listen. If the boy wakened, he was to come and tell him. He would be up on the hill at the Lookout.

At those times Jesus seemed a stranger, so pale and gaunt that James was always frightened, thinking that he too must have caught the plague. It was weakness that he showed, more than weariness, though of course he must have been mortally tired. It was as if his whole strong young body had been drained of its youth and vigor, as if he had somehow poured himself out in an effort to restore life to the small, pain-racked body lying within on its pallet. James would wait breathlessly, hardly daring to move, until finally Jesus would come back down the hill, the weariness apparently gone, his body strangely strong and young again, an amazing freshness in his sparkling eyes.

Once James got Jude to watch at the door for him and crept up the hillside after his Brother. Hiding low in the bushes just below the highest point, which they called the "Lookout," he heard Jesus speaking to someone. The words were low-spoken, and he couldn't get close enough to hear them, but they sounded familiar and intimate, as if he were talking to an old friend. James felt a quick surge of jealousy, remembering the other times when his Brother had come to this place, refusing his company and saying that he wanted to be alone. And to think that all the time he was meeting someone!

After Jesus had gone, James hurried furtively to the Lookout. But as far as he could see, over the whole barren hilltop, there was no one at all in sight, except Jesus going back down the path. James ran home another way, arriving before his Brother and taking Jude's place outside the lean-to door. He was standing there, pulses pounding and breath coming in short gasps, when Jesus returned, weariness and pallor having again disappeared, weakness transformed into a tranquil, seemingly inexhaustible strength.

Many people died in Nazareth that winter. The plague swept over Galilee, almost as deadly a scourge as that wielded three years before by the avenging hand of Rome. But Simon, the son of Joseph, was not among them. Spring found him playing as usual on the edge of the street before the carpenter shop, marching his tiny caravans and funeral processions up and down, a little paler and thinner perhaps, but with a mounting color in his cheeks which would soon match the strong, healthy ruddiness of his oldest brother.

Zeri also lived, but differently. The anemones blossomed as usual that spring on the hillside, in glorious, lavish brush marks of color. But the son of Malluch did not see them. Neither was his voice mingled with those of the other Nazareth children running in the streets, playing in the marketplace, roaming on the hillsides. For the grim terror of his long, dark battle with fever and delirium had left him both blind and dumb.

7

Time passed unhurriedly in the small peasant house on an obscure side street in Nazareth, like the smooth, even flow of clean, white shavings beneath the young carpenter's adz. Other springtimes came and went, wearing their lavish robes more splendid in color and texture than the raiment of Solomon, and then carelessly casting them aside, even as the shavings were swept up and thrown into the box in the corner. Farmers got out their light, one-handled plows, took them to the carpenter shop to have them fitted to new handles, used them and laid them away, presently bringing their sickles, forks, and fans to be mended or resharpened, that they might be ready for the harvest. The simple yet ever-varied pattern of daily living; the colorful flow of tongues and merchandise in the marketplace mingling together the sounds and sights and aromas of many languages and strange peoples and far places; the streams of caravans moving east and west, north and south, across the great trade routes of the Plain of Esdraelon—all these shifted constantly, yet ever remained the same, like the varying colors of a kaleidoscope turned slowly against the background of the seasons.

Here in this land of paradoxes, of simple peasants tilling their fields and kings building their lavish cities, of women weaving and spinning coarse fibers of camel's and goat's hair and merchants vending the costliest silks and finest velvets, of simple, homely contentment and fierce, seething, bitter nationalism, James, the second son of Joseph, grew to manhood.

Eagerly, in the half circle of boys gathered about Rabbi Nathan, the chazan of the synagogue, he absorbed more and more teachings of the Law, the Prophets, and the Mishnah, repeating them with a glibness that was the envy of most of his schoolmates and especially of his brother Jude. Dutifully, with a growing self-consciousness of his dignity and importance as a Jew, he went weekly to the Sabbath services, listening to the familiar intonations of the Scriptures, his sensitive fingers itching to touch the sacred rolls that were reverently rewrapped in their gold-embroidered covers of linen and silk and placed in their little niche behind the curtain, in front of which hung an everburning lamp. Curiously he watched each month with the rest of the townspeople for the first glimpse of the new moon, bowing his head as his Brother, now head of the household, repeated: "Blessed be Thou, Lord our God, who through Thy word didst create the heavens! Blessed be Thou, O Lord, who renewest the moons!" Then at the sound of the trumpet he would hasten to the synagogue to begin a holiday of feasting and universal rejoicing.

Joyously, thoughtfully, sadly, triumphantly, as the occasion demanded, he moved each year through the cycle of feasts and fast days: In June the Feast of Weeks, when vast throngs of pilgrims bore their offerings of first fruits to Jerusalem, the choicest of their crops, carried in baskets of willow or silver or gold. In October the Feast of Trumpets, followed by that Day of all Days, that Sabbath of all Sabbaths, the Day of Atonement, when every Jew in the village stood white-shrouded and white-capped in the synagogue, solemnly confessing his sins and the sins of his nation. Soon after, the Feast of Tabernacles, when for a week the whole family lived merrily out-of-doors in a house of twigs and green branches. In early spring the

Feast of Purim, with Rabbi Nathan reading the whole exciting drama of Esther, to the accompaniment of loud hisses and stampings and cursings every time the villain Haman's name was mentioned, and trying to repeat his name and those of his ten sons in one breath, thus showing that they had been hanged together. In April the Feast of the Passover.

James was twelve when he made his first trip to Jerusalem. Except for those few days years before when he had stood on the hilltop and witnessed in rapid succession rebellion and triumph and defeat and death, it was by far the most important thing that had ever happened to him. He was thrilled with it all—the arrival of pilgrims from the adjoining countryside; the night spent out-of-doors before their departure, to avoid sleeping in a lodging where a death might occur and so defile all those in the house that they might not attend the feast; the journey across the great plain and beyond the green hills that had heretofore seemed to his boyish vision the limits of the earth; the long, sweet rest in the camping ground at night, ended by the cry, "Arise ye, and let us go up to Zion unto Jehovah our God."

When finally they climbed the last hill and the Holy City lay before him, white and shining and splendid, James' heart was filled almost to bursting. He wanted to cry out with the rest,

> Beautiful in elevation, the joy of the whole earth,
> Is Mount Zion!

but the words stuck in his throat and made only a choking sound. His Brother, understanding, smiled and pressed his hand.

And, more wonderful even than his first glimpse of the Holy City or than the solemn, sacred ceremonies of the days that followed, was the feeling that came to James at that moment. For now, at last, his Brother had had no experiences in which he might not share. Their lives were now bounded by the same horizons. Their futures were committed to the fulfillment of the same Dream.

We're really comrades now, thought James with satisfaction.

At the age of thirteen, like all Jewish boys, he was solemnly initiated into manhood, becoming a "son of the Commandment." It was an exciting day in the household, that first Sabbath after he was thirteen years old.

"Are you sure you remember what you're supposed to do?" Mary asked him for the hundredth time as she adjusted his new blue-and-white praying shawl. "Don't forget the words of your portion, dear.

And above all don't be frightened. They're just your friends, the people you see every day."

James was not frightened, that is, not after the first awful moment when he stood on the platform of the synagogue, a vast sea of unfamiliar faces before him. He spoke the first words of his portion in a small, timid voice, stumbling a little. Then his Brother's face emerged, smiling and confident, out of the bewildering sea, and he finished clearly and triumphantly. Proudly he stretched out his left arm for Rabbi Nathan to tie on his new phylactery, a little cubicle case containing holy words of Scripture; stood confidently straight and still while the other little black case was fastened securely, exactly in the middle of his forehead.

It was a solemn moment, for now, he realized, he was no longer a child. He was a man, expected to know and observe all the intricate laws of his religion, and responsible for his own sins.

After that he did not attend the synagogue school. Reluctantly he took his rightful place beside his Brother at the carpenter's bench. He learned to make tables and yokes and cradles and chests and plow handles—not well, because his long, sensitive fingers would never be clever with tools, but passably. He went with Jesus to build frames for barns and houses, to construct doors and window frames, to repair sheepfolds, to fashion new booths for the storekeepers in the marketplace.

Even more than from the dull routine of work at the bench did James shrink from these intimate contacts with the people of the town and countryside. He hated the bold, crude jargon of the marketplace, the small talk of the farmers whose homes they visited every few months because they were under contract to keep their tools and their barns and their sheepfolds mended and in order.

"How can you!" he burst out impatiently after a particularly weary afternoon when, it seemed, Jesus had been more interested in mending people's complaints and quarrels than their barns and sheepfolds.

Jesus turned, surprised, a question in his widened eyes, and James continued hotly.

"How can you act so interested when people talk to you like that, old Enoch telling you that long story about how he became blind, and Reuben the herdsman talking to you about how lazy his wife is and about his horrible son, Gad? The way you listen to them anyone would think their troubles were the most important things in the world."

Jesus made no reply. James, looking up at him sharply, caught the peculiarly thoughtful, intent expression on his face, and, following his gaze, saw the figure of a young woman moving slowly along the street ahead of them. There was something arrogant, something vaguely seductive, about the way she walked, about the tilt of her head on which was poised a bundle of fagots. James frowned disapprovingly. It was Miriam, the daughter of Jothan. Though scarcely older than his own sister Tamar, she had already acquired throughout the village an evil reputation.

As she was turning into a doorway just ahead of them, her foot turned on a loose rock, and the bundle of fagots slipped to the ground, scattering in all directions. James walked straight ahead, his lips set in a firm, thin line of disapproval, but to his horrified amazement his Brother turned aside, set down his box of tools, and, stooping, helped the girl to gather up the fagots. James heard him say something in a low voice as he put the bundle in her arms, saw her eyes lifted to his Brother's face in a look that held gratitude, startled wonder, but, strangely enough, not a trace of coquetry. When Jesus again joined him, James maintained a fiercely disapproving silence.

He felt even more irritated a few minutes later when just before reaching home they encountered the wild, unkempt figure of Zeri, now, since his fresh affliction several years ago, more awkward and repulsive than ever. He had an uncanny way of turning up just when one least expected, especially when Jesus was around. No doubt he recognized his footstep. Now, fluttering grotesquely toward them, he burst into unintelligible cries.

"Peace to you, Zeri!" Jesus said as he put his arm companionably about the thin, stooped shoulders. Then, to James' utter dismay, he told the boy to wait there for him while he put his tools away. They would take a walk up on the hill together.

James shuddered with disgust. He felt a blind rage at Zeri, a desire to lift his bag of tools and strike him. For even more poignant than the feeling of disgust was that of bitter disappointment. He himself had wanted to go up on the hill tonight with Jesus, to be alone with him, to talk, perhaps, about the Dream.

Occasionally, in the months that followed, Jesus did other things that James did not understand. For instance, there was the incident that happened on the road to Sepphoris.

It was a hot day in summer soon after the Feast of Weeks. James was going with his Brother to the nearby city, where they had been engaged to construct the framework for several new houses. They were planning to stay the entire week, returning home in time to make their preparations for the Sabbath, and they were carrying not only their boxes of tools but also packs of food and extra clothing. With the heat of the sun pouring down upon them and their heavy loads, they were soon sweating uncomfortably.

And they were not the only ones. About a mile out of town they overtook a Roman soldier, his face red and dripping beneath his helmet, his shirt sticking in damp patches to his shoulders. He carried a heavy pack.

"Here, you!" he shouted curtly, after they had passed him. "You tall fellow, there!"

James' hand clenched on the handle of his toolbox. He knew what was coming. A despicable law and one that the Jews bitterly resented, that provision which gave a Roman the privilege of requisitioning a Jew to give him slave service for a mile!

Jesus turned back without apparent rancor.

"Take this pack," the soldier commanded brusquely, putting his hand to his sword hilt. "It's beastly hot, and I'm tired of carrying it." Jesus told him he would do so gladly.

The soldier gaped. His right hand, poised to frighten a sullen, scowling rebel into unwilling submission, dropped from his sword hilt.

Jesus shifted his own pack so that it hung at his side. He swung the soldier's heavier pack to his back, pulling his arms through both its straps. Steadying his own bundle with his left hand, he picked up his toolbox with his right and set off cheerfully along the road.

James had been hot before, but now he was seething. He was almost as angry at his Brother as at the despised foreigner walking on the other side of him. Jesus had to carry the pack, of course, but he didn't have to act as if he wanted to. Perversely, James did not offer to carry his Brother's bundle, though something told him he should.

As they walked along, Jesus occasionally passed a remark to the big soldier, his voice as informally friendly as if he had been talking to Reuben the herdsman. It *was* a hot day, he agreed, and he didn't blame him for getting tired carrying his pack. It was heavy.

"Yes," said the Roman. He acted embarrassed. When they got to the end of the mile—James knew it was the end, for he had counted the paces exactly—he reached out his hand. "All right. Here we are. I'll take it now."

Jesus smiled and shook his head. Shifting the heavy pack a little to make it rest more easily on his shoulders, he kept on walking.

James could not believe his eyes. Neither, apparently, could the soldier. "Y-you—you don't have to carry it any farther, you know," he said.

Then, all at once, he was no longer a burly, arrogant, red-faced soldier. He was a big, overgrown, homesick boy, talking to another boy about his age and telling him all about his old father and mother who lived in a little village on the Tiber, and about the girl he wanted to marry, and about the little farm he was going to buy sometime, if his term of service in the army ever ended.

James couldn't get it all, because he didn't speak or understand Greek so well as his Brother. Hearing him speak it now, almost as casually as if it were his own Aramaic, James wondered if he had picked it all up in the marketplace or if Ben Azel, the old rabbi with whom Jesus still spent long, mysterious hours, had taught it to him. If so, what else had his Brother learned about that hostile, pagan world beyond the borders of Israel? Was he, perhaps, intimate with the thoughts and teachings of personalities that were to James only the vaguest of names? Philo, Virgil, Livy, Aristotle, Plato? For Rabbi Nathan did not believe in tainting the pure waters of their fathers' faith with filterings from heathen philosophies.

He walked beside them moodily, straining his ears, his mind a hot, seething confusion of wonder, revulsion, and suspicion.

The second mile brought them to the gate of Sepphoris. The big soldier took his pack, and stood for a moment uncertainly.

"Maybe—maybe I can do something for you someday," he said and turned abruptly up the street toward Herod Antipas' new palace.

The Jews in his pathway saw him coming and began muttering curses. One of them made a vulgar gesture. Another spat directly in front of him. The Roman whipped out his sword, issued a curt command, began to swagger menacingly. He was no longer a big, overgrown, homesick boy.

James liked the mornings in the carpenter shop the best. In the afternoons after school let out, there were too many children about, not only little Joseph and his playfellows, but seemingly all the children in the village. Then the shop became a place of laughter, of small figures tossing about in the shavings, of bare fingers and toes continually underfoot.

Once James remonstrated. "Don't you ever get tired of having them swarm around you? You know you can't get half so much work done. Why don't you let me put them out."

"No," said Jesus, putting down his saw to comfort a tousle-headed urchin who had pinched his fingers between two boards. "Let them alone. Don't try to keep them from coming. The Dream belongs to such as these."

Then he sat down on a pile of boards and pulled the tousle-headed figure to his knee. Sensing that he was about to tell a story, the other children gathered around eagerly to listen. The story, Jesus told the tousle-headed one, was to be about a prince. He knew what a prince was, didn't he? Hadn't he seen them riding through town in their chariots? The child nodded, smiling gleefully through his tears.

"Once upon a time," began Jesus, "there was a prince who went away into a far country ..."

But in the mornings it was different. Joseph was usually with his mother, watching her knead the bread, helping her to fill the lamps, going with her to the well. James and Jesus were often alone then, working at the bench side by side. They had plenty of time to talk about the Dream.

For to James loyalty to the Dream and the deep comradeship he felt with his Brother were one. It was his Brother who, long ago, had given him the Dream, here on his knees among the shavings in this very shop, his warm, deep brown eyes on a level with his own. And it was his Brother who, through the years, had nurtured it within him. Just how he couldn't have told, except that it had grown slowly, with the patient unfolding of the seeds they had planted together in the garden plot behind the house. It had grown deeply, as they had inhaled the long draughts of coolness after a swift run up the hill, the sky held within their outstretched arms, the world lying at their feet. And it became clean-cut and firm of outline, like the crisp, curling shavings flowing smoothly beneath the blade of an adz. So many of the things Jesus had said stirred in his memory.

"See, little brother, how this great plant grew from the tiniest of seeds? Truth is like that....

"Come, little one, don't be afraid of it! It's the one thing worth seeking, worth striving for, the one thing the whole world is waiting for someone to give it! Lift your arms, fill your lungs full of it! It's *life!*

"The world is like this piece of white wood, rough and bruised and ugly, but whiter than the whitest dream inside. See, it's here in our hands, yours and mine, God's dream—waiting for us, perhaps, to make it a thing of lovely shape and whiteness."

James was eighteen, the age when most Jewish boys of Nazareth were well settled in a trade and married, when Jesus made his startling suggestion.

"You mean—" James repeated his Brother's words slowly, *"me—go to school—now—in Jerusalem?"*

Jesus' eyes continued to regard him calmly, as if he had suggested a casual trip to Capernaum.

Light leaped into James' dark eyes, then slowly faded. "But—I couldn't. You need me here."

With practical thoroughness his Brother answered all his objections. They could manage very well without him. Jude was getting old enough to do a man's work, and there was no more than enough business for the two of them. He could live with his Uncle Clopas in Jerusalem and earn his board by working as a carpenter, so it would not be too expensive. And besides, he reminded him with a sudden, clear, straightforward glance, it was time that he was getting ready for the work they had to do.

The eagerness flared again. "But—you—" James protested. "You're older, and it's your Dream, really. You ought to be the one to go."

The brown eyes twinkled. James flushed and laughed a little sheepishly. He knew what his Brother was thinking. How long would the carpenter shop stay open, he wondered, painfully conscious of his own limitations, if he were the one left to run it? And Jesus assured him that it didn't matter where he was. He would still be getting ready.

And so it was arranged. James was to go to Jerusalem and live at the house of Clopas and sit at the feet of the rabbis of the famous School of Shammai. Jesus was a little disappointed at this. He had wanted himself, years ago, to attend the School of Hillel, of whom Ben Azel was a disciple. But Rabbi Nathan had been a pupil of Shammai, and, rooted deeply in the convictions of his passionately zealous young teacher, James was firm in his desire. Seeing that his brother's heart was set on Shammai's school, Jesus made no further protest.

Mary quietly made ready for her second son's departure. She made him new tunics and sandals and four new cloaks, two of homespun linen for summer and two of striped wool for winter. His old garments she put aside to make over for the younger children. She was growing used, by now, to having her children go away. Both her daughters had married early and well—Esther to a well-to-do vine dresser over beyond Mount Tabor; Tamar, as usual more humble in her tastes, to an ambitious young farmer who lived in the nearby village of Cana. Each, thanks to her oldest son, had gone to the home of her husband with respectable strings of dowry coins hanging from either side of her headdress.

With each fine stitch that she took in her son's new garments she told herself that she was a fortunate woman. The years had been kind to her, leaving few marks on her fair, smooth features. Her dark hair was still unlined with silver. She had two daughters and five fine sons, all of them keepers of the Law and defenders of the God of Israel. One of those sons was now fulfilling her own and Joseph's dream. He was going to Jerusalem to study. He would perhaps become a rabbi, even a member of the Great Council. She was making him a cloak now. Someday, perhaps, she would be making him a *meil*, one of those fine, rich, embroidered garments worn only by men of special wisdom and distinction. She had always dreamed of making a *meil*.

But not for James, not for her *second* son!

"Dear God, forgive me," she prayed hastily. "What more could I want for Jesus than that he should take his father's place, that he should be loved and respected in his own village, that he should be known all about Nazareth as a clean and honest carpenter!"

But she knew secretly in her heart that she did want more than that. She wanted him to be—to be—Her brain whirled. There was the sound in her ears as of the whirring of mighty wings, the rushing of many distant waters. She was holding in her arms the sweet warmth of her firstborn, listening to unearthly cadences, entertaining dim, half-remembered shapes, tuning the ecstatic beating of her heart to strange, preposterous promises. Then, as always, it fled—the dream, the memory. Which it was she could scarcely have told herself, so often had she dreamed, remembered. And she was back again in the courtyard of her little house, the ecstatic beating that had set its tempo to divine promise no more than the firm, steady rapping of a hammer in the adjoining carpenter shop.

She picked up her needle and began to sew.

For the first time in his life James was venturing forth alone. His Brother went with him to the fork where the Nazareth road joined the great southern highway unrolling itself like a long, narrow scroll across the great Plain of Esdraelon.

"I won't forget," he answered the unspoken question in the steady brown eyes. "I'll be getting ready."

They exchanged a few casual words, gripped each other's hands, and his Brother went back up the hill toward Nazareth. Watching him go, James felt a sudden aching in his heart, as of a great loss. The simple, intimate comradeship of their youth was over.

But there was something better in store. Henceforth they were to be partners—partners in a task that James was only beginning to comprehend—partners of the Dream.

He set his face eagerly toward Jerusalem.

PART TWO
Partner

PART TWO

1

The girl standing in the doorway of the small guest room on the housetop swept the room and its furnishings with a lightning glance from a pair of bright, heavily lashed but very wide-open hazel eyes and pursed her pretty lips. Yes, it looked nice. Too nice, in fact, for the person who was going to occupy it. The thick, soft mat with its fine-textured embroidered covering, the cushioned stools, the big carved cedar chest, the low table with its lamp, its jug of water, its ewer, and its silver basin, the colorful rugs on the smooth stone floor—everything was just as it should be.

Her eyes returned to the graceful curving shape of the water jug on the table and twinkled into sudden merriment. With the unmistakable air of a person bent on mischief, she glanced quickly about, then tiptoed furtively back into the room and across the flat rooftop to the low parapet, where, leaning over as far as she dared, she emptied the water from the jug into the garden below. The water started to fall in a thin silver stream, then both the breeze and the sun caught it, splintering it into fine little rainbow darts of spray and scattering it like rain over the beds of anemones and cyclamens and even as far as the acanthus bush.

Ever fascinated by beauty, the girl set down the empty jug, dropped to her knees, and, leaning her small, pointed chin on her folded arms, watched the dazzling play of sunlight on the shimmering prisms, her own sun-flecked eyes almost as bright as the sparkling drops still clinging to the blossoms. Anemones, she thought wistfully, were surely the loveliest things in the world. What was it her cousin Jesus had said about them last spring when he had been here in Jerusalem? Something about their not making their own clothes. She wished she could remember. That purple one down there now, standing up so straight on its stem—didn't it look for all the world like a king wearing a long velvet coat? King—that was it! She had it now. Look at them, Jesus had said; they don't know how to weave or spin, yet Solomon in all his glory was never dressed like them.

She felt better after remembering. It somehow gave expression to the aching wistfulness that always seemed to fill her in the presence of beauty. Her eyes lifted, wandered over the vine-covered wall, climbed a ladder of flat, terraced roofs, and were caught again, fascinated, by the shining splendor of the Temple on the highest hill in the distance. Perfect as a dream, lovely and aloof as a mirage, it rested against the blue bosom of the sky like an exquisite white-and-gold cameo. The aching wistfulness came again, became almost unbearable. She wished she could always see the Temple like this—at a distance—without having to go down through the narrow, squalid streets, past beggars with their hungry eyes and plucking fingers, through dirt and dinginess and ugliness and poverty.

"Susanna! Sue, child, where are you?"

Susanna rose swiftly, snatched up the jug, and sped with it across the rooftop into the guest room, where she carefully set it down on the table, covering its top with the napkin. She was coming innocently out of the room when a young man came bounding up the little outside staircase, two steps at a time.

"Simon!" She greeted him eagerly, lifting her face with childish naïveté to be kissed. "I didn't know you were back. When did you come?"

"Just now. I went in to speak to mother first." He stooped and kissed her with brotherly casualness. "I say, what's the idea of running away from me and not answering when I speak to you? I heard you pattering away up here on the roof." He held her off to look at her more closely. "Aha! Up to some mischief, as usual. I can see it in your eyes. They're altogether too bright."

She lowered her long lashes. "I've just been fixing up the guest-chamber," she said innocently. "Huldah was busy and didn't have time this morning."

He glanced inside the room. "Expecting company?"

"More than just company. Didn't you know, Simon? He's coming here to live."

"Who's coming?"

"That's right. You don't know, do you? You went away before the message came. It's Cousin James. He's coming here to Jerusalem to go to school. And he's going to live with us."

"James? Let's see—" Simon lowered his short, stocky figure to the parapet and sat, swinging one foot meditatively. "He's the tall thin, dark one, with the eyes that seem to look right through you."

"Yes," said Susanna, sitting beside him and lowering her voice so it would not carry to the open courtyard beneath, where their invalid mother might be sitting. "I wish it were Jesus coming instead of James." Her pretty lips pouted a little. "James is so solemn and quiet, he keeps me wondering all the time what he's thinking. And he never laughs at all. That is, I've never seen him laugh when he's been here for the feast days."

"Jesus was coming to Jerusalem once to go to school," said Simon reflectively. "Years ago."

"I don't remember."

"You wouldn't. I was only about ten at the time. That would make you four or five."

"Why didn't he come?" asked Susanna curiously.

"His father died. He had to stay in Nazareth and support the family. That was the time we went to visit them. Remember?"

"Yes." The girl's eyes lighted as if two candles had suddenly been kindled behind them. "They had the nicest little house with vines growing all over it. And there were shavings to play in, and Aunt Mary made the nicest fig cakes I've ever tasted. And Cousin Jesus took me riding on his shoulders up on the highest hill in the world, I think, where you could see ever so far, and he told me stories and showed me how to make mud cakes. But I didn't like Cousin James, because he was so quiet and moody and—and stuffy."

Simon laughed gaily. "And I was beginning to think you were grown up!"

She pouted. "I am grown up. That is, almost."

"Let's see, how old would little Sue be now?"

"Fourteen," she said primly.

He placed his fingers beneath her chin and studied her small, heart-shaped face, noting with approval the high, narrow cheekbones, the white forehead with its two smooth wings of light-brown hair, the widely spaced, deep-fringed eyes with their dancing flecks of gold, the gaily curving lips.

"You're going to be a very beautiful woman, my dear sister," he said gently.

Pleased and embarrassed, she slapped childishly at his hand.

"Who says so?" she demanded scornfully.

"Well—Barabbas does, for one."

"Oh!" The color flamed into her cheeks, ebbing again almost instantly as she regarded her brother with sudden anxiety. "Is that where you've been, Simon? With—with them?"

His face hardened, and his hand dropped abruptly. "I've been away. On business."

"For father?"

"Yes, he sent me to Jericho to arrange about some balsam shipments."

"Oh!" Susanna looked relieved. Then her face clouded. "But—Jericho! Isn't it the road to Jericho where—"

Simon scowled. "Be quiet, can't you, Susanna? I knew Barabbas shouldn't have told you. You know too much."

"Then you have been with Barabbas?"

"Well, what if I have?"

The girl looked troubled. "I—I just wish you wouldn't, Simon, that's all. Barabbas frightens me. He's so big and strong, and his eyes are so bright they look as if they would shine in the dark. He makes you feel that if he really wanted anything very much, nothing on earth could stop him."

Simon leaned forward tensely. "You've felt that too? As if he were stronger somehow than fate? As if he had power to change human destiny? Do you know what it is he wants, Susanna?"

Again the color flamed into her face. "I—I'm not sure."

Simon looked swiftly around before he spoke. His voice sank to a whisper. "He wants freedom for our people. Deliverance from our oppressors."

"The Romans?" whispered Susanna, catching something of his tense eagerness.

"Yes. The Romans. And everyone who does business with them. The high priest too, and his whole family of whispering serpents. They've sold out our country to the enemy, that's what they've done. But their hour is nearly over. Israel's waited a long time for its Deliverer. Plenty of times people have thought he was here, but one by one each patriot has gone down. Mattathias and his sons, Thronges, Judas the Galilean. But this time, Susanna, there's going to be no mistake. There can't be."

"You mean—" the girl scarcely breathed in her excitement, "you believe Barabbas is the Deliverer promised to our nation? The Messiah?"

Light flared in Simon's eyes, then flickered. "I'm not sure," he said slowly. "Sometimes I think so, and then at other times—" Again the flame mounted. "But, after all, why shouldn't he be? Any man who can save our country from its enemies is its Messiah, and you yourself said that Barabbas is the kind of man who gets what he goes after, no matter what it is."

"Susanna! Simon!" called a querulous voice below.

The girl rose quickly. "There's mother calling. I'll have to go."

Simon moved beside her across the housetop. "I'm glad Cousin James is coming," he said. "If he's not a Zealot already, I think I can soon make him one."

"What makes you think so?" asked Susanna quickly.

But Simon, remembering the days he had spent in Nazareth years before, when together he and James had paid boyish homage at all the invisible shrines of Judas the Galilean, only smiled mysteriously.

At the moment when Susanna and Simon were descending the small stone stairway outside the house of Clopas, in Jerusalem, James was climbing the hill from the Valley of the Kidron to the eastern gateway of the city. He was very tired, for the trip from Nazareth had taken three days, and the bundle containing his clothes and tools was none too light. But there was no weariness in the dark, restless eyes that were lifted constantly toward the shining white-and-gold pinnacles of the Holy City. He had seen if often enough before—the great Temple rising, terrace upon terrace, above the lofty colonnades of the Porch of Solomon. He had come here many times in the past six years with his mother and brothers, mingling with the Passover pilgrims and singing to the sound of the flutes,

> I was glad when they said to me,
> Let us go into the house of the Lord;

bearing his wicker basket filled with his offering of first fruits and a pair of doves, with their wings bound, for a sacrifice; waving his palm branch and shouting with joy amid a great company approaching the gay, flower-bedecked city for the autumn Feast of Tabernacles.

But this time it was different. This time he came alone, and not as a pilgrim. This time he came to stay, and the great city, proud and mysterious and aloof, wearing its strange aura of divinity like a crown and wielding its mass of glorious tradition like a scepter, would become his, to absorb its strength, to fathom its secrets, to—yes, perhaps even to build its future.

As he paused, lifting his eyes for another last look before entering the gate, a whining leper crept closer. "Alms! Alms, in the name of Jehovah! May the Lord bless you and your seed!" The blessing changed to an imprecation as the young man quickened his step. "Curses on you! May your seed go hungry!"

James hastened through the sheepgate, glad for the law that forbade lepers entrance to the city and especially anxious to keep his own person undefiled in order that he might be free to worship in the Temple on the morrow. But there was no law against beggars! They swarmed about him, dirty and ill-smelling, plucking at his cloak with their filthy fingers, fawning and threatening, whining and clamorous. He escaped them finally, losing himself in the human stream flowing constantly toward the center of the city between the vast glittering Temple area on the left and the frowning battlements of the Roman fortress on the right. He had forgotten that Jerusalem was like this, dusty and stifling and swarming with so much dirty, noisy humanity— Arabs burnt dark from the desert suns; huge, dusky-skinned Negroes from Ethiopia; Egyptians and Greeks and Romans and Parthians. He had remembered only the white-robed priests, the haughty Sadducees with their silken garments, the Pharisees with their wide fringes and phylacteries, the shining pinnacles.

Down through the Valley of the Cheesemakers, with its busy, narrow, crowded streets filled with shops and booths, he hastened, up its terraced side through the streets of the butchers, the woolgatherers, and the goldsmiths, into the welcome seclusion of the upper city. Here were the dwelling houses of the more well-to-do and respectable citizens. Here, on a quiet side street, was the house of his dead father's younger brother, Clopas.

He mounted a flight of shallow stone steps, touched his fingers reverently to the *mezuzah* on the doorpost, removed his dusty sandals, and passed into a life different from any he had ever known—instead of a small, crude peasant's cottage, a house of many sumptuous rooms opening off a garden courtyard; instead of a village carpenter's shop, the ample stocks and warehouses of a prosperous city merchant; instead of his sisters and the other girls of Nazareth, with their ruddy health, their dark, voluptuous beauty, their colorful homespun, a cool, slender, remote creature, with a pale olive skin and hair the color of ripened wheat and clothes so soft and finespun that they must have sprung from those fabulous looms in the countries far to the rising sun.

He was not so much in awe of his cousin Simon, in spite of his city ways and expensive clothes, for there was the memory of the pilgrimages they had shared in the hills about Nazareth. Nor was he in awe of his Aunt Mary, who was a chronic invalid and much too interested in her own troubles, which were mostly imaginary, to scrutinize the awkward manners of a country relative. Nor even of his Uncle Clopas, who, he suspected, had always regarded his slender, sensitive-fingered, studious young nephew with something of contempt.

No, it was the presence of Susanna that made him awkward, self-conscious, tongue-tied, embarrassed for fear he was not displaying the correct manners at table, painfully aware, when he did manage to venture a remark, of the crude Galilean accent in his speech. It was her eyes, he thought miserably, hidden behind those thick fringes of lashes. For all he could tell, they might be hiding mockery or contempt or derision—or just plain laughter at his expense.

"So," said Uncle Clopas after the meal was finished, leaning his big frame on a substantial elbow and turning toward his nephew, "you think you want to be a scholar, do you?"

"Yes, sir," replied James, flushing under his uncle's disconcerting scrutiny.

"Pretty old, aren't you, to be entering one of the academies? Let's see, how old are you?"

"Eighteen, sir."

Clopas' thick brows drew together. "Hm! That is old. You should be settled by now in a substantial business, coming to me to arrange a profitable marriage contract, instead of starting off on a wild-goose chase after more knowledge."

James' dark eyes flashed. " 'Happy is the man who finds wisdom,' " he quoted promptly, " 'and the man who gains understanding. For her proceeds are better than the profits of silver, and her gain than fine gold.' "

Susanna moved closer and began to clear the table. James was sure now that there was laughter behind the thick, dark fringes, but he thought he detected also a faint gleam of approval. "Simon is nearly twenty, father," she said demurely, "and he's not married yet."

"But he's settled in a substantial business," returned Clopas quickly, too quickly, James thought, as if Susanna's words had prodded her father in some sorely sensitive spot. There was a spark of challenge, if not of actual belligerence, in the glance Clopas and his son exchanged across the table.

Simon smiled with his lips. His eyes, James noticed suddenly, were not smiling. "We were talking about Cousin James, weren't we?" he said with lazy good humor. "Why don't we leave business till later, when I tell you about the balsam shipments?"

"Very well," said Clopas briefly. But James knew instinctively that it was not well. There was dissension in the house of Clopas, and he wondered vaguely what part, if any, he would have to play in it.

He wakened the next morning when the first gray finger of dawn plucked at the dense black curtain shrouding Mount Moriah. Tense, wide awake, expectant, he lay on his mat and gazed out the open doorway, rejoicing in the luck that had given him a chamber facing not only the east but the Temple itself. Breathlessly he watched its majestic outlines emerge slowly out of the dim grayness, become shape instead of shadow, glorious reality instead of an elusive dream.

So startlingly clear was its outline, each marble and gold terrace, each tiny colonnade, that he imagined he could see the white-robed figure that would be the priest climbing to the topmost pinnacle, the dazzling pinpoint that would be his silver trumpet.

"Has the light reached Hebron?"

"Not yet. Not yet."

"Has the light reached Hebron?"

As if in answer to his own private little litany, the topmost turrets of the Temple burst into sudden, shimmering splendor, and three long sweet notes sounded across the morning air.

James sprang up from his bed. He had meant to be at the Temple before this, to see the great golden gates swing open, to be one of the first to enter for the morning sacrifice. And here he had been lying in a stupor, letting himself become fascinated by the familiar sight of breaking dawn. Hastily he put on fresh garments, being careful to stand on one spot as he did so. For it was one of the strict provisions of the Law that, having risen from his bed, an Israelite could not move four steps before washing his hands and face.

Even then he had to wash himself very carefully in the manner prescribed, lifting the ewer with his right hand and passing it to his left, then pouring the clean water three times over his right hand, with the fingers pointing to the ground. The left hand must then be washed in the same way, with water poured from the right, and the face must be washed three times. Then, with the palms joined and the thumbs and fingers outstretched, the words must be uttered, "Lift up your hands to the sanctuary and praise the Lord!" Other prayers followed. As far back as he could remember, James had repeated this ritual every morning of his life. It was as natural as sleeping, as necessary as eating and working with one's hands.

His dressing completed, James took the three steps to the table, removed the linen napkin from the top of the jug, and prepared to pour the water into the ewer. But when he tipped the jug, no clear, sparkling stream ran out. To his amazement and horror he found it was empty!

Carefully, without taking a step, he drew the low stool toward him and sat down. This was a predicament indeed. Not only must he miss the morning Temple service that he had so much anticipated, but he must remain here, all the morning perhaps, without taking a step until someone came. It did not occur to him that there was another alternative, that of breaking the Law. He would as soon have thought of reviling his parents or of rejecting his birthright.

The sun rose above the housetops, turning the white stones of the Temple to rose and jasper, causing its rich overlays of gold to gleam and scintillate like the burnished wings of seraphim. A spiral of blue smoke arose, thin and tenuous as a mist.

They are spreading the incense on the golden altar, thought James, and waited for the thicker, darker pillar that would indicate the morning sacrifice.

There were sudden light footsteps on the housetop, and Susanna appeared in the doorway. She carried a jug of water. Her eyes were very big and very wide open, and she stammered like a frightened child.

"I'm sorry," she said breathlessly. "I really didn't stop to think how it would seem—how mean and inhospitable. I just did it, that's all."

"Did what?" asked James curiously, noticing that her eyes were hazel instead of the dark brown he had thought them.

"Why, poured all the water out of the jug."

"Oh! I see." No, they were not exactly hazel. Amber, rather, because of the little gold flecks in them. "And why did you do that?"

The gold flecks were suddenly dancing. "Because you're always so sober and sedate and—and stuffy," she said frankly. "And you never think about anything except learning things and keeping the Law. I just thought it would be fun to see what you'd do."

James threw back his head and laughed heartily. "Wait a minute," he called as Susanna hastily set down the jug and fled. "I want to tell you something."

While he proceeded to wash, hurriedly but in the prescribed manner, he kept one eye on the door to make sure that the small figure in its blue flowing mantle was still lingering outside. "Listen, Susanna," he said, striding to the door. She turned obediently. "Until this morning I've always been afraid of you. You had such fine clothes and perfect manners, and you always seemed so far above us countrified Nazareth children. And now to find that you're just a child—and a mischievous one at that!"

"Oh!" exclaimed the girl, a little breathlessly. "So—so you think I'm a child, do you? I—I'll show you!"

Acting on a sudden ungovernable impulse, she came up close to him, stood on tiptoe, and kissed him full on the mouth. Then, aghast at what she had done, she turned with a little cry and fled.

James stood looking after her, not quite realizing what had happened but conscious of an unfamiliar stirring in his veins, a vague quickening of his pulses. Susanna might be a child, he decided, but she was also a woman. And a somewhat disturbing one.

2

James' life in Jerusalem soon settled into the routine that it was to follow for the next five years. Each morning he arose early, often before dawn, sometimes going to the Temple for morning worship, at other times pursuing his own careful ritual and taking a long walk, perhaps, out into the suburbs of the city. From the middle of the forenoon until well after midday he attended the School of Shammai. After that, until nearly time for the evening meal, he plied his carpenter's trade in a shop that Clopas fitted up for him in an end of one of his warehouses, or he went elsewhere to do repair work on some of his uncle's property.

Clopas was an exacting master, as critical of the joints on the sill of a warehouse doorway as of the cargoes of lumber or balsam or fish that were constantly moving in and out of it. His keen eyes inspected James' work thoroughly.

"You have your father's zeal, perhaps, but not his cleverness," he told his nephew bluntly. "No wonder you could be spared more easily than your brother."

James flushed, but the old blind desire for retaliation did not seize him. Words, he had discovered, were a far more effective weapon than physical violence. "My father," he said simply, "was a carpenter. You are a merchant. I shall be a scholar, perhaps a rabbi. Neither of us would choose to be all three."

Clopas said no more. He was better at driving a bargain than at repartee.

But in the School of Shammai James' abilities were forced to accept no slights. Each day he sat on his rug before the dais of his particular rabbi, his keen mind assimilating each fresh formula of the oral tradition like thirsty soil absorbing the rain. It had been no easy task to gain entrance into the school. For hours he had sat within a circle of exacting rabbis, answering their steady, rapid fire of questions, quoting long passages from the Law of Moses, even entering into an occasional bit of hot, eager debate. But Rabbi Nathan had done his work well. Not only did James pass his entrance examinations honorably, but within six months he had been transferred to the tutelage of the most venerable rabbi in the school, Ben Judah, the one upon whose shoulders had fallen the mantle of the great Shammai himself.

After that he was given more liberty to study as he wished. He was allowed access to the precious manuscripts in the school library, and he read avidly among the Haggadoth, the sayings and traditions of the prophets. Often he went with other students to the porches of the Temple, where companies of scribes and rabbis were almost always to be found in hot debate on such questions as: "Will the ten lost tribes ever return?" or, "If a dish becomes defiled and has to be broken, how small must the fragment be to become clean again?" Or if the company happened to be composed of Pharisees and Sadducees, "Is there really going to be a resurrection of the dead?" Often these debates were more than heated. They reached an intensity of bitterness that ended by the participants' spitting in each other's faces.

James did not always enjoy these arguments. He was sure his Brother would have thought some of them puerile and trivial—for instance, the frequent one about whether an egg laid on the Sabbath Day could be eaten on the sacred day or not. The School of Shammai held that it could be, provided it was laid by a hen intended not for laying eggs but to be eaten. The School of Hillel held otherwise. And, though the question had been decided long ago in favor of the latter school, rabbis still argued the matter hours upon end.

But he reveled in the majestic pronouncements of the Torah, that triumphant document of Jewish nationalism, and in the fiery utterances of the prophets, those fearless spokesmen of the past, who, like himself, had fashioned their hopes to the pattern of a Dream.

Only one other person in Jerusalem knew about the Dream. James told Susanna about it one evening when they happened to be walking in the garden, the red anemones and white cyclamens fashioning living mosaics of fire and mist in the dusk about them.

"You mean," she said softly, "you believe you and Jesus have some special work to do? Something that is very important to the welfare and happiness of our people?"

"Yes," he said simply, surprised to discover how easy it was to speak to Susanna about these intimate things, things so deeply embedded in his sensitive, reticent spirit that they had never before found expression in words. "It's really Jesus who gave me the idea, I think, though it was so long ago it seems as if it's always been a part of me. He's rather a wonderful person, you know—my Brother."

"Oh, I know he is," assented Susanna eagerly. "I've always felt it, even that time when we visited you long ago, when he carried me around on his shoulder. I can't just describe it, but he makes things intelligible, somehow. You feel all mixed up about things, or else you see something so beautiful that—that you can hardly bear it. And then Jesus just looks at you or says something, and things seem to be all right again." She laughed shakily. "I told you I couldn't describe it."

"I know what you mean," said James thoughtfully, wondering if any look or word of his would ever kindle such a light in Susanna's eyes, but, strangely enough, feeling no resentment at his Brother for having done so. He was, rather, grateful for this common bond of loyalty that drew them together.

"What kind of work do you suppose it will be?" asked Susanna curiously. "Have you and Jesus ever talked about that?"

James considered. "No," he said slowly. "I never thought about it before, and I guess we never have talked about it. We've just always known that there was some work for us, that's all—something that perhaps no one else in all Israel would be able to do." He laughed apologetically. "It sounds presumptuous, I know."

"I don't think it does," said Susanna quickly. "If you don't believe in yourself—the thing within you that makes you different—how can you have anything to share with other people?" She swung her slender body to a seat on the rock wall that edged the garden, so quickly and lightly that James had no chance to help her. He drew back his outstretched hand reluctantly.

"I suppose," he said slowly, a little gropingly, "that what we really want to do is give people a new vision of God."

"Yes?" The word was no more than a breath. Susanna leaned forward eagerly.

"We're a peculiar people," went on James more steadily. "There are two things we must have in order to live—freedom and God. The two go together. They can't be separated. We've already lost one. If we're not careful we'll soon be losing the other." His eyes flashed. "The high priest and his family care nothing for the keeping of the Law. They're traitors to their country. They've sold us all out to Caesar. Not only does a strange king sit on the throne of David, but the most holy place itself has become a nesting place for serpents. It's just a question of which is the more important to get back first," he went on more quietly, "our freedom or our God."

"Many people have tried to win back our freedom," said Susanna. "Some of them are trying right now—" She stopped abruptly. "How could you go about it to—to win back God?"

"How but by the Law?" retorted James quickly. "And by purifying our religion from every foreign influence that has contaminated it? God *is* the Law. How could there possibly be any other way?"

Susanna shivered. She slipped down from the wall. "I don't know," she said in an oddly disappointed voice. "I suppose there isn't, only the Law seems such a cold thing. And so lifeless, like an empty shell."

"The Law of Jehovah is perfect," James said.

"Yes, I know." She sighed. "I—I was just hoping, when you said you had some great work to do—"

"Hoping what?" he asked gently. They were walking back now

along the path toward the house, and he moved closer, so that his arm brushed the folds of her long, flowing mantle.

"Oh, I don't know. Only, there are so many people who need something. Lepers and beggars and those poor women with painted faces. And even father and mother and Simon—"

James frowned. He drew away to his own side of the path. "What do you know of lepers and beggars and harlots? They are unclean names to be coming from your lips. And certainly not to be mentioned in the same breath with the law-observing members of one's family!"

She shivered again. "It's getting cool, isn't it? There must be a wind from the sea. Shall we go in?"

Mary's eyes greeted them coldly. "I've been all alone," she said reproachfully to Susanna.

"I'm sorry," said the girl patiently, straightening the cushions behind the invalid's back. "I thought Huldah was with you."

The woman waved a white, shapely hand in an impatient gesture. "Huldah cares nothing for me. She runs away the moment one's back is turned. Anyway, a servant is a poor substitute for a daughter."

Susanna laughed. "It's all right now," she said cheerfully. "I'm back, and I won't be going out again. That is, not tonight."

Mary turned to James, her thin lips curving in a languid smile. "It's so pleasant having you here, nephew," she said evenly. "And what a shame it would be for all of us, you especially, if you were not able to stay!"

James opened his lips quickly, then, seeing the dismay in Susanna's eyes, as quickly shut them. He nodded his head abruptly and went up to his room.

After that he took no more walks with Susanna in the garden.

James had not been living in Jerusalem many months before the reason for the dissension in Clopas' household became apparent. Simon had no wish to follow his father's career as a merchant. Neither had Clopas' two older sons, James and Joses, who had left home and entered into other occupations somewhere in their father's native province of Galilee. Clopas resented this bitterly. He had built up a profitable business and one that was constantly enlarging, and to have all his sons, one after the other, turn their backs deliberately on a career that he had spent the best part of his life building for them was a bitter draught to swallow. That his own dominating and unyielding personality might have been to blame for his sons' reluctance to remain with him did not, of course, occur to him.

Simon was not outwardly rebellious. He did all the things his father asked of him—made trips to buy and inspect merchandise, paid frequent visits of inspection to the company's retail booths in the Tyropoeon, and appeared dutifully at all employees' and directors' meetings. But his heart was not in it—nor, frequently, was his body, for he was gone from the house for days at a time, on errands that had no connection with his father's business. During such periods Clopas was moody, Susanna worried, and Mary, strangely enough, less demanding and petulant than usual.

It was when Clopas was away on a long business trip to Damascus that James learned the secret. Simon came to him in the warehouse one afternoon, alert excitement displacing the usual veiled disinterest in his pale-brown eyes.

"We're having guests to dinner," he announced secretively. "John, the son of Zebedee, and a few others. I wanted to let you know beforehand."

"Certainly," said James, surprised. "But if you're entertaining friends, perhaps you'd rather I was not around. I know John, of course. He's my cousin. But the others—"

"No, no," said Simon quickly, in the same low, secretive voice. "That's why I'm telling you. I want you there. I've been waiting for a chance ever since you came."

James looked mystified. "Of course I'll be there, but I don't quite understand."

"You will." Simon looked around furtively. Then, reaching out his hand, he slowly drew some marks in the sawdust with his index finger. James stared in amazement at the pointed lines, the curves. Then sudden memory stabbed him.

"A fox!" he whispered.

Simon's lips closed in a soft, sibilant sound, more like a hiss than an acquiescence. "One does not even whisper it," he said.

John, the son of Zebedee, was a frequent visitor at the house of Clopas. Since the latter's visit to Nazareth years before, when he had met Zebedee at Joseph's house, a profitable fish wholesale had been added to Clopas' other commercial lines, and for some years John had represented his father's interests in Jerusalem, spending part of the year there and part in his own home in Capernaum. John was now about twenty-one, still unmarried, with a slim, hard, virile body and a flashing eye that indicated the continued aptness of the old boyhood nickname, "son of thunder."

Of the other three guests at the evening meal James had eyes for only one. So striking was the figure of the young man to whom Simon accorded the most honored position, so completely did he dominate the scene from the moment of his entering the room, that even the rugged and personable John seemed pale and colorless beside him. A giant of a fellow he was, standing, like King Saul, head and shoulders above the average person, yet with every huge muscle so perfectly, evenly poised that he moved with the utmost grace. His features were strong rather than handsome, their dark austerity lightened by sensitive, winsome lips and dazzlingly white teeth. But it was his eyes that most attracted James, eyes so intensely bright they looked as if sparks could be kindled from them. Never, James thought, had he seen such a vital person as this Barabbas.

Susanna served the meal. She had put on a soft, flowing, rose-colored garment that looked like a drift of flower petals, and she kept her veil drawn over the lower part of her face. Strangely enough, this seemed to reveal rather than conceal her beauty. The soft pink folds made a becoming frame for the high white forehead with its two close-folded wings of hair, the wide-set, long-lashed eyes. This was, to James, a new Susanna, more poised and mature than he had ever seen her, playing the part of the gracious hostess with the ease of one born to royalty. He thought she had never been more lovely or more desirable.

Apparently Barabbas thought so too, and was unhampered by James' reticence of expression. He paid compliments with the dexterity of a fencer.

"My lady of the rose petals," he greeted her with a graceful bow which would have seemed effeminate in one less virile. "You did remember, didn't you?"

Susanna tossed her head with an indifference belied by the faint stain of pink mounting to her forehead. "It is the duty of a good woman of Israel to please her guests," she replied primly.

Barabbas laughed heartily. "Then may heaven strengthen all lovely women in their sense of duty," he responded gallantly.

His bright eyes followed her every movement as she went quietly about, setting the food on the low table, placing the jug of wine, bringing the water for the preliminary washing of hands. Occasionally, when she passed close to him, he reached out with a light, intimate gesture to touch the folds of her dress, and when she brought the pitcher and basin, standing beside him while he washed, he deliberately prolonged the moment by another of his gallant speeches, carelessly brushing more than once with his strong brown fingers the small hand that held the basin.

Small things, unnoticed, no doubt, by the rest of the company, but James noticed them. "He's in love with her," he thought with a sudden swift stab of fear, remembering the faint suffusion of pink that had crept up to the roots of those smooth, soft wings of hair. "My lady of the rose petals," he had called her. He had seen her in that same flowing, bright-hued gown before, had complimented her, and she had worn it again to please him. Did that mean—

They took their places at the table, the wine was poured, the benediction spoken, the bread cut and dipped into the appetizer of salted meat. That Barabbas was an honored guest was indicated by the lavish display of food and the variety of the menu. There were fish, both fresh and salted, meats, cheeses, a half dozen different kinds of vegetables, pickled olives, fruits, and sweetmeats. When the after-dinner wine had been served and the second blessing spoken, Susanna quietly withdrew, leaving the men alone.

Instantly Barabbas laid aside his suavely genial manner. The languid, roving eyes became white-hot and intense. The careless fingers tightened into sinewy rods beating impatiently on the table. He nodded his head, and the two men who had been reclining, one on either side of him, sprang up and took their places beside the outer entrance.

"There's no one in the house," he asked Simon abruptly, "except your mother and sister?"

"Not even the servants," replied Simon. "I sent them all away."

Barabbas turned from James to John, fixing upon each the white-hot heat of his gaze, then back to James again, his eyes leaving the latter's dark, thin, serious face reluctantly. He turned again to Simon. "You're sure of these two, Ben Clopas?"

"As to sympathy with our program, no," replied Simon. "As to loyalty to the cause of our nation's freedom, yes."

"They're one and the same," retorted Barabbas. He leaned forward on his elbow, and instinctively James and John also moved closer.

"I'm going to speak plainly," he went on in a low, even voice. "You are men of Galilee, and in Galilee men do not whisper their thoughts in the dark. They let the sun shine upon their hopes and fears and—hates. They are not afraid to stand up and call a fox—a *fox*."

John stirred. "Herod Antipas," he muttered.

"Yes," assented Barabbas instantly. "Herod Antipas. A name so hated by Galileans, so indicative of all that is crafty and cunning and evil that when Jewish patriots sought for a symbol to denote our enemies, they chose the name they had called him in secret. A fox." He turned suddenly to James. "You know. You were born not five miles from the center of the hotbed. You remember Judas?"

Something stirred in James' memory—the sudden flash of a smile that was like a dark cloud edged with sunlight, the touch of a vibrant hand on his head, the echo of a half-remembered voice. "Perhaps sometime you will like to remember, little lad, that you once looked into the face of a strange man called Judas the Galilean."

"Yes," he said. He gazed steadily into the white-hot depths. "I saw him once. I was six at the time of his last rebellion. I saw hundreds of his followers die."

"Hundreds more of them are still alive," said Barabbas. "No, thousands of them. Many of them no longer call themselves the followers of Judas. Instead they are the followers of Barabbas."

"You!" echoed John.

"Yes." A flicker of vanity disturbed the steady, even flaming of his eyes. "Judas failed because he was not strong enough. He struck too quickly."

James turned his eyes deliberately from the magnetism of the man's kindling glance. "Perhaps he failed," he said thoughtfully, "because the people had already betrayed their country to the enemy, letting foreign customs taint their homes, their language, even their religion. Look at us," he went on, eyes suddenly flashing, "sitting here at meat, not in the old Jewish fashion, but on Grecian couches, eating foreign dishes, wearing clothes of foreign weave and fabric. I tell you, if we want to save Israel, we've got to purify her. We've got to purge ourselves of everything that ever came in from the outside and then keep ourselves separate, inviolate, a chosen people."

"Bravo!" said Barabbas, recalling James' wandering glance within the magnetism of his blazing eyes. "And we'll do it too."

"How?" demanded John bluntly.

James made a conscious effort to keep himself from falling beneath the hypnotic spell of those compelling eyes.

"By the Law," he replied firmly.

"By the sword," retorted Barabbas triumphantly.

James felt himself weakening, felt his eyes drawn back inevitably into that magnetic circle of flame. "Perhaps," he admitted. "But others have tried. For three hundred years men like you have been trying to win back our freedom. How can you be sure you will succeed any better than they?"

"Did you say men like me?" demanded Barabbas softly.

James stared at him, repelled and yet strangely fascinated. The vanity of the man who had the audacity to set himself above the Maccabees, above Judas! And yet—

"Suppose," it was Simon speaking, leaning across the table, "suppose it was the Promised One to whom you were speaking, the great Deliverer who is sure to come. Would you ask him how he could be sure?"

James gasped. Barabbas rose abruptly, with the true artist's instinct for the dramatic moment of exit, and took his departure—not, however, without a final fleeting glance toward the curtained doorway leading into the women's quarters.

Later James lay on his pallet, staring out at the stars, his mind a confusion of half-shaped questions. Had Simon actually meant to imply that this man—Did Susanna—Did Barabbas have the unspeakable presumption to believe himself—And yet, why not?

He fell asleep finally, to dream that he was walking in the darkness toward two lights that became two flaming eyes, a vast, limpid pool into which he was sinking, and that just before he sank out of sight, he glimpsed the final flutter of a pink drapery in the distance.

3

"There!" said Susanna, twining a garland of flaming sumac in and out among the contrasting green of the olive and myrtle and fir branches. "How does that look?"

"Not too bad!" said Simon critically. "Give me another strand of it, and I'll put some over my bower."

"Too frivolous," observed Mary dourly from the seat they had fixed for her in the shade of the olive tree. "Too much color is not a good thing on feast days. It distracts people's minds from their worship."

"Unnecessary," said Clopas practically. Nevertheless he reached for a piece, and fastening it over the entrance of the green tentlike creation that he was preparing for his son Joses, he stood off and viewed the result with some satisfaction.

"Like you," James felt like saying boldly, stealing another glance at Susanna's starry eyes, the rose-petal smoothness of her cheeks. "Like light and stars and sweet fragrances and laughter and beauty. Like everything that is lovely and desirable." But of course he didn't. "Mother would like that," he said casually and, at the risk of soiling his new white Pharisee's cloak, twined a piece of it in his own tent. Stepping back and stooping to brush off an imaginary fleck of dirt, he caught Susanna's eyes fixed upon him in laughing amusement.

"Look out, Cousin James!" she sang out, her sweet voice gaily derisive. "It's against the Law to get a spot of dust on it bigger than a pinpoint!" Then, seeing his thin, sensitive face flush, she took occasion to whisper soon after as she passed him, "It's really very becoming. Your mother won't be the only one who is proud of you today." James flushed again, this time because his gratitude for her approval was like a swift, upsurging warmth in his veins.

The household of Clopas, like every Jewish household in Jerusalem, was preparing for the annual Feast of Tents, or Tabernacles. It was the great event of the year. For a week the city would be filled with pilgrims, not only from Judea, Perea, and Galilee, but from Egypt, Persia, and the lands beyond the sea, all of them living in the gay, green, tentlike structures that had sprung up overnight in garden and on housetop, in every available outdoor spot from Olivet to Gihon, from Siloam to the farthermost bounds of the suburb of Bezetha. The Temple, that glittering focus about which the Jewish world revolved, would from dawn till dark be wreathed in sacrificial smoke.

From dark till dawn its great, blazing candelabras would make it a thing of ethereal, ineffable splendor. Only the frowning Fortress of Antonia was unadorned, ungarlanded; and the palace of Herod, where Valerius Gratus, the procurator, lived; and the great Roman theater on the shelf of the Tyropoeon.

The pilgrims came swarming along the Jericho road, dusty, tired, begrimed, sweaty, rapturous, exalted, straining toward the crest of Olivet and their first glimpse of the Holy City. Like animals, thought James, distaste mingling with his eagerness, and he almost wished that he hadn't come. It had been Susanna's suggestion that they walk outside the city to meet the band of Nazareth pilgrims, and James had acquiesced eagerly. It was three years since he had seen his mother and brothers. Mary had had a long, lingering sickness, and the family had not attempted the annual pilgrimages to Jerusalem.

"You're sure they'll come this way?" asked Simon, stepping aside out of the densely flowing human stream.

James looked anxiously to see if there was any mark where a fat, dusky-faced Arab had stepped on the blue border of his cloak. "Yes," he said. "They always come this way. The northern road leads through Samaria." To a Jew, he knew, no other explanation was necessary. For centuries the Jews had had no dealings with the hated Samaritans.

"Look!" exclaimed Susanna, her eye shining softly above her veil. "Look at their faces, James! They're tired, but they don't feel it. Look at that fat woman with the limp, and the sweat pouring down her face! She's forgotten that her feet hurt. She can't wait to get to the top of the hill. And look at their faces when they do get there! See them drop on their knees? It isn't just the Temple they're seeing, or the Holy City. It's everything they've ever hoped and longed for. James, it's the Dream!"

James' pulses stirred. He pressed her hand understandingly. Susanna was right. This living, moving, human flood—this was the bloodstream of Israel! And Jerusalem, with its Temple, its eternal Presence, its unchangeable Law, was the vibrant, beating heart. The stream was full of impurities: Witness that loud-voiced, ungodly Arab, that haughty Parthian, that swarthy Idumaean (symbol of the hated Herod!), that arrogant Roman flicking his whip from his high-stepping horse! It must be cleansed. And was not the very task of cleansing it a part of the Dream?

Eagerly James began to scan the approaching faces. Now that the moment was really at hand when he was to see his Brother again, he felt as if he could hardly bear the suspense. Three years was a long time. That they had brought changes in himself besides the mere outward detail of his having donned the Pharisee's dress he was well aware. Would they likewise have wrought changes in his Brother?

As they stood watching, the shadows lengthened. The garden on the western slope of the hill became thick with dusk. The trumpets of the priests sounded clear and sweet across the Kidron, calling the people to evening sacrifice. Yet still the stream of pilgrims flowed on unabated.

"Look!" Susanna suddenly clutched his arm. "The name on the banner coming up the hill! Doesn't it say 'Nazareth'?"

James' eyes strained through the half-light. The leap of his heart told him, even before he could read the letters. He knew that banner. Pure white it was, with its four characters of scarlet, and the pole to which it was fastened still had that little crook in it just halfway down. He would have known it even without the familiar sight of Jonathan, the pack driver, limping along with his clubfoot. Forgetting his new cloak, his dignity as a Pharisee, he ran toward them down the hill, his heart pumping furiously just as once, years before, he had run down the Nazareth hill to meet a returning caravan.

"Mother!" he cried, flinging himself toward the figure on the familiar little donkey, his heart constricting because her sickness had left her so wan and thin.

She kissed him and clung to him, then held him off and looked at him, her eyes marveling because he was so much taller than she had remembered. But all she said was: "James, my dear! You have a new cloak, haven't you?"

He greeted Jude, who looked just the same, except a bit heavier and stockier, and Simon, who looked very different, because in the three years he had grown to be a man, and his youngest brother Joseph, who was just turning twelve and intensely curious to reach the top of the hill and get his first view of Jerusalem. He met Jude's wife, Anna, whom he remembered as one of the sturdy, red-cheeked children who had frolicked among the shavings.

But everything else became strangely inconsequential when he felt his hands grasped in a firm, well-remembered grip, felt a warm vibrancy of strength flowing through them. He lifted his gaze hungrily to the beloved, familiar features, the deep brown eyes warm with tenderness and laughter and understanding, the full, smiling, mobile lips. And gladness such as he had never known surged through him.

"Peace to you, my brother," said Jesus. "Is it well with you?"

"It is well," replied James joyfully.

The gay green tents that covered Clopas' house and garden were filled to overflowing. James and Joses, Clopas' older sons, were there with their families from Galilee, as were Zebedee and Salome and their son James, since the house that John was building on an adjacent lot was not yet finished. There were also frequent callers. Esther and Tamar were visiting with their husbands' families in other parts of the city, and Mary, who seldom saw them except during feast days, urged them to come in often with their children.

The most interesting guest, James thought, was a distant cousin whom he had never met before, John, the son of Zacharias, one of the priests taking part in the Temple services. His mother had been Elizabeth, a cousin of Mary, now dead for some years. This John was a dramatic, compelling figure. Dedicated before his birth to be a lifelong Nazarite, he had become a severe ascetic, living a hermit existence somewhere in the wilderness down toward the Dead Sea and appearing only at stated times to pay his religious vows in the Temple. His spare, gaunt figure, thin almost to the point of emaciation, his long, thick, ragged locks which had never known the touch of a razor, his brilliant, piercing, dark eyes—all were intensely intriguing to James.

Apparently Jesus also found John interesting for they spent hours together in the guestchamber on the housetop. James listened to some of their conversations and became strangely stirred, for it was obvious that John too sensed that he had some definite work to perform. Listening to his passionate tirades against evil, his eloquence that was as dry and hot and scorching as the searing desert sirocco, James wondered if John might not be the great national Deliverer Israel was looking for, and he searched his Brother's face eagerly for some kind of kindred excitement. But Jesus said little, and only listened to his cousin gravely.

Finally, in one of their rare moments alone together, James asked him. "Could John be the one we're looking for?" he blurted out eagerly. "Would this work he wants to do fit in with the Dream?"

It was late evening, and they were sitting on the low wall surrounding the housetop, a little removed from the gay company in the garden below. Above them on Mount Moriah the great illuminated Temple swam mistily in the darkness, like a vast mirage.

Jesus was a long time answering, so long that James grew impatient. He leaned forward eagerly.

"There's another man I want you to meet," he said impetuously. "His name is Barabbas." With instinct born of long habit he lowered his voice cautiously. "He's the leader in this section of the nationalist party known as the Zealots. I believe Simon is one of them, though I'm not quite sure. You remember Judas the Galilean?"

Of course Jesus remembered him. The brown eyes were still and intent. James hurried on, his mind backing hastily from the dark, gaunt shadows that the name of Judas always conjured.

"Well, Barabbas is really the follower of one of the sons of Judas. Only some say that he's stronger than any of them—so strong that he may be the great Deliverer himself. " James' voice trembled with the tumult of emotion that the thought of Barabbas always roused within him. "I—I'm not sure myself what I think of him. There's something about him—he draws one like a magnet. When I'm with him, I can't help wondering. After all, isn't that what the Dream means, deliverance for Israel?"

Again his Brother was a long time answering. When he did speak, it was only to ask another question. Did James believe that this Barabbas was the Messiah? And did he think they should forget the work they had planned to do and join with him in trying to win political freedom for the nation?

James hesitated. "No—I—that is—I don't know what I mean—"

The dark eyes lighted whimsically, so that he could see their dancing even in the dark. "Come now, " they seemed to say in gentle, amused accusation. "A moment ago it was John. Now it's Barabbas. They can't both be the great Deliverer, can they?"

James floundered in the deep brown depths. "I—I'm rather mixed up, I guess. But after all, the Dream has to have a leader, doesn't it?"

The light in the brown depths became suddenly remote, like the pale shining mist that was the illumined Temple. When Jesus spoke again, there was no whimsical lightness in his voice. James was right, of course. The Dream must have a leader. And he would like very much to meet this Barabbas.

It was the last day of the feast. Meeting at the Temple at daybreak, the festive multitude separated into three companies. Some remained to watch the preparation of the morning sacrifice. Others marched in a gay procession outside the city of Mozah, where they cut willow branches and, bringing them back, built a leafy canopy above the altar. James and Jesus went with the third procession, which followed a priest carrying a great golden pitcher.

Out of the Temple they marched to the sound of music, a great throng of people in holiday dress, each one bearing in his left hand a piece of citron, in his right a lulab, a branch of palm woven together with willow and myrtle. Down through Ophel they passed, along the edge of the Tyropoeon Valley to the Pool of Siloam, where, with much singing and ceremony, the priest would fill his golden pitcher from its waters.

It was a gay, noisy procession, accompanied by much singing and dancing: A motley procession, where striped Syrian *simlah* merged into strange unity with Egyptian surplice and Greek stola and Roman toga, where haughty Sadducees walked side by side with ascetic, white-robed Essenes, where wealthy Alexandrian noblemen joined hands in dance with beggars; A strangely unified procession, all waving the lulabs, chanting the same Hallel, lifting their faces toward the same hilltop in fierce and loyal exaltation, scowling and muttering the same dire curses at sound of the sharp, staccato hoofbeats betokening the presence of an everwatchful Roman guard.

James walked along soberly, intent on his own thoughts. This was the last day of the feast, and he had not accomplished his purpose. Jesus had not met Barabbas. If he had not been so hesitant about broaching the matter to Simon, a meeting might have been arranged, but his cousin had been more cautious and reticent of late, and James had not wished to suggest it. Had he known the whereabouts of the Zealot's secret stronghold above the Jericho road, there would have been no opportunity to take Jesus there, for even on the half-holy days of the week no more than a Sabbath Day's journey was allowed. Tomorrow would be another sacred day, the octave of the feast, and Sabbath rest would again be enjoined. He felt uncertain and disappointed.

As the procession neared the Pool of Siloam, it moved more slowly, finally stopping entirely. The throng of people filling the great cleft where the Tyropoeon Valley merged into the Valley of the Kidron ceased suddenly to be an orderly procession and became a confused, disordered mass. Sensing the change, the eyes of the mounted guards became more wary, the flick of their whips more ominous, the hoofbeats of their horses more staccato. For they knew that with a mob like this almost anything could happen on a Jewish feast day.

And suddenly it did happen. Not ten feet away from where James and Jesus were standing the massive figure of a man was hoisted above the crowd. His feet planted firmly, each on a sturdy, invisible shoulder, he towered above the mass of milling bodies like a rock above restless waves.

"Men of Israel!" he cried. "How long—how long will you suffer the yoke of the unbeliever to hang about your necks, the sharp thrust of his goad to prick your backs? How long, I ask you? How long?"

A ripple swept over the waves, dying to ominous silence. James caught his breath, then clutched his Brother's arm. "Barabbas!" he whispered.

The towering figure dominated the silence. His glittering dark eyes swept the uplifted faces like a flail. "Are you sons of Abraham or babes of Caesar? How much longer will you let heathen lawbreakers police you while you keep the Law? How much longer will you have yonder *mokhes* for your priest, paying your tithes to him instead of to Jehovah? Are your bones water? Has the blood in your veins turned to milk? Woe unto you, men of Israel, letting yourselves be lulled to sleep by the whispering of serpents in your ears!"

Fifty yards away the Roman guard wheeled, circled the edge of the crowd warily, keen eyes suspiciously narrowed, fingers tightened on his sword hilt. But the towering figure had slipped into the tide, the waves closing over him. There was only a low muttering, barely perceptible, to indicate that the gay, festive spirit of the crowd had changed. He turned and rode back again, still wary, still uneasy, the sweat pouring down his cheeks, settling into the lines of his tight-drawn lips. These accursed Jews, these heathen smoke and water worshipers! One minute they were dancing and shouting like bacchanals, the next they were kowtowing and muttering. You couldn't tell whether it was part of their accursed heathen festival, or—

He suddenly wheeled again, as the muttering heightened to an ominous murmur, swelled to a burst of fury. His hand flew to his lips, and he blew three quick blasts on his bugle. Then he whipped out his sword, leaned forward in his saddle, and prepared himself for an onslaught, his lips tightening grimly, not so much from fear as from distaste. So—they were at it again, the crazy fools! Beating a few more of their blind brains out against the stone wall of Roman occupation! He would have to mow down a few more swaths of them with his sword, and there would be blood all over the place.

With sudden relief he discovered that he was not the target of their fury. They were headed for the customs booth on the main road leading to the city gate. The little tax collector sitting there saw them coming and crouched down into his booth, his face blanched with terror. The Roman's lips twisted grimly. So they were picking on one of themselves, were they, this time! How the Jews did hate these native tax collectors, to whom the Romans cleverly farmed out their taxes! Good riddance! Let them shed their own blood. It would save him the trouble.

No, he really couldn't do that. After all, the *mokhes*, as they called him, was entitled to Roman protection. He was collecting the empire's taxes. Though there probably wasn't much of him to protect by this time, the way the mob had lighted on him! By Jupiter, but these Jews were bloodthirsty devils! They were getting ready to stone the fellow now! He supposed he would have to kill off a few of them just to let them know that they couldn't get by with tricks like this. A half dozen, say? One good sweep of his sword? How many Jews would it take to atone for the carcass of a *mokhes?*

Reluctantly he spurred his horse forward. As he did so, a voice rang out over the crowd, clear and commanding, followed by a sudden silence. The Roman wheeled, suspicious and alert, his hand poised. The voice came again, startlingly clear and challenging, speaking in the native Aramaic language. And then an amazing thing happened. Instead of making a fresh onslaught, as the Roman expected, possibly toward himself this time, the mob slowly disintegrated, dropped their stones a little sheepishly, and drifted back into a more orderly formation. Far ahead, where the procession wound around the Pool of Siloam, the priest had filled his golden pitcher, and the marching had begun again. Joyous and festive, chanting their psalms and waving their lulabs, the end of the procession, erstwhile a mob of rebels, passed in orderly fashion around the end of the Pool of Siloam, up the Valley of the Kidron.

The Roman wiped his dripping face.

"Trouble?" asked the captain of the emergency guard that had rushed to the spot at the sound of his bugle.

"There was," replied the soldier, indicating the battered figure of the *mokhes* on the ground a few feet away. "I handled it all right."

The captain looked admiringly. "Good work! Not everybody can manage a mob of these devils without mopping them up in blood! I'll recommend you for a promotion."

After the captain had gone, the Roman lingered. A tall young man in peasant's dress was leaning over the figure of the *mokhes*, ministering to his wounds. Another young Jew stood by, one of those proud, white-coated, broad-fringed religious snobs with the queer harnesses on his arm and forehead. The Roman gave him only a casual, contemptuous glance. His eyes were all for the young peasant. Was it to him, he wondered, that that clear, challenging voice belonged? And if it was, what in Jupiter's name had he said that he could quiet the fury of a mob in less than a dozen seconds?

He wished he knew Aramaic.

James and his Brother went back to the Temple. The procession had long since gone in through the water gate to the threefold blast of the priest's trumpets. The water had been poured into the silver funnel at the base of the altar, the people shouting for the priest to raise his hand as he did so, to make sure that the water was really poured in. For it was a point of issue between the Pharisees and the Sadducees as to whether the custom had actually originated with Moses and was hence lawful. So bitter had been the argument waged that once, when the high priest had poured the water on the ground instead of into the funnel, there had been a severe riot, and six thousand persons had been killed.

When James and Jesus arrived in the court of priests, the special sacrifices had been offered, and the psalm for the day was being chanted. Dutifully James bowed with the throng at each threefold blast of the trumpet, joined his voice in the mighty paean proclaiming the final triumph of Jehovah over the heathen.

> Up, O God, rule thou the earth,
> The true God of all pagans—
> Senseless and ignorant, they blindly move,
> Till the world shakes to its base!

But his mind was not on the words. Even when the priests started their majestic march seven times around the altar, symbolizing the triumphant conquest of the Gentile stronghold, Jericho, his eyes kept wandering to his Brother's face.

Queer he had never noticed before how strong a face it was! He had thought Barabbas' face strong. But Barabbas had only aroused the mob. Jesus had stopped them. The words still rang in James' ears.

"Stop, men of Israel! Is there one among you who has never broken the Law? Then let him cast the first stone!"

James had not known at first that it was his Brother. He had only stood still in answer to an unwilling compulsion, dropping the stone that he had found himself holding in his hand.

Well, he had gained his wish. His question had been answered. Barabbas and Jesus? No. He had known long before his Brother had turned to him, after caring for the broken, battered body of the little *mokhes*—he had known before Jesus had said to him, "You see, James? It is my business to save people, not to destroy them."

The service was over. James raised his voice with the throng in the last great salutation of thanksgiving. He shook off the leaves of his willow branch before the altar and beat his palm branch into shreds. But it was his mind that was being torn, not the withered leaves of the lulab.

Jesus had done strange things that day. He had lifted his voice in an amazing, fearless authority on a fiercely controversial issue—and had taken the unpopular side. He had not only saved the life but bound up the wounds of a hated publican. And in speaking to his brother of the work they were going to do, he had said *my*, not *our*.

"It is my business to save people, not to destroy them."

Out of his confusion one fact emerged clearly—a startling fact, one that would perhaps change the whole nature of their partnership. Jesus would follow neither John nor Barabbas nor any other whom his brother James might choose. He would follow no one. For Jesus himself was a leader. He would expect others, including James, to follow him.

4

In Nazareth, time was measured by the slow, kaleidoscopic circuit of the seasons: After the winter rains, the burst of spring on hill and valley, the ripe scarlet of anemones and tulips, the golden splash of rock roses, marigold, and cytisus, the silver sheen of olive trees, the snow and flame of orange and pomegranate. After the spring the hot, steady, lavish ripening: fields whitening to maturity, branches heavy with long clusters, the golden purple richness of the harvest. After the harvest the winter rains again.

But in Jerusalem it was not so. The seasons were there, of course, playing their part in the unfolding drama, but as background, not as chief actors. The Temple was always in the forefront. Its ministers and worshipers were the cast; the Torah, its majestic playscript. The days were measured, not by the rising and setting of the sun, but by the sound of silver trumpets, the ascending of the smoky pinnacle from the morning and evening sacrifices. The earth turned slowly, passing through its various phases, not of summer and winter, seedtime and harvest, but of Purim, Passover, Pentecost, and Tabernacles.

Three times a year the Nazareth family came to Jerusalem for the feasts: at the Passover season in the spring, for the Feast of Weeks several months later, and for the Feast of Tabernacles in the autumn. But after that first visit their coming disturbed the even tenor of James' life very little. He was now a strict Pharisee, committed to the keeping of the Law in all its thousand and one intricate minor details, and this, he soon discovered, was a fulltime occupation for any man. He begrudged every moment that he had to spend in the carpenter shop or warehouses at tasks of manual labor, though he performed such tasks without complaint in fulfillment of his just obligations to his Uncle Clopas.

But when engaged at such labor he was always in danger of breaking some minute provision of the Law. For instance, there was the time when he was working with a crew of his uncle's employees on the framework of a new two-story warehouse out at the neighboring village of Emmaus, which Clopas had made the headquarters of most of his business. He was being especially careful to avoid all uncleanness, because it was the eve of an important feast day. And then, to his horror, one of the workmen slipped from a broken scaffolding and fell, breaking his neck, almost at James' feet! Not only was he unable to enter the Temple for that feast, but the prescribed washings to cleanse himself from the pollution of such close proximity to death took him seven days!

There were other reasons why he did not enjoy his labors connected with Clopas and his business. He had not been in Jerusalem long before he discovered that his uncle was heartily disliked by most of his employees. He paid poor wages, a circumstance made possible by the fact that Jerusalem merchants were banded together under certain agreements made to further their own interests, and, in order to secure employment of any kind, their employees must accept whatever wage was offered them.

James sympathized to some degree with the predicament of these workmen. The cost of living in the city was immeasurably higher than in the country village from which he had come, where food was plentiful and a workman often received his pay in ample measures of barley rather than in shekels. And he recognized that after paying their government taxes and their Temple tithes, to say nothing of the exorbitant prices charged for the required sacrifices on feast days, many of Clopas' employees were not able, literally, to get enough to eat. But he had no wish to become personally involved in any of their troubles. It was bad enough to be obliged to work among them a few hours each day, to come in close proximity to their odorous, underfed, ill-clad bodies, without entering more intimately into their private lives.

It was the day after this experience at Emmaus that one of the workmen came to James just as he was preparing to leave the warehouse at the close of the day. He was a thin, half-starved-looking Idumaean whose shoulders had become stooped from carrying Clopas' heavy bales. James would have brushed past him hurriedly, but something in the man's face, a certain watchful, desperate intentness, arrested his attention.

"You wish to speak to me?" he asked curtly.

"One minute." The man spoke haltingly, in broken Aramaic. "My brother. You know. Man killed yesterday on scaffold."

"Oh! That was your brother, was it?" James' face clouded with annoyance. "Well, what about it?"

"You there." The man spoke patiently. "You saw wood scaffold made of. You know what kind of wood. Rotten wood. No wonder my brother fall."

Ah! So that was it. James began to see light. He was conscious of other faces—all of them thin and gaunt and hungry-looking and possessing this same quality of desperate, watchful intentness—closing in about him, watching him, barring the way to the door. "Suppose it was," he said slowly, choosing his words cautiously. "What has that to do with me?"

"You can help us," spoke another voice less patiently. "Maybe the boss would listen if you said a thing was so. He couldn't make Jake alive again, but at least he could keep his children from starving."

"My brother have six children," went on the Idumaean gently. "Four fine sons and two daughters. Your Uncle Clopas, he have much money. He help my brother's children?"

James regarded the group steadily. "There's no law that could make him," he said evenly. "And you know there isn't."

"You help?" persisted the man doggedly. "You talk to uncle? You tell him wood scaffold made of rotten?"

James looked about the thin, gaunt circle, gauging its strength. "No," he said boldly, "I can't do that. It's none of my business. If Clopas chooses to make his scaffolds of rotten wood, that's his affair. Now—I'm late, and I must go. Will you step aside, please?"

There was a breathless instant when the watchful, desperate intentness hovered on the edge of something ominous and menacing. Then the circle of gaunt, hungry-looking figures broke. The men shuffled patiently aside. And James, picking up his tools, passed silently through them.

His five years at the School of Shammai were nearly over. James had been a brilliant student.

"What are your plans?" demanded old Rabbi Judah, on whose thin, bowed shoulders the mantle of the great Shammai had fallen.

James hesitated. "I'm not exactly sure. I thought I would go back to Nazareth."

The rabbi's shrewd, black eyes narrowed, then brightened. "To find a wife, my son?"

"No!"

The quick denial and sudden flash softened the brightness to a twinkle. "Ah! So that's the way it is. You do not need to go to Nazareth to find your wife. You've already found her here."

"No—I—that is, I—" James struggled to grope his way out of a burning confusion. "There—there's nothing arranged!"

"I see. Well, it's time there should be. How old are you now? Twenty-three? You should have married long ago. Unless you have a wife, you know, we cannot propose your name for the Great Council."

"The Great Council!" James gasped. "You mean—"

"Why not?" The pale lips smiled at the other's boyish, unbelieving eagerness. "Who would make a better defender of the Law of Israel? You have no other plans?"

James leaned forward impulsively. "Yes. I have plans. But I hardly know how to tell you. You see, my Brother and I—we've always believed there was some special work for us to do, something that will help to fulfill Jehovah's will for Israel."

"What sort of work?"

James stirred uneasily, conscious that the mood of informal friendliness that had prompted him to confide in the old rabbi was gone, that a cautious reticence, almost a veiled hostility, had taken its place. "Why, I—I hardly know—" he stumbled. "I—I guess I've always sort of left that to my Brother. It—it's really his idea."

"Who is your brother?"

"Jesus. Jesus of Nazareth."

"Never heard of him."

Something flared in James, a loyalty deeper and more instinctive than that nurtured by the School of Shammai. He looked straight into the old man's narrowed eyes. "Perhaps not," he said with dignity. "But I believe, sir, that you *will* hear of him."

The pale lips curled into a smile. "No doubt," said the old man indulgently. "But listen, my son. Let me give you some advice. If you want to be a good rabbi, take things as you find them. Don't try to change things. Don't try too hard, even, to change them for the better. The world, your own people—no, even your friends won't thank you for it. I'm an old man. I've lived a long time. I know."

The full, drooping lids curtaining the deep eyes lifted for an instant, and James saw that what they were hiding was not hostility. It was fear.

Susanna was eighteen. For four springs James had watched the small, piquant, heart-shaped face flower into fresh loveliness with each white burst of cyclamen in the garden; the slim, eager body become more softly rounded; the hazel eyes beneath their long fringes awake out of their gay, mischievous laughter to the first sweet, startled awareness of womanhood. Day after day he had met her in the casual intimacies of family living, every pulse of his body vibrating to her nearness. But he had never told her of his love, nor given evidence of it, so far as he knew, by look or gesture. True, his mother, Mary, had known it without his telling her.

"Be patient, son," she had said on one of her brief visits, her eyes very gentle and understanding. "I mean about Susanna, you know. If one cares enough and is willing to wait, things usually work out all right."

But if Susanna also guessed his secret, she had given no sign. He had kept it hidden all these months within him, at first because of the deep reticence that had always made expression so difficult; later because of fear, fear of the contempt of Clopas and the disapproval of his wife Mary, fear above all of the telltale flush that the presence of Barabbas always kindled in Susanna's eyes.

Until one day—

James came home early from the School of Shammai because the old rabbi was attending a meeting of the Great Council. He often attended these meetings himself and listened to their debates, sitting in the outer circle of scribes. But today he was anxious to do some special investigating concerning one of the minor laws of Sabbath observance and had obtained permission to bring several scrolls of the rabbinical sayings home with him in order to do so. Anxious for privacy, he took them to his room immediately without announcing his presence to the family.

To his annoyance, just as he was getting engrossed in his work footsteps sounded on the housetop. Clopas apparently was settling himself for conversation with someone just around the corner from the guestchamber door. James debated whether to announce his presence, rose finally to do so, then, his pulses pounding, he sank back on his cushion, powerless to move or speak. For it was Susanna's voice, unnaturally tensed and strained, that came in response to Clopas' deep rumble, and in a flash of intuition James knew that they were talking of her marriage.

"Must we discuss this now, father?"

"Yes, Susanna, we must. I wouldn't be doing my duty by you if I let the matter drift any longer. You are nearly nineteen years old. Most Jewish girls of your age are not only securely mated but have begun to fulfill their destiny by bearing sons and daughters."

"But mother—she needs me. She couldn't get along without me."

"That's what she thinks. And it's the reason I called you up here on the housetop to discuss the matter. Mary is an unnatural woman."

"She's sick, father. If she were only well again, she'd be different. I know she would."

"All right. She's a sick woman, then. But heaven knows we've paid plenty of denarii to doctors of one kind or another to get her cured. That's beside the point. I'm not going to see you sacrificing your woman's birthright to a faultfinding, self-centered shrew any longer."

"Why, father!"

"Shock you, did I? Well, no matter. The important thing is this. It's time you were betrothed to some good, solid, respectable man, such as—"

"Yes?" The girl's swiftly drawn breath made the words barely audible.

"Such as John, the son of Zebedee."

James felt his body freezing into numbness. Even his breath ceased to function. He waited during what seemed an intolerable eternity for Susanna's reply. It came at last, so low that he had to strain his ears to hear it.

"No, not John! Please! I—I don't love him."

James drew a long breath. Life flowed back again into his frozen body. But the momentary relief brought little satisfaction, for he remembered instantly that he had never remotely suspected that Susanna was in love with John. If Clopas had said Barabbas!

But James knew with sudden swift comprehension that Clopas would never say Barabbas. He would oppose Susanna's attachment to the daring young revolutionist as bitterly as he opposed his son's loyalty to the Zealot's cause. For Clopas was at heart a Sadducee, an opportunist, a believer in the *status quo*. Though loyal to his fathers' religion, he desired no political change. Why should he? Like Annas and his priestly clan, who had fattened their purses on the evils of the present regime by turning the Temple courts into a market shambles, Clopas had prospered under Roman occupancy.

"So you don't love John, my dear? May I ask if there is anyone else you would prefer?"

Again James strained his ears tensely, but there was no answer. Of course not. There wouldn't be, he reminded himself tersely after the first quick surge of relief. And, mingled with the sharp, stabbing jealousy there came a feeling of pity. He felt an overpowering urge to protect her, to guard her gentle, girlish reticences, even her love for Barabbas, from the cold, practical, prying eyes of Clopas.

"Very well. I thought not. Then there is no reason why we cannot go ahead with the plan. John is an honest, reliable Jew of good family and position. He will fit well into my future plans for the business. I shall speak to the marriage broker at once."

"Father—" Susanna's voice was desperate, "please don't! I tell you I don't want to marry John!"

"What's the matter with him?" Clopas was getting impatient now and anxious to end the conversation.

"Nothing. I like John very much. Only—"

"Well, then, that's sufficient." His voice became brusquely tender. "You'll soon find, my dear, that emotion is not at all necessary to a happy marriage. I've learned that from experience. Let's say no more about it. I'll go ahead—"

He stopped abruptly, amazed, as the tall, white-clad figure of his nephew appeared in the guestchamber doorway.

"I'm sorry. I couldn't help overhearing. You can't do this thing to Susanna, Uncle Clopas. You must not wed her to John."

Clopas' glance traveled deliberately over the tall figure, noting shrewdly the dark burning eyes, the taut lips, the tensed face almost as drained of color as the spotless white Pharisee's cloak beneath. "Why not?" he demanded with surprising good humor.

"Because she doesn't love him, for one reason. For another, I don't believe he loves her as a man ought to love the woman he makes his wife."

There was a twinkle in Clopas' shrewd, pale eyes. "And do you?" he asked pointedly.

James gasped. "Do I—"

"Do you love Susanna, James?"

"Yes," replied James steadily.

"Enough so that you would wish her to become your wife?"

"More than enough," replied James quietly. "So much that, if I knew she wished it, I would be willing to see her the wife of another."

Clopas regarded his nephew with a cool speculation that was not wholly unapproving. He turned suddenly to Susanna. "What about it, daughter? Would you be willing to have James for a husband?"

James felt himself submerged in a deep flood of shame and self-reproach. He dared not look at Susanna, knowing what humiliation this moment must be causing her. He had meant to protect her, to keep her tender, youthful emotions from being further violated, and here he had dragged them out for an even clumsier dissection. He waited in an agony of contrition for her answer.

"Yes," said Susanna quietly.

A rushing warmth flowed through his veins. His pulses pounded. Through the blinding radiance that seemed suddenly to engulf him, he saw Susanna's face, her lips smilingly tremulous and provocative, her eyes, with their deep fringes lifted, startlingly clear and candid.

"Susanna," he whispered, groping instinctively toward her.

"Wait a minute!" Clopas' voice was as crisply arresting as a dash of cold water. "This thing isn't settled yet, you know. Suppose we talk it over a bit. You say you love my daughter, do you, James?"

"Yes, sir." James' dark eyes flashed impatiently. It was astonishing how little Clopas seemed to matter at the moment.

"Very well. But do you love her enough to give up your books—all this foolish business of becoming a rabbi—for the sake of making her your wife?"

"Father!" It was Susanna who voiced James' horror. "You couldn't—"

Clopas' pale eyes narrowed. "Most certainly I could, my dear, I've always wanted a son to follow in the business. My own sons disappointed me. You're the only hope I have left. I'll admit I would have preferred John. He has a more practical mind. He's already proved his value in the business. But—" Clopas carefully traced with his white, stubby finger a seam in the stonemasonry of the parapet, "I'm not a hard man, I hope. I want you to be happy, my dear. If James is the one you want—"

Susanna gazed steadily at Clopas. "You mean," her lips were still tremulous but no longer smiling or provocative, "if James wants to marry me, he must give up the thing he's spent all his life working for? He must forget about the Dream?"

"Yes." The man's lips curled. "If that's what he calls it—these impractical plans he's been making. That's exactly what I mean."

James stared, fascinated, at the finger carefully tracing the narrow line between two stone blocks. His father's fingers had looked like that, short and square and blunt and curved up ever so slightly at the ends. But Joseph's had been rough and calloused instead of soft and white and carefully groomed. And Joseph had used his to make benches and cradles and tables, not to twist and distort the destinies of men and women.

The next few days were torture such as James had never experienced. It was like being forced to decide which eye one would prefer to have extinguished by a painful method, one's right or one's left—except that the choice now facing him, instead of involving mere physical loss, necessitated the uprooting of one of the two most deeply embedded life roots of his being. Whichever way he chose, he believed, it would mean betrayal, either of his love for Susanna or of his loyalty to the Law of Jehovah and, hence, to the Dream.

He saw little of Susanna, though apparently she did not try to avoid him and went about her daily tasks as usual. But she did not sing at her work, and she kept the curtains of her deep-fringed eyes tightly drawn. Looking at her, James wondered if he had imagined that smiling, candid clearness which, for that brief moment on the housetop, had seemed so revealing, and, if not, just what it had meant. Had it sprung from an impulse of relief that she need not be forced to marry John? Or from a conviction that, loving her as he claimed, he would in some way make possible her union with Barabbas? Or could it possibly—But at this point in his endless round of conjecture he must wait again for cold clarity to unseal the hot, clamoring flood of emotion, to still his hammering pulses. For of course Susanna was not in love with him. And, even if she were, the choice that he was about to make would soon kill whatever affection she might have for him.

For, being what he was, there was only one choice he could make. Loyalty to duty had always been, would always be, stronger than personal desire, stronger even than the loyalty that bound him to any human person—and he was capable of loving very deeply.

"I must speak to you," he said at last to Susanna.

She caught her breath. "Yes, James?" Her glance fluttered about the courtyard, through the open door into the women's quarters where Huldah, the maid, was vainly endeavoring to satisfy the whims of Mary, "Is—is it something you can say here?"

"Here as well as anywhere." Instinctively he reached out his hands toward her slim, blue-clad shoulders, then drew them back quickly, as conscious of the soft, warm vibrancy of her flesh as if he had actually touched it. He spoke hurriedly. "You won't understand, I know. You'll think I didn't mean what I said up there on the housetop. It doesn't matter, I suppose. The fact is, I can't do it, Susanna. I can't give up the Dream—the work I believe I was meant to do. I can't explain it, but if I gave it up, I wouldn't have anything left worth giving you."

The deep fringes lifted from her eyes, revealing a sudden swift radiance of—was it perhaps relief? "But I do understand, James," she said quickly. "And—and I'm glad. Really I am—"

She would have said more, perhaps explained why she was glad, if Matthias, Simon's personal servant, had not chosen that moment to enter the courtyard. He came straight to James.

"Excuse me, sir. A communication from my master."

"From Simon?" Susanna regarded the slim roll of parchment wonderingly. "But why should he be writing?"

James dismissed Matthias with a curt nod and, resentful of the interruption, broke the seal impatiently.

"What is it?" asked Susanna anxiously. "Has anything happened to Simon?"

James hesitated, then decided to tell her. "Simon has gone to join Barabbas," he said briefly.

"Oh! Then that means that Barabbas must be almost ready—"

"Ready for what?" he demanded, jealous of any intimate knowledge she might have of the young revolutionist.

"For whatever it is he is planning to do." She reached out suddenly and touched his hand. "James, there's more on that parchment, isn't there? Something you haven't told me."

"Suppose there is," he parried, still hurt and resentful and burningly conscious of the light touch of her fingers.

"James, he wants you to join him, doesn't he?"

"Well—" James covered his hurt with an air of defiance, "suppose he does? Is it any concern of yours—now—what I do?"

Instantly remorseful but powerless to recall the words, he watched her slim, blue-clad figure pass quietly out of the courtyard.

"So," Clopas hid his disappointment under a manner of mocking gruffness. "you decided that you loved your musty scrolls, your precious phylacteries, better than you did my daughter."

"Not the scrolls," replied James quickly, "nor the phylacteries. My duty to the God of Israel."

"All right, all right, call it what you want to." Under the edges of his mask of irony Clopas looked old and tired. "What you mean is, you don't want my business. Simon doesn't want it, either. He's gone and flung away his birthright on that fool agitator, that young upstart who wants to snatch the bread from out of our mouths."

"I'm sorry," said James. And he meant it. In that moment of weakness, with his mask loosened, Clopas reminded him poignantly of his father. "I wish there were something I could do."

The mask settled quickly into place. "There is," said Clopas abruptly. "Something you can do right now. I need a man I can trust to go to Caesarea. I was going to send Simon, and he's deserted me."

James looked doubtful. "I'd be glad to go, but you know I'm not much good at business."

"I know. But even you can do this. It's a matter of some money, and keeping the matter secret. I'll make it worth your while."

James left for Caesarea that evening, no one in the household except Clopas being informed of his departure. He carried a considerable amount of money concealed in his saddlebags among various innocent-looking bundles of food and clothing. His errand was to deliver the money to the manager of a wholesale house in the seacoast city, which he accomplished without incident. He was gone three days. When he returned, the house wore that too-clean, too-well-ordered air for normal living. He knew instantly that something had happened.

"The master," said Huldah, her dark eyes brimming with unimparted news, "wants to see you at once." She led the way, unable to resist the single whispered clue: "It's Miss Susanna."

"What about her?" he asked sharply.

"She's gone!"

But Huldah would say no more. Sick with apprehension, James followed her into Clopas' private apartment. His uncle lifted a white, haggard face, oddly naked and vulnerable without its mask.

"Ah! You've come, James. Thank goodness!"

Clopas gestured wearily toward the man standing discreetly in the background. "You tell him, Matthias."

Matthias cleared his throat, his small eyes shifting uneasily. He was obviously badly frightened. Three days ago, he explained, he had taken Susanna at her request to a certain spot on the Jericho road where he had been accustomed at various times to accompany her brother Simon. Perhaps James would know the place he meant.

James did. "The hideout of Barabbas," he murmured with stiffened lips.

Yes, that was it. He had taken her to a spot near the hideout, showing her the secret entrance. She had gone in alone, telling him she would be back soon, and he had waited outside. She had not reappeared.

Clopas groaned. "She's gone to join Simon," he said hoarsely. "She ran away from me because I was going to make her marry John. To escape from her own home she sought the protection of a brigand!"

James' nails bit his palms. "No!" The unuttered words twisted in his throat like a knife. "You're wrong, Clopas. What she did was to seek the protection of the man she loves!"

Clopas' white fingers fumbled helplessly with the folds of his *simlah*. For the first time in his life he looked at his nephew with eyes that held no contempt, only a desperate pleading. "She's all I have, James, now that Simon has deserted me. She's dearer to me than my sons, always has been. Do something, can't you? You love her too. You told me you do. Go and bring her back and take her to wife if you still want her. I don't care whether you're a merchant or a rabbi or just a common carpenter!"

5

Matthias paused where a blank, bleak wall of rock ascended sheer and vertical beside the Jericho road.

"This is the place, sir. Wait until the road is clear. We must not be seen entering. Stoop down and pretend there's a stone in your sandal, sir, while this caravan passes. Now! Follow me!"

Amazingly Matthias discovered an almost invisible oblique crack in the wall wide enough to let them through, and James followed his guide through what seemed to be a maze of twisting passages and tunnels, sometimes groping his way in darkness, sometimes finding the path lighted by rifts of light from above. At last, when they had been climbing so long that James was sure they must be at the top of the great barren cliff, they emerged into an open gully and began to clamber up its steep, rocky side. Matthias indicated a deep cleft in the rocks flanked by dark volcanic masses resembling two stone pillars.

"There! You'll have to go on by yourself, sir. This is as far as my master lets me go. Shall I wait?"

James looked back down the blind, tortuous path along which they had come. "No, Matthias, don't wait. It may take me longer than I expect." In fact, he told himself grimly, he might never come out. Barabbas was an unpredictable character. He would not welcome interference, even of a harmless verbal sort. With every sensitive fiber of his nature James shrank from the encounter.

Relieved, Matthias slithered noiselessly downward among the rocks and disappeared, the very furtiveness of his motions in keeping with the mood of the wild, desolate land about him. James shivered involuntarily. He had heard weird tales about these stark, barren cliffs above Jericho road, for centuries the haunt of brigands, escaped criminals, and guerilla warriors. Death seemed to hover above the land like a pall. Even the air hung still and sinister as a fever. James found that it took all his willpower to force his limbs to move. Wrapping his long cloak tightly about him, he climbed the few remaining steps and made his way through the crevice.

Within, a dark passageway stretched interminably. He groped his way down it, but he had gone only a few steps before a man appeared, holding a flaring torch. A sharp voice accosted him with a "Halt! Who goes there?"

"A friend of Barabbas," he answered boldly, conscious of the light focused full on his face in such a way that his inquisitor was still hidden in darkness.

"By name?"

"James, the son of Joseph, cousin of Simon ben Clopas."

"The sign?"

James' brain whirled. Then he remembered. He reached out a steady finger and carefully traced on the wall of the passage a series of little points and curves, the rough outline of a fox's head.

"Your business?"

"An interview with Barabbas."

He felt the probing scrutiny relax. "All right. Come this way and move carefully. Count ten steps down."

The passage descended, curved, rose abruptly, descended again, and they emerged into a cavernous opening lighted by flaring lamps. James gasped. Accustomed as he was to the caves in the hills about Nazareth, he had never seen anything like this. It was as large in area as the Court of the Gentiles in the Temple and almost as crowded as the latter on a feast day. There were men everywhere, sitting in groups, reclining about tables, sprawled upon fur skins on the stone floor, men eating, drinking, sleeping, arguing, carousing. The clamor of their voices reverberating from the echoing, cavernous walls was almost deafening. James glanced swiftly, apprehensively about, satisfied himself that Susanna was not there, then looked in vain for Simon. The guide, who turned out to be a small, squat, insignificant figure of a man wrapped in a frayed leopard skin, turned James over to another guard, who went to make his presence known to Barabbas. While he stood waiting, some of the men stared at him incuriously. None gave any indication of hostility or friendliness, even of curiosity.

So this, thought James, was the army of Barabbas, the hope of the political freedom of Israel! This motley array of rowdy adventurers, of social parasites, of fugitives from justice! He searched their faces in vain for some sign of that fiery idealism that he had seen gleaming in the eyes of their leader, graven, long ago, on the twisted lips of Daniel and on the sharp, compelling features of the great Judas, seared indelibly on the tortured forms of those victims hanging on their gaunt trees beneath the baking Galilean sun. Israel had indeed sunk low if it must look to such as these for its freedom! He felt an almost bitter triumph as he realized that his judgment had been vindicated. Before Israel could be saved as a nation, it needed the purging of a prophet.

"The captain sends greetings to the son of Joseph," said the guard, bowing low. "You are to be entertained today as his most honored guest. He will give you an audience tomorrow."

"But I must see him now," James protested. "I have important business. It cannot wait."

"Tomorrow," repeated the guard firmly. "It is the captain's wish. Come this way, please."

Unwillingly James accompanied the guard through another maze of subterranean passages with other cavernous rooms opening off at either side. He felt a growing amazement at the size and scope of the place. It was like a vast underground city. Inherited, no doubt, from past dynasties of brigands, it bore marks of a savage regal splendor. The flaring lamps shone dimly upon polished wood, rare tapestries, soft, colorful rugs, and gleaming pottery—the plunder, James thought likely, from many a passing caravan meeting grief on the road below. Through one of the openings he saw two women sitting on the floor weaving, and his pulse quickened at the thought that Susanna might be with them, but when he paused the guide hurried him on. They arrived at last in a small, cavelike room, which was well lighted and comfortably furnished.

"Wait here," said the guard, "until someone comes for you." He added significantly, "These caverns are filled with the bones of those who have tried to find their way out."

So, thought James, sinking down on the pallet, which was remarkably soft and comfortable, he was a prisoner. He had put himself at the will and mercy of Barabbas, on the chance hope of saving Susanna. From what? From the thing she herself desired? By now she was probably wedded to the young chieftain, with her brother Simon's blessing, and she would not welcome his interference. Or, if Barabbas possessed as little respect for custom and a woman's integrity as he did for law and order—James' blood grew hot at the thought. He got up from the pallet and, to relieve his tensed muscles, he began to pace the thick-carpeted floor. Once on a mad impulse he left the room and groped his way along the dark corridor, but before he had gone a dozen steps he knew it was no use. All the turnings and openings looked alike, and he groped his way back again in a panic, throwing himself down on the pallet, his body in a cold sweat. As the hours passed and waiting became more and more intolerable, he reproached himself bitterly for having been a fool.

An evening meal was brought to him, and after that he slept fitfully. When he thought it must be morning, he rose, and, using the water that had been brought him to drink, proceeded carefully with his ceremonial washings. Many hours later, when breakfast was brought, he decided it must be noon of the day following his arrival. Finally, to his infinite relief, there appeared before him one of the two men who had come with Barabbas that night to dine at Clopas' house.

"The captain will see you now," he said.

Barabbas was reclining on a thronelike couch in an atmosphere of barbaric splendor. His powerful body was clothed in an immense leopard skin, and it seemed to have imbibed some of that animal's more potent qualities: its sleek voluptuousness, its feline grace, its air of alert, yet lazy watchfulness. James felt the dark, compelling eyes leap out to enfold him, the vibrantly virile personality exerting its hypnotic spell. But this time he saw the rebel chieftain for what he was: a paragon of physical strength, but not much else, vain, fond of display, possessing the body of a great emancipator and the little soul of a despot. Suddenly his fear left him.

"I've come for Susanna," he said steadily.

Barabbas looked him up and down. "What makes you think she's here?"

"I know she's here," returned James quickly. "And whatever the reason she came, I'm sure of one thing. She doesn't belong here. She isn't your sort of person, and nothing you can do will ever make her so."

It was only a chance thrust, but apparently it hit the mark. The black eyes wavered. "Perhaps you're right," Barabbas conceded. "I admit I'm getting weary of her. Don't misunderstand me," he added with an ironical smile, noting James' sudden hot flush. "She's been most courteously entertained in the women's quarters. But I have talked with her."

He leaned forward suddenly forsaking his indolent pose. "You're both of you under the influence of some strong personality, something that keeps you out of tune, keeps you from responding to my will. I seem unable to reach either of you, no matter how I try." He bent his dark gaze on James. "Who is it?" he demanded abruptly. "Your brother?"

James gasped. "What do you know of my Brother?"

The black eyes gleamed. "So, it is he! I thought so."

"But how—"

Barabbas shrugged. "I have a good memory and many spies. I don't forget when a man raises his voice against mine and turns an inspired mob from an act of justice. It was your brother, wasn't it?"

"Yes," said James, lifting his head in sudden proud defiance.

Barabbas' face darkened. "I don't like him. I'll have nothing to do with him. Nor with you. Nor with this pretty sister of Simon's either. He's put his taint on both of you. Now get out!" He ended the interview abruptly. "One of the men will show you the way. You'll find the girl waiting on the road outside."

It was late afternoon when James emerged from the dark crevice between the two shapeless black pillars. The passageway between the rocks was heavy with brooding shadows, but sunlight still slanted across the clear blue above. In spite of the hot, heavy, stagnant heat of the air, he drew a long breath of relief. Following his guide down the long, tortuous path up which Matthias had led him, he tried vainly to memorize its bewildering twists and turns, knowing that if Barabbas failed to keep his promise, if he had deceived him into thinking

Susanna was free again merely to get him out of the way, he would somehow have to find his way back.

"Hsst!" The guide warned as they slid into what looked like an invisible crack between two solid walls. "Wait here! I'll see if it's all clear. All right," his voice hissed back a moment later.

The road was empty of life save for two figures, a man lounging against the cliff—the same man who less than an hour ago had conducted James to Barabbas—and the dark, heavily veiled form of a woman seated on a donkey. James hurried toward her, his body weak and trembling from relief. "Susanna!" he cried brokenly.

The fringed eyes above the veil burst into light, then as swiftly clouded. "James! Then you were there, after all. He said you weren't. He lied to me."

The lounging figure straightened. "We'll have to hurry," he told James abruptly, "if we're to reach Jerusalem before dark. The captain ordered me to go with you as far as the city gate. Then I'm to take the donkey back again."

They proceeded along the road in silence, mingling with the intermittent flow of late-afternoon travelers—artisans and tradesmen from the Jordan Valley, caravans of salt and balsam, an occasional priest or scribe or white-robed Essene—all in desperate haste to put the fevered haunt of desolation behind them, all lifting furtive, anxious faces toward the grim, ominous, danger-infested cliffs.

James stole a glance at the slim, straight little figure on the back of the donkey. She looked very small and absurdly young and helpless, and the eyes under the two smooth wings of hair held a hurt, bewildered look. Instinctively James moved closer, and placed his hand protectingly on the rein.

"I'm sorry," he said impulsively, his voice low, so that the guard, walking ahead, could not hear. "But you would never have been happy with him, Susanna. Believe me, dear, if I thought you would, I'd move heaven and earth to try to get your father to consent to your marriage to him. In fact, that's what I intended to do when I got Matthias to bring me to Barabbas' hideout yesterday."

She caught her breath. "When you—" The sudden clear light in her eyes was like one of the last rays of sunlight, enveloping him. "James, you weren't with Barabbas all the time? You didn't go to him when you received Simon's letter?"

It was James' turn to look bewildered. "Of course not. I went on an errand for Clopas to Caesarea. Then when I came back and found you had gone—to *him*—" He pressed his lips together tightly.

"James—" Her voice was low and insistent, "James, why do you think I went to Barabbas?"

He didn't look at her. He knew there was too much of naked pain in his eyes. "Because you loved him, of course," he said simply. "Because you wanted to find some escape from John and—and me."

"Oh, but you're wrong, James," she said softly. "I never loved Barabbas. Oh, he used to intrigue me a little, fascinate me, because I'd never seen anyone like him. But I never could have loved him."

James' hand trembled on the bridle rein. He walked with head bent, not daring to lift his eyes to hers. "Then why—" His voice choked on the words.

"Why did I go to Barabbas' hideout? Because I thought you were there, James. I thought you'd gone to join him, as Simon asked you to, and I had to see you, to talk to you, to try to show you that it was all wrong, that following Barabbas wouldn't fit in with the Dream. I had to do it, James, because—"

"Yes—because?"

Susanna laughed shakily. "You're going to make me say it, aren't you? All right, then. Because I love you! I think I've always loved you, James, ever since that first day, up on the housetop—"

He lifted his face then, and, though the sun had long since gone down behind the graying hills, James felt the warm, full blaze of it reaching out, enfolding him, from the clear, bright radiance of Susanna's eyes.

The little donkey was old and slow, and it was evening when they finally arrived on the crest of the Mount of Olives. "Suppose you walk from here," suggested the guide surlily. "It took us longer than I expected. I should be getting back."

"Of course." Susanna slid gratefully from the donkey's back. James slipped a denarius into the man's hand, and his face brightened. They heard his shuffling footsteps and the hoofbeats of the donkey grow fainter and fainter.

Before them the city rose in tranquil repose. Not that ancient citadel of the past, smoke-wreathed and battle-scarred, half savage, half holy, steeped in the blood of its kings and its prophets; nor yet that glittering white shell of the present, over whose pitiable emptiness a certain Man was soon destined on that very spot to weep; but a city white and remote, etched out of pearl and starlight, that new Jerusalem of the future, fashioned of things as eternal as a human life and as imperishable as a man's dreams.

"Look, James," said Susanna softly, "do you suppose that's what Jesus means by the Dream? Can't you see it? A city where life won't be full of hunger and hatred and fear and ugliness? And you and I having a part in building it together?"

For answer James took her in his arms.

Clopas kept his promise. He consented to the marriage of James and Susanna without stipulation as to the occupation of his future son-in-law. He would have been willing for the wedding to take place at once, before James' return to Nazareth, but Mary's objections overruled both Clopas' willingness and the young people's own wishes in the matter. She could not possibly spare Susanna, she maintained with querulous but stubborn insistence. Perhaps in a few months, or a year—

But at least the promise of their marriage was sealed, after the custom of the country, with a betrothal ceremony. Beneath a flower-bedecked canopy set up in the courtyard of Clopas' house, James gave to Susanna a piece of money and a parchment on which both their names were written, repeating before witnesses the sacred words, "Lo, you are betrothed unto me." Together they shared the cup of wine, the sacramental seal of their promises, and bowed their heads to the solemn cadence of the benediction.

"Blessed art Thou, O Lord our God, King of the world, who has sanctified us by His commandments.... Blessed art Thou, who sanctifiest Israel by marriage and betrothal!"

So Susanna, the daughter of Clopas, became the betrothed wife of James, the son of Joseph. Though not yet man and wife, they were bound in a relationship as sacred as if they had already been wedded.

Soon after, James made ready to return to Nazareth. His five years of study at the School of Shammai had been completed. He had distinguished himself as a brilliant student of the Law. His zeal to make his own contribution to the faith of his fathers ran hot in his veins. As yet his future was uncertain. He was anxious to get back home, to discuss with his Brother their plans for the future, to construct some concrete program of action out of the nebulous substance of the Dream.

So, though it was with a certain reluctance that he turned his back on the fair vision of Jerusalem and, especially, of his newly betrothed wife, it was with both eagerness and impatience that he set his face again toward Nazareth.

6

James' homecoming was gratifying and disappointing. Young Joseph had been watching for him almost constantly for two days, and before he had turned off the main road to climb the hill toward Nazareth, the news of his coming had been spread among the neighbors. By the time he reached the well a delegation had come out to meet him, including all the boys in Rabbi Nathan's school, who waved green branches and shouted, "Hail, James! Hail, son of Joseph!" with great exuberance, less perhaps on account of his coming than because of the half holiday declared for his benefit. For it was not often that a graduate of a synagogue school distinguished himself in further study, and Rabbi Nathan's pride in his pupil was undisguised. All in all, it was a triumphant homecoming. Many a rich man's son, returning to his native village, had received less acclaim.

Mary and Anna had swept and polished the small house until it shone. There were new cushions and bed rolls, fresh flowers in earthen jars, the aromas of newly baked loaves and his favorite savory meat stew filling the air. Neighbors kept coming and going for hours after his arrival, some bearing little gifts of food to help to "piece out" the evening meal (though they knew that Mary and her daughter-in-law had been cooking for days), some bringing other little tokens with their greetings and congratulations, but all friendly and all frankly curious. Most of them said little. They were afraid of the tall, serious stranger in his blue-fringed Pharisee's cloak, and James was glad for the wall of reserve that even their friendly curiosity was not quite able to penetrate.

"They're all so proud of you," said Mary, her radiant face belying the note of apology in her voice. "We'll have to share you with them first, I suppose, though we can hardly wait to have you to ourselves.

Later we're going to have a little feast to celebrate your homecoming, but tonight we thought you'd rather have things just as they used to be."

Just as they used to be! thought James with a sudden revulsion of feeling, the first instinctive pride and satisfaction yielding finally to deflation and disappointment. For them, perhaps. Never again for him. He sat with the other members of the family about the low table, his limbs, long accustomed to Clopas' comfortable couches, feeling cramped and awkward in the old familiar half-sitting, half-crouching position, and tried to appear as if he were enjoying himself. He dipped his bread into the common bowl, inwardly wincing at the rude manners of his young brother Joseph, and tried to convince his mother that her salted fish and fig cakes were the best viands he had tasted since leaving home five years before. He answered their questions about the Jerusalem household and about his betrothal to Susanna, inwardly conscious of the difference between his own quick, fluent speech and their crude, halting Galilean accent.

But even more disturbing than his consciousness of these deep changes within himself was his constant fear that in this more provincial, informal Galilean way of living he might in some small, obscure detail be breaking the Law. It began when the wine was poured. He glanced in quick dismay at Anna, waiting at one side with basin and towel and pitcher until the cups should be filled.

"We hold that the hands should be washed before the pouring of the wine instead of after," he said quickly. "I know it's a point that is hotly disputed between the two schools of thought, but we believe that we have rabbinical authority for our position."

Jesus' hand poised lightly above the tilted jug, staying the sparkling, golden flow of liquid. As suddenly the warm streams of laughter in the brown eyes became cold and crystal-clear. Did it really matter? He asked James the question with apparent carelessness.

"Of course it matters!" James warmed glibly to the familiar argument, unconscious of Mary's hurt, bewildered eyes regarding him. "So you see," he finished earnestly, "I couldn't conscientiously partake of a meal where I knew the ceremonial preparation to be wrong. I—I'd feel unclean."

Mary's thin hands fluttered anxiously. "But we've always done it this way," she said uncertainly. "I don't understand. Your father was always so careful—"

138

Jesus laid a steady hand on her fluttering fingers. It didn't matter, he reassured her. They would do it James' way tonight. Quietly he requested Anna to remove the wine already poured and bring some more.

After that James was uneasy all through the meal. He worried for fear the hollow dishes in which the food had been prepared had been touched by some defilement and not properly cleansed and for fear some part of the food he was eating had not been duly tithed. He remembered that in his boyhood the laws governing such matters had seemed relatively simple, involving not a hundredth part of all the manifold details that in the last five years had been added to his necessary ceremonial ritual. He was obliged to ask his mother some pointed questions about her household methods and kitchen utensils before he felt that he could conscientiously partake of the meal. Mary, hovering uneasily about the table as the men ate, answered them as well as she could and fell into a troubled silence.

After the meal the moment he had been anticipating finally came. The benedictions pronounced, the washings completed, his Brother turned to him with a smile and asked him casually if he would like to go up on the hilltop. Then, as young Joseph broke out in eager acquiescence, he shook his head gently. No. Joseph was not to go with them tonight. He and James had things they must talk over together.

James' heart gave a great leap. "I'm ready," he said confidently.

But after they had left the house Jesus seemed in no hurry to climb the stony, winding path leading to the hilltop. Instead he turned toward the square, ugly, weather-beaten cottage next door. Deborah would want to see him, he told James simply. She would never forgive him if he went somewhere else before coming to visit her.

James followed his Brother impatiently. Deborah had been away from Nazareth for long periods since Daniel's death, and he had not thought of her for years. She was an invalid now, a shapeless mass of strengthless muscle and flabby flesh, no more like her fiery ancient namesake than a shadow is like its substance. Both her pale hands and empty, hungry eyes reached out to enfold him.

"You didn't forget old Deborah, did you? *He* said you wouldn't. Tell me, what did they teach you in Jerusalem about my Daniel? Am I ever going to see him again? Is there going to be a resurrection of the dead or isn't there?"

James evaded the eager, reaching hands, but his eyes lighted. Did he believe in a resurrection of the dead? Could he tell her about it?

What Pharisee couldn't! Glibly he launched into a discussion of the pros and cons of the subject, enlarging on the differences of interpretation between the followers of Shammai and those of the more liberal Hillel.

Deborah listened in silence, the emptiness in her eyes unfilled. When he had finished, she shook her head. "It sounds very nice," she said, "if only it seemed to mean something."

Had it not been for his memory of that Sabbath eve long ago, James would have pitied her. But, remembering, he knew that her unbelief was not unmerited. The promises of Jehovah were for those who kept His laws. He was relieved when his Brother told Deborah gently that they must go now, but that he would come again, as usual, tomorrow.

As they went out, Jesus reached idly into the wooden bin in the corner and took out a kernel of unground corn. He came back and placed it in the pale, flabby hand.

"A—a grain of corn," she said, fingering it wonderingly.

His brown eyes glinted. Was it alive, he asked her simply, or dead?

"Why—I—I don't know."

He patted her hand. Put it in the ground, he told her gently. Cover it with earth, let God's sun and rain fall upon it, and wait. Then she would see whether it was dead or alive.

Out in the street again James fretted because they must waste so much time. The whole town, it seemed, was out sitting on its doorsteps, and, as usual, Jesus had to stop and speak with everyone he met. He must inquire after the health of Eliah the potter, who was suffering from boils, and help Milcah the widow to carry a heavy bundle of fagots up the path and into the house. He must ask after the son of Laban the merchant, who had joined the crew of a sailing vessel six months before and had just been heard from, and inquire if old lame Levi's rheumatism was any better now that the spring rains were over, and stop to admire the young son that had just been born to Hannah, the wife of Joshua ben Nathan. James made his own replies to their friendly, curious questions as brief as possible.

"Can't we take the short cut," he asked his Brother impatiently, "so we needn't meet so many people?"

The dark eyes shot him a quick glance. Jerusalem, Jesus reminded him, was even more full of people than Nazareth. Had he tried to take short cuts there too?

"In Jerusalem," replied James, "you don't need to know all your neighbors' genealogies and pains and secret worries. You can walk from Siloam to Bezetha through the crowded marts of the Tyropoeon and not once have your thoughts diverted from holy things."

They took the short cut. At the foot of the hill behind the town, however, where the path began to grow steep, Jesus turned aside. There was a family of lepers, he told his brother casually, who lived over there in a cave on the hillside. He wanted to look in on them once more before the day was over just to see if they needed anything.

James followed him reluctantly. "Is the cave near here?"

When Jesus told him that it was just above a certain ledge of rock visible from the path, James lagged behind. "I think I'll wait here," he said. "The wind seems to be coming from that direction, and there's always more danger of uncleanness—"

Jesus hurried on ahead. Throwing back his cloak, he began by the aid of the sparse, scrubby trees growing on the hillside to pull himself with long, swinging motions up the steep incline.

"Be careful to keep at least six feet," warned James, raising his voice enough so his Brother would hear, "or you'll make yourself unclean."

Jesus made no reply. He swung himself over the ledge and disappeared. James heard the shrill, weird cry, "Unclean! Unclean!" echoing over the barren hillside like the wail of a lost soul. He paced up and down impatiently until his Brother again appeared, and they swung into step up the path toward the Lookout.

Now, thought James, his eyes kindling at sight of the broad, familiar vistas stretching to each far horizon, *the time has come. He will ask me what I have learned in Jerusalem to prepare myself to be a messenger of Jehovah unto Israel. He will tell me new plans he has made. We will talk together of the Dream.*

They did talk together until the stars kindled their lamps above the Kishon—the same stars that once, so tradition said, "from their courses ... fought against Sisera." But his Brother asked him no questions, gave him no chance to frame the answers that lay glib and eager on his lips. And the Dream—the great Task, the salvation of Israel—was not even mentioned. Instead Jesus talked about some strange village, or city, or country—he didn't make clear exactly which it was. He called it the Kingdom of God. He talked about the lilies growing on the hillside and about seeds pushing their way up through the earth and about yeast hidden away in a loaf of bread. Trivial, homely, inconsequential things. And to his brother's annoyance he kept calling the God of Israel, the divine Judge, the Creator of all

141

things, whose ineffable name was too sacred even to be pronounced—Jesus kept calling him "Father!"

James went back down the hill, hurt and sullen and disappointed. For though they had not spoken of the Dream, there was in his Brother's eyes a light like that of long quiet embers ready to burst into flame.

On the first Sabbath after his return James was invited to be the reader for the day. Behind the lattice of the women's gallery Mary's eyes shone with pride and affection and a certain wistfulness. Rabbi Nathan, handing him the roll of the Law, lifted to his former pupil a face darkly eager and expectant. The elders of the congregation, in their raised seats facing the audience, listened to their young fellow townsman with deference. The congregation murmured its hearty and voluble approval. Truly, James, the son of Joseph, had brought honor both to himself and to his family.

The days passed, and still Jesus went quietly about his daily work, making no announcement of his plans. Reluctantly James donned his carpenter's apron, though there seemed to be little need of his services, since Jude was a most able and competent assistant, and fifteen-year-old Joseph was fast learning the trade. Simon worked in a vineyard outside the village and was awaiting only a favorable opportunity for acquiring a small farm of his own.

James tried to imagine Susanna in the small white cottage, now more crowded than ever by the addition of Anna and her two small children, Jeshua and Sara. Simon too would soon be bringing home a wife. He was already betrothed to Rachel, the daughter of Reuel the herdsman. The picture invariably aroused within him a feeling of panic. Not only was it impossible to picture Susanna in such surroundings, but he himself shrank from the prospect of spending many more weeks in the hot, congested little house. At night, lying on his pallet under the low, flat roof, the odors of warm flesh in his nostrils, the sound of vague stirrings and the baby's whimperings and Jude's little mutterings in his ears, he longed for the cool privacy of his room on Clopas' housetop. He even wished he dared to go up to the tiny guestchamber that his brothers had built on their own roof. The hot, cloudless summer days would have been well-nigh unbearable had it not been for the hope within him and that light as of glowing embers in his Brother's eyes. Surely, he thought, day by day, the time must be almost come.

But the weeks passed, and still Jesus gave no sign. He went quietly about his usual tasks, directing the work of the little carpenter shop and working long hours each day, making his contribution as head of a household to the services of worship, both at home and in the synagogue, paying daily visits to Deborah, the family of lepers, and a dozen other sick and troubled fellow townsmen, taking long walks, often alone, either early in the morning or after the day's work was done in the evening.

James also settled into a routine. Gradually he ceased to watch for the flaring of those glowing embers and settled himself to a period of outwardly resigned but inwardly fretful and impatient waiting.

As the weeks passed and the colors of the backdrop shifted from green to ripened gold, from gold to the dry, parched tints of sunbrowned ivory, from ivory to the warm rich russets of newly plowed soil and the crimsons and purples of the autumn vintage, the lines of the players also changed. There was a filtering of new names through the jargon of the marketplace, in the casual gossip of the women about the well, as constant as the flow of the never-failing spring that bubbled from the hillside.

Pilate—

"A new governor in Judea, you say? Let's hope he's no worse than Gratus!"

"What's that you're saying! Jehovah pity us, you say, from Caesarea?"

"Not the golden eagles! Ordered them brought up from Caesarea to Jerusalem, you say, and set up right within sight of the Temple?"

"But no Roman governor has ever dared—"

"Surely the anger of Jehovah must strike him down!"

"Heaven knows Antipas is bad enough, but at least he has some Jewish blood! He wouldn't commit a blasphemy like this!"

Barabbas—

"Have you heard? At least there is some red blood left yet in Israel!"

"Yes! Surrounded the palace in broad daylight and tore down those heathen standards!"

"Bared their necks, you say, to the swords of Pilate's soldiers, and the procurator did not dare make resistance?"

"They say he has a hideout in the hills toward Jericho."

"A new Judas, do you think, come to life?"

"Praises be to Jehovah, he escaped safely, you say?"

"Give thanks, for the abomination is removed! Pilate has ordered the heathen emblems taken back to Caesarea!"

"If this Barabbas has really escaped, if he's plotting something even more daring in his hideout, then there may be hope."

John—

"Yes, you should see him! A wild man he looks like, dressed in the coarsest camel's hair!"

"Down in the desert beyond the Jordan!"

"Yes, all Jerusalem, they say, is flocking to him!"

"And have you heard what he said about Antipas? He actually dared to accuse him of his infamous sin in plain words!"

"And the things he says about the priests!"

"They're calling him the Baptist now, because he's started baptizing people."

"Yes, right there in the river!"

"Yes, actually! Vipers! He dared to call them."

"Elijah, some say, returned from the dead!"

"No, I've not seen him yet, but I'm going to! The next feast day."

"A voice, he calls himself, one crying in the wilderness!"

And then one day Jesus said quietly that he was going away.

James lifted his face from his work at the carpenter's bench.

He saw that the light as of long-quiet embers in his Brother's eyes had burst suddenly into flame. And his heart stood still.

Jesus continued to speak in the same quiet voice. It was James' turn now to be the head of the family. He would find Jude a good helper. In fact, he was a better carpenter than either Jesus or James had ever been, because he seldom lifted his eyes above the adz.

Before James could speak, the coldness within him had reached his lips. "You're going alone?" he faltered.

The deep brown eyes met his in a glance of swift, penetrating, strangely pitying appraisal, then became slowly remote, as if already they were beginning to adjust themselves to longer, broader perspectives. Yes, he was going alone.

Dazed, hurt, bewildered, too stunned as yet fully to fathom the bitterness of his disappointment, James stood in the doorway of the carpenter shop and watched his Brother climb the hill into the sunset.

PART THREE
Antagonist

1

The afternoon sun was already casting long shadows down the village street. As if anxious to atone for the hot, merciless glare of midday, it gathered the rows upon rows of neat, square houses into its soft, caressing glow, its slanting rays threading them along the terraced hillside into jeweled strings of roseate, gleaming whiteness. It passed with lighter, more indulgent footstep over the flat, unsheltered roofs, the narrow, dusty streets, the heat-drenched gardens, leaving cool sanctuaries for tired children beneath the gnarled, spreading fig trees, laying its long fingers along the fronds of feathery palms, touching the tips of olive trees with silver.

James, however, hastening homeward and lifting his eyes in a brief, all-encompassing glance, noticed none of these things. He saw only that it lacked two hours until sunset, and he quickened his step. But it was no use. The more he tried to hurry, it seemed, the more his fellow townspeople kept stopping him.

"James! Wait a minute! I want to ask you something."

"James! James ben Joseph! I heard your brother is coming."

"Is it true that he's going to be at the service tomorrow and will give the sermon?"

"Seems funny to think it's Joseph's boy they're making all this fuss about! Why, I remember the time he was no bigger than my Asa here."

"My old grandfather's been sick since the first of Nisan, but he says if Joseph's young one's going to speak, he'll be there if he has to be carried today on his bed!"

"Well, James, how does it feel to have a famous person in the family?"

He stopped and answered them all, his fine, straight features ill concealing his impatience. Did they suppose he, the head of a house, had time to spare for street gossiping, with guests coming and the Sabbath not two hours away? Suppose in her excitement his mother should forget some of the necessary preparations! It wouldn't be any wonder. She had been busy enough these last few days, even with Anna and Susanna to help her!

Yes, he told them briefly, his Brother was coming. Perhaps even now he might be entering the town and starting up this very street. And he would, of course, be at the service tomorrow morning. Had any of them ever seen one of the sons of Joseph neglecting his religious duties? As for his being asked to give the sermon, that was for Rabbi Nathan to say. However, they all knew the custom of inviting well-known guests to take part in the morning service, and he would tell them this much. He was himself returning this moment from the rabbi's house, where they had had a most satisfactory conversation together.

He escaped from them at last, feeling soiled and ruffled of person as well as temper, and wondering if there were finger marks on his cloak. A glance downward, however, at its long, immaculate smoothness, its broad blue border, its elaborate fringe, reassured him. His townspeople had evidently forgotten for the moment that he was James the Pharisee, ardent student of the Law, pupil of the School of Shammai the Great, and remembered only that he was James, brother of a simple country carpenter. He wasn't sure yet that he enjoyed this change, in spite of the by-no-means-unwelcome honor that it was bringing him. If it meant that people were going to crowd about him, crush his garments, break through the barrier of his dignity, treat him with the casual intimacy which they had always accorded his Brother—

His reflections were interrupted by the harsh, grating sound of a saw plunging through heavy timber, and he became suddenly conscious that he was passing the house of Malluch. The sight of the short, wiry figure in the open doorway of the carpenter shop, back bent to its labor like a tautly drawn bow, aroused in James, as it always did, that swift surge of anger as poignant as a sudden pain. All his muscles tensed, and the blood surged to his temples.

So, he thought grimly, *Malluch is deliberately flaunting his law-breaking this time! Starting a task that can't possibly be finished before sundown and the beginning of the Sabbath!*

As if the shaft of disapproval had hit its mark, the curved, taut lines of the figure relaxed, the thin lips broke into a smile, and the carpenter lifted his hand in airy salutation. There was a mocking jauntiness in the gesture, and it infuriated James. His hands clenched at his sides, and his pulses pounded against his temples with a suffocating sense of futility. Words crowded to his lips, words that needed no thought or preparation in their forming, because they had been such a long time in the shaping, like barbed shafts sharpened slowly to a point.

"You son of Satan, you lawbreaker, thief, and murderer! Yes, that's what you are in the sight of a just God—a murderer! For it was you who killed our father, Joseph. You worried him into his grave with your cheating, blackmailing schemes that took away more and more of his business, and with your infamous lies that tried to ruin his reputation! May the God of Israel requite you according to your iniquities!"

But he did not say them. For hardly had he opened his lips when a strange figure emerged from Malluch's house and came groping its way toward him, uttering unintelligible cries like the shrill mouthings of a trapped animal. A grotesque figure it was, half man, half boy, with arms outstretched in what resembled the fluttering motions of a bird, and wide, bright, sightless eyes that stared unblinkingly into the sunlight. The passing years had brought but few touches of maturity to Zeri, the son of Malluch.

James moved aside with revulsion as the creature veered toward him, then he realized with dismay that he himself was the object of its excited attention. Whichever way he turned, Zeri uncannily followed him, until he suddenly found himself with his back against a wall, the groping hands, disturbingly grimy, plucking hungrily at his long, immaculate cloak.

"You son of the Evil One, get away from me, do you hear?"

He lifted his arm to strike, but at the sound of his voice the man fled away, whimpering like a whipped dog. Malluch thrust himself forward belligerently.

"Oh, so you'd strike my son, would you!" he cried shrilly. "You worthless offspring of an inferior carpenter!"

James could feel the phylactery on his forehead tremble. "It's no wonder," he retorted bitterly, "that your son is such an ugly, misshapen creature! The sins of the fathers are in his case certainly visited on the children!"

The little man seemed suddenly to wilt. For a moment his brown face looked almost as white as his beard.

"He wasn't doing you any harm," he muttered. "He likely thought you were your brother. Your step sounds the same. He heard your brother was coming back. Jesus was always friendly to my boy."

James drew himself up to his full stature. "And you think," he said scornfully, "that there could ever be friendship between the house of Joseph and the house of Malluch?"

As he walked swiftly on toward home, he felt vindicated and elated. Not only had he seen his father's old enemy abashed and confused, but also he had stumbled on a most vulnerable weakness, his love for the unfortunate Zeri! There was justice, then, after all, in Israel! As long as the son of Malluch was an object of contempt and derision among the people of Nazareth, a pitiful apology for a son, Joseph and his family would in some measure be avenged.

In the street alongside the neat white house with its adjoining carpenter shop a crowd of people was gathered. Even at a distance James recognized some of them. There was old blind Enoch from out on the Sepphoris road, and lame Levi, and Jonathan the mule driver who had a clubfoot, and Reuben the herdsman, with his son Gad who was possessed of a devil. And that figure on the pallet under the plane tree—Yes, it must be. It was Eliah the potter, whom nobody in the village had seen for months, but whose body, everybody said, was covered with festering sores. And there were Lemuel, the hunchback, who had fallen from his mother's arms when a baby; and Reuel the tentmaker, who had had to give up his trade because his broken arm had not healed properly; and Amrah, the daughter of Jered the merchant, with her twisted eyes and harelip. Queer! It looked as if everybody in the village who had anything the matter with him—

James stood still, struck motionless by a sudden startling suspicion. It wasn't possible, of course. It was ridiculous even to imagine for a moment. And yet—He moved forward, a smile of amusement playing about his lips. But as he approached the group, as he came near enough to note the still, grim, tenseness of the faces, the smile faded.

"Where is he?" someone shouted hoarsely, and, as if the words had been a signal, questions and commands broke suddenly against him from every side, like missiles.

"Is he in the house?"

"Bring him out to us!"

"We've been waiting here for hours."

"Trying to hide him from us, are you?"

"Where is he? We want Jesus. We want Jesus, the son of Joseph!"

James tried to pick his way through them, but they pulled at his cloak, held him powerless to move. He stared, amazed, at their strained, unfamiliar faces. Was it possible that they actually believed these wild tales that were being bandied about the country, that his Brother possessed magic powers of healing? Why, it was ridiculous, preposterous! They had known him, lived with him intimately, for thirty years. Surely they must have more intelligence.

"Where is he? Bring him out to us, we tell you! We want Jesus, the son of Joseph!"

James felt a sudden chill pass over him. Why—these were not his neighbors, his townspeople, with whom the sons of Joseph had worked and played and gossiped and laughed and suffered and worshiped all their lives! These men with their hungry eyes and tight, strained faces—they were strangers!

"Listen," he said in a loud, clear voice that commanded silence. "If it's my Brother you're waiting for, he hasn't come yet. We're expecting him, and he ought to be here any time. But it's no use your waiting to see him tonight, you should know that. Look at the sun! It's less than an hour to the Sabbath. Have you forgotten that your clothes must be changed, your houses put in order, your lamps lighted? Do you expect to commend yourselves to the son of Joseph by neglecting your sacred duty to the God of Israel?"

They went away then, hastily, casting hurried glances at the sun, anxiously remembering all the last-minute things that needed to be done. The four men who had brought Eliah the potter, two of them his sons and two his neighbors, picked up his pallet again, each one taking a corner, and, to the accompaniment of his groans and sharp admonitions to "go easy," carried him as gently as possible up the street. James stood and watched them go, his emotions a strange mixture of relief, amazement, and vague uneasiness.

The staccato strokes of a hammer, a bit sharper and less leisurely than usual, gave evidence that Jude was still at work, trying to finish something before the Sabbath. Casting another swift, worried glance at the fast-narrowing angle of sunlight before passing through the doorway, James hastened through the outer passage and into the inner court.

His mother rose eagerly from where she had been sitting close to the door. "Oh! It's you, James. I thought—"

"Don't worry," he assured her with all the competence that his new position as head of the family aroused in him the moment he crossed his own threshold. "He will come soon. It's less than an hour to the Sabbath."

Expectantly James' glance circled the courtyard, rested for a moment on its only other occupant, the woman with the thin, dissatisfied face, her listless body shrouded in coverlets and cushions. Her lips curved into a mirthless smile, both petulant and shrewd.

"Susanna," said Mary the wife of Clopas, "isn't here. She's gone to the well to get some fresh water for me."

James flushed and felt his usual irritation toward his aunt mounting. He had been looking for Susanna, of course. But she didn't have to make him feel like a boy suffering from his first attack of romance. He had naturally been overjoyed when Susanna had brought her mother to Nazareth a few weeks before in the hope that the country air might benefit Mary's health, but he had soon found that their presence was not an unmixed blessing.

He found it increasingly hard to understand how a person so utterly beautiful and desirable as Susanna could be the daughter of a shrewish misanthrope like the wife of Clopas. He would be glad when she tired of visiting her husband's poor relations and returned to her own sumptuous house in Jerusalem, except that when she went Susanna would be going too. Unless—They had been betrothed for nearly a year now. Surely he had a right to expect, to demand, that in spite of her mother's tenacious, clinging hold upon her Susanna should soon become his wife. But, no. Always at this point the cycle of his reasoning brought him to the same dead end. He couldn't ask a girl like Susanna to share the life of a dull, plodding, country carpenter.

He turned his back abruptly on his aunt. "Everything is in readiness for the Sabbath? The lamps are filled, the food laid away, the water drawn?"

Mary's gentle face lifted in surprise. "Why, of course, James. The lamps are ready, and Anna is putting away the food right now. Have you ever found us lacking in reverence for the holy Law?"

James frowned. "Not you, perhaps. But Jude isn't so careful as he might be. I've seen him wait till after sunset to put away his tools."

The staccato hammer beats seemed to intrude themselves suddenly, like a defiant personality.

"He's so anxious to get his orders filled on time," said Mary apologetically.

"Does that excuse a man for Sabbath-breaking?" James shot back at her swiftly.

"Of course not. Only—you might have helped him, James."

"I had more important work to do," replied James abruptly, stifling the momentary compunction that her words aroused. "I've been talking with Rabbi Nathan."

"Oh, James!" She lifted her eyes to his in a full glory of sunlight. "Did—did he say—"

In his eagerness James felt his dignity slipping from him. "Jesus is to lead the service in the synagogue tomorrow." He blurted out the news excitedly. "Not only as the messenger of the congregation, to read the Law, but as the preacher."

Mary turned eagerly to the woman swathed in coverlets and pillows. "Did you hear that, sister Mary? My son is going to preach Jehovah's word in his own synagogue."

"I could have told you that," returned Clopas' wife dryly. "Did you think that after all the talk they've heard, the curious people in this town would let a chance like this slip by? The place will be crowded. If you don't believe it, look at the mob that's waiting outside the door right now."

"They're not there any longer," said James. "I sent them home."

"Oh, are you sure you should have?" asked Mary doubtfully. "Jesus might not like it. He would never turn anyone away."

"Neither would he like them to break the Sabbath," returned James almost curtly. He stooped suddenly and fingered the soft white mass of something in his mother's lap. "What's this?" he demanded. "You haven't started a new garment, have you, before the Sabbath?"

Mary's hand fluttered over the thing possessively, with the tenderness of a mother bird protecting its young.

"Oh, no! It's a cloak that I started long ago. I wanted to finish the embroidery on it before he came. It's almost done now."

James' eyes narrowed as they noted the fine, even texture of the wool woven all in one piece, the elaborate crimson embroidery, the wide fringe.

"But—this is no *simlah!*" he exclaimed sharply. "No ordinary cloak! This is a *meil!*"

"Yes," replied Mary softly. "It's a *meil*."

James felt a sudden swift upsurging of jealousy and knew it for the emotion that had all that day been struggling within him for supremacy. There had been no reception like this for him when he had returned from Jerusalem. Oh, there had been the small crowd that had come out to meet him, mostly schoolboys. And he had spoken in the synagogue on his first Sabbath, and on many Sabbaths since, as any young scholar would be asked to do. But there had not been all this preparation, this town-wide excitement. And, though by his superior education and attainments he had surely won the right to wear it if anyone in the family had, had his mother made any *meil* for him?

"After all," he asked himself, "what has my Brother done that the whole village should become so excited over his paying it a visit?"

Jesus had been away from home for a few months, attracted crowds here and there, propounded some ideas that had gained him a handful of followers, most of them either relatives or life-long friends. There were his two cousins, James and John; and Simon and Andrew, whose father was now in charge of Zebedee's wholesale in Bethsaida; and a couple of other young men whom James had never met, one of them from Bethsaida, the other from Cana, not far from Nazareth. He had spent some time with his cousin John down in the Jordan Valley, until John had become so violent in his accusations of Antipas that he had gotten himself arrested. Then Jesus had come back to Galilee, stayed for a short time in Capernaum, visited a few villages, gained a few followers. That was all. What was it that made him any different from the other young men of Nazareth who had left their home town in the hope of bettering their fortunes—except, possibly, the Dream?

Even now the thought of his disappointment was like a twisting knife within his flesh. The Dream was so much a part of him—had always been—that without the hope of its fulfillment his life seemed like an empty shell. In vain he had tried to persuade himself that its fulfillment did not depend upon his Brother, that hidden within himself alone there was a Destiny. But it had been no use. His Brother—and the Dream. The two were linked together, somehow, inseparably, like the seed and the budding plant, like clean-washed air and the breath of life filling your body, like the fresh, unshaped timber and the object of beauty hidden away in its unsullied whiteness.

His Brother *was* the Dream.

The curtain covering the passageway was hastily drawn aside, and

Susanna entered the courtyard with Jude's two small children. Her coming was as quietly unobtrusive as a refreshing breeze or a ray of sunlight, and as stimulating. Mary glanced up from her work with a welcoming smile. James hastened to relieve her of her pitcher, his dark, moody features alight with a transforming eagerness. Even the sallow-faced woman beneath the coverlets lifted a wan smile.

"Well, Susanna, so you're back. And about time, I should think. I suppose you had to stop and listen to all the village gossip while your poor mother's throat was parched for some fresh water."

But for once Susanna had no ears for her mother's reproaches. Her eyes, sparkling clear as the water in her pitcher, were brimming with excitement.

"He's come," she said breathlessly. "I saw him at the well. He'd be here now if the people didn't crowd about him so. And Salome is with him, and James and John, and a lot of others. And James," she turned to him with a sudden radiant look of understanding, "he wants you. He's asking for you."

James' heart leaped. He set down the pitcher of water and hastened out the door, pausing just long enough to satisfy himself that the sun was still a good half hour from setting. If they hurried, Jesus would still have plenty of time to make all his preparations for the Sabbath—the necessary cleansings, the changing of raiment. As a sudden afterthought he hurried back into the courtyard, lifted the covers from the great water jars, and peered inside to satisfy himself that there was plenty of water drawn to last over the Sabbath. It took him only a moment, but in that brief interval Mary had passed him, run down the little path and out into the street, all the radiance of the sunset seeming suddenly concentrated in her gentle, quiet features.

"My son!" she cried eagerly. "Jesus, my son!"

James felt a quick stirring within him at sight of the tall, familiar figure that emerged from the crowd and came to meet her. This was his Brother, whom he loved, had always loved, better than any other living person, whose life was indissolubly linked with his own, whose Dream had become through the years the very air he breathed, the very rhythm to which his pulses moved. And his Brother had come back and was asking for him.

What could that mean? That Jesus needed him, of course, had been unable to fulfill the Dream without him, had come back for him. Probably he had intended to do so all the time.

Proud, confident, elated, James went down the street to meet him.

2

James looked about him with satisfaction. The synagogue was full, fuller than he remembered ever having seen it, not excepting those rare occasions when there had been famous visiting rabbis from Jerusalem. Even the time when the great Hillel had been there, long before James could remember, there could hardly have been more present than today. For the crowd overflowed the main body of the building into the corridor outside the double colonnade, and many of the latecomers were standing.

His keen, dark eyes swept the crowd appraisingly, noting with unerring swiftness those of special wealth and distinction, before returning to the figure of the young man who occupied the slightly raised seat in the center of the synagogue. Just the sight of him gave James a warm glow of pride. One might think to see him sitting there so straight and calm, his healthy young body so poised, that he was as used to crowds as the great Shammai himself had been.

No, James corrected his own thoughts swiftly, *not quite. Shammai would never so far have forgotten his dignity in public as to let his eyes light with eagerness at sight of a familiar face, especially if it belonged to a wandering shepherd like Joab, who is as careless of the Law as of his shekels!*

James' brows drew together in a faint annoyance. There was much that he could teach his Brother. In the first place, he was sure that Jesus had made a mistake in allowing these fishermen relatives and boyhood playmates to attach themselves to him as his followers. If he didn't look out, he would get them branded from the start as "that fisherman crowd." The words stirred some vague, discordant chord in his memory. He felt the disagreeable, rocking motion of a boat, the sound of a hearty, rollicking voice, his cousin James' saying:

"I'll tell you what! We'll all help you. We'll form a corporation and call it 'The Galilean and Company, Fishers of Men'!"

Then Jesus' voice, thoughtful, clearly resonant, more than half serious, "When the time comes, I will remember."

Foolish, impulsive, childish words! Yet the memory of them aroused the same vague, quick resentment which, hearing them, he had felt years before. Surely Jesus had not taken this silly boyhood compact seriously! He must see that for a leader who sought to restore the foundations of Israel to choose as his helpers a crowd of crude, unlettered fishermen—Why, only last night at supper that impulsive fellow Simon had misquoted his benediction and would surely have neglected his ceremonial cleansing after the meal if James had not sternly called his attention to it! Of course John, with his Jerusalem background, was more well-bred. And this Philip, together with his friend Nathanael, seemed a better sort, but—Oh, yes, there were many things that he, James, could teach his Brother.

As the time came for the service to begin, he leaned forward, his annoyance forgotten, watching the tall, familiar figure ascend the platform, approach the lectern, and begin the well-known litany.

"Blessed be Thou, O Lord, King of the world, who formest the light and createst the darkness, who makest peace and createst everything. With great love hast Thou sought us, O Lord our God."

The beloved, well-remembered voice seemed to endow the ancient words with a peculiar freshness, to separate them somehow from the smoking grandeur of a distant altar and make them as simply human as a loaf of bread or a hammer and adz. Even James, accustomed as he was to the phrasing of the long, smooth-flowing cadences, felt his spirit quicken. Like the crowd pressed about him, hushed and expectant, he too was caught in the spell of this half-strange, half-familiar personality.

But, looking covertly at the faces about him, noting the rapt eagerness, the still intentness, he was suddenly startled. He remembered the crowd outside the door of the house yesterday, their tight-strained lips, their tensed faces, and the same uneasiness that he had felt then crept over him now. It was as if in this one brief, illuminating glimpse, he had read their thoughts.

Here again was old blind Enoch, his sightless eyes staring upward toward the sound of the voice like two great hungry pools. "Joseph's son, is it, talking like that? I wouldn't have believed it. Supposing he is a prophet, like people say! Prophets *do* have strange powers—"

And lame Levi, his big body twisted with rheumatism: "I always said he was different. I remember once he just took a little lame bird and touched it and—"

Jonathan the pack driver, who had the clubfoot and moved slowly, but whose little eyes darted here and there with the swiftness and avidity of a ferret: "I don't believe these stories that are going around, not really. Why, we've known this carpenter's son ever since he was a boy. He's run alongside of me for the last twenty years on our trips to the feasts at Jerusalem! And they say he did a magic trick of healing on that nobleman's son in Capernaum just within seven days! It isn't possible, of course, and yet—there's just a chance— And if it should be true, why, I'm right here, with my clubfoot—"

James again stirred uneasily in his seat. He was glad when the eulogies were over and the rabbi approached the sacred niche in the wall and brought out the scroll of the Law. While the descendant of Aaron and the Levite and the five ordinary Israelites were reading the sections as prescribed, it gave him time to think.

The feeling of exaltation that had come to him the night before had not left him. He was no longer jealous of his Brother. He was glad even that his mother had prepared the *meil,* for it lent to the young carpenter's powerful, slender figure an aspect of almost regal dignity. This was the day of his Brother's triumph, the fulfillment of his mission. Perhaps in this very address that he would make this morning, his first address to the people of his home town, he would declare his purpose, sound the theme note of his plan for the restoration of the glory of Israel. And presently he himself would be sharing that mission and that triumph. For was not that the real reason for Jesus' coming home, because he knew now that this thing he had started was too big for him? Had he not practically said so in that brief moment that they had had alone together last night on the housetop?

"I need you, my brother," Jesus had said simply, throwing his arm in comradely fashion about James' shoulders. "When I go back to Capernaum, are you going with me?"

James' conflicting emotions had risen swiftly into words, half gratefully eager, half accusing. "Why didn't you take me before? You must have known I wanted to go."

"Because," Jesus had returned quietly, "I wasn't sure that you were ready."

James still experienced the startled hurt of that moment, the blow to his wounded vanity. Not ready, indeed! Not with his five long years of painstaking study under the greatest rabbis of Jerusalem, his brilliant record as a student of the history of his people, his constant, eternal vigilance that kept the thousand and one intricate provisions of the Law glibly at his tongue's end? He had thought at first that his Brother must be joking, but the brown eyes had been as cool and remote as the starlight.

"Then what makes you sure I'm ready now?" He had not been quite able to keep the hurt resentment out of his voice.

"I'm not sure yet," had been the reply. "Perhaps something will happen that will make us both sure."

He had wanted to talk with him more, to ask him many things, perhaps make some suggestions for the improvement of his present program of activity. But there had been no further opportunity, for Jesus had spent almost the whole evening talking with the wife of Clopas. Talking, of all things, about such inconsequential subjects as birds and sunshine and flowers! And this morning, when he had risen early, knowing that it was Jesus' custom to be up and out-of-doors before the sun rose, he had found him already possessed of a companion for his morning walk—of all people, that dumb brute, the son of Malluch!

The attention of the crowd about him wavered, relaxed, then surged upward again, and James realized suddenly that the most important moment of the service had arrived. The readings from the Law were finished, and his Brother was even now unrolling the Book of the Prophets. The portion for the day was from the Book of Isaiah. James recognized the section the moment the first words were uttered, and a sudden eagerness flamed within him. The very aptness of the passage served as tinder to his swift imagination.

> The Spirit of the Lord is upon Me,
> Because the LORD has anointed Me
> To preach good tidings to the poor.

James' quick brain leaped ahead of the quiet voice, creating picture after picture from the stately, heroic language.

> He has sent Me to heal the brokenhearted,
> To proclaim liberty to the captives,
> And the opening of the prison to those who are bound;
> To proclaim the acceptable year of the LORD.

The acceptable year of the Lord! Was not that the very substance of the Dream itself, preparing Israel for the great Year of Jubilee when the Law would be upheld through all the land and Jehovah's name would be exalted? James wondered if Jesus realized what an opportunity was now given him, what a magnificent text coincidence had provided. He almost held his breath when the quiet voice finished and the strong, steady fingers, which had shaped themselves more often to the hammer and adz than to the scroll, rolled up the book and returned it to the chazan.

"The time has now come," went on the quiet voice, as simply as if it had been speaking of a yoke or a plow or of the family's daily bread, "for all these things to happen. God is ready to give us all these blessings. The Year of Jubilee for which we have been waiting so long may be even now at hand."

James was suffused with a great warmth. Pride in his Brother, enthusiasm for the work they were to do together, an overwhelming zeal for Jehovah and the Law seemed to take possession of his mind and soul and body. He looked about him and realized that others were stirred in the same way. There was not a sound in the whole synagogue. All were held fast in the spell of the words that fell from the young carpenter's lips. James was filled with a sense of exaltation so great that he could scarcely bear it. This beloved, familiar figure, this gracious leader among men, this bewildering personality whom he had always known, yet apparently had never known—this was his Brother.

When the sermon was finished, the crowd relaxed and, as was the custom, began immediately to discuss what had been said. James waited breathlessly for the reaction. It was old blind Enoch who made the first comment.

"Is that really the carpenter's son?" he demanded in his thin quaver. "I can't believe it. Why, I remember—"

The comments came then, thick and fast, starting with a low buzzing murmur and rising to a quick crescendo, like a flying object gathering momentum.

"Imagine! Joseph's son!"

"I never would have dreamed—"

"Such words of grace—"

"His mother must be so proud!"

"Why, I remember when he was just a baby. One time—"

"It can't be true, though, all these things they say—"

"That's right! Without even touching him. Just by mumbling some magic words!"

"Some rich man's son in Capernaum—"

"If he's got magic, how about working it on us?"

"His own folks, for a change—"

"I'd have to see some sign before I believed!"

"That's right. A sign—"

"Give us a sign, a *sign!*"

"A SIGN!"

James looked apprehensively toward the tall, straight figure sitting quietly on the platform. He had been afraid this would happen. Those empty, hungry pools in the face of old blind Enoch; those powerful muscles of lame Levi, twisted and locked in his great frame like the gnarled roots of a giant tree struck dead; those little ferret eyes of keen, clubfooted, miserly old Jonathan, as shining and round as the yellow coins he was so fond of saving; that sea of strained, tensed, unfamiliar faces! They had gone away quietly enough yesterday, because they had had this to look forward to. But now—

He thought he knew well enough how his Brother had gotten himself into this situation. It was that unfortunate interest of his in people, not just people in crowds like this, but people as individuals. All people. The Roman soldier on the road to Sepphoris as well as the righteous Pharisee. The fawning beggar and ill-smelling leper equally with the rich merchant and respected landowner. Even that despised little *mokhes* by the wayside of Jerusalem! And he had always had the queer idea that somehow he was responsible for all their troubles, that just by being born into the world he had taken upon himself all the problems and sorrows of the entire race.

Doubtless he had made friends with one of these poor, half-dead wretches that he was always choosing as his companions and coaxed and cajoled him into good health just by sheer willpower. Then, most likely, someone had started these stories about him, and, as stories will, they had grown by leaps and bounds.

What would Jesus do now? James leaned forward breathlessly. The tension of the crowd was like the crest of a wave, poised in mid-air, ready to slip back or surge forward in a tumultuous burst of energy.

The young carpenter rose and faced them. His warm, sympathetic eyes had become suddenly intense and cold, and his voice, when he spoke, was keen and cutting as a blade.

Was this the reception his own people gave him? Next they would be saying to him, "Doctor, cure yourself!" "Do here in your own town all we have heard you did in Capernaum!" No prophet was ever welcome in his native town or among his own people. Even Elijah and Elisha found more faith outside of Israel than in it! There were many widows in Israel in Elijah's day when the famine came over the land, but did Elijah minister to any of them? No! He was sent to a woman in the foreign town of Sidon! And there were many lepers among his own countrymen when Elisha lived, but he was able to help none of them. Only Naaman the Syrian! The dark eyes flashed. He had come speaking to them of the things of God, and they had asked him for a sign! Did they think that to men like them belonged the Kingdom of God!

The crest of the wave held itself poised for another moment after he had finished, then surged suddenly forward, seeming to gather unto itself some new, dark, mysterious energy out of unplumbed depths. James felt himself being swept along with it, his emotions keeping pace with the rising hysteria of the mob about him.

He forgot that the man standing there alone in the center of the synagogue was his Brother. He knew only that his pride and integrity as an Israelite had been outraged, that this ordinary carpenter of Nazareth had presumed to set himself up as an authority, had even dared to compare them unfavorably—*them*, keepers of the Law!— with the outcasts of other nations. It wasn't until he was out of the synagogue, amid the hysterical, enraged human mass that had arisen and borne the tall, quiet figure out with it on its crest, that he remembered.

"Out with him! Away with him! Run him out of the city!" cried someone, and, moblike, the crowd took up the cry, "Away with him!"

A man on the edge of the crowd picked up a stone and threw it. James turned just in time to see the quick arc made by his bony arm, the righteous zeal inflaming his thin features. It was Malluch the carpenter.

Blindly, with a swift revulsion of feeling, James struck out toward him. Malluch! It was he who had first shouted, "Out with him! Away with him!" in the synagogue. He knew it as surely as if the shrill accents had been reproduced by his mocking lips. Malluch was to blame for all the misfortunes that had ever come to them. If he could once get his fingers about that long, thin throat, clamp his bare hand down on that triumphant smile! But the crowd carried him on with it, even as it had carried that other straight, calm figure through the narrow, winding streets of the village, past the deserted bazaars of the marketplace, up toward the hill behind the town.

James' brain was steadying now. Out of the torturing conflict of his emotions one thought emerged. He must find his mother. Susanna was young and strong. She could look out for herself. But Mary was small and frail and delicate. She could easily be trampled upon in this crowd. And how they must be trampling on her heart already! He remembered the way her hands had looked that morning smoothing into place the soft, finely embroidered folds of the new *meil*, tenderly caressing and gently curving inward like a white bird's wing; how her eyes had been alight as with the flames of soft-glowing candles; how she had turned back proudly so many times to watch them after they had left the house and separated, the men to hasten eagerly along the main thoroughfare, the women to take the back streets, as was the custom, to the synagogue.

"I do so want them to like it," James had heard her say and felt a little stab of jealousy. "I'm afraid I've never wanted anything so much."

He felt no jealousy now, only a deep, consuming pity. He longed to find her, to shield her from this unbelievable thing that was happening, but he was helpless against the solid mass pressing against him. These were not people, he thought swiftly, his mind rendered strangely clear by the helplessness of his body. They had merged their separate personalities into a composite whole which in itself possessed personality vaster and stronger than the sum total of its several parts.

They were capable of anything, this mass of unknown, familiar humanity about him. How odd it was to see faces you knew so well, gentle, kindly faces that had laughed over your childish antics and wept over the death of your loved ones, now distorted with rage and hatred! Hands that had patted you on the head and fed you figs and dates and brushed the dirt off your tunic when you tumbled down, now closed avidly about murderous weapons! Now and again, through a gap in the crowd, he caught a glimpse of his Brother's face, still and calm as a bit of blue sky seen through a rift in stormy clouds, an angry stain of red over his temple where Malluch's stone had hit its mark.

Suddenly a voice rang out somewhere up ahead, a woman's voice, tearfully shrill and pleading. "Listen to me, please listen! You don't know what you're doing! This man is Jesus, Joseph's son, your friend. You can't—" Then the sound was muffled, as by the sharp impress of a heavy hand.

James knew that voice. He pushed his way frantically toward it. It was like battling a fiercely stubborn current, but at last he managed to reach her side.

"Susanna!" He gathered the slight, trembling figure into his arms. "Darling, they haven't hurt you?"

"James," she sobbed, clinging to him, "what are they going to do to him?"

Deliberately he turned her away from the mad confusion of faces, his own eyes meanwhile searching for a single familiar face. "Have you seen mother?" he asked anxiously. "I hoped she was with you."

"She's back there somewhere with Jude," replied Susanna, her voice smothered in the folds of his cloak.

"Good." His lips set grimly. "I hope he managed to get her home. At least she isn't seeing this."

"Oh, James!" The girl lifted her face again, the eyes above the soft white veil so wide open and piteous that they seemed bereft of their protecting fringes. "How could they do this to him—his own friends, his neighbors! I never knew him to do an unkind thing to anybody anywhere—not ever!"

James pressed her head back against his breast. The top of it came just to his shoulder. He knew suddenly that in this moment they were closer than they had ever been, that, strangely enough, in their common loyalty to his Brother and the Dream, they had found a bond uniting them even more completely, more indissolubly, than their love for each other.

James looked again for the rift and found it closed. With the erasure of those calm, serene features had gone the last steadying verity in a treacherous and bewildering uncertainty. His feet stumbled as they struck a sudden sharper incline, and he felt the impact of the crowd holding him in mid-air, tossing him forward like a bit of flotsam, before he regained his balance. He managed, however, to keep a firm, protecting arm about Susanna's shoulders.

"Keep close to me," he commanded, "whatever happens. And don't try to talk to anybody."

The mob spirit, which had been first hysteria, then blind energy, now, with the feeling of that sharp incline beneath its feet, became subtly transformed into purpose. Up, up they climbed, panting, as the broad panorama of Esdraelon stretched away before them. They knew now where they were going.

Susanna clutched his arm. Her mouth shaped the words silently. "The cliff!"

Yes. That was it. The cliff. The crowd was heading straight for the western edge of the hill, where it fell abruptly forty feet at least to the valley below. James' whole body felt cold. He moved without conscious volition. His brain felt active, but it refused to accept the thing that was happening. It was as if it must pass through years of accumulated memories and emotions before arriving at the stark reality of the present.

They were passing the Lookout now. There, standing on that highest point, his Brother had taught him to lift his face, to stretch his arms wide. "See, little one? You don't need to go to the Temple or even the synagogue to worship. God is *here*." "Can't you feel him—all about you—inside of you?" "Down there where the hills begin, that is Samaria, and somewhere over toward the sea is Phoenicia. But look as hard as you will, little one, you can't see any lines between them. God can't, either." "See that great man riding along in his chariot? He looks small, doesn't he, even smaller than the slave that runs along beside! Maybe the slave's face is black, but it doesn't show from here. That is the way God sees things, little one."

There, just a few feet away on the left, was the tiny gorge that had been in its turn the Red Sea, the Valley of Aijalon, the murky, rushing torrent of the Jordan over which Joshua and his brave pioneers had crossed. There on the ledge above was the cave which in their childhood games had been used for everything from Pharaoh's palace to the fiery furnace and the dark, secret haunt of the witch of Endor. Sometimes Jesus had played with them. Occasionally he had made a suggestion such as, "Let's play a new game, shall we? Let's pretend there aren't any Jews anymore, or any Greeks, or Romans. Let's make believe we're all just one big family!"

Yes. Jesus had really said these things. Strange that until today he had never fully understood their implications. And now it was too late. There was not time even to think. The past was gone. There was no future. There was only the present—the hoarse shouting of a mob, Susanna's stricken face, and ahead a vast curve of shimmering blue and nothingness.

So this was to be the end, was it, of the Dream? And the man whom the crowd was slowly, inexorably crowding, inch by inch, toward the edge of darkness and oblivion was his Brother. No, no! It mustn't be. He wouldn't let them—no matter what he had said and done. Leaving Susanna abruptly, he began to push his way forward with sudden vigor, his every muscle tensed for struggle.

But, strangely enough, there was no need for struggle. The mysterious cohesion of hysteria that had bound the crowd together had as mysteriously vanished. It parted easily before him, like a pathway. And down that pathway, walking steadily and quietly, came a tall, straight figure. On he came, through the gaping crowd, stopping once to lay his hand briefly on the thin shoulder of Zeri, the son of Malluch, and once as he came face-to-face with his brother James.

"Are you coming?" he asked quietly.

James stared, amazed, his whole being a sudden hot flood of conflicting emotions. Bitter disappointment, unwilling admiration, an old and passionate loyalty, the pride of an Israelite wounded to the quick—all struggled within him for the mastery, while two pairs of eyes attempted to leap the barriers between them. For an instant he hesitated, and his glance seemed about to kindle into fire. Then his fine brows drew together. Hot words of censure rose to his lips, but before he could speak them, his Brother was gone.

"Where is he?" "Where did he go?" "You know we asked for a sign!" "Do you suppose this could be it?" "Did you see the way he looked? They just let him pass through!" "I tell you—magic!"

They went back down the hill toward their homes, a little sheepishly and with a righteous slowness of pace as they remembered that it was the Sabbath and they were returning from, not going to, the synagogue. The women bethought themselves of the noonday meal, which had been cooked the day before and laid away in the storing chest. The men covertly brushed the dust off their hands and rearranged their Sabbath raiment. The anger and hatred left their faces, and their features returned to their normal contours—smiling, kindly, shrewd, petulant, gracious, tired, hopeful, worried, unsatisfied. All very human. All a little ashamed. And all curious.

"I tell you, he didn't do a thing! Just stood there and looked at us!"

"Where did he go? Where? *Where?*"

James knew where. There was a path they had found long ago, with an entrance almost as completely concealed as that to his own secret hiding place. It led down over the hill by a succession of steep, rocky ledges and, if one followed it far enough, came out finally on the main-traveled road called the Way of the Sea. He knew that his Brother had gone. Alone. And he would not return.

"It must have hurt him terribly," said Susanna sadly as they were walking back down the hill together. "After trying so hard to make them understand."

"Hurt *him!*" All the bitterness and disappointment of the past hour rose up within him and concentrated themselves in the scathing reproach of James' reply. "So it's he you're thinking about, is it? What about us whom he has left behind? What about me? Do you think it's nothing to have it all come to an end like this? It was he who taught me to dream—up on this very hillside, out under the stars, at the carpenter's bench. We would work together, he said, side by side. We would prepare a way for the coming of God, and we would go out together and show that way unto men. He made me dream." The harshness of his voice was like a sob. "And I, like a fool, thought he shared my dreams with me. I thought he understood."

Susanna put a gentle hand on his arm. "Perhaps—perhaps, James, dear, it is you who did not understand."

"Well, at least I understand now," James returned sharply. "He has turned against the promises of Jehovah, condemned and betrayed his own people, just at the moment when he had it in his power to fulfill our Dream and become their leader. And now the Dream is over, and he is gone. I don't even want to hear his name."

"Oh, my dear!" The girl's eyes were wide with pity and reproach. "Don't speak so! He's your brother!"

James lifted his hands in that peculiar, irrevocable gesture of the Israelite about to rend his garments.

"Jehovah bear witness," he said solemnly, "he is no longer my Brother! Hereafter the house of Joseph shall have no part with him!"

3

It was late April when the young carpenter of Nazareth turned his face with finality from his native village, and after that time his name was not mentioned in the house of Joseph. That is, it was James' command that it should not be mentioned. In the first bitter heat of his resentment, the impulsive words of denunciation hot on his lips, he delivered an ultimatum to the family.

"Don't let me hear his name again. With his own words this day he has condemned himself. He no longer belongs to the house of Joseph."

"But—" quick protest showed through the hurt bewilderment of his mother's eyes, "not that, James. You can't—"

"What has he done?" Susanna interposed quickly. "It's you who are condemning him. How then can you say he has condemned himself?"

The glance that James turned to her was hot with misery and anger, misery because he felt that since that moment of closeness up on the hill some indefinable barrier had risen between them, anger both at himself and at her for allowing it to do so. Couldn't she see now, with his Brother gone and the wreck of the Dream around him, he needed her sympathy and understanding as never before?

"You know what he did," he tried to explain it to her patiently, though it amazed him that she should even ask the question. "He dared to compare us, the chosen people of Jehovah, with the outcasts of other races. You heard him. He implied that the heathen were more worthy than we to receive favors from Jehovah."

Susanna returned his glance steadily. "Perhaps they are," she said quietly, "if his own friends and neighbors are any sample."

"They did what they thought was right," retorted James. "They acted impulsively, perhaps, but what he said was enough to arouse any loyal Jew."

"If you ask me," said the wife of Clopas sagely, "it wasn't their Jewish loyalty that got offended. The trouble was, they thought they were going to get something out of him, and they were disappointed. I saw that crowd around the house yesterday, and I know what they came for. Jewish loyalty fiddlesticks!"

"You mean," asked Mary wonderingly, "they thought my son could heal them?"

168

"No," returned the other bluntly. "They didn't really think so. That was just the trouble. If they had, maybe—"

"Maybe what?" breathed Mary.

The wife of Clopas shook her head. Her dark eyes, bright and snapping and less mocking than usual, seemed to share some secret with her daughter. "Nothing," she replied laconically.

"What mother meant," said Susanna gently to Mary, "was that the people didn't really give Jesus a chance—"

"You heard me," interrupted James sharply. "You're not to talk about him at all. He is no longer one of us."

"But James," Mary lifted a hurt, stricken face, "this is your brother you're talking about—your brother Jesus!"

"Don't!" The words twisted cruelly in the deep, raw wound of his disappointment. "I tell you I don't want to hear it. I don't even want to hear his name!"

But he did hear it often enough in those next few weeks, while his anger was cooling into an aching, stolid resignation. The name of his Brother was on every lip, in the street, the synagogue, the marketplace. For Nazareth soon forgot its mad pilgrimage up the hill on that spring Sabbath morning. The carpenter's son was again the subject of curiosity, conjecture, and conversation, the popular hero of the hour. And the reason for this turnabout was simple. They had asked for a sign, and they had been given one. Their wounded ego had been both salved and healed by what they chose to call the mystery of his disappearance.

James strongly suspected too that the forbidden name was mentioned in his own household. Jude was usually taciturn and a bit sullen in his older brother's presence, but James frequently, when approaching the shop, heard him talking to young Joseph volubly enough. Once he managed to move cautiously enough to make out the words above the harsh grating of the saw.

"I can't say I remember anything different about him when we were growing up," Jude was saying, his speech flowing with a surprising fluency. "But that's no sign. Maybe David's brothers didn't notice much about him, either, except that he was a pretty smart young shepherd. Well, you and I could say the same thing. Jesus was a pretty smart carpenter."

"You really think our brother might be another David?" asked young Joseph eagerly.

"If he's what people are beginning to say he may be, he's even greater than David," replied Jude with obvious satisfaction. "Of course I don't believe for a minute he is, but, after all, you never can tell. At least James can't keep people outside the house from talking, and they are talking plenty." The words were spoken with a sharp venom and accented by the staccato beat of hammer strokes. "If it weren't for mother's sake, I wouldn't stand his condemnable bossiness, not for a minute. Telling us we can't mention the name of our own brother! If I didn't have a family to feed, wouldn't I move out of here quickly!"

James withdrew quietly, managing somehow to stifle the hot, bitter words that came flooding to his lips, the futile anger behind his clenched fists. It was better to pretend that he had not heard.

There were those times too when he came suddenly into the court-yard and found the four women sitting there—his mother, with her hands in her lap, strangely idle; Anna busily sewing on a new, small garment, her smooth dark head bent so that her passive but strongly intelligent features were hidden; Mary, the wife of Clopas, with that new, intense eagerness seeming to possess her thin, sensitive body; Susanna, her pure young face half-lifted with that look of a flower slowly unfolding from simple, immature bud to fragrant blossom. Always there would be at his approach that hum of excited conversation, that hush like a quickdrawn breath, that swift, deeply audible silence.

"We were just wondering," the wife of Clopas ventured on one such occasion, "how your Aunt Salome is getting on these days. It's the busy season on the lake, I suppose, right now. But, then, she's a woman who'd always have something to take up her mind, even without worrying about those two young daredevil sons of hers."

James glanced at his aunt sharply, but there was the most guileless of looks on her face. Of course it was barely possible that they had been talking of his mother's sister without reference to the fact, already common gossip, that Jesus was making the house of Zebedee his headquarters and that James and John were among his most ardent followers. But was it at all likely?

Another time she greeted him lightly, "I was just telling your mother and Jude's wife here that since the coming of—of the spring I've been a different person. It seems as if I've never really lived before."

Indeed, as the spring days lengthened and ripened into summer, Mary, the wife of Clopas, did seem to be a different person. Her uncertain, tottering steps became firm and confident. Color and fullness came into her thin, wan features, and, most marked difference of all, the sharp petulance mellowed into an invigorating, if slightly tart, good humor.

"It's a miracle," said Susanna, to whom the spring had brought its own gift of starry-eyed maturity. "And it's just because—"

"Because what?" James demanded sharply, jealous because he knew that no words of his had kindled that starry-eyed look.

"Because she knows the secret."

"What secret?"

"The secret of Life," the girl replied softly.

They had walked to the top of the hill together after the day's work was finished, and as they stood there side by side watching the sun go down behind Mount Carmel, she suddenly threw back her veil and stretched out her arms in a quick, spontaneous gesture that was to James poignantly familiar.

"Can't you feel it, James, all about you? It's here, everywhere. It's flaming in the beauty of the sunset and pulsing in the earth at our feet and throbbing in the song of every bird and flowing upward through the stem of every flower. And it's in us too. It's in every man, a great soul beat of harmony that links us somehow with everything that's ever been and shall be and makes us a part of the Dream that's in the heart of God himself."

"Don't!" commanded James sharply, not, as she supposed, because he was angry with her for venturing on forbidden subjects, but because he could no longer bear to see her standing there as his Brother had stood so many times, holding out her arms as he had held out his to this same broad vista of earth and sea and sky, speaking words that were as familiar as his own thoughts.

He longed to express some of these things to Susanna, to share with her all those doubts and fears and yearnings that seemed these days to be consuming him, but the barrier of silence he had himself erected seemed in this moment more insurmountable than ever.

But Susanna recognized no barriers. Her happiness was like a living spring, overflowing and engulfing him in an unstinted flood of tenderness. She was patient with him in all his sullen moods and silences, understanding perhaps even better than he the struggle for adjustment through which he was passing. And when finally by midsummer Mary, the wife of Clopas, was ready to return to Jerusalem and Clopas arrived with his servants and his expensive carriage to take his family back home, James felt a hopelessness akin to despair.

Now that all prospect for the fulfillment of the Dream was gone, life was indescribably empty. Except for the bright, shining thread which was his love for Susanna, the long dark tapestry of his life stretched out ahead of him, monotonous and dubious of color. And there was no immediate prospect of marriage, even if he himself had wished it, for Clopas, bluff, shrewd, practical, as usual, with that streak of hardness in his stocky, close-knit body which had been utterly foreign to his kind, slow-moving, patient brother Joseph, looked askance at the tiny carpenter shop, the meager piles of lumber, the slow, blundering fingers of James, and the short, blunt, skillful but unimaginative ones of Jude.

"So this," his look implied, "is the end of all that education my money helped to pay for! As if your being a dreamy, impractical rabbi wasn't bad enough! Oh, I may have said once I didn't care what you were, but you had me confused just then, and you know very well I didn't mean it. You'll have to do better than this, young man, before you're ready to marry my daughter."

James had no wish to argue the matter. He was even more unwilling than Clopas that Susanna should become the wife of a common country carpenter, like Anna, who dragged herself wearily about her endless household tasks, her slim, comely body again becoming heavy and shapeless; or like Rachel, Simon's new wife, who worked from morning till night on the tiny farm Simon had at last managed to purchase on shares, out toward Mount Tabor; or like his own sister Tamar, whose hands were scored and roughened by constant contact with the soil and whose face had long since lost its vivid girlish bloom. Just once, and then only for a moment, did his purpose waver.

It was on the last evening before Susanna's return to Jerusalem. He saw her go out into the garden and followed her, finding her under the almond tree, her slim body pressed hard against it and shaking with sobs. And in that instant all the barriers between them slipped away.

"Susanna, beloved," he murmured, his arms closing hungrily about her. "My darling, what is it?"

"James, please—please don't make me go back to Jerusalem! Let me stay here with you."

Emotion choked him so that he could hardly speak. "My dear! You—you mean—"

"Let me become your wife now, James, before father and mother go back to Jerusalem."

He tried to think clearly and steadily, to let reason still the mad, tumultuous beating of his pulses. "But you couldn't, dear. I have no place to take you."

She lifted her face, and even in the dark he could see the tears clinging to her long lashes. "Why not? This is your home, isn't it? You're the oldest son, now that—" she hesitated over the forbidden word, "now that Jesus is gone. You have a right to bring home a wife just as much as Jude."

"Yes, of course, but—" He pressed her face back into the folds of his cloak, knowing that with those shining wet eyes upon him, those softly curved lips so close to his, he could never think clearly. "You're not like Anna, dear. You're not used to being poor and working hard with your hands and living with a big family in a cramped little cottage like ours. I couldn't let you. Besides, your father would never consent."

The bright eyes, the eagerly insistent lips, refused to stay covered. She lifted her face again, shining and wet and tremulous. "When I became your betrothed wife," said Susanna simply, "I promised to share your life, whatever it was. Nobody ever said anything about living in a palace or about never having any work to do. And my father consented then. I don't see that he really has very much to say about it."

James felt himself yielding, his will becoming submerged in the shining, tremulous flood. "You really mean this, Susanna?" he asked humbly. "You'd be willing to stay here—in this crowded little hovel—"

She lifted firm, quick fingers to his lips. "You shan't call it a hovel," she said. "It isn't. It's little, but it's clean and sweet and homelike, and I love it. Please let me stay, James."

For her sake he had to make one more effort. "But your mother—you've always said she needed you."

"Not any longer, James. Can't you see for yourself? She's a different person since Jesus made her well again."

"Since—Susanna!" James' voice was suddenly sharp. "What's that you're saying?"

"Of course, James. Didn't you know? Surely you must have known that it was Jesus who did it!"

James' pulses steadied. "You mean," he said slowly, "that you really believe my Brother made her well again?"

"Of course," said Susanna simply. "And she doesn t need me any more now, James. It's you who need me." She lifted her arms impulsively. "I can't bear to see you like this, hurt and bewildered and mixed up about things. I'm so happy myself. Everything seems so wonderful and so alive since Jesus came and I found out the secret. Please let me stay and help you to find it too."

The bright, tremulous flood receded, leaving James' body cold and strangely devoid of feeling, but his mind clear. So Susanna was sorry for him. She wanted to help him. It was pity, not love, that had prompted her request. And he had imagined in that first mad, reckless moment when he had almost yielded that it was because she felt the need of him, could not be happy without him! When all the time it was his Brother—

Gently but firmly he reached up and removed her soft, clinging fingers from his shoulders. "No," he said, the bleakness of his eyes belying the light, mocking tone of his voice. "It's no use. I couldn't possibly let you make such a sacrifice. I'm not worthy of it."

Susanna, more conscious of the bleakness than of the mocking lightness, sighed. "All right, dear," she said patiently. "Let's go in, shall we? If I'm going home tomorrow," her voice broke a little, "I must be getting ready."

With Susanna gone, James felt a dull resignation and an even greater sense of futility each time he laid aside his embroidered Pharisee's cloak to don the carpenter's leather apron. He loathed the work at the bench, and his fingers, it seemed, had gained no more skill with tools in spite of his long years of apprenticeship in Nazareth and his service for Clopas in Jerusalem. Sometimes he thought of leaving home and finding another village where he might teach and preach, even of becoming a wandering rabbi. But his ambition was dead, and he could not bring himself to make the decision. Besides, he would merely be exchanging the old, familiar bench for another belonging to a stranger, because all rabbis were expected to support themselves by the work of their hands. Nathan was a weaver of cloth, Ben Azel a potter, and even the great Shammai had been a mason.

Jude, in spite of his lingering resentment over James' arbitrary assumption of authority, was surprisingly good-natured and uncritical. He had got word through Zebedee of a contractor's business that was soon to be put on sale in Capernaum, and by saving painstakingly he had been able to lay by almost enough money to make a part payment. In fact, he was finishing the last orders before making the trip to Capernaum to complete the deal when an incident occurred that upset all his plans.

James heard the sound first, that harsh, weird, unintelligible outcry that could come from the lips of but one person in Nazareth, so loud that there could be no mistaking its proximity. He looked up with a frown from his work at the carpenter's bench.

"It's the son of Malluch," he said shortly, striding out of the shop into the courtyard, Jude and Joseph both close behind him. They found Mary hastily attempting to propel the grotesque figure of Zeri through the outer passageway.

"It's only the poor dumb one," she said quickly, placing her own body between the crippled youth and the threatening figures of her three sons. "Don't hurt him! He came here to find Jesus."

"I won't have that man in my house," James persisted stubbornly. "His father has always been our enemy. Have you forgotten all the things Malluch has done to us? Here, Jude, help me to get him out of here."

"Zeri! Zeri!" cried a voice suddenly from outside the courtyard.

"It's Malluch," warned Jude. "You'd better not touch him."

But James had already thrust his mother aside and seized the wild, unkempt figure by the shoulders. Zeri gave forth his weird, unintelligible cry, and at the rough, unfamiliar touch, he redoubled it in pain and terror. Malluch appeared in the doorway, his small, crafty eyes alert and menacing.

"Oh, so you're attacking my son, are you! A fine keeper of the Law you turned out to be! I could have you before the judge for this."

"He isn't hurt, Malluch," said Mary, quietly stepping between the two belligerent figures. "He came here to find my son Jesus. He's often been here before, and I don't mind having him a bit. But he's going now." With gentle but firm persuasion she piloted the groping figure out the door.

"Yes," said James threateningly. "And his father had better follow."

Malluch bowed in mock humility. "As you please, James ben Joseph," he replied amiably. "And in return for your most pleasant hospitality, let me give you a piece of news. I'm leaving Nazareth for good."

James regarded him steadily. "That is news indeed."

The thin body still held itself in its curve of servility, like a bent bow, but into the crafty eyes came two little gleams of triumph. "I am leaving," Malluch spoke the words slowly as if he relished each juicy syllable, "because I have just purchased a most profitable contractor's business in Capernaum. You know it probably. The one belonging to old Benjamin."

When Malluch had gone, Jude's big hands trembled with a suppressed fury that shook his stocky, powerful body. Beneath the cry of outraged anger that rose to his lips was all the hurt bewilderment of a child who sees his last fond plaything being helplessly trampled.

"I should have known it!" he exclaimed bitterly. "Never has the house of Joseph desired any good thing but Malluch has not snatched it from our fingers. As long as I live there'll never be another chance like that. I think I could take these two hands and kill him!"

"May he be punished according to his sins!" exclaimed James bitterly. "May he cry out for mercy in the hour of his death and none be there to answer him!"

If before his work at the bench had seemed an empty and futile thing, it now became well-nigh unbearable. For Jude's bitterness was like a canker, spreading and consuming his every word and action. The strokes of his hammer became sharp and vindictive, and the blade of his adz, though no less swift and smooth and skillful, often bit into the wood savagely as if it had been the quivering flesh of Malluch. Even the arrival of his third child, a healthy, sturdy son, did little to alleviate his sullen moodiness, his coming being but another reminder that a man with a growing family should, if he had any ambition, be providing for the future. Most of the time he would work in brooding silence, then, like a vessel in which the steam has been tightly sealed, he would reach the point of explosion.

"If only Jesus had stayed here at home, this would never have happened. We'd have had enough money by early summer to close the deal. He was a real carpenter, not just a lily-fingered bookworm dressed up in an apron! Our father Joseph would be proud of that yoke you just made, wouldn't he? It might fit the head of a donkey, since it was obviously a donkey who made it!"

They quarreled often and bitterly, in low voices so that Mary would not hear them, for in spite of their selfish preoccupation with their own troubles, neither could bear the thought of adding to her worries. They watched her covertly as she went about the house, silently as a shadow, sharing the work of the household with Anna, folding the sleeping mats, kneading the flat wheat cakes, weaving warm woolen cloth for their winter garments, all with the mechanical detachment of one who walks in a dream.

It was the silence that disturbed James most, for always his mother had been wont to sing at her work. And the occasional idleness of her hands distressed him. He had looked at them once, lying still in her lap, and they had reminded him oddly of the wings of a little white bird that he had once held in his fingers. The wings had fluttered for a moment in one last, terrified, agonized attempt at freedom, then had gone suddenly still.

James knew that Mary got news of Jesus—at the village well, perhaps, where she went with Anna and the children each day, sometimes twice a day, for the fresh supply of water. He could even tell what the nature of the news had been, simply by a casual glance at her face. At first, when all Galilee was humming with the news of his popularity and each day there came fresh tales of his sayings and wild rumors of his magic acts of healing, she wore an air of suppressed excitement, of wondering, tremulous expectancy.

"She hoped it was he," thought James pityingly, coming into the house suddenly one day. "Our step sounds the same. She always hopes a little when she hears me coming. She doesn't quite know whether to believe these stories or not, but she's hoping. By all that's holy, I believe she actually toys with the idea, secretly, that her son is the Promised One of Israel!"

"What are you making?" he asked gently one day, seeing her smooth dark head bent earnestly over a mass of soft, striped wool.

She looked up, startled, tried to draw the floating end of her drapery over the fine scarlet embroidery. "Just a cloak," she said lightly.

But James knew that it was more than just a cloak. It was another *meil* for her eldest son, and, in spite of the disgrace, the disappointment that he had brought upon them, she was weaving into the delicate, elaborate pattern all the secret hopes and dreams that had gone into the making of the first. This time James felt no jealousy, only a great tenderness and pity. Were all mothers like that? he wondered. Would Susanna, perhaps—

Then the look of tremulous expectancy changed to a puzzled, thoughtful preoccupation.

"She is hearing the whispers now," thought James. "She has heard, no doubt, that he is seen rather too often with people who haven't a good reputation and that he has a tax collector called Levi among his most intimate friends."

Then one day when the puzzled preoccupation changed to a sudden lowering of her clear brown eyes, a troubled, haunting fear, he thought sadly, "Now she has heard about Mary, the Magdalene."

That afternoon, when Jude and Joseph were working away from the shop, she came in and stood beside the bench.

"James—"

He saw her hand first, fluttering a little as it rested on the end of the board he was planing, like those same little white wings trying uncertainly to find a resting place.

"Yes?"

"James, I know you have forbidden us to mention his name, and I've tried hard all these weeks, but the time has come now when I must speak."

"Well?" He kept his eyes resolutely on the white planed surface, knowing that if he lifted them she would read his secret and know that his bitterness was only a mask covering a great frustration and loneliness.

"James, they are saying things about him. I hear them in the marketplace and when I go to the well. Strange things."

"Yes," he said quietly without lifting his eyes. "I know."

"If only we could go to him, James, and talk with him! We know him so well, you and I—things about him that other people wouldn't understand. He does these strange things because he never thinks of himself or cares what other people think of him. To Jesus it doesn't matter who a man is, or what he is, or a woman, either. If he thought someone needed him, nothing else would matter."

"Yes," said James thoughtfully. "You're right. Nothing else would matter."

The white hand stopped its fluttering, moved steadily, persuasively, along the planed surface. "If we could just go to him and talk with him, James, we who understand him—"

"No!" He turned toward her then, and looked full into her pleading eyes. He was sure of his bitterness now, of its concealing potency. It rushed over him in a warm flood of memory, constricting all softer emotions, remolding the softened lines of his mask into something hard and impenetrable.

"You're wrong," he said. "We don't understand him. We never have. I'm beginning to see that now. When you come to think of it, he's always done strange things. Remember the time he carried the soldier's pack two miles instead of one? No, you wouldn't remember, but I do, because I was there. And the time he broke up the riot and saved the life of that miserable *mokhes?* Oh, there are dozens of things if you just stop to think. He's never done things like other people. Even the stories he used to tell—wasn't he always making out that foreigners were just as good as Jews? So why should we be surprised now when he chooses such friends? People with whom a good Pharisee wouldn't be seen on the street! Beggars and lepers and tax collectors and harlots!"

She winced at the word. "Then you won't go and talk with him?"

He turned back resolutely to his work. The adz gouged deeply into the white wood. "No," he said abruptly.

She went away, quietly and unprotestingly, and he had a strange feeling that it was her small white hand instead of the wood that he felt quivering beneath his adz. He was almost relieved when he saw the deep gouge that his tool had made in the planed surface, even though it meant that Jude would be angered, and justly so.

But he had been forced to hurt her, or else tell her of the struggle that was still going on within him. For he knew now that the choice he had made that day of his hot, impulsive denouncement had not been final. It had been the hasty whim of a vain and disappointed boy. He had still to make the mature, thoughtful decision of a man.

The Dream was not dead. He knew that now. In his own way Jesus was trying to bring it to fulfillment. But his way was not James' way. And probably it never would be. If he wanted to have a part in it, he would have to take second place, perhaps third, perhaps even less. He would have to associate with people whom he had been taught to shun as unclean, to despise. And he was not ready to do that, not by any means.

Susanna's communications were the one bright spot in an otherwise almost unbearable existence.

"There is a great deal of talk here," she wrote once, "about—shall I call him by name and thus risk your displeasure, or shall I just say, 'about him who was once your brother'? It is considered quite the thing by people in the more fashionable sets here in Jerusalem to take a pleasure trip to Capernaum just so they can say they have seen or heard him. Simon is much interested in the reports that come to us of his sayings."

Simon, the hotheaded young Zealot, and Jesus? How absurd, thought James. Jesus was concerned with leading his people back to a true zeal for the Law, not in raising an army. Or was he? After all, what did James know of his plans or ambitions? He had thought he knew them. He had assumed that Jesus' attitudes and purposes were the same as his own. But he had had no reason to do so. In all the years of their living together his Brother had said little about his actual hopes and plans.

During these days he sometimes wondered if he might not have misjudged Jesus. After all, it was the things a man did that were important, more so than what he said. It was easy to misunderstand a man's words, much harder to misinterpret his actions. After all, so far as James knew, Jesus had done nothing reprehensible. He had broken no law. The worst thing he had done was to associate with the wrong kind of people. And that was nothing new. He had always done that. Perhaps all he needed was a little steadying influence and advice—a balance wheel, so to speak—such as he, James, with his finer sensibilities and superior education, could give him. Perhaps—But how could he find out if he stayed here in Nazareth plying the saw and adz? Jesus would not come to him, he was sure of that. He had come once and given him his chance. Now there was only one way.

Later Susanna wrote: "I must tell you, dear, all that has happened even at the risk of your displeasure. Jesus—yes, I am even going to speak his name—has been here at the feast. He brought only James and John with him this time, and they stayed here at our house. He and Simon had many long talks together. Perhaps I haven't told you before, but Simon is no longer with Barabbas. I think they quarreled. I believe Simon felt that Barabbas was more concerned about gaining position for himself than about making his country free. Anyway, the wonderful thing about it is that since Jesus' visit father and Simon have been in complete accord. Father is becoming more different every day. He isn't so bluff and cross as he used to be, and he doesn't keep worrying about business.

"They say that Jesus did another wonderful thing while he was here, that on the Sabbath Day down by the Pool of Bethesda he healed a man sick with some nervous ailment. All Jesus did, they say, was to tell the man, 'Arise, take up your bed, and walk.' That is very wonderful, but not half so much as the miracles he's performed on father's and mother's dispositions."

James pondered over this news for some time. He was sure that

Susanna must have made a mistake. It could not have been on the Sabbath Day that Jesus had told any man to arise, take up his bed, and walk. It was unlawful to carry a burden on the Sabbath. But, then, as she had said, the story was just hearsay. He wished he knew—

"I've been thinking," he said to Jude, "that we should be going to Capernaum soon. Uncle Zebedee must have some boats that need repairing. And we ought to be ordering some new supplies. Father always liked to see his lumber before he bought it."

"What business is it of yours—" Jude, who had done all the planning and buying since Jesus left, opened his lips for a hot rejoinder, then closed them again, for he remembered suddenly that Malluch was in Capernaum. "I'll go with you," he said gruffly. "Only I'll do the buying, and I'll make the arrangements about the boats."

"You're welcome to," returned James shortly. "Surely you're not blind enough to think I want the job!"

Jude regarded his brother curiously. "Then why—" His pale eyes lighted with a sudden ironic gleam. "Oh! I see. So that's what you're going for!"

"What do you mean?" demanded James, flushing.

Jude paused to drive a nail with one single expert stroke of his mallet. "You're caught in your own net, aren't you?" he said with surprising astuteness. "You want to know what's going on in Capernaum, and yet you've told everybody to keep still so you won't hear a thing about it. You've heard something about Jesus, haven't you, and you wonder whether it's true or not? What is it? Maybe I could tell you."

James turned on his heel abruptly, then hesitated, torn between a sense of outrage at his shattered pride and a desire to find out what Jude might know about their Brother. "I guess we will postpone the trip for a while," he said uncertainly.

"I'll be ready to go when you are," Jude threw back at him.

Then Susanna wrote: "Simon has gone to Capernaum to join him. Life seems rather empty and futile now that he and his enthusiasm are gone. They say that Jesus' followers grow in number every day, though he is not quite so popular with the social set here in Jerusalem. I have heard that there are some women among his followers."

Finally there came the brief note that at one stroke shattered James' silent, brooding indecision.

"When you receive this, I shall have gone to Capernaum. I must go, James, my beloved. Please try to understand. It's Life that calls me, for I believe he—Jesus—has found the secret of real living, and I want to find it too."

That very night James said to his mother: "Jude and I are going to Capernaum on business. You may go with us if you like. We are starting in the morning."

4

"I wish I'd known you were coming," said Salome with a brisk cheerfulness. "I'd have had things in better order."

She moved about the room with a bustling efficiency, straightening coverlets that were seemingly straight, flicking imaginary grains of dust from polished surfaces, her tongue meanwhile keeping up a steady chatter and her sharp, dark eyes making a swift, but complete inventory of her visitors' appearance. Salome was that kind of woman. She could do three things at once—or more, if necessary—and do them equally well.

"I didn't know myself until just before we started," said Mary with a gentleness of accent oddly in contrast with her sister's brisk staccato. "James and Jude had some kind of business here that couldn't wait. They didn't tell me what it was. But you needn't make apologies, Salome. I've never seen your house look neater. And all your fine new furniture and curtains—"

"Oh, you noticed them, did you?" Salome straightened one of the perfectly straight draperies, her plump fingers lingering on the lustrous folds with satisfaction. "You like them? They're a new pattern, brought from the East, beyond Babylon. The trader who sold them to me said there were no others like them this side of Damascus."

"They're beautiful," replied Mary softly. "But you almost frighten me with your magnificence. It looks more like a merchant's house than a fisherman's."

Salome laughed, a deprecating but pleased little laugh, and managed to relax long enough to seat herself beside her guest, though her fingers were soon busy with a thread and needle and length of striped wool. Seated so, side by side, it was almost impossible to believe that they were sisters. Mary's clear, fair skin and small features, delicate as a fine etching, were the ethereal counterpart of the others' vivid, dark, voluptuous coloring. Her movements were smooth and even and quiet, like the sure swiftness of a bird in flight, while Salome's were quick and spasmodic, like the same bird bobbing along on the ground. There was a light in each pair of eyes, the soft brown and the black, but that in Mary's was like a steadily glowing candle, while that in Salome's was more like a firefly, darting hither and thither, swiftly spending itself in each fresh outburst of energy.

"Yes," said Salome, her needle slipping into a swift rhythm that kept pace with her tongue, "Zebedee is much more prosperous than when you last visited us. He owns at least twenty fishing boats now and has twice as many men working for him, and the wholesale in Bethsaida has been growing by leaps and bounds. He's even been thinking of opening up a branch business in Magdala and maybe in Tiberias, but now that James and John have lost interest, Zebedee hasn't the same incentive for getting ahead. It was quite a disappointment to him when they just dropped everything and went off with their cousin Jesus. But you know what James and John are when they've made up their minds. It isn't for nothing that all these years they've been nicknamed 'sons of thunder'!"

"Salome!" Mary's voice interrupted with gentle insistence. "Where have they gone—Jesus and James and John? I'm afraid we must return to Nazareth soon. Is there no chance of seeing Jesus?"

Salome considered. "Well, that depends. Jesus may return to Capernaum today or tomorrow, and then again he may not. There doesn't seem to be much system to what he does. He just goes where people need him. For the past few weeks he and his friends have been traveling through the villages."

"And when he returns," interposed Mary eagerly, "Will he come here? To this house?"

"Either here or to the house of Simon ben Jonas."

"Suppose—" the light flickered in the brown eyes, "suppose he came and I should not know?"

"You'll know," Salome assured her. "He won't be in town ten minutes before half the sick folks in Capernaum will be crowding in the streets. And they'll be coming here to look for him. They always do. There is never a day that goes by but some poor wretch comes crying and asking for the Master. Yesterday it was the son of that horrible Nazareth carpenter who's bought out the contractor's business down the road." She shuddered. "An awful creature."

"You mean Zeri?" asked Mary, diverted.

"I guess that's what his name is. I've always had a grudge against his father for what he did to poor Joseph. I guess the son came by his ugliness rightly. If only Zebedee had known in time, he could have kept the scoundrel from buying into that business. It wasn't till afterward that he found out Jude had wanted it. If only Jude had told him—"

"Jude doesn't like to ask favors of anybody," replied Mary.

"The worst of it is," her sister's eagerly darting mind had already pounced back on the previous subject, "these poor creatures don't come and stand outside and ask for him politely. They come right into your house without being invited. Why, only yesterday—"

"Salome!" This time Mary placed a firm hand on the fingers that held the needle. "Tell me, what has Jesus been doing all these months since he left Nazareth?"

The fingers slackened as Salome stared. "You haven't heard?"

"Oh, I've heard gossip after synagogue service, and whisperings in the marketplace and at the well. They say that Jesus goes about with tax collectors and sinners and that he has women of evil reputation among his followers." Her hand clutched Salome's tensely. "Is it true?"

The fireflies in the dark eyes began to dart about. "Well, yes, I suppose it is. Levi, the tax collector, is one of the twelve, and Jesus went to a dinner at his house to which half the tax collectors in town were invited. And of course Mary of Magdala is among the women who follow after him."

The light like a candle flickered downward and was still. "I heard she was," said Mary quietly.

"You know what she is," said Salome significantly. "Though I will say that since she began to follow Jesus she seems like a different woman."

"The Law says," Mary's lips moved mechanically, "that such women shall be stoned."

"Yes, but Jesus doesn't. I shouldn't worry much about her, though," Salome assured her cheerfully. "There are many noble women in his company. There's Joanna, the wife of Herod's steward, and of course your own niece Susanna."

"Susanna!"

"Why, yes. Didn't you know that?"

Mary shook her head. She felt torn with emotion. Rising suddenly, she moved across the room to the courtyard entrance, longing for a breath of fresh air. Desire to see her firstborn son consumed her, tortured her with an agony that was almost physical, as if once again he had become knit with her own flesh. Yet in some way he had severed the link that bound them together, made himself a stranger to her. Why did he do such things—arouse the hatred of his neighbors, make friends with publicans and lawbreakers? And yet, stranger though he was, was he not still her son?

"You're an envied woman in Capernaum, Mary," said Salome, as if reading her thoughts, "being his mother. You should see the crowds that flock after him, Mary!" The chattering voice deepened, became low and intense. "He talks to men about some kind of new Kingdom—the Kingdom of God, he calls it—of which he's going to be the Leader. Sometimes I can't help wondering if he may not be—Messiah!"

"Messiah!" From sheer weakness Mary leaned against the doorframe. There was the sound of rushing waters in her ears—or was it the wheels of chariots? Through the sound, Salome's voice came from a great distance.

"I'm not the only one who thinks so. James and John believe that if his popularity keeps growing, his followers will become strong enough to crown him king."

So it was chariots—the sound of wheels turning and feet tramping. A mighty host. And the rushing swiftness was that of wings—a mighty phalanx of angels.

"Mary! Sometimes I have a dream. I see your son at the head of a great company with my sons beside him, riding through battle and fire and darkness."

The rushing sound became a great flood, enveloping, engulfing. "No, no!" cried Mary faintly.

"And then the darkness becomes light, and I see him sitting on the great high throne of David, and James and John still beside him, the one on his right hand and the other on his left." Salome stopped breathlessly.

Mary lifted her face. The rushing waters had parted, lifting her on a wave of ecstasy, and were becoming a mighty chorus of voices swelling upward to the very heavens. But there was something the matter with one of the voices. It soared above the rest, weird and insistent and unintelligible.

"What was that?" she asked suddenly.

Salome sprang up. "Oh, dear!" she cried in vexation. "It's that man again!"

Mary followed her sister out of the room into the courtyard. "Zeri!" she exclaimed, as the ugly, unkempt figure of Malluch's son appeared suddenly before them. Hearing the familiar voice, he came groping his way toward her.

"Look out!" cried Salome sharply. "Don't let him touch you!"

"But I know him, Salome," Mary demurred without retreating. "He's never done anyone any harm."

Her sister clutched the striped cloth with both hands, assuming that instinctive gesture of one about to shoo away disagreeable insects. "He must have," she replied firmly. "Either he or his father, or the evil spirit wouldn't have taken possession of him."

"He's looking for Jesus," said Mary gently.

"Well, he won't find him here. I told him so yesterday. Get out of here! Get out, I say!"

At that moment a step sounded in the passageway. Zeri uttered a hoarse cry and sprang toward it. Mary felt her limbs grow suddenly weak, her pulse beat wildly in her throat. But it was not Jesus who drew aside the protecting curtain. It was James.

After arriving in Capernaum James had left Jude to attend to whatever business he considered necessary. Having satisfied himself that neither of his cousins was at home and that Susanna was not staying in Zebedee's house, James went immediately to the house of Simon. He found it easily enough, having visited it several times with James and John as a boy. He was disappointed to find the house apparently deserted, except for the grotesque shape of a man, hideously crippled, who sat close to the threshold, a pair of crutches propped beside him. James contemplated this creature in dismay, unwilling to pass close enough to him to approach the door, for fear of ceremonial uncleanness, yet loath to leave without securing the information he sought. Unwittingly the cripple solved his problem.

"If it's the Nazarene you're looking for," he said sociably, "he's not here. He's been away from Capernaum for a week or more."

"He has?" James was surprised at the revealing flatness of his own voice. Until this moment he hadn't admitted even to himself just how much he had been counting on his Brother's presence. "Where has he gone?"

"Don't ask me!" The hunched shoulders arched themselves still farther. "To find some poor beggars like me, probably, though there are plenty of us here in Capernaum. If you don't believe it, come look at this street when he gets back. You'll see so many sick devils about you'll think you were down at the pools of Tiberias."

"When will he get back?" asked James, despising the creature and yet loath to leave until he had found out all he could.

The hunched shoulders shrugged again. "You tell me. Anyway, I'm not taking any chances. I'm going to be right here when he comes."

"How long have you been here?"

"Four days."

James stared at him. "You mean you'd sit out here in the hot sun like this for four days just on the chance that my—that this—this Nazarene can do something for that ugly body of yours? You don't expect him to—to—"

"To straighten out all my humps?" The man supplied the words dryly. "Well, no, I can't say I do. That would be too tough a job for the Almighty Himself, I guess. But he might get me so I could hobble around a little. You'll notice my legs are all here." He spat deliberately in James' direction, then leered good-naturedly as the young Pharisee backed away. "What's the trouble? Afraid I'll pollute you? You're like all the other good religious people. You think I'm a terrible sinner, I suppose."

"Naturally," said James coldly. "Either you must have sinned or your father."

"Well, all right, maybe I am." The man's eyes blazed up at him defiantly. "But I won't be much longer. You just wait till the Nazarene comes back. He'll forgive me my sins."

James' eyes narrowed. "He'll do what?"

"He'll forgive me my sins. You wait and see."

"You'd better be careful what you say," retorted James sharply. "Only God can forgive sins."

"Maybe so," the cripple returned cheerfully. "I don't know as I care who does it so long as it's done."

"Does he—" James tried to keep his voice from trembling, "make it a practice to go around telling people their sins are forgiven?"

The man considered. "Well, yes. I guess you might say he does. There was that paralyzed fellow they let down from the gallery here in the courtyard of this very house. The crowd was so big, you see, his friends couldn't get him in. The Nazarene told him his sins were forgiven. And only a little while ago there was that woman over in the Pharisee's house. Probably you've heard about her."

James shook his head. He could not trust himself to speak.

"Well, she came in while they were eating. Poured ointment on his feet, she did, and wiped them with her hair. She was a sinner, believe me, if there ever was one, and Jesus said the same thing to her."

James turned away blindly. "I say," the man called after him. "You don't believe what I'm telling you, do you? You don't think this Nazarene has any power to change people?"

James stopped. "I—" He choked. The words would not come.

"You don't have to take my word for it, you know. There are plenty of folks around here who can tell you. See that man over there mending his nets? The one with the gray beard and the shoulders stooped almost as bad as mine?"

James looked in the direction of the pointing finger. "I see him," he said.

"Well enough to see what he's doing? Whether he's working with both hands or not?"

"Yes. He's working with both hands."

"One as well as the other?"

"I should say so."

"Well, then." The cripple's leathery, sunburned face cracked in a triumphant smile. "That's Obed the fisherman. A few weeks ago he couldn't use his right hand at all. It was as no good as a dead fish. But one Sabbath he was in the synagogue and this Nazarene was preaching, and he told him to stretch out his hand, and he did. And now look at it. Spry as an eel. I guess that's proof enough the Nazarene can change people."

James wet his lips. "You're sure this was on the Sabbath?"

"As sure as—" The man's eyes narrowed suddenly. "I say, are you one of those smart religious fellows that have been trying to make trouble for this Nazarene? By all that's holy, you look like one of them! Long fringes, boxed-in prayers, and all! Do you know what he calls people like you? Whitewashed tombs. You look fine on the outside, but inside you're nothing but dead bones. Come closer and let me spit at you again!"

He began edging his grotesque body forward by a series of jerks, at the same time revolving his toothless jaw suggestively, and James backed away. Desiring only to put as much distance as possible between himself and the sickening creature, he hastened down the street, not noticing which direction he was taking. But he was obliged to slacken his steps at last, to face these disturbing facts that he could no longer evade. His Brother was not only a social radical. He was a heretic.

5

"James! James ben Joseph! Peace to you!"

James looked up, startled. So deep had been his concentration on the problem now facing him that at first he failed to recognize the tall, energetic, sharp-featured young man who accosted him.

"What! Don't you remember me? Abdiel, your fellow pupil."

"Of course. I must have been thinking of other things. Peace to you, Abdiel ben Sirach. I would have recognized you at once on the streets of Jerusalem. But here! What brings you to Capernaum?"

"I might ask you the same question," returned the tall young Pharisee. "But, no, you live in Galilee, don't you? Then you're just the man I'm looking for. You can help me. Come, James, here's the house where I'm staying. We'll go up to my room on the housetop."

James followed willingly. He had known Abdiel ben Sirach well in Jerusalem, in spite of the fact that they had been in different classes and had studied under different teachers. Though they were nearly the same age, Abdiel had been finishing his courses just about the time James had started, and he had stayed on in the School of Shammai to become one of the younger rabbis. James' admiration for Ben Sirach had at times approached envy. The young rabbi possessed all the qualities that he himself had, and more: a brilliant mind, razor-sharp and swift, and a facile and easy tongue to go with it; an irreproachable zeal for the Law, together with a smooth urbanity which made him an accepted guest in almost any household in Jerusalem. There were rumors even that he was intimate with the high priest's family and had considerable money invested in the Temple booths, from which Annas and his clan derived such enormous profits by the sale of animals for Temple sacrifice. But James had never seen any reason to believe such rumors. So far as he knew Ben Sirach had always been a model Pharisee.

"I'm here in Capernaum on business," he told James now, when the two were ensconced in a guestchamber whose size and appointments would have made Salome's proud display look like the pitiable pretense of a peasant's hovel. "They sent me down from Jerusalem with a couple of scribes to investigate this fellow who's been stirring up the common people. Probably you've heard of him. Jesus, his name is."

James felt his lips going dry. He ran his tongue carefully between them. "Yes. I've heard of him."

Ben Sirach's tall figure lolled aimlessly against the soft cushions of a couch. Like many men with intensely energetic brains, he was a slouch when it came to bodily posture. The muscles of his spare, dark face, however, were never in repose. Now they were drawn taut. "Ever seen the fellow?"

"Not recently," replied James. "Not since he began doing all these strange things, breaking the Law—"

"Ah! Then you know he's been breaking the Law? You have evidence?" The words shot from Ben Sirach's lips like well-aimed coils, ready to pull their victim taut.

James hesitated. He knew he must choose his words carefully, that both his own integrity and his Brother's safety were at stake. "No," he said. "I have no evidence. I know only what I've heard. I knew this Jesus very well at one time, and I think I can truthfully say that to my knowledge he never once wittingly broke the Law."

The slouching figure straightened, became animated. Ben Sirach rose from the couch and paced up and down, his long fingers laced behind him. "There are plenty of instances where he's broken it," he said. "All we need is to get the evidence."

James leaned forward. He had to ask the question, yet he dreaded the answer. "What instances, Abdiel?"

"Enough," retorted the other, "so that we could hail him before the Sanhedrin tomorrow if we wished to. He's broken the Sabbath on a number of occasions, causing people to do unnecessary work by his healing, letting his followers pluck grain, shell it out, and eat it right before his very eyes. Then a number of times he has been known to eat with unwashed hands. But we don't want to have him before the Sanhedrin, not yet, at least. There's a better way."

"What way?" James' voice was no more than a whisper.

"Get the people to turn on him themselves," was the triumphant answer. "Why do the crowds follow him? Because they believe the things he tells them? These crazy, preposterous things about loving your enemies and going a second mile and turning the other cheek? No! Because they want to get something out of him. Once we prove to them that this magic he does is evil instead of good, they'll turn on him soon enough!"

"And how do you expect to do that?" asked James, surprised that his own voice, arising out of such inward tumult, could sound so quietly natural.

The fingers locked and interlocked nervously. "I'm not sure yet. That's what I'm here to find out. Maybe you can help me. But I have an idea." He bent his searching dark gaze full upon James. "Have you heard how this Nazarene appears to get his power?" he demanded abruptly.

James shook his head. He could not speak.

"They say he goes off by himself every day into some lonely place, a desert, a mountainside, the top of a hill, almost anywhere. He lets no one go with him, not even his closest followers." The dark eyes snapped sparks. "Suppose we could convince people that he goes, not, as his followers claim, to commune with God, but to hold intercourse with some evil power, with which he is in league."

James stared into Ben Sirach's eyes as if spellbound, but he saw nothing in their dark, blazing depths. He was probing deep back into the past, trying to recapture something that had been for years forgotten. And at last he found it. He was a boy again, standing outside the door of the carpenter shop, straining his ears for the low whimperings that meant that little Simon was still alive. As clearly as if it had happened yesterday, he saw his Brother emerge, saw the desperately weary lines of his body, as if all the strength had gone out of it; saw himself, his thin, small face distorted with morbid, jealous curiosity, climbing the hill after him, hiding, listening, creeping out and finding no one there—only his Brother, his tall body again firm and erect and vigorous with a contagious strength, going back down the hill to Simon. To Simon, who had lived when almost everybody else who had been visited by the plague in Nazareth had died!

"What's the matter?" asked Ben Sirach sharply. "Are you ill?"

"No," replied James. "I just wasn't listening, I guess. You were saying—"

"That the man has a certain kind of power. We have to admit that. And he must get it from somewhere, even if it's only from within himself. He breaks God's laws. Therefore it can't come from God. Where then but from some source of evil?"

Where, indeed? James felt suddenly weak and shaken. As Ben Sirach said, his Brother must have a certain power over men. Where did he get it? Was it a thing of evil? Those frequent pilgrimages that he had made all his life to the hilltop, refusing even his brother's company! James had jealously resented them, yet they had seemed natural enough. Jesus had always had queer ideas about God. He called him "Father"—a name that had always, to James, seemed to rob Him of his proper dignity—and he talked to Him in the most intimate, unconventional language and in the most surprising places. James had grown to accept these peculiarities, but now he wondered. After all, people did not go away by themselves to worship Jehovah in loneliness and seclusion. They went to the Temple, or, when they could not get there, to the synagogues, and daily they used the prescribed forms of worship in their own houses. Suppose—suppose this Being whom Jesus worshiped so spontaneously, so unconventionally, was not Jehovah at all! Suppose it was some other Entity, vastly powerful and mysterious and, if not the one true God Jehovah, therefore a Thing of Evil!

James' brain whirled. The tumult in his mind met and merged with a sudden growing tumult in the street outside, so that he was barely conscious of the sound of many shuffling feet, the excited murmur of many voices. Ben Sirach frowned and strode to the parapet, where he stood for some moments watching the motley crowd of people passing the house. Presently he returned to the guestchamber where James still sat, intent on his thoughts.

"Come, Ben Joseph," he said abruptly. "This Nazarene has evidently returned. We must get busy."

James roused himself with a start. "He's here, you say?"

Fearfully, expectantly, his pulses racing, he followed Ben Sirach out of the room, across the housetop, and then down the stairs.

The street in front of Simon ben Jonas' house was full to overflowing. James regarded the throng of people in amazement. It was as the cripple had said. Surely all the lame, the halt, and the blind, not only in the city of Capernaum, but through all Galilee must be gathered here in this narrow street! One might well have imagined himself at the healing baths in Tiberias or Magdala, to which flowed a steady stream of unfortunates, not only from Galilee and Judea, but from Damascus and the lands even farther to the east and from the Grecian cities of Asia Minor.

"We must not go too near," Ben Sirach warned James and the two scribes who had come with him from Jerusalem. "Be careful to keep the regulation of six feet. This is a veritable pit of corruption."

James drew his Pharisee's cloak closer about him and followed Ben Sirach about the edge of the crowd to the outer staircase of a nearby house, where they could get a clearer view of the scene. In spite of his precautions, he feared he had not succeeded in guarding himself from ceremonial uncleanness. It had been impossible to avoid contact with some of the unfortunate creatures. But later he would observe an elaborate cleansing ritual. Now he had other things to think of.

"See!" said Ben Sirach, pointing. "That man over by the door! It must be he!"

James looked. His heart seemed suddenly to miss a beat, then to pound furiously, sending a strong, swift suffusion of warmth through his veins. He knew every line of that tall, supple, graceful figure, every distinctive gesture of those strong, shapely hands, every contour and feature and fleeting expression of that beloved face. His Brother looked tired, he thought with sudden compunction. And no wonder, with that clamoring horde milling around him! Hungrily his eyes scanned the familiar features, then hastened on to the group of people surrounding his Brother. No, Susanna was not there. She was in the house, perhaps. He certainly hoped so. The very thought of her pure, unsullied person in intimate contact with a throng of untouchables like this was maddening.

The door of Simon's house opened, and a group of women came out. James' pulses leaped again, then slowly subsided. For Susanna was not among them. One of the women approached Jesus, touched his arm, and said something to him. Jesus shook his head and turned again toward the crowd. She was trying to persuade him to come into the house and rest, no doubt. Did she actually think he would, so long as he had the faintest notion that one of these poor devils needed him? Even James knew his Brother better than that!

"Watch him," said Ben Sirach, gripping James' arm. "He's got them all worked up to a frenzy. They believe they're healed, whether they are or not. And maybe some of them are, who knows? I tell you, this fellow is powerful. He's dangerous. If we're not careful, he's likely to upset our whole way of life."

James watched. He saw a lame man throw away his crutches, take a few tottering steps, which became firmer and steadier as assurance possessed him. "Look at me!" he screamed. "I can walk! I'm a good man, and I can walk! I'm no longer a sinner, I tell you. My sins are forgiven!"

The crowd burst into cheers, abandoned themselves to a wild frenzy of rejoicing, then began pushing and jostling each other, every man for himself, in a vain, frantic attempt to get to the center of things, jabbing with their elbows, clawing at each other's garments, trampling each other ruthlessly underfoot—like a hungry mob to whom someone has thrown a single crust of bread.

James watched his Brother's face. *How he must hate this!* he thought with a sudden sharp, stabbing comprehension. *All these people crowding around him just for what they think they can get out of him! The way he used to hate to have us children quarreling! But he has to do it. He can't turn them away. It's the way he's made. He's never been able to turn anybody away who needed him.*

For a moment he felt a rush of sympathy, almost like the old comradeship and understanding, until he remembered that his Brother had forfeited all right to sympathy and understanding, that he was no longer his Brother but a stranger, that he had betrayed the faith of his fathers.

"Give us a sign!" Ben Sirach suddenly shouted, his voice carrying above the clamor of the crowd with such startling clearness that the confused medley subsided into silence. "Give us a sign to show us whether the things you do come from good or from evil!"

The tall figure in the center of the crowd straightened. The dark eyes swept the small group on the stairway of the adjoining house. For an instant James felt their familiar, penetrating warmth probing deeply into his own. He lifted his head and gazed back fearlessly, defiantly.

The mood of the crowd had changed. They were silent, watchful, waiting for his answer. Like the hungry mob, they were always ready to fight each other for the crust, but equally willing to turn on the person who threw it if it happened to be sour or moldy.

Jesus did not appear to be angry. He seemed rather to be amused. There was a warm twinkle in his dark eyes as he lifted his hand and pointed over their heads to where the high, spreading branches of a fig tree showed above a garden wall. He spoke quietly, but his voice carried easily to the stairway where James and his companions were standing. Would someone bring him a fig from that tree?

"Sure!" A boy about a dozen years old shinnied obligingly up the wall and tossed a ripe fig over the heads of the crowd. Jesus caught it adeptly and bit into it, waving his hand at the boy. He turned, smiling, to the people nearest him. "A good tree," he said simply, "cannot bring forth bad fruit. Neither can a bad tree bring forth good fruit. You can't gather figs from a thorn tree, can you, or grapes from a bramble bush?"

A ripple of laughter swept the crowd. "No," they agreed volubly. "Of course not. Whoever would be so crazy?"

"Well, then," continued Jesus, "isn't it the same way with people? The good man does things that are good, and the evil man things that are evil. By a man's fruits you shall know him." He turned swiftly back toward the group on the staircase, the warmth gone from his eyes, and James felt his body swept by a sudden coldness. His Brother's words, once spoken, droned on and on in James' ears:

"You scribes and Pharisees—you who ask me for a sign, but don't even know the difference between good and evil! You who delight in your long, fringed cloaks and your wide phylacteries and your long public prayers, but haven't even enough godliness to lift the burdens of oppression from the shoulders of the common people! You who keep the Kingdom of God from becoming a reality, because you are unwilling both to share in the building of it yourselves and to let others build it! You who are so religious about trifles, who even tithe the spices you cook with, but are pagans when it comes to the really important things, like justice and mercy and kindness! I tell you, all who have your kind of religion are accursed!"

James muttered something to Ben Sirach and slipped away. He almost stumbled over a crippled figure lying by the roadside, and the fringe of his coat brushed against an unsightly creature whose body was covered with sores. But he did not notice. He did not even see the girl who, watching him with pitying, comprehending eyes from the doorway of the house whose stairway he had just occupied, drew her veil closer about her face and prepared to follow him—to follow him though he had passed close enough to touch her.

Jude detached himself from the edge of the crowd and joined his brother. "I heard him," he muttered. "I heard what he said, and I don't blame you for being angry. I guess you're right, after all. Sometimes I think he must have gone mad."

James did not speak, and the two walked on in silence. As they turned into the street leading to Zebedee's house, Jude's attention was suddenly diverted. "Look!" he clutched James' arm. "There's Malluch's place now. Look what it says."

James lifted unseeing eyes to the sign which read, "Malchus. Master Carpenter and Contractor." "I see it," he replied dutifully, though he couldn't have told what it said.

"Malchus!" Jude spat out the word disgustedly. "Do you know what he's done? I just found out today, and this sign proves it. He's gone and changed his name, so it will sound more Greek, and he will get more foreign customers. They say he will build any kind of heathen contraption, even carve images of the emperor, if he gets enough money for it. He's getting more business every day and adding to his apprentices. While I, who try to keep the Law and live honestly—look what I get! Isn't there any justice?"

While Jude fumed, James walked beside him, the hot flowing of his brother's complaints as unheeded as the distant patter of rain by a man deep in a dungeon. It wasn't until he had passed down the street to Zebedee's house, stepped through the passageway and entered the courtyard, where he almost stumbled over a crouching figure, that he became conscious of his surroundings. He saw the awkward, uncouth shape of Zeri, his mother's concerned face, his aunt's bristling elbows, and took in the situation at a glance. His features, already white and strained, constricted into sudden hardness.

"What is that son of the Evil One doing here?" he demanded.

Mary lifted a thin, deprecating hand. "James, please, the son of Malluch never did you any harm. He's just looking for Jesus."

"Then let him go and find him," retorted James harshly, all the bitterness of the long day of intense shock and disillusionment finding release in his voice. "He's at the house of Simon just around the corner. Malluch's son will be quite at home among the sinners and unfortunates crowding about the door!"

"Then James and John must be here too," cried Salome excitedly, bustling toward the kitchen. "And there's no knowing how many they'll be bringing for the evening meal. I must be getting things started."

Mary's face showed an exquisitely sweet relief, mingled with both fear and excitement. "He is really here in town? My son is here?"

James pondered how to tell her. Was it worse, he wondered, to feel his own soul plunged hopelessly into darkness or to be obliged to quell that ineffable radiance of motherhood in her eyes?

"No, not your son," he said slowly. "A stranger."

"James—" There was in Mary's voice all the desperation of those months of patient waiting. "He *is* my son! Let me see him just once before we return to Nazareth!"

They stood looking at each other, measuring each other, almost, each with his own peculiar strength of will—the man's hard and unbending as a blade, the woman's soft and suppliant but unyielding, like a thin stem which can be twisted and crushed but cannot be broken. Neither of them noticed that Zeri's ugly figure had vanished from the threshold and that another had taken its place, as straight and fair as Zeri's had been awkward and uncouth. Jude noticed and would have spoken, but Susanna put her finger to her lips.

"You call him your son," James spoke slowly, hating to hurt her. "But do you know what others in this town are calling him? They call him a glutton and a winedrinker, the friend of tax collectors and lawbreakers. They call him blasphemer—*heretic*—"

"Some of them, yes," said Susanna clearly. "But others call him teacher, friend, and savior."

James turned swiftly, the thing within him that was like a blade lighting as if a ray of sunlight had struck it, yet losing none of its firmness. "Susanna!" he cried eagerly.

The girl put her arms about Mary. "I've been looking for you at Simon's house," she said, smiling. "They told me you were here." Then she turned to James, both hands outstretched. "I thought you would come," she said simply, her eyes telling him all that the reticence of her voice held back.

His glance leaped out, enfolded her in its warm embrace, but his hands remained motionless at his sides. It was as if the struggle through which he was passing made of him two separate men, the one humanly tender and responsive, the other uncompromising and inexorable. "What were you doing in the house of Simon?" he asked deliberately.

"Why, I—" her voice wavered, but her eyes did not falter, "I just went there with the other women."

"What other women?"

"The—the women who follow Jesus."

"And you—" James' voice held the slow precision of a blade poised and ready to strike, "are one of them?"

The girl's pause was barely perceptible. "Yes," she said quietly. "You know I am. Didn't I tell you I was going to follow him?"

His anger quivered for an instant in the air between them, then shot out at her. "You—my betrothed wife—leaving your father's house and roaming the country like a shameless vagabond! Making free with tax collectors and harlots!"

"James," said Susanna faintly. "Please, dear, you're hurt now, I know. Terribly hurt. But please try to understand."

Suddenly the anger was gone from his voice. "Listen!" he said earnestly. "I want to tell you something. I came here to Capernaum today to see Jesus. I had to come. I couldn't stay away any longer. I wanted to be with him, to work with him. I decided that even if he did strange things and had strange friends, perhaps it didn't really matter."

"James!" It was Susanna and Mary both who spoke, their faces eagerly alight.

"No, not yet. I haven't finished." The softness in his eyes faded, became again that cold, inflexible hardness. "Do you think I could have any part with him now, after the things I have seen and heard today?"

"What have you heard and seen?" asked Mary fearfully.

"What would you say," demanded James sternly, "if I told you that your son—*your son*—had been unfaithful to the Law of Israel?"

She recoiled as if he had struck her. "My son couldn't—"

"He has."

She turned away from him in an agony of distressed emotion, then, head lifted, she spoke defiantly. "I don't believe it! To turn against the Law is to sin against God, to deny the faith of our fathers. Jesus would never do that."

"He has done it," pursued James relentlessly.

"What—what has he done?"

James dipped wearily into the confusion of facts which the day had been pouring relentlessly into his mind, wondering which one to tell her first. "Well, for one thing," he began reluctantly, "he and his followers are said to eat repeatedly with unwashed hands."

Mary lifted her own hands and looked at them, almost as if she expected them to be befouled with some uncleanness. "No!" she persisted helplessly. "I've always taught him the proper cleansings. Surely Jesus knows—"

"He knows," James completed the statement for her firmly, "that to omit them is sacrilege, a sin against God."

"Cleanliness within is more important," interposed Susanna gently. "It is the unkind words he speaks that defile a man."

James spun about. "You too!"

"I've heard," declared Jude with the blunt directness of a hammer stroke, "that he has broken the Sabbath."

Mary made no comment. Her mind, like her body, seemed stricken into a dull numbness. She crouched in one corner of the wooden settle, her eyes following the intricate pattern of circles in the fine new tapestry that Salome had bought of the traveling merchant. Round and round and round—Her son had broken the Law, he had turned against the religion of his fathers. No, no, it was impossible! Any of her other sons, perhaps, even the dutiful James, but not he— not Jesus! Why, she had never had to worry about him, even in the little things, whether he had his toys put away before sunset on the eve of the Sabbath, or remained dutifully quiet in the synagogue service or—

"He has permitted his followers to pluck corn on the Sabbath Day," James' voice went on and on, like the little golden circles, "and not only to pluck it, but to rub off the husks and eat it. That involves two acts of labor, both reaping and threshing; hence, it is a double sin. But that is not all."

Not all? Of course not. There was no end to circles.

"Only lately he entered into the synagogue here in Capernaum and told a man with an impotent hand to stretch it out that he might be healed."

"Jesus believes," Susanna said simply, "that the Sabbath was made for man—to help each other—not man for the Sabbath."

Mary turned to look at the girl, and, as if the movement of her body gave her mind release, her thoughts began slowly to clear. She remembered things she had not thought of for years. The Sabbath Day, for instance, when they had gone walking up on the hilltop and found the little lamb caught in the brambles. "Look, mother, it's hungry. I'm sure God won't mind if I pull a little grass to feed it. God likes lambs." And the time when old Matthias the shepherd had been ill and Jesus had slipped out one Sabbath Day to visit him. "I carried him a little loaf, mother. I knew you wouldn't mind. And God wouldn't want him to go hungry, even if it was a little farther than I should have walked on the Sabbath Day."

"Suppose—" she spoke very softly, "suppose there is something greater even than the Law."

"How could there be?" retorted James with finality. "It is our only way of knowing God."

Yes. Of course James was right. The Law was the beginning and ending of all wisdom. Without the keeping of the Law, even the smallest part of it, there was no salvation, no hope for Israel. And yet—

"My son knows God," she said softly. "I have seen it in his face as he has come down from the hilltop at eventide."

James opened his lips, preparing to release at last the full torrent of his bitterness, to tell her of the final, unbelievable indignity that her son had committed in publicly attacking his country's most respected religious leaders, his own brother among them. But instead he strode to the door leading into the courtyard, sharp premonition written on his face. For outside, in the street, there was the unmistakable sound of a crowd approaching. If his Brother dared to come here—

"The fishing boats are in, most likely," said Jude uneasily.

Mary stood up. Her knees felt suddenly weak, and she had to hang on hard to the back of the settle. A crowd. Did not Salome say there was always a crowd where Jesus went? And outside in the street now there was a crowd. It was coming closer. The sounds of its coming grew louder and louder. It was in the street outside. It was forcing itself into the passageway—

There was a loud, weird, inarticulate cry. Then a strange voice, high and quavering, a voice unfamiliar yet bringing with it a faint, haunting reminiscence of the past, called out, "Where are you, mother of Jesus?"

"Mother of Jesus!" Yes, that was what she was. No matter what he had done, what people thought of him, she was—would always be—that.

Swiftly Mary made her way to the door, past Jude's stolid bewilderment and Susanna's newly acquired courage and serenity, past James' tortured, ravaged face and restraining hands, into the courtyard. People were crowding in through the narrow passageway, filling the square space inside, overflowing into the covered porch which ran the full length of the court, while Salome, appearing from the kitchen, her hands smeared with barley meal, attempted in vain to shoo the encroaching crowd away from her precious potted palms and imported fountain.

Mary scanned the clustered faces eagerly, but the one she sought was not among them. The figure of a young man occupied the center of the crowd's attention—a slim, straight figure with wide-open eyes and a face so radiant that it seemed abounding with energy. Something about his unkempt hair and the shape of his features seemed vaguely familiar, and she stared at him with growing amazement.

"Zeri!" she exclaimed softly.

The wide-open eyes, which had been roving uncertainly from Salome to Susanna, rested upon her with sudden joyous recognition. "There you are, mother of Jesus!" the young man exclaimed happily. "I know you by your face, as well as your voice. Look at me! Listen to me! I can talk! He told me I could—and I can!"

"The son of Malluch!" muttered James.

Zeri wheeled toward him. "And you are his brother," he said clearly. "I can tell by your voice. It is firm and strong and steady like the blows of a hammer." Stretching both arms wide, he turned to the crowd thronging in through the door, his joy overflowing. "Look at me, everybody!" he cried excitedly. "See what he has done for me! I was blind, and now I can see! I was dumb, and now I can speak!"

6

The crowd in the courtyard of Zebedee's house buzzed about the figure of Zeri like flies about an unfamiliar object, noisy, inquisitive, and, if the occasion arose, rapacious. Now and then a few words in the buzzing became distinguishable.

"The son of Malluch—"

"Just now at the house of Simon ben Jonas—"

"The Nazarene—"

"Him that was possessed of a devil—"

"Son of him who seeks favor from the Gentiles—"

Mary placed both her hands on Zeri's slim shoulders. In her face there were delight, amazement, incredulity, mingled with a wild, daring glimmer of hope. "Who did this to you?" she demanded breathlessly.

Zeri looked surprised. "Why, your son, of course."

"Jesus?" asked Mary tremulously.

The radiance of the young man's face was dazzling. "I opened my mind—my eyes—my lips. I saw. I spoke."

"Jesus did that?" whispered Mary.

Regarding the scene through narrowed eyes, James was shaken with an impotent anger. It was bad enough to see the son of their old enemy radiantly, joyfully displaying his good fortune, without having it proclaimed publicly that it was done by the son of Joseph!

"It's not true!" he cried sharply in a voice loud enough to surmount the crowd's excited murmuring. "The man is lying, like the son of liars that he is. Do you think my Brother would use his power, if he has any, to benefit the son of his worst enemy? I tell you, none but the Evil One himself could cast out evil from Malluch's son!"

Hardly were the words out of his mouth when he realized what he had done. The murmuring of the crowd grew suddenly sinister.

"Listen to him!"

"He speaks the words of the elders!"

"Didn't those scribes and Pharisees from Jerusalem tell us that this Jesus casts out demons by the power of demons?"

"This man too is a Pharisee—"

As if James' words had through the very intensity of their bitterness possessed some magic power to conjure up the object of their hatred, the crowd about the entrance parted to make way for Malluch.

"Where is he?" demanded the little old man belligerently. "Where's my son?"

Zeri sprang forward at the sound of the familiar voice.

"Father! Look what Jesus has done for me! I can see! I can speak!"

The sharp little eyes opened wide in amazement and joy, bereft for an instant of their cold craftiness, then they slowly darkened. "Jesus? You say Jesus has done this? Is he trying to trick me, the son of my old enemy?"

Zeri stretched out his hands. "But don't you understand, father? I can see! And I'm speaking to you now!"

Again the keen old eyes lighted, became pathetically eager. "Yes, yes. So you can. So you are. My son—" But as Malluch stumbled across the courtyard toward Zeri, the crowd suddenly ceased to be individuals, because group thought, composite, reached out its hands, like tentacles, to restrain him.

"Don't touch him!"

"He's a thing of evil!"

"If you value your life, don't go near him!"

The old man paused, bewildered. "Don't believe them, father," cried Zeri, going eagerly toward him. "Jesus said there was no demon in me."

"He says there was no demon," cried a voice loudly from the back near the door, "when we all have heard him crying from his lips! See, the greater demon of falsehood that now possesses him! I tell you, this Jesus casts out demons through the power of demons!"

The crowd assented, muttering, shrinking back before the steadily approaching figure of Zeri. "Father, believe me!" he pleaded. "Jesus has set me free. You do believe me, don't you?" As Malluch drew back, shaking his head and cowering, the young man turned to James and Jude. "Do you not believe me—you, his brothers?"

James' face, turned in silent reply, was tortured but bitter; Jude's hard and expressionless. Eagerly and with a ringing certainty in his voice, Zeri addressed Mary. "Surely you—"

Her gentle brown eyes stared out at him between the folds of her veil, dark and ravaged, like sunken pools in a deep abyss. She turned away uncertainly. "Oh, I don't know! I don't know what to think!"

The crowd pressed forward, muttering.

"Let us take the man—"

"Show him to the Pharisees."

"How can we? We dare not touch him!"

Zeri faced them scornfully, eyes flashing, seeming, in spite of his gaunt thinness, to tower in dignity above them. "I'll go with you," he said contemptuously. "I'll be glad to go. I want everybody to know what Jesus has done. I'm not afraid of you or of the Pharisees. It's you who are afraid." His glance swept over them triumphantly. "I am free!"

They shrank away, leaving him a path to pass through, then, crowdlike, swarmed after him. All but one. Malluch remained to face James and Jude, his thin body quivering.

"I hate you, hate all of you!" he exclaimed stormily. "I hate you.

James ben Joseph, for your smug religion, and you, Jude, for your narrow, self-righteous jealousy. And I hate your brother Jesus worst of all. I hate him because he won't leave me in peace to live my life as I want to live it. If I want to sell my soul for the success I couldn't have gotten any other way, what business is it of his? Must the very bread I eat be made bitter by the memory of his condemning words? Must the very images I carve in the temples of Israel's oppressors take on themselves the likeness of his accusing face? And now—now he has done this thing to me! He has brought my son into the light only to thrust him into greater darkness! Is this Jesus of Nazareth going to follow me forever?"

James listened to the long, bitter tirade in contemptuous silence. Almost more than he had hated the man for his evil-doing did he despise him now for his lack of self-control. His miserable little eyes were getting bleary with tears of self-pity. In another minute he would be groveling, calling upon the gods he had spent his life cursing to deliver him from this fresh misfortune. If his mind had not been so concerned with his own bitter suffering and disappointment, James would have laughed at the irony of it.

But Malluch did not grovel. Instead he suddenly straightened, shook his fist at James and Jude, and a gleam that was almost fanatical came into his hard little eyes.

"No!" he cried. "I won't let Jesus follow me. There are others who hate him as much as I do. I shall go to them, to these good religious people who are afraid of him because he dares to condemn their smug authority, their self-righteous piety—people like you, James ben Joseph! And together we shall destroy him! In the name of the narrow, unmerciful intolerance you call God, we shall destroy him!"

The laughter died on James' lips. Without a word he watched Malluch lower his trembling hand and depart, presumably to carry his threats into action. Ben Sirach, he knew, would be glad to welcome him.

Mary turned, panic-stricken, toward her sons. "Did you hear what he said? Jesus has enemies—"

"Did you suppose he didn't?" demanded James, his voice unnecessarily harsh and curt to keep it from trembling. "Did you think he could deny the very faith of Israel and have no one condemn him? All the really religious people must be against him."

"Now don't you go to worrying," comforted Salome with her usual genius for appeasing people's emotions. "I used to worry at first when James and John started going around with Jesus, but it didn't do the least bit of good. He'll just go ahead and do what he wants to without caring a mite what people say."

Susanna gently put an arm about Mary and led her to the settle. "They cannot really hurt Jesus," she said quietly. "He is stronger than they."

Mary sank down with a little shuddering sob. "Oh, I don't understand him!" she cried out in an agony of desperation. "Why does he do these things? He must be beside himself."

Beside himself! The tumult in James' mind suddenly cleared, like fog blown away by a fresh wind. How blind, how foolishly stupid he had been! It was all so very plain.

"Yes!" he exclaimed. "He is. I can see it all now. I understand what we must do. Mother—Jude—"

Mary rose quickly and went to him, responding instantly to the new note of decision in his voice. "What? What is it, James?"

"We must go to him," said James confidently. "We must persuade him to come home with us."

"Yes—home—" Mary lifted her face with the happy serenity of a child.

As the new conviction became stronger, James became more and more confident. He even began to lose some of the intense displeasure he had been feeling toward his Brother, and the new rush of tenderness brought a sense of sweet freedom and release. He could pity him, yes, but he need no longer despise him. Why hadn't he thought of it before? It was so very obvious that no man in his right mind—certainly no man like his Brother—could turn his back on the faith and traditions of his people as Jesus had done. Those long years in the carpenter's shop, struggling to make both ends meet; those sacrifices for his brothers and sisters, one after the other, each one striking a little more deeply into the living, throbbing heart of his own dreams! Oh, they had been blind, this family who loved him!

"My Brother—" James repeated the word, it had such a sweet flavor on his lips, "my Brother is indeed beside himself. We must save him from these enemies his madness has created, save him from himself."

"You are wrong," said Susanna quietly. "He is not beside himself. He will not go with you."

Mary smiled at the girl with a sweet, pitying tolerance.

"You don't know his loyalty," she said confidently, "to those he loves."

Susanna's eyes, steady and grave and equally pitying, met hers. "It is you," said the girl slowly, "who do not know his loyalty to those he loves."

For Mary now there was no waiting. She was not only going to see her son, she was going to take him home with her. She would persuade him—or, if he would not be persuaded, command him, lovingly, but firmly. Never yet had he disobeyed her word or set his will at variance with hers, except—Strange that she should remember it now! It had been such a long time ago, and he had been such a little lad that first time they had taken him with them to Jerusalem—only twelve—

"Come!" she said hastily. "Let us all go. Let's not wait even another minute!"

All radiant eagerness, the suppressed emotion of those long months of inactivity seeking release at last in action, she seized Jude's arm impetuously.

"I'm not sure yet." He held back stubbornly. "Maybe he's not beside himself. Maybe he knows better than we do what he's doing."

But Mary's long-starved eagerness would brook no opposition. "Come," she commanded him, half-laughing, half-sobbing. "It's the only way. Everything will be all right now. He will be safe. If only we can persuade him somehow to come home again! Come, James!"

They had reached the door leading into the street before James realized that Susanna was not with them. "Wait for me here," he said abruptly.

She was still standing in the room where they had left her, her slender body almost as still as the painted figures on Salome's draperies. James went swiftly toward her. "Beloved!" he said softly, holding out his arms, and in another moment Susanna, uttering a glad, smothered little cry, was within them. James gathered her to him hungrily, with a fierce possessiveness that sought to atone for the long, lonely months of separation, pressing his lips against her eyelids, her lips, the soft, smooth wings of her hair.

"Beloved," he whispered again. "It's all right. I love you. I forgive you everything, only don't ever let anything come between us again. I understand how it happened. You were carried away with all the rest of the crowd. But it's over now. Thank heaven we found out the truth before it was too late!"

"James—" He felt her slender body tensing within his arms and silenced her lips by the quick pressure of his own.

"Not yet, sweet. Don't try to explain to me yet. I understand. You're going with us now to help us persuade him. You'll be glad enough to when I tell you. Listen, darling!" He spoke swiftly now and with a matter-of-fact briskness. "I found out this morning that Jesus has enemies. They are spying on everything he does and says, trying to involve him in some charges that may bring him before the Council. And heaven knows there are plenty of them! Don't you see now, dear, that we have to do something to save him from this madness?"

"James—" The tenseness had become resistance now. She drew away from him, pressed both her hands hard against his breast. "James, you don't really believe this, do you—what you said? That Jesus is beside himself? It isn't true. You know in your heart it isn't."

"It must be true," he insisted stubbornly. "Either he is out of his mind or he is under the control of some evil power, one or the other. And I can't believe that there's evil in him."

Susanna lifted her hands to his shoulders. Her eyes, with their thick fringes parted, were wide and yearning. "Oh, James, dear," she pleaded, "can't you understand? It's neither. He's not out of his mind, and surely you can see that there's nothing evil—only good—in the things he does! Don't you see? He's just trying to make the Dream come true for everybody!"

Slowly James reached up and removed her hands from his shoulders. Then he deliberately moved away and stood looking at her. "So," he said coldly, "it's come to this, has it? It's actually come to a place where you've got to make a choice between me and my Brother? I guess I've known this was happening. He's been coming between us for a long, long time—much longer than I like to think. I'm not sure but that it's always been true. It was partly our loyalty to him that brought us together in the first place, and even that meant that he was there—between us. I guess you'd better decide right now which one of us you want most. You can't have us both."

His voice choked in his throat, and he turned hastily toward the door, knowing that if he kept looking at that beloved figure, those quivering lips, those lovely, unsheltered eyes, wide with unbelieving hurt, he would surely take her again in his arms. And he must not do that. It would make it only infinitely harder for them both.

At the door, he turned deliberately. "Well," he said, "will you come?"

She knew what he meant. For while his dark eyes held a yearning hunger, about his thin, finely molded lips there was the firmness of steel. He meant not only: "Will you come with me? Will you help me persuade my Brother that he is making a grave mistake?" But: "Which one of us are you going to choose? Whatever happens, will you be a dutiful daughter and return to your father's house? Will you become once again the woman I have loved and wanted with all my heart for my wife? Or—"

Susanna knew that he meant all that. She knew too that she loved the tall, proud, fine-featured young scholar more deeply at this moment than she had ever loved him before. She yearned with all her heart to fling herself at his feet, to make herself soft and yielding and submissive to his will, as the women of her race had for generations been taught to merge their souls and bodies into the stronger, more dominant personalities of their mates. Yet she couldn't. Not after knowing for these few brief days this exquisite freedom of the spirit. Why, only yesterday she had held a sick, wretchedly dirty baby in her arms and helped with soap and water and an infinite amount of patience, while Jesus brought about a miracle of health and cleanliness. She had held within her own hands the mystery of creation, placed her fingers on the living, throbbing pulse of the whole world. If only there was some way of making James understand!

"Beloved," she began eagerly and then stopped, knowing it was no use. Jesus had tried too and had failed. She lifted her head. "No James, I can't come with you. I believe in the life Jesus has shown me, and I must be true to my faith."

He stood quietly, without moving. Only his stern, tortured face gave any indication of the intense struggle going on within him. "You understand what that means? That it's all over between us?"

She drew a long breath, "I understand."

She heard his steps across the flagstones of the courtyard, swift, methodical, the footsteps of a man who followed inexorably the path of duty, even though it meant the trampling of his own fondest hopes and dreams. Then there was silence. Susanna sat very quietly on the settle. She didn't jump to her feet, as her woman's heart bade her do, and run after him across the courtyard, out into the street, madly, joyfully, humbly promising all he wished. She didn't even follow the bidding of her tense, quivering emotions and slip to her knees, burying her face in her hands and weeping. She just sat quietly.

Jesus had said something once about people's needing to be born again. Was it painful, she wondered, that mysterious, spiritual rebirth? And was this it, this pain that was so all-consuming it seemed to leave you bodiless and free? This feeling of being torn and swept by a storm of conflicting desires and purposes, until, having become one desire and one purpose, the soul within you was washed clean?

Outside the house of Simon ben Jonas Mary lifted her face.

"Listen!" she said softly, her eyes shining through the folds of her veil like morning breaking through a mist. "It's Jesus' voice! Oh, we must see him! We can't get through to him because of the crowd. But please—somebody—tell him we are here!"

While He was still talking to the multitudes, behold, His mother and brothers stood outside, seeking to speak with Him.

Then one said to Him, "Look, Your mother and Your brothers are standing outside, seeking to speak with You."

But He answered and said to the one who told Him, "Who is My mother and who are My brothers?"

And He stretched out His hand toward His disciples and said, "Here are My mother and My brothers!

"For whoever does the will of My Father in heaven is My brother and sister and mother."

(Matt. 12:46–50)

PART FOUR
Enemy

1

The visit of Jesus to Nazareth had marked the erection of a wall, high and impenetrable. The visit of his family to Capernaum was, for his mother at least, the closing of the last open door in that same wall. Hitherto there had been some slight inkling of what was going on on the other side—the sound of footsteps which at any moment might be approaching; the echo, much repeated, of words he had spoken and deeds he had done; and always the possibility that at any moment the door might be widened, the wall swept away. Now the door was closed, definitely, irrevocably. And there was only silence.

During the months that followed Mary heard no more gossip at the village well. She did not stop to listen. Whenever possible, she went early in the morning or late at night, or let Anna go for her, to avoid meeting anyone. And if she found a knot of women gathered there, loitering over their brimming jugs, she drew the veil closer about her face and exchanged only the barest of civil greetings. She who had always displayed the healthiest and kindliest interest in the pleasures and woes of every person in the village!

They were talking about my son, she thought when at her approach the little knot would loosen itself, draw apart into an embarrassed silence. *Perhaps they were telling each other about some new thing he has done—some act of wonder the whole countryside is talking about. They probably know where he is, what he is doing at this very moment, while I, his mother—*

No, not his mother—not even that to comfort her in her loneliness, the knowledge that since he had been so intimately linked with her body, there must always be between them a special bond of soul! He himself had publicly renounced the bond, had put their beautiful, intimate relationship upon an auction block, as it were, that all who would might buy. "Whoever does the will of My Father—" The women in his following perhaps—Susanna, Salome—strangers she did not know? These women here at the well, with their curious, pitying eyes? Other women—strangers, in Capernaum, or Nain, or Cana, or some other town he might be visiting? Even—may she hide her face in shame!—the Magdalene?

Later, when the faces of the women at the well became a little less curious, a little more calculating and secretive, she thought: *He has done something else to turn people against him. These women know what it is. If I asked them, they would tell me. They would probably be glad to tell me. I can see it in the parting of their lips, the eager glint of their eyes. They aren't even going to wait for me to ask. No, no! I mustn't let them. I must hurry. Dear Father, help me—help me to fill my pitcher quickly, before—*

Had it not been for Anna and her children, Mary would have been unbearably lonely. Jude's wife was a cheerful, practical person who talked little about her neighbors and seldom listened to gossip. She was one of the children who had romped in the shavings on the floor of the carpenter shop, and she had known and liked Jesus all her life. Anna was shrewd but not sensitive. She could go to the well and talk with the women as usual, noting neither their sudden silences nor their excited, buzzing undertones. With Anna, Mary could be herself, unreservedly and without pretense. And in Anna's children, Jeshua and Sarah and baby Joseph, she relived something of the blessedness of her own early motherhood.

Indeed, so much was Jeshua like her own firstborn that sometimes, seeing him romping on the earthen floor, marching his little weddings and funerals up and down in the yard, walking with her to the well carrying his own little jug, she could almost imagine that the intervening years had not been. He was like Jesus not only in name and in physical characteristics—the same wiry, slender body, the same wide-set brown eyes, finely arched forehead, and sensitive, mobile lips, even the same little habits of walking with his head upraised, as if listening, and of crinkling the fine skin about his eyes when he smiled—but in other, more elusive qualities as well. He liked to go up on the hill and lie for hours watching the bold brush marks of caravans across the broad canvas of Esdraelon, the more softly blended colors and shadings of a more expert Artist in the ever-changing skies above Mount Carmel. He was fond of birds and flowers and trees and animals.

"Come, look!" he would say, pulling Mary by the hand to see a bed of flaming new anemones. "See what lovely clothes God dressed the flowers up in!" Or, "I've had the most wonderful time, Na Na, up on the hill God and I have been playing together!" And her heart would be stabbed by such sweetly, sadly poignant memories that she wouldn't know whether to laugh or cry.

The boy had been barely four when Jesus had gone away, but he still remembered him with a vividness that was at times amazing. To Jeshua Mary could talk of her eldest-born to her heart's content. She never spoke of him as in the present—always in the past. It was as if, in reliving those long-distant days in which he had been simple and childlike and understandable, all hers, she managed in part to erase the memory of those bitterly revealing hours in Capernaum, so that at last the high wall with its inexorably closed door, separating her from that strange outer world in which he lived and moved apart from his family, became a shelter as well as a barrier.

Only once did the door swing, ever so briefly, ajar.

She was sitting outside the door of the house one evening, making use of the last bit of sunlight to sew on a new carpenter's apron for Jude, when a woman came sidling up to her. She recognized her at once as Miriam, the daughter of Jothan, who lived down in the poorer section of the town, and, knowing her to be a woman of evil reputation, her first impulse was to rise hurriedly and go into the house.

Something in the woman's appearance, however, held her—a certain eagerness perhaps, a springiness of step where there had always been a slouch, an unaccustomed, newly washed look of cleanliness. Whatever the reason, she remained where she was, even when the woman left the street and came deliberately toward her.

Her black eyes were sparkling, and she looked a little breathless. Coming straight to Mary's side, she reached out her hand with an eager, friendly gesture. But as Mary shrank back from her touch, she quickly withdrew it. "I'm sorry," she said. "I didn't mean to touch you. I just wanted you to know what Jesus did for me, because you are his mother." Her voice too sounded breathless, as if it were full of the sparkle of clean, fresh air. "I heard about—about that other woman, you know, the one they call the Magdalene, and I thought maybe he could help me too."

She was more reticent now, the breathlessness quelled, perhaps, by the calm steadiness of Mary's gaze. "And so I went to him, and he did help me. He said my sins are forgiven. It's all over and past, like—like the falling of this year's leaves."

The breathlessness was there again, unquenched, unquenchable. "I'm going to be a new woman now. I'm really going to live. I had to tell you. I thought you'd like to know, because you're his mother."

She was gone as suddenly as she had come, and Mary sat in the open doorway looking after her, the carpenter's apron falling unheeded from her lap. She sat so for a long time, without moving; then she got up slowly and went into the house and closed the door.

The winter passed, the rainy season came and went, and the world ripened into another spring. The carpenter shop, thanks to the removal of Malluch, prospered better than it had done for years. Jude lost his look of sullen resentment, and spent his energies lavishly on yokes and plows and household chests as if they had been the houses and synagogues and palaces he had once dreamed of building. He began to talk of opening a shop in Sepphoris, now that Joseph was old enough to take his share of the work along with James. There came into his eyes at times a look of calculating shrewdness which held just a glint of ruthlessness, a look such as Malluch at about his age might have had. His straight, sturdy back, too, began to bend ever so slightly, shaping itself by its constant homage to the carpenter's bench more and more into the curved tautness of a bow.

James' back did not bend. He had never been intended for a bow but for an arrow, and, though ensheathed apparently without hope of release, he must remain firm and straight and poised. He worked faithfully beside his brothers at the bench or on the houses and barns and sheepfolds of Nazareth and the neighboring communities, and the yokes and plows and frameworks that his hands fashioned were, though not perfect, at least passable in workmanship. And if the fathomless dark eyes held shadows in their depths—vague, tortured shapes of lost dreams or restlessness or vain regret—they lay too deep beneath the surface for even Mary's loving watchfulness to penetrate. She knew only that he never climbed to the hilltop these days, nor wandered to the door to lift his face toward far horizons.

"James is settling down," said his neighbors approvingly. "It looked for a while as if there might be another queer one in the family. But, no, he's going to be hard-working and steady like his father."

Scrupulously, meticulously, with even more ardor than formerly, if possible, James adhered to every last tenet of the Law. It was as if all the zeal of his ardent, vigorous personality had of necessity become concentrated on this one outlet. His many washings and ceremonial purifications took so much of his attention that Jude grumbled because he had so little time to spare for carpentering. He watched the household routine with a sharp eye, making sure that the cleansing of the vessels, the preparation and tithing of the food, even to the spices used, was all in accordance with rabbinical specifications. And when on one Sabbath he discovered the boy Jeshua climbing the hill outside of town, carrying a small basket in deliberate profanation of the Sacred Day, he was furious.

"What have you there?" he demanded, gripping the boy's arm with a pressure that must have hurt.

Jeshua looked up at him, his deep brown eyes sober but unafraid. He raised the napkin covering the basket and disclosed some small, round loaves of bread, a handful of figs, and two little pats of cheese.

"For the lepers," said the boy gravely.

"What lepers?"

"The ones that live in the cave up on the hill. Uncle Jesus told mother and me about them. We can't go near them, but we can go as far as the big stone at the foot of the path. Mother and I go there and leave food, and the lepers come and get it."

"But you mustn't carry them food on the Sabbath," James returned sharply. "Don't you know it's wrong? Haven't you been taught that it's sinful to carry a burden on the Sabbath Day?"

"Yes, I know." The dark eyes were very wide and clear and untroubled. "But I couldn't come yesterday. Mother wouldn't let me. I didn't feel well."

"Does your mother know you're here now?" demanded James with sharp suspicion.

"No, but she wouldn't mind my taking the bread and things. Really she wouldn't."

"I'm not talking about your taking the food," said James impatiently. "The thing that matters is that you've broken the Law. You're a sinful, wicked little boy, and you must be punished."

"All right," said Jeshua cheerfully. "Wait a minute, and I'll be right back." He ran swiftly ahead along the path at the foot of the hill, stopping at the big rock that marked the intersection with another path leading up the steep incline—the same spot where, months ago, James had stood and waited for his Brother. He waited now, watching with a strange tumult of emotion while the small figure knelt, removed the food from the basket, covered it carefully with a pile of leaves, and ran back again.

"There!" There were gaiety, bravado, and a hint of roguish mischief in his face as he looked up at his uncle. "Now you can punish me. It doesn't matter, I guess, so long as the lepers don't go hungry."

James took the small hand firmly in his and led the boy back down the hill, into the carpenter shop. "Wait here," he ordered curtly. Going out into the garden, he cut a tough, slender reed from a clump of low bushes and, returning with it to the shop, closed the door. "Now," he said sharply, "perhaps this will teach you not to disobey the sacred Law of Jehovah."

He lifted his hand, and the reed curled about the slender body, leaving red, angry marks on the small, quivering legs. Again. Again. His hand trembled so that finally the reed thrashed futilely upon nothingness. There was such a ringing in his ears that he did not even hear the opening and closing of the door.

"What's this? What are you doing to my son?"

Facing Jude, his arms gripped hard by his brother's viselike fingers, James felt the hot flood of his emotions recede, the coolness of reason flowing slowly back into his body.

"I caught him breaking the Sabbath," he rejoined curtly. "He was carrying a basket of food to some lepers outside of town. Just the kind of thing our Brother might have done. He's very much like him, Jude—his face, the things he says. If we don't look out, he'll grow up to be another lawbreaker, another heretic!"

Jude relaxed his iron grip, but his eyes still blazed. He stooped, felt carefully over Jeshua's hard, thin, little body, and satisfied himself that the child was unharmed. "Go to your mother," he said briefly. Then he faced James, his stocky body planted firmly, his feet wide apart. He stood looking at him a long time, eyes narrowed, lips grimly compressed. Then he spat in the shavings.

"Jesus was right," he said finally, his voice deliberate and contemptuous. "If all the Pharisees are like you, I don't blame him for saying what he did. You'd let a man starve, wouldn't you, before you'd break the Law! What is it he says about such as you? That you choke on an insect and swallow a camel? I see what he means now. And he's right. Maybe he's right about other things too. I'm beginning to wonder."

He swung abruptly on his heel, then, a sudden thought occurring to him, as abruptly turned back again. He picked up the reed which had fallen from James' hand and fingered it, a mocking glint in his eyes. "A new reed," he said slowly, "freshly cut. And on the Sabbath."

James' face grew hot with shame. He faced his brother silently, the swift, bitter reply dying on his lips. Jude was right. He had broken the Sabbath by cutting the reed, broken it more grievously than little Jeshua, since his act had involved not only the carrying of a burden but the beginning of a new task, as serious an infringement of the Law as to start the building of a house or the making of a garment. And in his heart he knew there was an even deeper reason for shame. He had punished Jeshua, not for breaking the Sabbath, but for looking and acting like his Brother. He had vented the sharp anguish of his disappointment, the bitterness of his disillusionment, upon a child. He could atone for his breach of the Sabbath by fastings and ritual observances. But how, he wondered suddenly, could one make amends for an injustice done a human being?

Jude and Joseph went alone that spring to observe the Passover feast in Jerusalem. Mary felt that she was not strong enough to take the trip, and James gratefully volunteered to stay at home with her, though it was unnecessary, with Anna there. But it gave him an excuse that sounded genuine, and both he and Mary understood each other's motives perfectly. It would have taken more courage than either of them possessed at this time to face the possibility of seeing Jesus.

James had another reason for not wanting to go. For even greater than his reluctance to chance a meeting with his Brother was his dread of a possible encounter with Susanna. If Jesus were in Jerusalem for the feast, she would probably be there too. And even if she weren't, there would be the dilemma of either going or not going to spend the Passover at Clopas' house. It would mean explanations and embarrassment either way. For according to Jewish law, Susanna was still his betrothed wife. The contract made between them was as sacred and binding as the marriage rite itself and, like the latter, could be broken only by his giving her a legal bill of divorcement. As yet James had not done this. His mind had continually toyed with the thought and as often rejected it. For he still loved her with a passion which with absence and the passing of time seemed to grow but more all-consuming. He dreaded the inevitable moment when Clopas would demand that he set his daughter legally free. In fact, he found it surprising, knowing Clopas, that he had not done so long before this.

With the bond of bethrothal unbroken between them, there was always the possibility that Susanna might discover her mistake and return from this amazing errancy. If she did, he knew that he would take her back. He would insist on a long period of penance, an acknowledgment of complete submission, but he would take her back. Merciful heavens, yes! If only he could have the chance!

The return of the Galilean caravan was preceded by a piece of news which swept the countryside, kindling the patriotic zeal of every ardent Jew to white-hot heat. Pilate, the despised Roman governor, had again profaned the Temple. For a second time he had ordered the imperial standards to be brought up to Jerusalem from Caesarea and set up within the holy place. The deed had been done under cover of night, and in the morning the people, going into the Temple with their sacrifices, had found them there. Their hot, fierce passions aroused, several of the bolder Galilean pilgrims had risen in fury and flung them out, whereupon Pilate had set his guard upon them and slain many of them at the foot of the altar, thus mingling their blood with that of their own sacrifices. Other uprisings had followed, in which Barabbas and his guerilla warriors had figured, but they too had been unsuccessful, and the bold young chieftain had been thrown into prison, charged with murdering a Roman guard. Excitement throughout the country ran at feverheat. The volcano which slept beneath the green hills of Galilee and the pleasant pastoral lives of its people proved to be alive and smoldering. It awaited only one kindling touch to burst into an eruption as devastating and far-reaching as that started by the bold son of Hezekiah.

James waited in a torment of anxiety for the return of the Galilean caravan. He and Anna tried to keep the news of recent events from Mary, and they were in part successful, for few things of the present left their stamp on her these days. She lived, dreamy and aloof, within the past, and they were glad that it was so.

When Jude and Joseph finally arrived, with all the other Nazareth pilgrims, unscathed, the village breathed more easily. It learned that Herod Antipas, also present in Jerusalem at the feast, had objected dutifully to Pilate's insults to his subjects, had even been prepared to take his protests to the Emperor Tiberius had not the hated emblems been removed. The heat of the volcano gradually subsided, and James' vague fear, unacknowledged even to himself, that his Brother might have been involved in the tragedy, changed to a burning curiosity.

He longed to ask Jude and Joseph questions about Jesus and Susanna and Clopas, about the present attitude of the religious leaders toward his Brother, but he would not. Instead he watched and listened, tortured by a consuming impatience and curiosity, until, from their broken conversations in the shop, their remarks dropped at random, he discovered some of the things he wanted to know. Jesus had not been at the feast, probably because the opposition to him among the religious leaders was becoming too intense. His popularity, however, was still growing among the people of Galilee, and only a few days before the feast a crowd of Galileans, many of them Passover pilgrims, had gathered around him—at least five thousand of them—and would have crowned him king had he permitted it.

Simon, Clopas' son, had been at the feast, however, with his brother James, now a disciple of Jesus. Simon had not forsworn his loyalty to the Zealot cause by leaving Barabbas. He had only transferred it. Jesus, not Barabbas, was to be the great national Deliverer, to overthrow his country's enemies, and, from what James could gather, Simon had been intensely disappointed because Jesus had not come to Jerusalem for the Passover, feeling that by not being there to assert his leadership when the populace had been aroused, his cousin had lost a supreme opportunity.

Surprisingly Simon had imbued Jude mildly and Joseph intensely with his nationalist ideas. James contemplated this change in his brothers with secret amazement, but he marveled still more at the lack of change in Simon. Was it possible that Jesus' own followers, who professed to know and follow his heretical teachings, could so misunderstand his purposes, his motives? Why, even he, James, his bitterest and harshest critic, knew now that Jesus was no nationalist. What a huge, ironic act of justice it would be if, after all these months of laboring to imbue men with his heresies, of telling them to turn the other cheek and go the second mile and love their enemies—if even his own followers should have missed the point entirely!

2

With the coming of spring James began to awaken from his lethargy. He discoverd that, though the Dream as he had conceived it during all these long years of preparation might be dead, the purpose and zeal that had sustained it within himself was still actively, vitally alive. It was Rabbi Nathan who helped him to make this discovery.

"I'm disappointed in you," he told James bluntly one evening after the two had been engaged in a spirited but friendly argument as to whether it should be lawful for a parent to take his child in his arms on the Sabbath Day.

For a moment James looked bewildered. He had been about to point out the difficulties of permitting such an act, supposing for instance that the child had a stone in his hand when the parent lifted him and hence should cause the parent to carry the stone, which would involve labor, when Rabbi Nathan's cool statement had broken abruptly into his thoughts.

"Why?" he asked lamely.

"Because you've believed all your life you have a work to do, and yet, now that you've prepared yourself to do it, do you proceed to go about it? No. Just because something went wrong with your original plans, you sit in a corner and sulk."

James was too amazed to be angry. "But—" he stammered, "you know why—"

Rabbi Nathan's black eyes snapped. They were the only thing he possessed that was still youthful and exuberant. The fierce abundance of his energy had burned itself out, like a furnace allowed to run full blaze, and now he found himself at middle age, with a frail, nervous body afflicted by a malady that might at any time prove fatal, an irate disposition, and a pitiably small career as a small-town rabbi—nothing, in fact, but a little pile of ashes, unless he succeeded in fanning into fresh blaze the dormant energies of this favorite pupil of his, this live coal through which he had once hoped to perpetuate his own fire.

"Of course I know why," he whipped out at him accusingly. "Because all these years you've let your Brother dominate you. Because you believed in him more than in yourself. Tell me the truth. Do you believe in him now, Ben Joseph?"

"No. You know I don't."

"Why not?"

A faint flush appeared in James' cheek, like the slow emergence of life in a banked fire that has been breathed upon. "Because he breaks the Law and is untrue to the religion of his fathers. Because he's a blasphemer and a radical and a heretic. Because he's a rank internationalist who denies our God-given racial superiority. Because he's an enemy of our faith!"

Rabbi Nathan rose from his cushion. He could breathe on the fire more recklessly now, without fear of killing it. He crossed his thin arms, straightened his stooped shoulders into a semblance of towering dignity, and bent the full blaze of his pitiful store of unconsumed energy on his pupil.

"And yet you sit here at home and make stools and cradles," he spat out contemptuously, "and poor ones at that! You believe that the very foundations of your national heritage are threatened, and yet you do not lift a finger. You, with your swift hammer-stroke mind and your keen blade of a tongue and your zeal which used to be white-hot, like metal on an anvil, working with the dull, clumsy tools of a country carpenter! What wouldn't I give if I had your youth and strength and training!"

After James was gone, the rabbi sank back wearily on his cushion. He would probably have another severe attack now, another sharp reminder of the malady that was slowly but steadily consuming him. It would clutch him about the throat, wind its fingers tighter and tighter, torture him into thinking that every gasping breath he drew would be his last, until it finally grew tired and released him. Sometime, he knew, there would be no release. Perhaps this time—

But it had been worth it. He had succeeded in fanning the blaze alive. His work should not all be dead ashes, even if he had had nothing but a peasant's brazier of a small town to burn in! Ben Azel should not be the only one in Nazareth to produce a famous pupil! Confound Ben Azel, with his wise old eyes that seemed to pity you even while they looked straight through you, his kindly, serene old features, as fragile and finely molded as rare porcelain! He must be nearly a hundred. Was he going to live forever—outlive him, Rabbi Nathan, who had been young when he, Ben Azel, had been old? Had that pupil of Ben Azel's, that troublesome young upstart whose questions he had never been able to answer, had never even tried to answer for fear he might find their implications too disturbing—had he, perhaps, given the old rabbi some secret?

There! It was coming. The fingers were upon his throat, winding, tightening. His breath came in great, long, choking gasps, and he expected every one to be his last. But release came finally, and he lay, spent and exhausted, breathing heavily. Not this time, then. He might yet outlive Ben Azel, might even outlive that strange, disturbing pupil of his who had the same confounded, indestructible serenity.

God of Israel, what wouldn't he give for such a serenity as that!

Once fanned to life again, the coal glowed hotly. James began to make plans immediately. The next Sabbath, with Rabbi Nathan's permission, he spoke in the synagogue. Even as he stood up to read the portion from the Prophets, the change in him was apparent. Was this the second son of Joseph, the people wondered, this tall, towering figure with the clear, ringing voice and eyes that plunged into their complacency like rapiers?

After reading the portion and sitting down, he spoke to them in eloquent language of the Law and the part it had been destined from the beginning to play in the salvation of Israel. "You are looking for a Deliverer," he told them finally, the coal glowing. "Do you think he will come as long as the people of Israel go running after false leaders, as long as they go about seeking healing for their bodies at the price of their souls? Has one come among you telling you that this God-given heritage of our race does not matter, that the individual, being more important than the Law, can break any one of its provisions and go unpunished? That a man, if he is weary, may sit down to meat with his hands defiled or, if he is hungry, may go into the fields on the Sabbath Day and harvest grain and thresh and winnow it and eat? Then, beware, for I tell you such a one is not good, but evil. Were he my own brother, I should condemn such a one. I should consider it my duty to destroy him."

There was a smothered cry from the women's gallery, a breath of stunned silence, and then a murmur which began with a faint, almost inaudible stir and swept in a rising storm of comment over the congregation. Every soul in the synagogue knew exactly what and whom James meant. When the Sabbath ban lifted at sunset, the news would have reached every corner of Nazareth, would have been well started on its swift relay race to the neighboring towns and villages, that James, the second son of Joseph of Nazareth, was in open enmity against his Brother.

Rabbi Nathan raised his eyes in discreet triumph toward the old, old man who occupied the chief seat among the elders on the platform, the triumph changing slowly to a grim, thwarted look of defeat. By all that was holy, what was Ben Azel made of! Could nothing mar that confounded serenity, that accursed tranquillity? The old rabbi's thin, transparent lips were moving, as if they were repeating something, and the soul in his great, sunken eyes looked as impenetrable as death itself. Rabbi Nathan would have given much to know what he was repeating. Had he known, however, he might have been disappointed, for the old rabbi was merely quoting some words that he had heard reported as coming from the lips of his favorite pupil.

"I came to set a man at variance against his father, and the daughter against her mother, . . . and a man's foes shall be they of his own household."

Before the next Sabbath a delegation came from the neighboring village of Nain to ask James to come and speak in their synagogue. He went, and this marked the beginning of many such visits into nearby centers of Galilee. Gradually a small group of admirers gathered about him, some of them ardent legalists, others individuals who nurtured some special grievance against his Brother, still others—and there were more of these—of that fly-by-night genus which flutters hopefully about every fresh flame, so long as there appears to be no immediate danger of getting singed.

Among these were lame Levi, and Jonathan with his clubfoot. James was not pleased when he saw their faces—Levi's, long and heavy and angular, Jonathan's with its little darting ferret eyes—in his congregations Sabbath after Sabbath, in Nain, in Cana, even once when he spoke in one of the synagogues in Capernaum. He remembered too vividly the clutching fingers of the group huddled in the street the day his Brother was expected home in Nazareth; the hot, rasping voices in the synagogue, demanding, "Give us a sign!"; the bleak, hostile faces of the mob sweeping with a grim purpose to the top of the hill. They were not here, he knew, because his words had stirred them to a great zeal for the Law of Jehovah. Uneasily he waited for the moment of crisis which he was almost sure would come.

It came finally toward the end of summer in a small, obscure Galilean village close to Nazareth, where he had been speaking in the synagogue on a weekday. He was finishing a circuit of some of the smaller towns and was now about to return home, flushed with righteous zeal and a sense of victory. This latest trip had been successful beyond his greatest hopes. People had flocked to hear him, had been stirred to loud, emotional demonstrations, had even in some instances proclaimed James himself the great Deliverer. His Brother had been steadily losing ground in popularity that summer. Since his refusal just before Passover to let the people crown him king, the crowds had not followed him. He had withdrawn first to the seacoast, then to northern Galilee, so that James had unwittingly chosen the psychological moment for his campaign of opposition. His path had not once crossed that of his Brother, though former admirers of Jesus, their hopes of political leadership proving unfounded, gladly swarmed to hear their new, reversed appraisal of their former hero vindicated.

James came out of the synagogue and found a crowd waiting for him. Foremost among them, not ten feet away, stood Levi and Jonathan and between them the familiar, ungainly figure of Gad, the herdsman's son, his great, awkward body convulsed and shaken by one of his nervous fits.

"There he is!" shouted someone excitedly. "Ask the Rabbi James what to do!"

"Who knows? Maybe James can heal him!"

"His brother casts out devils. Why not he?"

"Give us a sign, James. Show us Jehovah is really with you!"

"If your words are true, give us a sign!"

"Yes, a sign! A sign!"

James gazed in horror at the choking, writhing figure. The sight of Gad had always revolted him, and he had traveled a mile out of the way more than once to avoid passing the farm where the unfortunate herdsman's son lived. He remembered the first time he had ever seen him in a fit. He had been walking along that road with Jesus, and they had come upon Gad—a child then, not much older than James— eyes staring, teeth clenched, twisting in the grass. James had hidden, shaking, behind a tree, while his Brother had sat in the grass beside Gad, for hours it seemed, rubbing his forehead gently, speaking low, quieting words, until finally the fit had passed. He stood shaking now, while Levi and Jonathan, both limping, dragged the horrible creature toward him. There was a hushed, expectant silence before he found his voice.

"Stop!" he cried sharply. "Don't bring him any nearer! Would you make both yourselves and me unclean? Have you forgotten what the

Law teaches about one like this? You know very well that he is suffering for his own sins or his father's. And you come to me expecting me to heal him? I wouldn't do it even if I could! Here I come to you speaking of the holy things of Jehovah, and you ask me for a sign!"

He stopped suddenly, for the words had a familiar ringing in his ears. Turning abruptly, he went back into the synagogue and waited for the crowd outside to go away. He leaned against one of the wooden columns, his body weak and trembling, his head aching from the strain, feeling more lonely than he had ever felt in all his life before.

People—the narrow, bigoted, myopic, self-centered, jealous, demanding pettiness of people! Jonathan, walking through life with his little ferret eyes focused on his clubfoot! Levi, his whole life perspective twisted into the contours of his rheumatic body! People—dabbling in a little pot of gold while Sinai thundered in majesty above them! People—how could his Brother stand them, let them pluck at his garments, jostle against him, each one intent on his own petty ailment, or grievance, or silly little problem! Good heavens, didn't his patience ever break, didn't he ever become so mortally tired of people's littlenesses that he'd like to give up the whole thing! And if he didn't, why not? What was the secret?

It was in the fall, not many days before the Feast of Tabernacles, that James looked down from the platform of a village synagogue and saw Ben Sirach in the congregation. Conscious of the distinguished Pharisee's dark, appraising eyes upon him, he spoke more eloquently even than usual, and he was not surprised when he came from the building to find Ben Sirach waiting for him, his whole demeanor gracious and warm with approval.

"You are a true servant of Israel," he said, linking his arm with James' in comradely fashion. "We have heard of your zeal in Jerusalem. At first we could not believe it, because—" He hesitated, coughed discreetly.

"Because the man I am publicly denouncing is my Brother," supplied James promptly. "Is there anything so strange in that? Can a man not love his brother much but his duty to Jehovah more?"

"Well said!" approved the other. "I thought I could count on your loyalty. That's why I came all this way to find you, because we need your help."

"What can I do," asked James, "that I'm not already doing?"

Ben Sirach explained guardedly, with his keen dark eyes fixed full upon James' face. The religious leaders in Jerusalem were in a quandary. They wished to stamp out this heresy that his Brother was spreading. In fact, they must do so, or the whole political and social foundation on which the Law rested might be put in jeopardy. It was a dangerous philosophy that his Brother taught. Its implications were so far-reaching that if people took them seriously, it might upset the whole structure of society, turn it upside down.

Take his attitude toward the Samaritans, for instance. As if it weren't enough to put up with them in their villages, treat them as equals, he had gone on record as telling one of them that it was unnecessary to go to Jerusalem to worship, that God, being a spirit, could be worshiped anywhere. With such propaganda as that abroad, how long would it be before the Jews lost their pride in the pure superiority of their race and, worse yet, refused to pay taxes to the Temple!

And this insidious doctrine of loving your enemies! It sounded innocent enough on the face of it, but suppose somebody should interpret it as applying to the Romans! Where would the hope of Jewish independence be then! As for these libelous insinuations he made about the scribes and Pharisees—naturally the people couldn't believe him, one who maligned the best religious people in the country! But it was unhealthy, nevertheless. Already people were beginning to ask questions.

At last Ben Sirach came to the point. "We can't touch him," he said, "as long as he stays in Galilee. He's still too popular, and the people up here are too touchy. Their emotions blaze like tinder. And then, too, Antipas is slow in acting. Of course, he did act finally in the case of John the Baptist, but that was largely an accident. We must get Jesus to come to Jerusalem—if possible, to the Feast of Tabernacles this fall."

"What action do you plan to take against him?" asked James steadily.

Ben Sirach pursed his lips. His black eyes wandered evasively. "Oh, the usual procedure. Catch him in some indiscreet act or utterance, bring him before the Council, inflict some punishment that will be sure to silence him. Perhaps even—" his eyes came swiftly back again, "excommunication!"

James winced. He felt as if a cold flood had passed over him. Excommunication—herem—that dread pronouncement which not only debarred a man from public worship, but also set him apart from all others, outcast, accursed, doomed him in life to sit on the ground, unbathed, unanointed, unshorn, an unclean thing like a leper, in death to be carried unmourned to his grave, with stones thrown at his coffin!

"Does the word frighten you?" asked Ben Sirach softly.

James' face hardened. "No," he returned steadily. "It is a just punishment for a man who betrays his faith."

Ben Sirach suddenly quickened his tempo, as a man speeds up his oar stroke in smooth water. "Then bring him to Jerusalem for the Feast of Tabernacles next month."

"I!" James stared in bewilderment. "But I haven't seen my Brother for over a year! How could I—"

"You can do it. Work through your relatives. Appeal to pride, sentiment, loyalty to his friends, devotion to his cause—whatever he thinks it is. You can find some way."

James found the way. Not many days later he deliberately sought out his youngest brother Joseph when he was working alone in the shop. He stood watching him for a few moments in silence. Both the man and the boy were embarrassed. There had been few words of late between James and his brothers. As the summer had progressed and his trips into neighboring villages had grown more frequent, James had spent less and less time in the carpenter shop. He knew that his brothers did not approve of the thing he was doing. The seed that Simon had planted had taken root and grown, not abundantly, but its sparse offshoots were still thriving. While neither Jude nor Joseph had sufficient confidence in Jesus to ally himself publicly to his cause, their minds were still toying with the possibility that he might, just barely might, be the long-expected retriever of Israel's national glory.

"That's a good yoke," said James finally. "I wish I could make as good a one."

Joseph's thin face flushed with embarrassed pleasure. "You can do other things," he said modestly. "I'd give anything if I could talk in front of people the way you can. Only I wouldn't say the same things you do," he added with a burst of boyish defiance. "I don't think you're being fair to Jesus."

James spread his hands flat on the bench. The muscles of his long fingers tightened. "Do you actually believe," he demanded, "that Simon is right about Jesus?"

Something flared in Joseph's face, like a flame, carefully guarded, fanned by an unexpected gust of wind. James recognized it instantly. He had seen it before, in other faces he had known. In Daniel's, with its ugly scar and burning, unquenchable eyes. In Simon's. In Judas the Galilean's, also, and in Barabbas'. But there it had not been carefully guarded. It had been bold and flaring like a beacon, held high for all the world to see.

"Why not?" replied Joseph in a burst of boyish frankness. "After all, it could be, couldn't it? Just because he happens to be our brother, and a Galilean, that's no sign. Judas was a Galilean, wasn't he? And the Maccabees weren't anything so terribly big to start with—"

"Judas is dead," said James. "So are the Maccabees. None of them succeeded in freeing their country."

"That's because none of them was the real Deliverer," Joseph answered promptly. "When he comes, he can't fail. You believe that, don't you?"

"Yes," said James. "The Sacred Writings all teach that. But isn't it preposterous even to think—"

"Yes, but it could be, couldn't it?" Joseph was so excited that his hands were trembling. "You know yourself he's done wonderful things, and a lot of the people here in Galilee think he may be the Messiah."

"Here in Galilee, yes," said James carefully. "But how about Jerusalem? What do the people there think of him?"

"Why, I don't know. Of course he hasn't been there so much. He hasn't really shown the people what he can do."

"Then why doesn't he?" James answered quickly. "Why didn't he go to Jerusalem last Passover? If he really wants public recognition, why should he keep his actions so secret, hiding himself away up here in an obscure corner of the country? Why doesn't he let the people in Judea see some of the things he can do?"

"That's right," admitted Joseph thoughtfully. "Maybe he's never thought of it that way. It's too bad somebody can't—I wonder if Simon—"

Having planted the seed, James left it to take root. He laid aside his cloak, donned his apron, and took his place beside Joseph at the bench. But he was of little use. Now his were the hands that were weak and fumbling. Joseph's mood of frank, eager intimacy, a tribute to his sudden lowering of the barriers after many months of hostile silence, aroused in him a sense of shame. He felt like a traitor and despised himself for feeling so, knowing that he had only done his duty. And he had said nothing but the truth. If Jesus had been the national leader Joseph hoped he was, he should most certainly be gaining a following in Judea. Jerusalem was the political center of the country. It must be the hub of Israel's future hopes. Did it make any difference that James knew Jesus was not that leader? That if he went to Jerusalem to the Feast of Tabernacles this year, it would only give his enemies a better opportunity to bring him to justice?

James reached for another length of terebinth wood and started all over again with his measurements. His adz had slipped, and he had spoiled the first one. Perhaps Joseph would make no effort to persuade Jesus to go to Jerusalem to the feast, after all. Perhaps his Brother would continue to stay here safely in Galilee. Safely? With Herod Antipas sending spies to watch his every move and squirming worriedly on his meager little throne for fear this bold peasant who dared to call even foxes by their proper names was another John the Baptist risen from the dead? Herod had killed John. He could kill Jesus too, if he happened to want to. At least, the Council in Jerusalem could only punish. It had no power over life and death. But, there! What was he doing? Thinking of his Brother's safety again instead of his duty as an Israelite? Jesus was a heretic, a lawbreaker, an enemy!

James' forehead broke into a cold sweat. He became suddenly conscious that the adz had bitten deeply into his finger, that his blood was creeping across the white surface of the terebinth wood.

Neither James nor his mother went up to the Feast of Tabernacles. Jude and Joseph went, starting two days early, not in the direction of Jerusalem, but toward Capernaum. James knew that they had gone to try to persuade Jesus to go up to the feast with them. He found out later that they had not succeeded, but had joined the Galilean caravan and gone on alone. Jesus, however, had followed later. James waited in an agony of apprehension for the further news that his Brother had been arrested and summoned before the Council!

It did not come. Jude and Joseph returned home, still perplexed, secretive, taciturn, and it was many days before James discovered what had actually happened. Jesus had appeared openly in the Temple, had spoken to large groups gathered in Solomon's Porch. On the last great day of the feast he had done a startlingly dramatic thing.

Just after the priest had poured the water from the golden pitcher and the hallel had been chanted, Jesus had shouted, so that all in the Temple courts could hear: "If anyone thirsts, let him come to me and drink. He who believes in me, as the Scripture has said, out of his heart will flow rivers of living water." James' pulses quickened in spite of himself as he tried to imagine this scene. How gloriously could a moment like that have been made to fit in with the Dream! If only the water that Jesus proposed to give them had been the pure, holy sacrament of the Law!

At some time during the feast officers had been sent to arrest Jesus, but they had not done so. James did not learn why. He only knew that he felt a sharp reflex of two emotions, relief and apprehension. For heresy must not go unpunished. It might even become his duty to help to see that it did not. And when that day came, God pity him!

It was the longest winter, Mary thought, that she had ever known. The early rains, which she had once awaited eagerly because they brought such blessing to the parched, thirsty soil, fell like leaden weights. Sometimes she sat in the doorway, her slight body wrapped in a heavy woolen aba, and tried to count the drops, or closed her eyes and listened to them—soft at first, like the patter of babies' bare feet in dust; then dull and hard and thudding, as if each drop were a bit of clinking metal; then sharper and sharper as they mingled with the rhythmic pulsing of Jude's hammer, beating, pounding. She watched the farmers bring their plows into the shop to have them fitted to new handles, watched them come and take them away again, and wondered idly if the earth was at all like a human heart, if it hurt when a blade tore through it.

But spring came at last, strangely enough, just as it always did. She was amazed to find that the anemones were just as bright a crimson as always, the olive leaves just as pale and shimmering a silver, the sky above the hilltop just as breathtaking, unbelievable a blue.

And with the coming of spring something deep within her awakened.

"I must make you a new cloak before we go up to the Passover," she said one day to James. "The fringe is getting worn on your old one."

James looked at her and drew a long breath. It was a relief to have it decided so simply, the question he had been hopelessly pondering for months. "Yes," he said.

"And I think," continued Mary with decision, "that we will take Jeshua with us this time. He's very young, but somehow I'd like to have him go."

So it was that, when in April, called Nisan, many of the people of Nazareth prepared, as usual, to go to Jerusalem for the annual Feast of the Passover, James, the son of Joseph, and his mother, Mary, and his two brothers, Jude and Joseph, and his little nephew Jeshua, were among them.

3

It was good to be back in Jerusalem. His nostrils full of the sweet savor of incense, his spirits lifted in selfless exaltation with the great, coiling spiral rising from the early morning sacrifice, James left the Temple and set out resolutely down the familiar street toward the School of Shammai. He went alone and with purpose in his every motion, for he had a definite task to perform. Even the crowds, flowing and eddying about him like mountain streams swollen by the spring rains, failed to move him from his remote concentration.

The Temple services with their majestic, solemn ritual, the long days of preparation for this festival of his nation's freedom, had plunged him, cold and irresolute and tormented, into their hot, glowing crucible, from which he had only just now emerged, a new being. He was no longer James, the son of Joseph of Nazareth, one of the great motley throng of pilgrims come to Jerusalem for the Passover, brother of a strange, disturbing man called Jesus. He was the essence of some quality as ageless and inexplicable as his race. He was Abraham laying his bound son on the altar; Moses descending from the mountain to hurl relentless curses on his wayward brother; Jephthah unflinchingly surrendering his beloved daughter in fulfillment of a vow. In short, he was an Israelite about to fulfill his duty to Jehovah, no matter what the cost.

It was Thursday of Passover week. The family had been in Jerusalem now for two days, and as usual they were staying at the house of Clopas. Jesus was, fortunately, not a guest there. He was visiting at the home of some of his new friends in Bethany. But both Simon and Susanna were at home.

James' meeting with Susanna had been more and less disturbing than he had anticipated. More, because he found he had forgotten just how lovely she was—how the long fringe of her lashes swept the smooth-petaled ovals of her cheeks, how her little, firm, pointed breasts rose and fell beneath the blue bodice of her dress, how gently fragrant and completely desirable was her slender, gracefully poised young body. Less, because she seemed to accept the new relationship between them as simply and naturally as the old.

"You're looking thin, James," she had said with genuine, friendly concern on his arrival. And his whole being had leaped into warmth and gratitude, until a few moments later he had seen her gentle eyes light with the same sympathy for the troubles of a loathsome beggar at the gate.

Clopas too, soon after James' arrival, had relieved the situation of all strain and embarrassment. When James seized the first opportunity to suggest awkwardly that, knowing how the family must feel about him, he didn't wish to intrude on their hospitality, his uncle only placed a friendly hand on his shoulder and said: "Let's talk about you and Susanna later, shall we? As for me, I want nothing but the happiness and well-being of both of you. I've made a great many mistakes in my life, and some of them have been in my relationship with you. You're my brother's son, James, and however much we may differ about some things, you will always be welcome in my home."

"Thank you, sir." James was too amazed at the friendliness and humility in his uncle's manner to reply properly. The cool, correct words of explanation, so carefully prepared, died on his lips. The spectacle of Clopas shorn of his mask, the hard, blunt craftiness replaced by kindly consideration, the cynical patronage by sympathy and generosity, was enough to silence one completely. He was even more amazed later to learn that his uncle was reorganizing his business in accordance with some queer notions he had developed, that the men who worked for him were just as much entitled to share in the profits their labors had created as he was himself. More of his Brother's influence, of course. Jesus had always been unreasonably concerned about hirelings of one kind or another—the miserable, underfed pack drivers of rich caravans, the water carriers straining beneath their yokes, even the gangs of dirty, naked slaves, chained together in long, taut rows, dragging stones from the quarries to build Herod's massive palaces and amphitheaters in Sepphoris and Tiberias.

"I'd like to have you go over to Emmaus with me someday while you're here," his uncle told him casually. "Things have changed over there since you knew the place. I'm trying a little experiment—letting the workmen themselves run the shop for a change—with guidance and advice, of course. I go over about once a week to help them to plan things. We're building some new houses now. Like to have you and Jude look at them. In fact, there's enough work there to keep you busy for months, if you wanted to stay. The man in charge of the building project is an Idumaean. You may remember him. Had a brother who was killed about the time you were here."

"You mean you're building houses for those—those miserable workmen!" exclaimed James, remembering the circle of starved gaunt figures that had surrounded him that day in Emmaus.

"No," replied Clopas, "they're building them for themselves. Mary and I plan to move out there as soon as they get enough homes built for all of us. We hope to have quite a community of us there when we get through."

"A community?" echoed James.

"Yes," Clopas smiled. "That's one good thing about the Kingdom of God. You can start a little of it right where you are. You don't have to wait for it to come. Simon seems to think you do, but he's young. Youth always expects trees to grow overnight."

James' first amazement at this inexplicable behavior on the part of his uncle changed to grim determination. Ben Sirach had been right. A philosophy that could make a man like Clopas not only loosen his purse strings but change his whole way of living was dangerous, indeed. You couldn't tell where one of its strange ramifications was going to break out next. Before it got through it might upset the whole basic structure of society!

James had seen little of Simon since their arrival. He assumed that his cousin had been spending most of his time with Jesus. He had seen enough of him, however, to convince him that Simon was living these days in a fever of disappointment, excitement, and anticipation. James could guess why. His cousin was constantly expecting Jesus to rally the multitudes about him, sweep with an avenging host through the city, and drive out the Roman cohorts. On Monday, when Jesus had dramatically driven the despised, profiteering agents of Annas from the courts of the Temple, he had, Simon felt, missed a heaven-sent opportunity. Recklessly in James' hearing he had confided his disappointment to Jude and Joseph.

"He was standing there—you should have seen him!—lashing out with that piece of rope, and those cheating, fawning dupes of Annas' scuttling away as if it had been a two-edged sword! I tell you, we all thought the time had come. What more could he have asked for! The whole city packed with Jewish loyalists, all ready to be touched off, like tinder! Why, it couldn't have failed! Pilate and his Roman garrisons would have been so outnumbered they wouldn't have had a chance."

"Barabbas tried it," Jude put in slowly, "last Passover. And now he is in prison."

"Barabbas!" Simon dismissed his erstwhile hero with a flick of his fingers. "Of course he didn't succeed. Barabbas wasn't the Deliverer, was he? You don't believe Jesus can do it, do you? You're still doubting. But you wait! Wait till tomorrow! You'll see! He must strike soon. If only he doesn't wait too long!"

That had been Tuesday. Tomorrow had come and passed. Now it was Thursday, and James, who had also been waiting, decided to do so no longer. At the suggestion of Ben Sirach, whom he had met in the Temple yesterday, he was going this morning to take counsel with the men who were plotting to arrest his Brother.

He turned in at the familiar gateway, lifted his fingers reverently to the mezuzah on the doorpost, and, removing his sandals, passed quickly inside. Then he moved swiftly, with unerring steps, down the long corridor to a paneled door at the end. He knew where he would find them.

They were sitting in a tight circle about the dais of his old teacher, Rabbi Ben Judah, at least a dozen of them, some of them with familiar faces. A few of them he had gone to school with, Ben Sirach among them. Others had been frequent visitors in the School of Shammai. Still others he vaguely recognized as belonging to the School of Hillel, and remembered having seen them in the Council chamber.

They greeted him with sudden silence, looked at him askance at first, and of course he knew the reason. With his usual arrow-swift directness he came straight to the point, setting their warily cautious minds at rest.

"I know why you are silent," he told them boldly. "You were talking about the man called Jesus, and you think because he is my Brother I would protect him from the punishment he so justly deserves. But I tell you he is no longer my Brother. A man's religion is more sacred than the bonds of blood. It is you who are my brothers. I too am a Pharisee, a servant of Jehovah and a defender of the faith."

"He speaks the truth," confirmed Ben Sirach quickly and described, in brief but glowing terms, what he knew of James' ministry in Galilee. They welcomed him then, made a place for him in the circle, confided to him certain of their plans for the further entanglement and, possibly, the apprehension of the man called Jesus.

"We must teach him a lesson," they told him frankly. "He will probably be reproved, publicly, by the Council. It may even be found necessary—" Here they spoke guardedly, studying his face to see if he really meant what he said, "to confine him for a while in prison. And if you really wish to render a service in the cause of justice—"

James did not flinch. He was ready to do his duty, he told them proudly, his straight young body unbending beneath its long, embroidered Pharisee's cloak, face thin-lipped and stern. Yes, he would even be willing to testify before the Sanhedrin.

"As soon as—say, tomorrow?"

He caught his breath, but his eyes did not waver. Yes. If that was the way things worked out. He would be ready. Even if it should be tomorrow.

They then resumed their conversation which his coming had obviously interrupted, but in a strained and guarded manner. They were discussing the charges that were going to be brought against his Brother in the Council. James sat and listened uneasily. He knew some of them were still wary because of his presence. He followed the arguments intently, hoping for some opportunity to reassure them further.

"Of course," said Ben Judah, looking around the circle carefully, "we must make the most of all this various testimony against him, including things that we know are relatively unimportant. We all recognize, I think, just where we stand. While the arguments we have been discussing here today must of necessity become for the moment the center of our attention, we all realize that there are vaster issues at stake."

A puzzled frown appeared between James' dark, intent eyes. What more important issues could there be, he wondered, than the ones they had been discussing? He thought that in the few moments since he had been listening they had covered the whole case against his Brother—ceremonial defilement, the breaking of the Sabbath, association with Gentiles, the blasphemous forgiving of men's sins.

"Until Monday of this week," put in a stout Pharisee whose pale slits of eyes were almost hidden in the deep folds of his flesh, "I believed the man comparatively harmless. Of course there's always a certain danger from people who go about upsetting custom and tradition, but you might also say there are certain advantages derived therefrom. It keeps the public resentment of authority from being under too severe a pressure. But when he started interfering with our economic system, it was plain that something had to be done."

James stifled an exclamation. He could not believe his ears. If there was one action of his Brother's that every devout Jew would heartily approve, it was surely his clearing the Temple courts, if only for a few hours, of the shameful, degrading trafficking of Annas' despised profiteers. He waited for the group's instant outraged reaction.

"Yes," agreed the stout man's neighbor on the left, one of the scribes who had accompanied Ben Sirach on his mission into Galilee. "But don't forget I warned all of you long ago that if he was allowed to persist in his radical blabbings, the time would come when none of your financial investments would be safe. Now maybe you'll believe me. If this Temple-cleansing business were to be carried much further, how long do you think you'd be getting your hundred percent dividends from the money you invested in the booths of Annas?"

"There's another side to that too," threw in Ben Sirach. "This time he happened to use a tangible weapon, a little cord of rope. But there are other weapons just as potent that he's been wielding right and left. How long do you think a poor peasant will be willing to pay a silver denarius for a couple of pigeons to sacrifice to Jehovah if he once thinks through some of this Galilean's rash statements, such as the one about God's being a Spirit, with the implication that he can be worshiped anywhere a man pleases?"

"He's an enemy of the *status quo*," said another Pharisee decisively. "That's apparent to all of us. However much we may deplore the Roman occupation, the subjection of our beloved country, I am sure that we are all agreed that at this time nothing is to be gained by change. It is better to keep things as they are."

James stared from one to the other of the faces before him, from the round, fleshy mass with its little slits of eyes to the scribe's beside him, thin and cold and narrow-lipped—Ben Sirach's, lean and arrogant and intense—on around the circle. The looks on their faces were unmistakable. Stern and white-lipped, he impulsively rose to his feet.

"My Brother," he said with clear emphasis, "has broken the Law of Israel. By his words and actions he has betrayed the faith of our fathers. For the sake of that faith which must be kept pure and inviolate, that Law which must be written in the heart of every Israelite before the divine promise of deliverance can be fulfilled, my Brother's heresy must be punished. Is this not so?"

He looked straight at Ben Judah as he spoke, and the old rabbi returned his gaze for a full moment without answering. Perhaps he was remembering another time when the two had spoken together, words that had throbbed in the air between them, words now strangely pregnant with meaning.

"Who is your brother?" Ben Judah had asked.

"His name is Jesus. Jesus of Nazareth."

"Never heard of him."

"Perhaps not. But I believe, sir, that you will hear of him."

Ben Judah's gaze was the first to waver. The lids drooped over his keen black eyes, leaving his face looking very old and drawn, its skin parchment-thin. He slowly twined the fringe of his embroidered cloak about one white, transparent finger.

"Of course, my son," he said. "You have stated the case just as we would all wish it. In fact, you have stated it so accurately, so concisely, that there is nothing more to be said."

Alone in the street again, James laughed to himself bitterly. And he had thought their zeal to be a pure flame burning before the Holy of Holies! They cared nothing for the Law, these pretenders, these gluttons who fattened themselves on the meager savings of the poor, these sticklers for the Law who made themselves so clean on the outside but were full of filthiness within, these—these "whited sepulchers"!

As the word leaped to his mind, he stopped short, aghast. Well—suppose he had been thinking in terms of his Brother's accusations. Suppose Jesus had been right about some things. He was still a heretic. And James had suffered disillusionment before. He could take it. It meant only that now he must stand alone. Regardless of what other men might do or say, he was still a servant of Jehovah. He had promised to testify in the Council against his Brother, and he would do it, because, God pity him, it was his duty. Though he were the only man in all Israel who kept the Law with a singleness of purpose, he would be true to the faith that was in him.

"It will be good," said Mary, "for so many of us to be together again. It's been such a long time since all my sons sat down at the same table to eat the Passover feast."

James stared uncomprehendingly at his mother. "What did you say?" he asked deliberately.

She repeated it for him. But it was the radiance of her face, rather than her words, that told him what she meant. She expected Jesus to come here to Clopas' house. She expected her two oldest sons to sit down and eat the Passover supper together.

And why not? James asked himself after the first astounded dismay had given place to grim apprehension. What stupidity on his part not to have foreseen such a probability and acted accordingly! For were not Clopas and Mary in sympathy with Jesus' teachings, and was not Susanna one of the women who followed him?

Susanna. James found her presence almost more disturbing than the prospect of his Brother's. The sight of the slender, fair young figure moving so familiarly about the house; the smiling, serene face, concerned, it seemed, with everything and everybody except himself; the firm, white hands deftly spreading the festal table, preparing the sacred lamps, performing a hundred and one little services for the comfort of the many guests. All these things set his pulses racing, filled him with an agony of hopelessness and jealousy.

In spite of her smiling serenity Susanna was, he knew, worried. About Jesus, no doubt. And well she might be. Simon too had been worried last night. He had come in hurriedly, snatched a hasty meal, and departed, presumably to that unknown haven where Jesus had secreted himself. But mingled with the worry, there had been that air of impatience, of subdued excitement, almost of elation. For the Zealot in him would not be quelled. He was still expecting a miracle to happen.

Poor, deluded Simon! And poor Susanna! Would that look of calm serenity be shaken from her face if he should suddenly take her by the shoulders and say: "You're afraid it's coming, aren't you, the end of this pretty little dream of yours? And you're right. Sooner than you think. Did you actually think he could defy our very religion and suffer no consequences? Monday he brazenly ordered the high priest's henchmen out of the Temple, and, whatever we may think of them, Annas and his party have power. Tuesday he antagonized the most prominent religious leaders of the city. And tomorrow—tomorrow—"

The pleasant fragrance of fresh-roasting meat filled the house. The paschal lamb, which Clopas had taken to the Temple that afternoon to be killed according to the ceremonial law, was turning on its pomegranate spit, carefully placed so that it did not come in contact with the oven. The other things too were ready for the feast—the unleavened cakes, the bitter herbs, the mixture of vinegar into which the herbs must be dipped, the wine for the four cups. The lamps also were trimmed and ready.

Mary hovered over the table, anxious that everything should be just right. At the sound of each approaching footstep her eyes sought the door, eagerly at first, then hopefully, finally with a fevered desperation.

"He must come," she kept telling herself. Why, the Passover was sacred to the home! All over the city families were sitting down together, congregated from every part of Judea and Galilee, even from those Jewish outposts in the far corners of the world. They were all here, James and Jude and Simon and Joseph, all her sons. All but one.

As the moments passed and still he did not come, the intense lines of eagerness on her face deepened into weariness, and when the time came for the males of the household to sit down to the feast, she took her place listlessly among the women, scarcely noticing when Clopas, reclining at the head of the table, partook of the first cup and pronounced the majestic opening benediction. The lamb, symbolic of Israel's deliverance, was brought in, steamily fragrant, and Clopas, dipping the bitter herbs into the vinegar mixture, handed some to each person seated at the table, beginning with James, who, by reason of the unexplained absence of Clopas' own sons, sat on his uncles's left.

His face looks hard, thought Mary, watching her son from the shadows where she sat. *And it is hate that makes it so. Oh, what have I done, what have I failed to do, that my son should hate his brother? If only they could have sat down to the sacred meal together!*

Clopas lifted the second cup. "This is the bread of misery which our fathers ate in the land of Egypt. All that are hungry, come and eat; all that are needy, come—"

Hungry. Needy. Yes, that was what she was. Hungry and needy for the sight and presence of her son. She didn't care what he had done, how many laws he had broken. She knew it now. All these months she had been eating bread of misery. The unleavened cake was dry dust in her mouth. The wine was bitter on her lips.

A high childish voice broke in on her thoughts. "Wherein does this night differ from other nights?" asked little Jeshua in his prescribed role as the youngest child at the feast. "For on other nights we may eat leavened and unleavened bread, but tonight only unleavened."

Once, long ago, her own oldest son had been the youngest child in their household and had asked that question. She closed her eyes and, to the rhythm of Clopas' slightly droning voice recounting the long narrative of his nation's birth, her mind drifted back over the years, back—back—She could see him sitting beside Joseph, his dark brown eyes now grave with solemnity, now dancing with merriment and laughter. How he had loved the gay, jingling rhythm of the *Chad Gadya* chorus! If she kept her eyes closed very tightly, she could almost imagine she was hearing it tonight—his clear treble rising gaily above all the rest.

"*Chad Gadya! Chad Gadya!* One only kid of the goat! And a cat came and devoured the kid which my father bought for two *zuzim*. *Chad Gadya! Chad Gadya!* And a dog came and bit the cat which had devoured the kid which my father bought for two *zuzim*. *Chad Gadya!*"

"Where is he?" her heart cried soundlessly. "He knows we are here. He must know. Why hasn't he come, on this night of all nights, to keep the sacred tryst with his mother and brothers?"

His mother and brothers—

Who is my mother and who are my brothers? For whoever does the will of my Father in heaven is my brother and sister and mother.

The feast was eaten and cleared away and the evening far spent, but still Simon and his brother James did not come home. The wife of Clopas looked worried.

"I don't see where they can be. Of course it's natural that they might want to eat the feast with Jesus, but, wherever they were, they should be home by now. I've a good mind to run over to John's house and see if he and his brother have also been away. Salome and Zebedee would be there, and they would know."

Susanna's eyes danced. "If anybody knew their whereabouts, it would probably be Salome," she said without malice. "But I wouldn't worry if I were you," she added more gently. "They've just changed their plans, that's all."

"But it isn't like them. I—I can't help wondering—"

"Hush!" cautioned Susanna with a quick glance at Mary's still, white face. Going to her, she put a strong young arm about her shoulders. "Come, Aunt Mary. You're tired and need your rest. Let me take you up to your room on the housetop."

Mary accompanied her with a docility born of indifference. Dutifully she closed her eyes, permitted herself to fall into a troubled sleep. Then suddenly—hours later, or was it minutes, or only seconds?—she was abruptly, vitally awake. Firmly, purposefully, she dressed herself, drew a cloak about her, and, leaving the little housetop chamber, crept softly down the outside stairs.

"Yes—yes—" As the voice that called to her had been inarticulate, so now was her answer. "Just a minute. Wait for me—wait for me— my son. Mother's coming!"

At the foot of the stairs she paused uncertainly, then a waft of fragrance came to her out of the night, and she turned toward it gratefully. Of course. The garden. Need she have questioned, she who knew him so well? If he were in trouble, needing help, where else would he go but to a hilltop?—or to a garden?

The coolness was like the touch of a hand on her brow. She moved forward into it, closing her eyes, letting the fragrance steal about her like an enveloping, invisible presence. Yes, he was here. Not to be seen or heard, but only felt, as she had once felt the burden of him, infinitely, agonizingly sweet, beneath her breast.

"Here I am," she breathed softly. "Mother's here—little one."

She stretched out her hands and felt the gnarled, twisted trunk of an olive tree. Its little pale-silver leaves made a shimmering cloud above her in the darkness. Kneeling beside it, she pressed her face hard against it, until the bruising roughness cut deeply into the tender flesh of her forehead.

Pain. She welcomed it, embraced it hungrily, certain that it was out of some peculiar agony that she had heard her son call. Pain. She had welcomed it once, long ago in a stable, had drunk deep, intoxicating draughts of it, for his sake.

Now here, again, with her face pressed against the gnarled trunk, she seemed to enter once more into her first hour of travail. As his being had once been merged with hers, so hers became suddenly, inexplicably merged into his, and by that same sacrament of pain that had set his spirit free, there came to her also a knowledge of release and a strange new sense of peace.

Blind that she had been, thinking that a mother had to comprehend, to understand completely, when all that was necessary was to love!

4

It was Salome who brought the news the next morning, a strange-looking, unnatural Salome with her headdress all awry, her garments untidy, and her usual bustling energy dissolved into a flabby helplessness.

"May the Lord have pity on us!" she exclaimed, dropping down on the stone settle in the courtyard. "It's happened. Oh, the Lord have mercy upon him—and upon us!"

"Is it Jesus?" asked Susanna in a whisper. And Salome, unable to speak further, only nodded.

With deliberation and poise Mary went straight to her sister and took her firmly by the shoulders. "Salome," her voice was low and quiet. "Salome, what has happened to my son?"

James stepped forward. Fearful of missing a message that might come from Ben Sirach, he had not gone with his brothers and Clopas to the early morning sacrifice.

"Yes," he said sternly, his tall figure suddenly towering above the two women. "Stop being hysterical and answer her."

Salome rallied. "Nothing, yet," she admitted with an almost reluctant regaining of composure. "But they say the men came and took him in the night and carried him away with them. And they say he wouldn't even lift his hand to stop them but just stood there. Oh, dear, what's going to become of us! They've taken him somewhere, and James and John are gone too. And they say—"

"They say!" repeated James witheringly. "Have you come here to stir up the household with nothing but idle gossip?"

"But they *have* taken Jesus," Salome persisted, turning with relief from James' sternness and Mary's still whiteness to the shocked, sympathetic faces of Susanna and the wife of Clopas. "John sent a messenger to tell us. The soldiers of the high priest went out secretly and surrounded him when he was in a garden with his disciples."

The face of Mary came suddenly, startlingly alive, as if illumined by a light from within. "You say Jesus was in a garden?"

"Yes. Among the olive trees on the slope across the Valley of the Kidron. He goes there often to pray and meditate and be alone."

"Among the olive trees," repeated Mary softly. Then she turned and went slowly out through the door of the courtyard into the garden. Susanna started to follow, but her mother with a quick gesture restrained her.

"Not now. She doesn't realize yet. She's moving in a kind of dream. Let her be."

"Where is he now?" asked James quickly.

"Oh, dear, I don't know!" Salome was again close to hysteria. "I tried to find out, but nobody seemed to know what happened after they took him before the Council!"

It was James' turn now to come alive. His dark eyes probed her terrified uncertainty. "You say they took him before the Council?"

"Yes. That is, I think so. Somebody said—"

James turned quickly toward the door. "Then I must go. I promised. They may need me to testify. Even now I may be too late."

Susanna followed, clinging to him breathlessly. "Oh, yes—do go! You have influence with the scribes and elders, James. If you'll only testify for him, it might save him from—from something terrible!"

His senses flamed at her touch, but his eyes were cold. "You think I could testify *for* him?" he asked slowly.

She recoiled as if he had struck her. "James," she whispered. "You—you wouldn't—"

The other women gazed at him in horror, as if he had suddenly been stricken with leprosy. Salome stretched out a quivering, accusing finger.

"You too! You are one of those who have stirred up the people against Jesus! I knew you had opposed him, but I never would have believed this! You have betrayed your own brother!"

James surveyed them all calmly. He felt as if a knife were slowly turning within him, but he did not flinch. "My brother," he said, "is he who keeps the Law of a just and righteous Jehovah."

"There is a higher Law than that," said Susanna clearly.

Her eyes were like two lights shining steadily toward him through a great darkness. He made a fumbling gesture toward them. "What could be higher?" he asked earnestly.

"The Law of a merciful and loving Father."

He looked at her a long moment, intensely, as if trying desperately to span the distance between them. Then slowly he shook his head and turned abruptly toward the door.

The lights in the girl's eyes flickered and went out, "He's gone," she said bleakly.

"Yes," said Mary, returning quietly from the garden. "And we must go too."

"Where?" demanded Salome in sudden terror.

"To be with my son," answered Mary, "with Jesus."

"But you can't," wailed her sister. "It isn't safe. You can't tell what they might do to us. Even all his followers ran away except my John, and I don't dare think what's become of him!"

Mary looked at her tranquilly, a little pityingly. It seemed so strange to see Salome's bustling competence reduced to quivering helplessness, almost as strange as seeing the sensitive, thoughtful James frozen into unforgiving hatred.

"My son is in trouble," she said kindly to her sister. "Can't you understand? Nothing else matters. I must go to him."

"Oh, why did he come to Jerusalem!" exclaimed the wife of Clopas with almost a return of the old petulance. "He must have known that he was walking into the very face of danger! If only he had remained in Galilee, he would be safe."

Mary lifted her head proudly. "My son has never been afraid of danger."

Salome stared at her sister, for the moment forgetting her own anxiety. "What's happened to you, Mary?" she asked curiously. "You sound as if you believed in Jesus. What's happened to make you understand?"

Mary shook her head. "I don't entirely," she said quietly. "Some of the things he does and says are as strange to me as every line and feature of his body are familiar. When I try with my mind to follow the way he has chosen, it is not always clear. But that doesn't matter right now. He is my son, and I must go to him."

The light kindled again slowly in Susanna's eyes. "I'll go with you, Aunt Mary," she said simply.

And together they went out into the street.

James went straight to the Temple. Early as it was, the streets near the Temple area were thronged with the people who had gathered for the early morning sacrifice. James moved cautiously among them, careful even in his haste to avoid all forms of contamination, such as going too close to a Gentile or a sick or crippled person or an unclean animal, for such contact would have prevented his partaking of the festive sacrifice later in the day.

But he acted subconsciously, not deliberately. Even when he passed through the great Royal Porch with its double colonnade and entered the Court of the Gentiles, though he stopped to lift his gaze reverently to the Temple itself, rising sheer and white and glittering, though his nostrils quivered at the mingled odors of incense and burning flesh, and though his lips fashioned a prayer, he was not conscious of what he said and did. For both body and mind were consumed by a white-hot singleness of purpose.

Passing through the Court of the Gentiles, he came to that particular room in the section occupied by the booths of Annas where the Council was in the habit of meeting, wondering if he were too late. Jesus, Salome had said, had been taken before the Council. But the chamber was empty. It showed no signs of recent use.

Turning away, he felt a soft touch on his shoulder. "We were looking for you, James Ben Joseph."

James turned swiftly. It was Rabbi Ben Judah. Had he not been so intent on his purpose, he would have been shocked anew by the changes that the brief years of his absence had wrought. So fragile seemed the old man's features, so transparent and tenuous the parchment-thin flesh stretched above them, that they looked as if the lightest touch might crumple them to dust. Even the contact of his fingers seemed to impart a penetrating chillness. Yet life lingered robustly in the pale, smiling lips, the gleaming eyes, almost as if it derived an ironic pleasure out of the paradox it had created—that one who had rebelled so relentlessly against change should have become the living prototype of the greatest change of all!

"Am I too late?" asked James quickly. "I came as soon as I heard. But the Council room—it seems to be empty."

"The Council has already met," returned the old rabbi, smiling.

"Not in the chamber. At the high priest's house."

"Did you—did they—"

"Yes," replied Ben Judah, smiling again. His eyes, James thought, were like the windows in a closed house, gleaming but oddly tenantless. He laid his hand again on the young man's arm, gently, almost caressingly. "Come, James ben Joseph."

James went with his former teacher through the Temple courts and out at the western gate. They had to make their way slowly at first, as against a current, weaving their way through a crowd of worshipers approaching the Temple. But as they passed over the bridge spanning the Tyropoeon and into the narrow streets of the upper city, James felt a subtle change. They were no longer moving against the current but with it. It surrounded them, lifted them as on a slowly rising tide, bore them along on its crest.

The mood too and the tempo of the crowd had changed. It elbowed and pushed and jostled. It muttered to itself, softly, unintelligibly, like the barely perceptible rumblings of an approaching storm. The warm wave of fervent devotion which had seemed to draw the worshipers together, sweeping them upward toward the lofty, smoking pinnacles of the Temple, was no longer perceptible. Somewhere along the way it had changed to a deep undercurrent, chill and swift and sinister.

James lifted his eyes to the frowning, glittering battlements of what had once been Herod's palace, now the *praetorium,* office and seat of Roman authority in Jerusalem. He clutched the old rabbi's arm.

"Where are we going?" he asked sharply.

The heavy black eyebrows lifted in quizzical arches above the vacant windows. "You mean you don't know? They are trying your brother before the Roman governor. It was to formulate our charges against him that the Council met this morning. He had already been tried before a committee of the scribes and elders—and condemned."

"But—" James spoke with sudden stiffened lips, "why? Why should they be taking him to Pilate? The Council has jurisdiction over all religious matters. It can render its own verdicts and decree its own punishments."

The windows were still gleaming but no longer tenantless. Before James' stricken gaze they had become peopled with a thousand ironic, grinning shapes of torment.

"Except death," replied Ben Judah.

The next hours were to James a series of pictures flashed against the background of his torn and tortured senses—rough-cut and jagged, possessing no sequence, bearing no relation to time or space. Brief and sharp in outline, their straight, harsh lines cut clean as if by a scalpel, scored deeply in gaunt grays and blacks and raw crimsons.

He was standing beneath the great balcony of the *praetorium,* looking up at two familiar faces, two faces etched sharply against a vast confusion of mass and sound and color. Barabbas and his Brother. One bold and dark and arrogant; the other—heaven help him, had he ever thought they had anything in common?"

He lifted his hands, pushed hard against the human wall that shut him in on both sides, pressed upon him in front, smothered him so that he could hardly breathe.

"Easy, James ben Joseph," said the old rabbi's voice in his ear. "What are you trying to do?"

"I've got to get through here," he gasped, tossing off the thin, parchmentlike fingers. "Got to tell them something, make them understand—"

The wall was soft and yielding, but impenetrable. "Men of Israel!" he shouted hoarsely, but against the clamor of the crowd his voice was like a murmur. He drew in long, choking breath and in desperation tried again. "Men of Israel, for God's sake, please listen!"

A firm hand was clamped over his mouth. The fingers were not dry and tenuous like parchment, but thick and soft and moist with the sweat of excitement.

"What's going on here?" demanded Ben Sirach roughly. "Can't you keep him in hand?"

"I told you we couldn't depend on him," said Ben Judah with withering contempt. "And you thought he'd make a good witness in the Council!"

"Well, at least it's too late for him to do any damage!" Ben Sirach's dark eyes shone with satisfaction. "Hear that mob shout for Barabbas? We've got them now right where we want them. What dupes people are when you put a little pressure in the right places! Listen to that, James? Hear what they're shouting?"

James heard. The sweat poured off his face. Beneath the band of his phylactery the pulses at his temples throbbed suffocatingly. "You didn't tell me you meant to kill him," he said hoarsely.

Ben Sirach raised his eyebrows mockingly. "I told you he must be silenced. Even I know him better than to think he could be silenced any other way."

"But do you hear what they're saying? They—they want to— to *crucify*—"

"I'll take care of him," said Ben Sirach in a low voice to the old rabbi. "He won't make any trouble, I promise you. You've done your duty. Go back home and rest. Now pull yourself together, James ben Joseph. Remember your duty to the Law of Jehovah!"

The pulsing in his forehead became a steady, rhythmic, whirring beat which made him wince sharply at every stroke. He was standing before a great gate, looking through, and the beating in his temples was the sound made by the whipping, curling motions of a lash curving about raw flesh. He pushed his way through a knotted mass of bodies, his arm almost grazing the spear of a bewildered Roman sentry, and flung himself at the gate.

"You heathen dogs! I'll teach you. In the name of the God of Israel, stop, I say!"

The hand of Ben Sirach bit deeply into the flesh of his arm. "Ben Joseph! Fool! Shut your mouth! Have you gone mad?"

"They're flogging him, can't you see? They're flogging my Brother!"

"Suppose they are. What do you think you can do about it? Be quiet, can't you?"

"But it's my Brother—my Brother, I tell you! Let me go! I—I'll change places with him! I'll do something—"

"Fool! Softhearted, blubbering idiot! Do you want these soldiers laying hands on you, a Pharisee? Quick! Down this alleyway!"

The beating at his temples became a dull, steady pounding, the sound of a heavy hammer striking hard and firm upon a nail. It thudded in long, measured strokes through his body, each one like a rapier point thrust deeper and deeper into the very core of his being.

He was alone now. There was no need for Ben Sirach's restraining touch. There was nothing James could do. There was nothing any man could do. Even the slow, interminable motion of one's feet— creeping, shuffling, stumbling, climbing, feeling the dust sift thinly, thickly, cloggingly into one's sandals. That was over too. There was no longer any need for motion. He stood very quietly, unresisting, while bleak comprehension swept over his tortured spirit.

So this was to be the end. Another rough slab of wood stretching its two gaunt arms against a gray horizon. And the figure of a man upon it. The end of another dream. And of another dreamer. Nothing unusual about that. The horizons of his boyhood had been graven with those same rough slabs, each one marking the end of a dream and of its dreamer. Nothing to distinguish this one from all others. Nothing in that steady, rhythmic pounding to touch him, so that his every pulse beat became a nail driven into his own quivering flesh. Nothing in that slow, agonized ebbing of a man's life to drain the very life streams of his being. Nothing—Dear God, everything! For this time the dreamer was his own Brother.

The pounding at his temples became so intense that he could bear it no longer, and without conscious volition he tore off the strap binding his phylactery, letting it fall unheeded at his feet. The sweat ran down his body, clung to his chilled fingers, and he wiped them automatically, leaving grimy, wrinkled marks on his long, immaculate Pharisee's cloak.

Suddenly he felt a fierce, swift surging of desire to push through the crowd, to stumble blindly up the grim hilltop, to clasp his arms about the beloved figure on the rough wooden slab, to say—God pity him, what could he say?

The fierce surging receded, and bleak darkness swept over him.

When he went back long afterward, the hilltop was strangely deserted. After the day's mad, panting confusion it lay relaxed and quiescent as a spent, exhausted child, its grim toys lying meaningless and forgotten on the ground. Two men were there, bending over a still figure. They lifted mute, inquiring faces.

"He was my Brother," said James simply.

The older of the two, a tall man with spare, patrician features and tortured eyes, nodded understandingly. James recognized him as Nicodemus, a member of one of the oldest and most highly respected Jerusalem families. He had seen him often in the Council.

"Come with us," he said to James. "We need another to help us."

James bowed his head gratefully. His tears rained down on the beloved, serene, familiar face. So many times he had seen him lying just like that, the lines of the day's weariness smoothed away in sleep, a little smile playing about his lips, tenderly, amusedly reminiscent yet vibrantly expectant, as if he were dreaming of a full day well spent and of an even more adventurous day yet to come. For a fleeting moment the years slipped away, and James was a child again.

He's tired, he thought with tender, swift compunction. *He's had a hard day. We must be careful not to awaken him too early.*

Then, as he stooped to lift his corner of the clean linen cloth, awareness smote him, and again cold darkness swept over him.

PART FIVE
Brother

1

The execution of an obscure Galilean agitator, whether religious or political, was no stupendous event. It made but a momentary ripple upon that even surface of cult and custom and tradition into which the opponents of change have virtuously through the centuries flung all such agitators, blissfully unaware that those same harmless ripples release the energy that will set vast tides in motion. Jerusalem, its proud coronet of smoke an incense not even blown awry by an event that was destined to crumble thrones and reduce crowns to dust, merely smoothed its rumpled skirts, brushed the lint of peasants' garments from its fingers, and went on about its aloof, traditional business.

The leading members of the Great Council, satisfied that their way of life had again been made safe from alteration, washed their hands the prescribed number of times, assembled an exultant crowd, erstwhile a howling mob, and departed to the spot across the Kidron where the day before the first barley sheaf had been marked for cutting. Arrived at the appointed place, the throng surrounded the three prescribed reapers with their sickles and baskets and shouted their enthusiastic affirmatives to the prescribed questions.

"Has the sun gone down?"

"With this sickle?"

"Into this basket?"

"On this Holy Day?"

"Shall I reap?"

"Yea, yea!" responded the ecstatic voices which but a few hours before had hoarsely shouted, "Crucify!"

Then they passed back into the city and through the gates of the Temple, shouting with religious fervor, shunning the outcast leper, muttering curses at the hated heathen overlord, reviling the despised Samaritan, seeking divine favor by throwing pittances into the laps of ever-present beggars, keeping the regulation six feet from every miserable foreigner, ecstatically proclaiming their divine birthright of freedom, as their fathers and their forefathers had done before them, on the evening of the fifteenth of Nisan, for centuries.

By sunset the hilltop outside the city was silent and deserted, its grim work finished. Apparently unconscious of its three gaunt shadows, the white glittering mass of the Temple arose, proud, serene, aloof, jealously gathering unto itself all the waning light of a departing day and era. A white-clad priest mounted to the topmost pinnacle and, poised like a toy puppet between earth and heaven, blew on his silver trumpet the thin, flutelike notes that proclaimed the coming of the festive Sabbath. And as the day drew to a close there were but few people who recalled the incident on the skull-shaped hill with more than passing interest and morbid curiosity.

Annas and Caiaphas, keeping their sensitive, diplomatic fingers carefully tuned to the pulse of public opinion and computing to a nicety just when it would be safe to move the family business back into the Temple booths and lift back to normal the prices on sacrificial lambs and pigeons: "Regrettable that it should have happened at the beginning of Passover. Let's see, how did the sale of lambs compare this year with last? Tut, tut, all that difference? But just think what the fellow might have accomplished if he had lived! Tell that to the shareholders!"

Barabbas, returning to his hideout above the Jericho road, exulting in his amazing freedom, his keen mind already plotting new underground ventures against the army of occupation: "That blind fool of a dreamer! Nailed to a gibbet when he might be sitting on Herod's throne! If I'd had his chance!"

Pilate, his hard, brittle armor of superstitious vanity pricked by the strangely penetrating weapon of nonresistance: "A strange man! Even now I don't know what to make of him. I can't get away from him. His face still haunts me. Standing there so tall and serene and silent, so invincible! That's it, that's the word I've been trying to get! By Jupiter, he was invincible!"

A soldier, tossing down his weapons in his bare barracks: "I tell you I've never seen anything like it! I've seen men die before—brave men, cursing the enemy with spears stuck through them! But this man—No, confound you, I'm not growing soft! Only this man was different, I tell you. He reminded me of someone—someone I met a long time ago, up on a road in Galilee."

A little group of women, among them Mary, the wife of Clopas, and Salome, and Susanna, returning slowly to the city, huddled together in their grief: "Can you remember the place?" "One of those men looked like James, I thought, but of course it couldn't have been." "Look, the sun is already setting! We must hurry to make our preparations for the Sabbath." "I'm glad it's such a lovely spot, aren't you? A garden!"

A comparative handful of his devoted friends and followers and relatives, most of them terrified for their lives, all of them bewildered, uncertain. But none of them more stunned, more stricken, more completely solitary in his loneliness, than was James, his brother.

The streets were nearly empty now and very dark. Twice that day the sun had hidden its face, once in an impenetrable cloud, again in a repentant blaze of glory, pointing long, crimson fingers clear across the sky. The Holy City, suddenly aware, perhaps, that that crimson blaze had been but the first of a long array of pointing fingers, interminable and accusing, lay cowering and silent in the darkness.

"Here! Look out where you're going, can't you! Curses on you!"

James knocked against a figure in a narrow street and knew it for a beggar by its touch, its imprecations, its clutching fingers. Absently he reached into his girdle, took out a couple of coins, and dropped them toward the crouching shape. The imprecations changed to benedictions, but he walked on unheeding—through the dark, deserted streets of the city's remote suburbs, along dim, starlit ribbons of country road, back into the holiday confusion of crowded thoroughfares. He walked aimlessly, not caring where he went.

He was like an empty vessel, out of which all emotion has been drained. The world too was a thing of emptiness, the heavens a vast, inverted shell of nothingness. The very dust over which he walked seemed a hostile thing, since it had added this day to the measure, already full, of human suffering. It had blinded eyes already dim and smarting, mingled itself with the salty, sharp, bitter tangs of blood and sweat and gall, ground itself deep into the defenseless pores of quivering flesh. Dust. The sight of a thornbush. The fresh, acrid odor of green wood.

"Will these things always be reminding me?" he asked himself dumbly. "Will I ever again be able to hear the sound of hammer striking on a nail without—"

The footsteps of a Roman sentry echoing hollowly through the stillness beat against his senses, receded, died away, became irrevocably mingled with those other sounds already indelibly recorded on his consciousness: the shrill, harsh clamor of a mob demanding, "Crucify!"; the scuffling and stumbling of interminable pairs of feet; the rhythmic, whirring, whipping, brutal flaying of a lash.

A light hand touched his arm, and a face, caught in the pale blur of a lighted window, peered up into his. A woman's face, boldly etched in crimson, unveiled, provocative. He shook off her clinging grasp impatiently, let her painted features slip forgotten into the darkness. But he could not erase the memory of those other faces: Ben Sirach's, smug and cold and righteous. Susanna's, stricken yet calm, like snow in moonlight. Mary's. The Magdalene's. Queer! He had never supposed she could possibly look like that, so pure! That other, so strangely, so magnificently tranquil, which he had only just now looked upon in the garden of Joseph the Arimathaean.

Once he had seen Simon's face too, through a rift in the crowd. Piteous, dazed it had been, yet amazingly, dauntlessly expectant. Poor, mistaken, stubborn Zealot! He had probably still hoped to the end that his idol would descend in triumph, magically change those degrading nails into spearheads, and rout the Roman legions. Strange that he, James, his bitter antagonist, his enemy, should have known him better in this, his last hour, than his friends! God in heaven, what his Brother must have suffered! To have tried all these months and then not to have been able to convince them! Not to have made them understand even yet that he was less interested in all the vast pomp and panoply of Caesar than in those two gaunt wrecks that had hung on either side of him!

It was the thought of his mother, Mary, that led his feet at last to pursue a definite course. Where was she? With Jude? With Susanna or her mother? With John, to whose care Jesus had committed her, believing, no doubt, James accused himself bitterly, that he who had been unfaithful as a brother could hardly be depended upon as a loyal son?

Pushing aside the heavy, embroidered curtain forming the entrance to the living room in Clopas' house, he was relieved at first to find the room empty. A lamp was burning dimly, a fire glowing softly in the brazier, and Mary's blue cloak was lying on the back of the settle. The warmth, the quiet, reached out and engulfed him, melted the hardness within him. He groped toward it blindly, flung himself on his knees beside the cloak, and buried his face in his hands. It was so that Susanna found him.

"James—James, my dear—"

And then suddenly her arms were about him, his head pressed hard against her breast, his body shaken by long, convulsive sobs. She made no effort to soothe him, only held him quietly, her cheek held gently against his thick, disordered hair, until finally the storm of long-pent emotion exhausted itself.

He raised his face, unabashed because it bore the ravages of tears. "He is dead," he said dully.

"I know."

"It was his enemies. And I was one of them who hated him, who killed him."

She shook her head. Her clear eyes were steady, compelling, like the glow of a lighthouse beam glimpsed across stormy waves. "Yes, dear," she said gently. "You misunderstood him, and you hated him for a while. But you never stopped loving him."

He lifted his face toward hers, eagerly, uncertainly, even as his troubled spirit struggled gratefully upward toward the assurance in her troubled eyes. "You really believe that?"

"I know it," she said quietly. "You have always loved him, just as he has loved you. There has never been a moment when you wouldn't gladly have given yourself to save him."

Yes. Susanna was right. In his heart James avowed the truth, freely, gratefully. He loved his Brother. God knew he loved him! He would gladly have taken his place today—bared his back to their pitiless scourging, bowed his shoulders to the weight of his burden, yes, even suffered the agony of those nails driven into his hands. But what good was the knowledge of his love now, when it was too late? He had failed his Brother when he had most needed him. At Nazareth, when friends and fellow townsmen had turned against him. At Capernaum, when his enemies had first plotted to destroy him. At Jerusalem.

"I think Jesus understood how you felt," said Susanna gently. "He wouldn't have wanted you to follow him, feeling as you did. He always wanted people to believe in him, to count the cost before deciding to follow him."

"But I could have been loyal to him," returned James, in bitter self-reproach. "I could have shared his failure, his sorrow, his defeat. I could have loved him even if I didn't understand why he said and did the things he did."

He suddenly rose to his feet, laid his hands firmly on the girl's shoulders. "Tell me, why did he do it?" His voice held an agony of entreaty, "Why did he choose this strange, bewildering, lonely way to travel? He must have known where it would lead. Why did he do it? Why?"

But before Susanna could answer, Salome entered from the courtyard, wan-faced but immaculately neat of dress, bustling competence reduced through grief and fright to flustered nervousness.

"Oh! Is that you, James? I shouldn't think you'd have the face to show yourself around here, after what you've done! Perhaps you're planning to have all the rest of us arrested now, your mother included. Is that what you've been doing?"

James' hands dropped reluctantly. "No," he replied shortly. Then with sudden swift compunction he remembered. "Where's mother?" he demanded. "Isn't there somebody with her? Have you left her all alone?"

"A fine time for you to be thinking of her!" reproved Salome tartly. "She might as well have no sons for all the help you've been to her. If it hadn't been for my John—"

"Aunt Mary is here," put in Susanna quickly. "She's resting, I think. Mother is with her. We are all grateful to John for taking care of her and bringing her home."

"Resting!" exclaimed Salome incredulously. "How can she! After seeing her own son—" She shuddered convulsively. "I should think she'd be beside herself with grief."

"Perhaps she is." Susanna's clear eyes looked troubled. "She doesn't seem to realize what has happened. She talks as if she thought he—he were still alive!"

James uttered a smothered cry. "God pity her!" he muttered hoarsely.

Salome regarded her nephew curiously. "I saw you in the crowd," she said "after it was all over. Where did you go?"

James hesitated, but only for an instant. "With Joseph, the Arimathaean, and Nicodemus, members of the Council. We took the body of my Brother to Joseph's tomb."

"Oh!" exclaimed Susanna. "Then—then it *was* you!"

Salome's eyes widened as she retreated. "Then you have touched the dead! You have made yourself unclean, according to the Law!"

James' eyes pursued her, unwavering. "Is the Law more important than my Brother?" he demanded sternly.

"And you have not changed your raiment!" Salome's upraised hands were like two shocked exclamation points. "Go quickly and do so and cleanse yourself for the seven days of purification before the wrath of Jehovah falls upon you!"

He turned on her in sudden fury. "Raiment! Purification!" he repeated scornfully. "When the Brother I loved lies dead? You think it matters what clothes I wear when my spirit is bowed beneath sackcloth and ashes? Or if I cleanse these hands when the sinful stain of disloyalty is on my soul?"

Susanna's deep glance was like a sudden probing radiance. "James! You—you talk so strangely—"

"Can't *you* understand?" He turned to the girl, no longer scornful, but eager, appealing. "These things don't matter! It's my Brother who matters."

"It's strange," she said softly, as if to herself. "You say you don't understand the things he said, and yet your own words sound like his."

"What do you mean?" asked James slowly.

"Why, just that he also loved his brother with a love so great that he would have given his life for you. But to him all men were brothers worth dying for."

A startled look came into James' eyes. It was as if the radiant, probing glance had kindled some answering spark, if not of complete understanding, then at least of faintly dawning comprehension.

"You say—" he began.

But this moment of contact, like that other, was doomed to interruption, for Jude entered from the courtyard, dragging an obscure shadow of a figure with him. The spark in James' eyes flared an instant later, not into dawning comprehension, but into suddenly awakened hatred.

"Look!" exclaimed Jude indignantly. "I found this fellow skulking in the lane outside the garden."

He roughly pulled the figure within the circle of lamplight and turned to berate him further, then stopped openmouthed as he recognized the stranger's identity. "You!"

"The son of Malluch!" muttered James under his breath. He felt a sudden surge of fury rise up within him, tightening his muscles, inflaming his whole body. He had been, it seemed, on the verge of discovery. A door had been slowly opening before him and then had been suddenly slammed shut. Instead of dawning understanding, the cold, blinding darkness of this old, almost forgotten hatred! Instead of the lineaments of a beloved, familiar face, its vague outlines at last becoming comprehensible, this despised and hated visage!

Zeri came forward eagerly. He was a miserable-looking figure, dusty, ragged, almost as forlorn as he had looked in the old Nazareth days, except that his shoulders were straighter and his eyes bright and shining. They glowed like watchfires in the pale, tired desert of his face.

"I'm looking for the house of Clopas," he said weakly.

Susanna came forward graciously. "This is the house of Clopas."

The watchfires flared, lighting the pale face with an indomitable purpose. "Where is Jesus?" demanded the son of Malluch earnestly. "They say he comes here sometimes when he's here for the feasts, and I must find him! I've been traveling for hours, and even now it may be too late. Tell me, for God's sake, where is he? Where can I find the Master?"

The silence reared itself about him like a wall. Only Susanna, it seemed, dared thrust it aside. "The Master is not here, Zeri," she said gently. "He has gone."

He looked at her, puzzled, the watch fires flickering. "Where? I must find him and take him back with me! My father lies dying. It's been hours since I left him—"

James felt himself moving slowly forward. "You say your father is dying?"

"Yes," returned Zeri, eager recognition in his face, "and with but one request on his lips—that he might see Jesus, your brother, and ask his forgiveness. He has sinned against him and against the house of Joseph, and now that his hour is come, the shadow of his sin is upon him, and he is afraid. He would find peace for his soul."

Again, without his volition, it seemed, James felt his muscles moving, twisting his lips into a hard, ironic smile. Words formed themselves before his eyes, swiftly, connectedly as flame—words that he himself had spoken.

Let his bread be bitter in his mouth. Let him cry out for mercy in the hour of his death and there be none to answer him!

Malluch, with the cold sweat of death upon him, gasping for

forgiveness—in vain! Never could he have devised a punishment so cunningly ironic, so devastating, as this that fate had provided. At last Joseph was to be avenged. There was justice in Israel!

"Jesus will speak peace to his fears," said Zeri confidently. "There is that within him which is stronger than all fear, stronger even than the fear of death. Only tell me where I can find him, before it is too late."

"It *is* too late," James heard himself saying with a coldness akin to triumph. "This Master of yours who was stronger than the fear of death is dead!"

"Dead—" echoed the man faintly.

"Yes." James repeated the details with that strange satisfaction which the tortured sometimes derive from torturing. "His enemies have killed him. They nailed him on a cross. Just before sunset we took him down—and sealed his lifeless body in a tomb."

Zeri listened, stood very still while James was speaking, then said quietly: "So he's done it already. I didn't think it would come quite so soon."

James stared. "You mean you—expected him to die?"

It was Zeri's turn to look surprised. "Of course. If he didn't, how could he show us that there's nothing to fear, that his love and power are stronger than everything—even death?" He turned suddenly to Jude. "It was against you and your family that my father sinned. Will you come with me in your brother's stead?" he demanded eagerly. "Will you grant him your forgiveness?"

Jude looked horrified. "I grant forgiveness to Malluch!" He laughed harshly. "I would sooner let these hands commit murder!"

"Jesus would have done it," insisted Zeri earnestly. "He taught men to love their enemies. He would have gone with me no matter what it cost him."

He turned wearily away. The watch fires in his eyes flickered out.

"Where are you going?" asked Susanna anxiously.

"Back to my father."

"Wait!"

James stepped quickly forward. He no longer moved without volition. The impulse, the act, the words, were all suddenly the integrated expression of his will. "Where is Malluch?" he asked quickly.

The man turned back, his muscles quivering. "In a little village the other side of the Jordan. We were on our way here to Jerusalem, to keep the Passover, when he was taken sick."

James' brows drew together, and his eyes became swiftly calculating. He was no longer the scholar, the dreamer, but the man of action. "We could get there by morning," he said with decision, "if we traveled through the night."

The watch fires in the tired eyes again trembled into flame. "You mean—"

"My Brother would have gone with you," said James simply. "So I will go."

Zeri almost sobbed his gratitude. "May heaven bless you!" he prayed fervently.

"But you can't—not tonight!" Salome interrupted, distressed and horror-stricken. "You can't travel on the Sabbath!"

The Sabbath! The words struck deep into James' consciousness with the swift poignancy of an arrow. He had forgotten it was the Sabbath! For the first time in his life since he could remember, sunset on the sixth day of the week had come and gone, leaving him unconscious of its passing. Swiftly, almost without his volition, his mind surveyed the hours just passed. Luckily he had broken no law. Or had he? Those long, weary stretches of dusty road—that woman who had touched his arm—the beggar—Had he unwittingly traveled more than the prescribed two thousand cubits? Had the woman or the beggar been a foreigner?

Well, suppose they had been, What did it matter? It hadn't mattered to his Brother. Jesus would have sat down beside the beggar, no doubt, given him his cloak and sandals; stopped and talked to the woman, rested unsatisfied until she had known the forgiveness of her sins and the freedom of purity discovered by the Magdalene.

"The man is dying," said James abruptly. "If we wait, it will probably be too late. We must go tonight."

Zeri threw himself on his knees and kissed the hem of James' long, fringed, embroidered cloak. "May the blessing of the Father of all men rest upon you!" he prayed fervently.

Stooping, James lifted the kneeling figure to his feet. As he did so, Jude's face, amazed and outraged, thrust itself into his line of vision.

"Are you forgetting that this dying man is our enemy who helped to kill our father, that he has brought nothing but misfortune to our family, that we have sworn to avenge ourselves upon him?"

"I'm not forgetting," replied James, turning to him. "Can't you understand that the reason I'm doing this is just because I'm not forgetting? I'm remembering, not Malluch, but Another."

He hastily made ready for the journey, exchanging his fine-textured cloak for one rougher and more serviceable. As he came out of the guestchamber on the housetop, Susanna met him with a small bundle containing fruit and unleavened cakes. Her eager eyes probed his face.

"You do understand, James?" she asked breathlessly. "Is that why you're doing this?"

James returned her gaze steadily. He wanted desperately to satisfy that questioning, breathless eagerness, to wipe out this one last barrier that separated them. But he knew that in this moment there must be nothing but honesty between them.

"No," he said slowly. "I'm afraid I don't. I'm doing this because it's what Jesus would have done, not because I understand why he would have done it. It's the only thing there is left that I can do for him."

"I see," she said quietly.

She tucked the small packet of lunch into the leather bag at his girdle, then, just as she had done long before in almost that very same spot, she raised her slender body on tiptoe and gently touched her lips to his.

With a little broken cry James swept her into his arms and for a brief moment held her close. Then swiftly he went down the narrow staircase to where Zeri was waiting.

"We must hurry," he said abruptly. "Come, son of the Evil—" He stopped suddenly, a slow light kindling in his eyes. "Come, my brother," he finished firmly.

2

"Is she still there?" asked Mary, the wife of Clopas, anxiously.

Salome peered out the doorway of the courtyard into the garden. The early morning sun was bright, and she was nearsighted. So, in order to satisfy her instinct for detail, she had to shade her eyes with her hand.

"Yes," she said finally. "in the very same spot. Sitting beneath the olive tree. And with the same look on her face, that listening look, as if she were waiting for someone."

The wife of Clopas turned quickly, her fingers, which had been plucking dead leaves from her potted plants, suddenly still. "I believe you're right," she said thoughtfully. "I think that's just what she's doing."

Salome regarded the other woman curiously. "You mean for her son?"

"Why not?" asked Mary slowly. She seemed to be speaking more to herself than to Salome. "That would explain, wouldn't it, why she's acted as she has these last two days? Her seeming lack of grief doesn't mean necessarily that she's insensible to all that has happened. I think she realizes it to the full, so deeply, perhaps, that the pain of it can't find expression in mere outward signs of grief, and still, in spite of it all, she has this strange inner certainty that he will come back."

Salome bit off the end of her thread with strong, white teeth. Even in a strange city and in another woman's house her hands could not be idle but were busy mending a tear in the cloak of her son James. She tapped her head significantly. "After all Mary has been through these last few days it's no wonder her mind's a bit—"

"But the Magdalene said she saw him," said the wife of Clopas musingly.

Salome pursed her lips. "The Magdalene is always saying queer things. Besides, she herself admitted her eyes were so dim with weeping she thought at first it was the gardener."

The other woman moved closer, her eyes suddenly alight with an insistent eagerness. "Salome," she said breathlessly, "Did you hear nothing—see nothing—when we stood there in the garden this morning before the tomb?"

Salome neatly clipped a frayed edge before answering. "Hear? See? Why, I heard and saw what you did, of course."

The wife of Clopas bent closer. "Did you? Did you see the radiance of the men who spoke to us?"

"The sun was bright," assented Salome doubtfully. "It almost blinded me."

"And did you hear what they said?" Mary caught her breath. "Did they not say triumphantly that Jesus was not there, that he is not to be found among the dead? Did they not remind us of his own words, that he would be crucified by sinful men and on the third day rise again? And did they not say he is even now going before his disciples into Galilee, very much alive?"

Salome's eyes widened. "Alive!" she exclaimed. Her glance shot furtively toward the garden, then back to rest warily on Mary's face. "You—you can't mean you too believe—"

There was a quick step in the passageway, and a moment later Jude pushed aside the curtain and entered. He cast a worried glance about the room, and, seeing only the two women, frowned.

"Where is Clopas?" he asked abruptly.

Mary returned to her plants. With sure, deft motions she began to loosen the dirt about the roots of a potted acanthus. "He went to Emmaus this morning," she replied, adding with a quiet satisfaction, "And Simon went with him. They had a lot of new plans to attend to."

Jude frowned again. "You don't mean he's still going through with this crazy idea of his?"

"Why, yes, of course," returned Mary simply. "Why shouldn't he?"

Jude dropped his heavy body on the settle and sat twisting his big hands, fumbling for words. "Well, I just thought—After all, it's over, isn't it? What I mean is, now he's gone, I shouldn't think it would really matter—"

"You mean," asked Mary quietly, "that now Jesus is dead, the hope of the Kingdom of God is dead too?"

"That's it." Jude looked relieved. It was always an effort for him to put his ideas into adequate words. "That's what I was trying to say, I guess." He wiped his forehead on the sleeve of his cloak. "Well, it is, isn't it?"

Mary pressed the dirt firmly back about the roots. "That depends," she said thoughtfully. "To you who were expecting Jesus to establish some sort of earthly kingdom—yes. I suppose the hope is dead. But you see, Clopas and I never expected that. We believed the things he told us, that the Kingdom of God is like a seed, or like a bit of leaven. It must start very small, perhaps—take years, maybe even centuries in the growing. But once it is started, nothing, nothing on earth can destroy it, anymore than it could destroy—"

She stopped abruptly, conscious of their stupidly staring, bewildered faces. "You're worried about something," she said kindly to Jude. "What is it?"

"It's a good thing somebody's worried," threw in Salome tartly.

"What with my boys both gone and you and Susanna acting as if things could go on just as they always have and Mary walking around in a dream and James gone off with his worst enemy nobody knows where—"

"Yes, fool that he was!" exclaimed Jude bitterly. "Perhaps now he'll be sorry for his madness."

"Why, what is it?" Salome's pale features quivered. "What's happened now?"

Jude leaned back wearily. He had gotten little sleep in the last two days, and his face looked haggard. His big hands, awkward in their emptiness, fumbled at his girdle. "Some of the Council members," he said worriedly, "have heard about his journey. Someone saw him leave by the Jericho road the night of the Sabbath."

Susanna, busily rolling the mats in one of the adjoining sleeping rooms, had paused at the first mention of James' name. Now she moved swiftly to the door leading into the courtyard and entered. The preceding days had taken their toll on her also. The oval of her face was pale against the deep blue of her flowing headdress, its heart-shaped outline more sharply pronounced than usual. But her eyes remained sun-flecked and serene.

"James is in danger?" she asked quietly.

"We're all in danger," returned Jude gruffly. "I know they've had spies watching us ever since it happened. And if there isn't any danger, why don't James and John and Simon come back home? I'll tell you why. Because they're frightened. They know it isn't safe to show their faces. And now, to make it worse, the Magdalene starts this story. She's telling it all over the city that Jesus isn't dead, but alive. Of course, no one will believe her, but—"

"I believe her," said Susanna with sudden clearness.

Salome and Jude looked at her in amazement, but the wife of Clopas continued quietly to pick dead leaves from the shining, dark-green clusters of the acanthus plant.

"What *are* you saying?"

"Susanna! You can't—"

"Why not?" she returned calmly. "He came to give us never-ending life with God the Father, didn't he? Why should we think it so strange that he should possess it himself? I know this new life I now have with the Father isn't just physical. It's spirit. And the death of my body cannot destroy my spirit. I know it can't. Oh, I do wish I could make you understand!"

They continued to stare at her stupidly. Only in the face of the wife of Clopas did her eager, glowing words kindle any response. "What you mean is this," said Mary thoughtfully. "The life he has given us is the same eternal life he revealed by rising from the grave. And because we no longer need to fear death, we can freely give to others the love, goodness, and truth he has put in our hearts."

"Yes, yes, that's it," assented Susanna gratefully, "That's just what I was trying to say."

Salome turned to Mary, her pale eyes suddenly aflame. "You mean," she said breathlessly, "you actually believe that Jesus is alive?"

"Yes," returned the wife of Clopas with growing confidence. "I do. And not only that, but I believe it's going to be possible for him to share our life with us." As the certainty of her conviction grew, Mary's delicate features became more and more radiantly alive. "I believe he's going to be with us whenever we show his love to others."

Bewildered but pathetically eager, Salome's practical mind lighted on the single tangible foothold emerging from a sea of baffling abstractions. "But if he's alive," she said excitedly, "he'll be coming back again, won't he? Will he come to Jerusalem, do you think, today? And will he be here to supper—in this house?"

"Don't be a fool, aunt," said Jude gruffly. He rose impatiently and, leaving the courtyard, went out into the street to see if by any chance James was coming.

But the wife of Clopas laid her hand gently on Salome's tensed shoulder. "My dear!" she chided affectionately. "Must these eyes of yours always see and these hands always touch to know truth for reality?"

Salome looked hurt, bewildered, disappointed. "But I thought you said he was alive—"

"He *is* alive," replied the wife of Clopas gently. "Can you not believe it without seeing his body?"

Out in the garden Mary leaned her head back against the seamed, twisted trunk of the old olive tree.

"Perhaps," she thought, "if I close my eyes and keep very still, so still that it will seem there is no life left in me at all, perhaps I will feel him near to me again."

But it was no use. Keep as still as she would, strain her ears until it seemed their sensitive strings must be tuned to rhythms above and beyond the gamut of sound, make her whole body as empty as it had felt in those first bleak, terrible moments when she had ceased suddenly to partake in full measure of another's pain and had become achingly, devastatingly conscious of her own—still it was no use. The beautiful, intimate comradeship was gone.

But not because her son was dead. She was sure of that. Strange that she could be so sure. They thought she was just a little mad, touched in the head by her grief. They were kind to her and pitying, not understanding that the more deeply she had been able to drink of his agony, the more real she had found his presence. Even later, after it was all over and John had brought her home and she had sat here in the garden spent and exhausted, her flesh still quivering to the pulse beat of those driven nails—even then he had been with her. That was why she was so sure.

Now there were others too who believed he was alive. Mary, the wife of Clopas, was beginning to. And Susanna. And that strange, calm-faced woman who looked as if her eyes had been lighted from within, the Magdalene. She had come to her only this morning to tell her that she had seen him, thinking that she, his mother, should be one of the first to know that he was alive again. As if she had not known already!

So—it was the Magdalene now who enjoyed that blessed sense of comradeship, that comforting knowledge of his presence. While his mother, who surely loved him better than any stranger possibly could, sat waiting, alone! The sweet feeling of release and peace that had come to her in the sharing of his pain was submerged in this new torturing flood of loneliness and self-pity.

"Come to me, come to me," she prayed voicelessly. "You showed yourself to her—that woman. Surely my love is greater than hers. Here I am, waiting—your mother—"

Who is my mother and who are my brothers? . . . Whoever does the will of my Father in heaven is my brother and sister and mother.

The words smote her suddenly out of the past, flooding her spirit as with a chilling wave. Although the spring sun was warm upon her shoulders, she shivered and drew her mantle closer about her. For a little time she had forgotten them. She had told herself that they did not matter. She had believed for a while that loving was all that was necessary, and indeed it had been so, as long as she had been able to feel the comforting consciousness of his presence. But now—What now that the loved one had been taken away?

She felt a light, timid touch on her arm and, looking down, saw a child's face looking up at her. So like was it to that other face that had looked up into hers so often long ago that she thought for an instant prayer had been answered, and she caught her breath sharply.

"My son," she whispered brokenly. "My little one."

Then her vision steadied. And she saw that it was little Jeshua standing there and that his wide, clear eyes were blurred with tears.

"Na Na—"

Her arms went about him with swift tenderness. "Why, beloved, what is it? Tell Na Na what the trouble is."

The child's lips quivered. "What will all the people do, Na Na, now that Uncle Jesus is gone?"

"The people, beloved?"

"Yes. Like the poor lepers that live up in the cave. And old Deborah, that he asked me to go see every day. And all the little children, Na Na, that he used to love and tell stories to? What will they do now?"

"Why, I—" The woman looked into the child's clear eyes with a sudden strained intentness, "I don't know."

"He told me I could help him, Na Na, when I grew up."

She looked back at him steadily. "And so you can, beloved," she said earnestly. "And you don't need to wait until you grow up. You can help him now. We can both help him."

"How, Na Na? How can we?"

"Well—" The stillness suddenly left her fingers. She lifted them and smoothed back a lock of hair that had fallen over the tear-stained face. "We'll go back to Nazareth and start in right away, shall we? First of all, of course, there are the lepers. They will have missed you, and mother may not have had time to take them things. And then there's Deborah. I believe we'll have something to tell her now that will take away that terrible hunger from her eyes. Yes, I know we have, beloved! And then there's Miriam, the daughter of Jothan. She came to me once, and—oh, I failed her miserably! There's so much to be done, beloved. Can't you see?"

The eager radiance in the child's clear eyes struck through her whole being like a poignantly familiar shaft of light. She reached out and drew his pulsing, vital little body close to her, feeling the warmth flow into the deep, cold, inner recesses of her spirit, letting his need of her fill the hungry emptiness. It was not little Jeshua, her son's son, whom she held in her arms. It was not even the blessed, healing memory of her firstborn. It was all the helpless children who had ever lived, all the human beings who had ever needed a mother's love and tenderness and pity.

And suddenly she understood. Jesus had not been shutting them outside of his life by those words spoken long ago in Capernaum. He had been including them. He had not withdrawn himself from the circle of her love. Instead, he had widened the circle to infinite horizons. He had given her the whole world to love.

"My son," she whispered softly. But in her heart she said, "And who is my son? Whoever has need of a mother's love—that is my son and my daughter."

3

The road between Jericho and Jerusalem is an uphill one, dangerous and frightening, especially for one who travels it alone. The rocks tower high on one side, stark and ugly and full of lurking evils, only to descend on the other into cavernous depths down which a man might easily slip and become lost among the shadows.

James walked slowly because of an intense weariness but with a rhythmic steadiness like the living beat of a pulse. He had slept only a few hours since leaving Jerusalem two days ago, but he was not conscious of being tired. His mind was too keenly, too vitally alive, reliving the experiences and emotions of the last few hours.

He had accomplished the purpose of his journey and left the little town in Perea across the Jordan as soon as sunset had brought an end to the Sabbath. He had spent the previous night at an inn in Jericho, rising long before dawn in his impatience to continue his journey back to Jerusalem. The first long, golden shafts of sunrise streaming across the red cliffs of Moab had found him high up among the barren, wrinkled hills. He would have been farther along his way had it not been for the aged slave whom he had met stumbling beneath a heavy burden not many miles outside the walls of Jericho. He had turned around and carried it for him a little way, while the other travelers on the road, laborers and artisans scheduled for work in the city at dawn, had stood and stared at him, confounded by the sight of a respectable Jew with the burden of a slave on his back. Well, they had stared at *him* too, not many hours ago, carrying another burden.

The wild road wound up and up through savage glens and along the edges of sheer, bare precipices, between steep, overhanging cliffs, their faces seamed with erosive scars and honeycombed with black caves, through a country as starkly barren and desolate as if it had been stricken with some leprous disease. As the sun rose higher, the air grew more dense and stagnant, until James' body beneath the heavy, enveloping cloak ran rivulets of sweat. But still he hastened on, pace undiminished, barely conscious either of bodily movement or of discomfort.

Only once he stopped, lifting his eyes curiously toward a black cliff rising like a sheer blank wall straight up from the roadside. Somewhere in that vast, solid expanse, he knew, there was a rift. If he hunted, perhaps he could find it—wedge his way through, climb up the tortuous path which led to an opening between two massive black pillars of rock. Doubtless Barabbas was back there now, in his hideout, lolling negligently upon his leopard's skin, exulting in the luck that had restored life and freedom to him and brought death to that dreaming fool of a Galilean. Life? Freedom? James' lips twisted into a pitying smile.

He was about to travel on when he saw the queer, shapeless object lying at the bottom of the rocky gully below the road where he was standing. After a moment's hesitation he made his way toward it, edging carefully down the steep, slippery incline. Coming closer, he saw that the object had both form and shape, that it was the figure of a man stripped of his clothes, his body bruised and torn, apparently lifeless. Even without the battered helmet lying close by, he would have recognized the pale, unshaven face, the sharp, clean-cut features as belonging to a Roman.

Barabbas, he thought grimly, remembering the looted splendor of the rebel chieftain's hideout. Trust the loyal patriot to combine zeal for country with the acquisition of a good Arab horse and a stout suit of armor!

He had turned indifferently away and started to climb up the side of the rocky ravine when he remembered that he had chosen to take on this journey, not his own way, but Another's. Driven by the same inner compulsion that had already caused him to do many strange things in the last two days, he turned back toward the recumbent figure. As he came nearer, he noticed that it stirred slightly and a faint moan escaped its lips. He stopped short, repelled. He had meant only to satisfy himself that the man was dead. He had not dreamed—

As he stood staring down at him, the stiffened lips moved and mumbled some foreign jargon, of which James caught only the single Greek word, "Water!" But at the sound of the voice his pulses seemed suddenly to stand still. He glanced about eagerly, involuntarily, as if he half expected to see other lips from which the sounds might have issued. Strange! He could have sworn—Was he going mad? There had been that moment too when he had looked into the pleading eyes of Malluch—and later when he had reached out to grasp the hand of that sweating, stumbling slave. Was his mind so distorted with grief that it must create his Brother's likeness in every face, his accents in every voice, his touch in every hand?

Abruptly he knelt beside the still figure and, removing the water skin from his girdle, pressed its mouth gently between the stiffened lips. He took off his cloak and wrapped it carefully about the bruised body. Then, lifting it in his arms, he half dragged, half carried it up the rocky incline to the edge of the road. The few passers-by looked askance at the spectacle of a disheveled, cloakless traveler begging succor for one of those luckless victims of the lurking brigands of whom all were in constant terror. And with hastened steps and averted faces they passed by on the other side of the road. But he finally found an old Arab peddler with a donkey who agreed, for half a denarius, to let the wounded man ride as far as an inn which James remembered having passed, several miles back toward Jericho. He went with them himself, walking beside the donkey, and arranged with the innkeeper to care for the man until he should be well again, leaving enough money to provide food and clothing and oil to dress his wounds. Then he went on his way. But not alone. For now he knew for a certainty that Another journeyed with him.

It was late afternoon when a man, watching patiently in the shadows of the great eastern gateway, saw the tall, straight figure ascending the hill toward the city. He waited for another minute or two to make sure of its identity, then with a satisfied smile he slipped away among the crowds moving toward the Temple area, where he knew that certain members of the Council would be waiting.

Without slackening his pace, James climbed the last familiar, dusty, well-trodden slope and passed through the gate. Above him, towering high, the great dome of the Temple caught the sun's slanting rays and flung them against the deep topaz of the sky like the wings of a thousand seraphim.

But for the first time in his life James barely lifted his eyes to its majestic grandeur. He was too busy seeing the people whom he passed on the streets—the young hastening buoyantly to finish some task before the close of the day; the old huddled on their thresholds to catch the last pale warmth; the tired, the sick, the hungry, the worried, the lonely, the oppressed. He saw them all with a strange new sympathy and discernment, as if he were looking at them not through his own but through Another's eyes.

As he entered the outer passageway of his uncle's house, the sound of voices came to him from the inner courtyard—Salome's, high and excited; Susanna's, low and gentle and blessedly familiar; Mary's—

"But I'm not tired, Salome, dear," she was saying gently, "and I'm quite well enough to return to Nazareth at once. Can't you understand? I must go. I have so many things to do!"

Quietly James pushed aside the heavy curtain and stepped inside. And in the first moment he was conscious of the eyes of the woman he loved, reaching out toward him, enveloping him in their warm embrace. He knew suddenly that there need be no questioning, no explanations, between him and Susanna. As well as if she had gone with him on his journey, thought his thoughts, experienced his emotions, she understood.

"I'll get some water for your feet, James," she said simply.

"My son!" cried Mary joyfully, coming toward him with outstretched arms. "You've come back!"

He turned wearily toward the other women. For them, he knew, there must be many questions and explanations.

"Yes, mother. I'm back."

"You're tired. And your garments are all stained with dust. You have had a hard journey."

"Yes," he replied, "and a long one. But I was not too late."

"Then Malluch—"

"Malluch died with the blessing of the son of Joseph in his ears and peace upon his lips."

Susanna brought a basin of water for his feet and knelt to wash them, while James, too weary to make remonstrance, found the touch of her soft hands more refreshing to his tired body than the cool, fresh water. The other women hovered about solicitously.

"Why don't you tell him the good news?" demanded Salome, able to restrain herself no longer. Then, without waiting, she herself blurted out eagerly, "Jesus is alive!"

"Yes," replied James. "I know."

Salome's face fell. "You—you do? You met somebody that had heard the Magdalene's story?"

"No. What do you mean? What did the Magdalene say?"

"She said she saw him in the garden outside his tomb this morning, not just in a vision, but *himself* — just as we knew him — alive again!"

James nodded, the weariness in his face suddenly vanishing into radiance. "Praise God! I believe it. Then he really is alive — and not only in memory and spirit! I understand now the things he said. It wasn't enough to tell us about the power of his love. He had to *show* us — that it's great enough to endure even death — and to conquer it. I should have known he was alive when he seemed to go with me on my journey every step of the way."

Salome looked even more bewildered. "You mean," she continued to stare at James, her gaze blank with stupefaction, "you have really seen him — heard him — touched him?"

James' eyes locked for an instant in a swift understanding with Susanna's before they turned steadily toward the other woman. "No," he said, "not in the way you mean, Salome. But when I looked into the face of my enemy, whom I hated, and when I had spoken to him words of pity and forgiveness, behold, it was somehow my Brother's face I saw. And in the same way I have heard him speak. For when I turned aside from my journey to help a stranger lying by the roadside, it somehow seemed to be my Brother's voice that called to me. And again, in this same sense I have touched him. For when I saw a slave stumbling beneath a heavy burden and reached out to help him, the hand that I clasped seemed to be my Brother's hand."

Hardly had he finished speaking when Jude rushed in from the street, flushed and panting. Seeing James, he flung himself toward him, grasping him roughly by the shoulder.

"Come!" he cried hoarsely. "We must get you away from here, James, before it's too late. There's a crowd of people outside the house now, and the high priest's guards are with them. Here, through the garden—"

James slipped on his sandals and rose to his feet. But he resisted the constraint of his brother's hands. "Wait a minute!" he said slowly. "What is this? Suppose there are people outside. Why should I—"

"Don't ask questions," ordered Jude sharply. "Just come. There's no time to lose."

Salome, who had been peering out through the passageway, now returned excitedly. "They're coming! They're turning into the lane! They're going to take us all! Heaven help us, what shall we do?"

"They don't want us," said Jude roughly. "It's James they want."

"What do they want of me?" asked James, surprised.

"Jude is right, James," interposed the wife of Clopas firmly. "These people are your enemies, as they were Jesus' enemies. They found out somehow that you broke the Law, that you journeyed beyond the Jordan on the Sabbath. And they're determined to make an example of you. They would like to destroy you, just as they did Jesus."

"It's the priests and Council members again," threw in Jude harshly. "They have stirred up the people. They've heard all this talk about Jesus' being alive, and they're determined that someone shall be punished. They want to frighten the rest of his followers. And they've chosen you because you're his brother and because you're like him."

A light kindled slowly in James' eyes. "Because I am his brother," he repeated. "Because I am like him."

"Now will you come?" Jude seized him forcibly by the arm, as a low murmur of voices outside made itself apparent. "They're your enemies, I tell you! They're coming! They're here!"

James turned his face toward the low murmur, growing steadily louder, like the dull drone of waves as the tide rises higher and higher. It was not a new sound. He had heard it before. In Nazareth. In Capernaum. In Jerusalem.

Is not this the son of Joseph? Away with him.

I tell you, this Jesus casts out demons through the power of demons.

Take this man, we say, and give us Barabbas.... Crucify him!

"Go, James," said his mother firmly. "Go with Jude. Jesus would want you to."

"Yes," said Susanna a little breathlessly, coming close to him. "You must go, beloved."

He put his hands on her shoulders, looked steadily into her eyes. "*You* want me to run away?" he asked quietly.

Her eyes fell before his, but she continued hurriedly, "Yes, James. For—for *his* sake. You must save yourself to be a leader, to help to build the Kingdom of God."

James turned away, unable to face the tender pleading of her eyes. Even Susanna, he realized, could not help him now. She was human and she loved him. Now that the hour of testing had come, there was only One who could help him, only One who really understood. And yet how could he be sure? What would his Brother want him to do? Was there any way of really knowing?

"Breaker of the Law—"

It was the voice of the crowd without, drawing steadily nearer, its murmur becoming intelligible.

"Traitor unto Moses—"

"Come out of the house and dare to show your face!"

"Brother of him who called himself Deliverer—"

"Alive, is he? Then let him show himself!"

"Come out if you dare—"

"We'll show you what we do to lawbreakers!'

James flinched.

"You and I," said Susanna breathlessly, "we have all our lives ahead—years to spend in making the Dream come true—together!"

The Dream! Yes, that was it. That was what mattered, what had always mattered. "Yes," he said suddenly. "I am needed. I must live, for his sake, for the sake of the Dream!"

"Then come!" Jude grasped him hastily and pulled him toward the door leading to the garden. "In the name of all that's holy, come quickly!"

James followed, his pulses beating in a frenzy of relief and fear. But one glance out through the door showed them that there was no possible escape through the garden. The Council members had gathered together enough of a mob to surround the whole house. Jude dragged him swiftly back. "Quick!" he gasped. "We'll have to hide you!"

Back in the inner court the high, shrill voice of the crowd pursued them, insistently, relentlessly. "We know who you are, James, son of Joseph, Sabbathbreaker! If your brother is alive, show him to us!"

"Show him to us! Show him! Show him—"

Suddenly James stood still. And as suddenly he knew what he must do. "No, no!" he cried, loosing himself from Jude's grasp. "What am I doing! God forgive me!"

Deliberately he turned and passed through the door leading into the outer courtyard.

"James!" It was Susanna, pale and trembling but clear-eyed. "Where are you going?"

"Out yonder," he said, "with my Brother."

"Come out unto us, brother of the Galilean!"

James lifted his face. "I am coming," he called clearly.

"You're mad!" cried Jude harshly.

Salome hid her trembling features in her veil. "They'll kill you," she sobbed.

James turned slowly. "No," he said, "I do not think they will kill me. But even if they do, they cannot touch my spirit anymore than they touched his. The eternal life with which he conquered the grave is now mine as well, so I can face them not with fear or hatred, but with his truth and love."

Mary stretched her hands toward him. "My son," she said brokenly, but her face was radiant. "My beloved son!"

"But the Dream?" questioned Susanna, her eyes searching his, no longer frightened and pleading, he noticed gratefully, but clear and fearless.

He gestured toward the doorway, toward the moving, impatient mass surging confusedly beyond the threshold. "This is the Dream," he said simply.

He was conscious of her face, steadily smiling and shining like a white flame, every beloved feature purely and indelibly outlined, until, standing at last on the outer threshold, he found its contours merging into a whole sea of faces. Hostile, curious, indifferent, bold, timid, eager, contemptuous, indignant, self-righteous, smug, tired, fretful, worried, lustful, hungry, and all unsatisfied—they stared up at him.

And suddenly James knew. These people had not come to kill him. They had first come, as they had come to his Brother, because with all their eager, hungry, unsatisfied little souls they desired something he had to give. They didn't want death for him. They wanted life for themselves. Sometime—years later, perhaps, but surely as a straight road leads to its inevitable ending—they would meet him at some other crossroads, and there would be no hunger in their faces at that time, only the hatred and violence and death with which they had finally attacked Jesus. These things would come, as they had come for his Brother. But not now. Not yet. Before that time there would be a long road to travel through sunshine and shadow, with Susanna by his side, while together they tried to show the way of his Brother unto men.

"Whom seek you?" he asked gently in the sudden silence.

The voices rose again, but less shrill and less insistent, like the subsiding of a wave that has already mounted to its crest.

"The brother of the Galilean!"

"I am he," replied James quietly.

As he went out to meet them, he reached out his arms toward them in a simple, friendly, all-inclusive gesture. "Peace to you, my brothers."